JENNA WOLFHART

THE FALLEN FAE

Court of Ruins

Book One of The Fallen Fae

Cover Design by Gene Mollica Studio

Copyright © 2020 by Jenna Wolfhart

All rights reserved.

No part of this book may be reproduced in any form or by any electronic or mechanical means, including information storage and retrieval systems, without written permission from the author, except for the use of brief quotations in a book review.

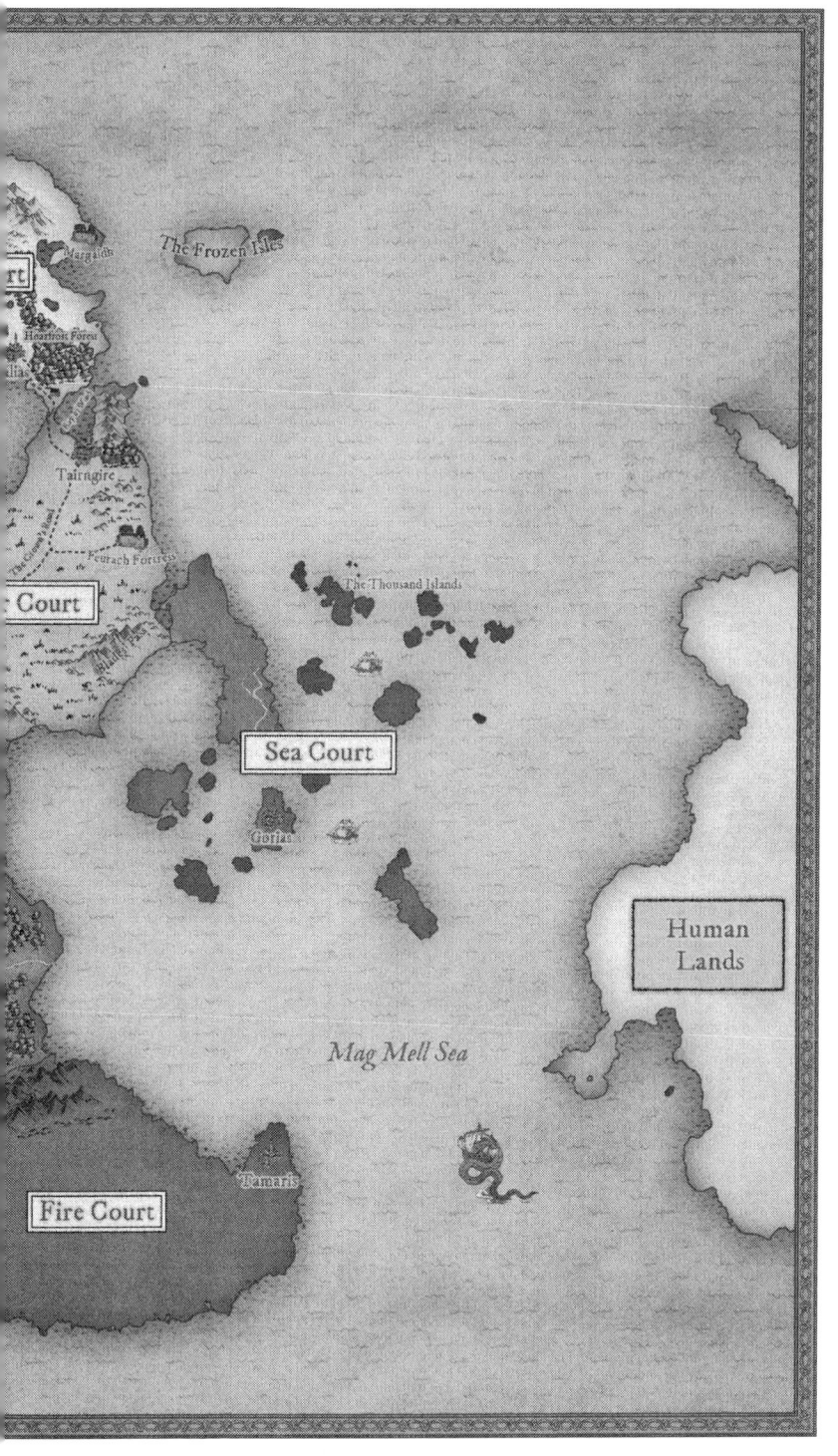

I

REYNA

"There's another village full of the dead." Reyna stood on the crest of the snow-packed hill, the orange sunset streaking across the sky behind the smoldering buildings. Her snow owl perched on her shoulder, his long talons curling around her hoarfrost cloak. "Perhaps a few have survived the attack. We should go down and check."

Her sister stood beside her, small and wispy but stronger than she looked. Her billowing cloak was the color of the ice blue sky and her hair as silver as steel. "No. We should tell Father."

Reyna frowned at Glencora. "By the time we return to the castle and alert Father, any survivors will be dead. We should check the village now."

Glencora was silent. She surveyed the wreckage of Pinehallow, her silver eyes as distant as they had been for weeks. Her mind was not in the present. Betrothed to the Air Court's only prince, she would be leaving these lands for a safer kingdom soon enough. The Ruin would no longer be her concern.

"These attacks, if that is what they are, are becoming more frequent." Reyna cut her eyes across the sweeping lands of the Ice Court. From the vantage point on the top of the hill, the snowy lands seemed endless. Indeed, Reyna had never stepped foot outside of her court. Too dangerous, Father always said. The great continent of Tir Na Nog had been plagued with endless war from the very day of her birth. Reyna did not know peace and could barely comprehend it. Hence, Glencora's agreement to wed. It would cease the skirmishes between the Air and Ice Courts, and that was a start.

Glencora swore beneath her breath. "He instructed you to merely scout, to ensure the Air Court have called back their bands of fighters. And he only allowed it because he was certain of their retreat. Father will tan my hide if I let you get anywhere near the Ruin."

She whispered her final two words, as if the very act of speaking 'the Ruin' aloud would bring the darkness tumbling down on top of them.

"It will not kill me," Reyna said, though she could hardly be certain of that. No one knew what caused the Ruin, and no one understood how it left endless darkness behind it. But kill it did. Anywhere the Ruin was found, bodies would lie in its wake. Recently, entire villages had been reduced to nothing but ash. Corners of the great ancient Ice Court were covered in shadows, darkness, and soot.

Still, Reyna set off down the hill. Wingallock pushed off from her shoulder and soared just ahead, his outstretched wings pulsing against the winter air. Reyna's leather boots crunched into the snow as thorny branches covered in tiny, translucent hoarfrost worms whispered by her ears. Sometimes, she swore she could hear them singing to her, a song that no one else could hear. When she tried telling

Glencora and Eislyn about it, they always laughed, but their mockery never doused the voices that filled her head.

Now, the trees were silent, as if in mourning for the dead.

"Reyna!" Her sister quickly followed behind but did nothing to stop Reyna's advance on the forsaken village. As they drew closer to the blackened buildings, a strange heat pulsed from the stone houses whose thatched roofs were nothing more than charred, smokey pits.

Reyna came to a sudden stop at the very edge of the village where a strange line had been dug into the snow. It stretched from right to left, encircling the buildings. The ground inside of it was black, unlike the ice that appeared untouched where Reyna stood outside of it.

"That is unusual," Glencora said, suddenly far more interested in their findings. "What do you reckon that's about?"

"I am certain it is nothing good."

"And you are still pigheaded enough to look for survivors? With a mark like that on the ground?"

"It looks more like a boundary than a mark." Reyna gave her sister a slight smile and stepped over the line. "Come along. Or I'll tell Father you left me to search the village all by myself."

Glencora scowled.

As always, Reyna simply ignored her. She did not have to follow Father's strict orders as Glencora did. She was not a future queen, to be wed to a High King's son. She was not even a princess or a lady anymore. She had shrugged off her courtly duties to fulfill the desires of her warrior heart. Appearances did not matter to her in the least.

What did matter to her were the fae of the Ice Court. She had not taken a vow to protect them, not like the other warriors had, and she never would—former princesses were never allowed to become true sworn Shieldmaidens. But she would protect them all the same.

Reyna took a deep breath and stepped across the boundary. For a moment, she stood and waited, cocking her head to listen with ears that curved into sharp points at the top. The trees were silent in the distance. Not even the ground beneath her feet pulsed with life. In the sky above, Wingallock circled the village. Through his eyes, Reyna saw no stirrings, not of darkness nor of light.

With a nod, she drew her ice dagger from the sheath she wore belted around her waist at all times. The dull light from the cloud-scudded sky glinted off the sharp blade. It had been her mother's dagger, along with the matching ring she wore on her left hand and the black hoarfrost cloak around her shoulders, held in place by a brooch painted with the Ice Court's sigil—a silver-blue pair of ice wings. The items gave her strength. They filled her bones with courage. Remembering her mother reminded her of why she fought so hard.

Reyna's boots crunched as she slowly crept through the ruined village. Every building was covered in soot as if a fire had raged there for days. But Reyna knew the truth. The Ruin did not come from fire. It came from something else, something hidden in the skies.

She had once seen the Ruin take an entire village. As a small child, she had not quite understood what she'd witnessed. It was a heavy darkness that fell like a blanket, as familiar as snow. At first, the specks of black were soothing to the skin. A soft caress against the cheek. But then the darkness squeezed tight, trapping everyone in place. Their charred bones were the only thing left behind, the only sign that there had ever been life.

She shuddered and pressed forward. Casting her gaze across the blackened ground, she searched for survivors, her heartbeat thumping loud in her ears. Her palm had gone slick around the dagger's silver hilt, and her leather tunic suddenly felt far too tight. Fighting the Ruin was her calling, but that did not mean she was immune to fear.

A soft moan drifted out from the husk of a building just before her. Her footsteps faltered as she came to a sudden stop. The building was small, its thatched roof charred from whatever magic had tormented this place. There had once been a single door, but no windows. Through a gaping hole in the side of the building, she could see a single room. Three beds had been pushed up together along one wall. Beneath those beds were three huddled forms.

And they were alive.

Reyna's footsteps were loud as she charged into the hut. "Glencora! In here!"

She slid to her knees, her trousers ripping on the rough floor, and peered beneath the bed. Three pairs of frightened silver eyes stared back at her. The survivors were all young. Barely ten years old, if that. Reyna's heart flickered as she reached out a hand to the nearest one. "Come. Take ahold of my hand."

Tiny fingers slipped into her palm, and she squeezed them tightly. One by one, she pulled the frightened children out from their hiding place beneath the bed. When all three were safely in front of her, she checked for wounds.

"Does anything hurt?" she asked, brushing the silver hair away from tiny faces full of fear. "How long have you been hiding here?"

"Days," the youngest whispered. He was a tiny, little thing, bundled up in ragged blankets with only his head poking through. Soot flecked across his ruddy cheeks, but he was not bleeding.

Reyna cupped his cheek with her palm. "I am so very

sorry. No word has reached the castle of an attack or we would have come sooner. But my sister and I are here now, and we will get you to safety. Tell me your names."

"I'm Aeron. That is my twin sister, Abria, and my eldest sister is named Arianna."

"Are you Princess Reyna?" the eldest, Arianna, said. Slight and willowy with gleaming silver hair, she was the spitting image of a younger Glencora.

Reyna did not have it in her heart to correct the girl. She was no longer a princess, but there was no need to explain that to her now. "I am. And my sister, Princess Glencora, is here with me."

As if summoned by her name, Glencora appeared in the blackened doorway, eyes wide. Wind whipped at her ice blue cloak. "You found survivors."

Her words were laced with shock. Reyna could not blame her for that. The Ruin rarely left the living behind. In the past three villages that had fallen, not a single soul had been found. Only corpses.

"Come, Glencora," Reyna said, standing and lifting Abria into her arms. "Help me get the children back to the castle."

"I can walk myself," said Arianna, lifting her chin. "I do not need to be carried."

"Very well." Reyna bit back a smile. She had seen what could happen to a child's spirit when confronted by the Ruin. Her sister, Eislyn, had gone years without speaking before she recovered. Perhaps these lucky souls had not witnessed the gruesome deaths themselves. Hiding may have saved them, in more ways than one.

Glencora gathered Aeron into her arms, and together, the two sisters trekked through the village, rushing in the direction they had come. Reyna could not help but want to turn back and continue her search through the rubble.

If these children had survived, perhaps others had as well.

"Glencora," she said, as they reached the boundary of the village. Up ahead loomed the snow-blanketed Hoarfrost Forest through which they would find the Rowan Road that would take them back to their home in the Ice Court's capitol city, Falias. "You are capable and strong. I am certain you can get the children safely back to the castle alone."

A deep frown fell across her sister's face. "In the name of the Dagda, I swear to you Reyna, do not do what I think you are about to do."

Reyna gestured at the village where her snow owl still circled overhead, her heart torn at the thought of leaving any surviving low fae behind. "We have not searched the entire village."

Glencora huffed as she moved the child from one hip to the next. "Honestly, Reyna, I cannot believe you are suggesting you will stay and continue the search alone. It is far too dangerous. What if the Ruin returns?"

"The Ruin has already done all the damage it can. It will not strike the same village twice. It never has before."

"I cannot lie to you. I am fiercely against this decision. In fact, I refuse to return to the castle without you."

"You must." Reyna flicked her eyes down at the eldest child who was watching their exchange with increasingly frightened eyes. "The children must be taken to the castle at once. Alchemist Naal will need to ensure there are no hidden wounds or brewing illnesses."

Glencora shook her head, her silver hair rippling in the winter wind. "One of these days, you will be the end of me, Reyna."

Reyna's heart ached at her sister's words. Soon, Glencora would no longer have to deal with such a troublesome sister. Even as understanding as her family had been, Reyna knew her choice to become an unsworn Shieldmaiden had caused them nothing but strife.

With a huff of irritation, Glencora stepped across the boundary, still cradling the child in her arms.

"Do not go angry. Let me help you take them to the horses," Reyna said just as her sister's leather boots crunched snow.

Glencora screamed.

Her sister fell to her knees, her arms loosening their hold around the child. The snow blanketed their fall, but Glencora's scream did not fail. Reyna's heart pounded against her ribs as she wildly scanned the forest ahead for a hidden attacker. She had not seen an arrow whistle by, but ice fae often used small poison darts in stealth attacks such as this.

Reyna rushed toward her sister, and the blackened ground began to rumble. A wild wind whipped at her face. The snow suddenly ceased. The clouds overhead went black, their bellies heavy with darkness. Her footsteps slowed, her hand flying to clutch the brooch at her neck.

A rumble much like thunder rolled across the sky. The clouds flickered, their shadows cracking open to reveal a strange light hidden within just as dark flecks rained down like black snow.

Reyna's heart pounded. She had seen this once before. Memories flooded her mind that she had tried so hard to bury deep inside. Her mother's screams filled her ears, drowning out Glencora's own cry for help. And then the forest began to hum, dragging Reyna out of her reverie. It was a strange, melancholy sound, one that made her ice dagger quake.

"Wingallock!" Reyna shouted. "Come!"

The children began to cry as Reyna dropped to her

sister's side. Her knees dug into the cold snow, but she did not feel the chill. Ice fae never did. Reyna gathered Glencora into her arms, pulling her head into her lap. Glencora stared up at the sky, horror flickering across her face. A few grains of black fell onto her face. Her eyes widened. And then a single fleck pierced her gaze.

Screaming, Glencora clawed at her eyes.

Reyna curled over her sister's face, blocking the Ruin. She glanced up and caught the gaze of the children who had huddled together in the snow. They held their rags over their faces. The youngest boy cried.

"Don't look up at the sky," Reyna whispered to them. "Keep your eyes shut tight."

The children squeezed their eyes shut, tears leaking down their cheeks.

Reyna reached back and flicked up her hood, shielding her own face from the onslaught of the Ruin. She twisted to Wingallock, who had settled on her shoulder, his claws piercing her skin. "Fly ahead. Warn Father."

Wingallock gave a hoot and took off through a sky full of dark soot. She prayed to her forsaken god that the snow owl would make it out of the Ruin alive. Reyna did not know how she could survive without her familiar. Their souls were as linked as her heart to her veins.

Glencora still screamed, a high-pitched noise that cut through the terrible silence.

Reyna gave a whistle, and their two grey-speckled mares galloped out of the forest. She wrapped her arms tight around Glencora, shushing her screams. "Sister, listen to me. I've got you, but I need you to calm down. None of us will make it out of this alive unless you swear that you will trust me."

Glencora's sharp breaths shook her body, but she quieted and clung tightly to Reyna's arms. With eyes wide and unseeing, she gave a quick nod. Reyna pulled her sister to her feet, thankful for her training. If she had not spent so much time wielding a sword, she would not be able to bear her sister's weight, even as slight as she was. Slowly, she helped Glencora onto her horse's back. All the while her sister was silent, her eyes shut tight.

"Go on then," she whispered into Mannin's ear, slapping the horse's rump. The horse took off through the forest, snow spraying up from the ground.

Reyna turned to the children. "You're next."

She lifted them onto her own mare's back in turn. They were small enough that all three fit. "Enbarr knows the way. Just hold on tight."

The children disappeared into the forest on Enbarr's back. With one last glance behind her, Reyna shook her head. Even she would not risk a continued search of the village. It would not take long for the Ruin to seep through her cloak and eat the flesh off her bones.

Specks of black clung to Reyna's cloak as she took off through the forest. She ran toward the Rowan Road, her pace slow as she struggled to find purchase in the snow. When the thick canopy of trees finally twisted together overhead to shield her from the falling Ruin, she unclasped the brooch and tossed her mother's cloak off her shoulders, leaving it behind on the ground.

She continued on, but risked a single glance over her bare shoulder. Where the cloak had fallen, the crisp snow had transformed into a pile of pulsing soot.

Reyna shook her head and carried on. She did not know how she had survived, but that did not matter to her now. She had to get home to her sister.

F ather's expression was grim as he stepped out of Glencora's bedchamber. "Alchemist Naal says she may survive, but it will be a long fight. And she may never regain use of her eyes. She may be blinded. Permanently."

Reyna steadied herself on the slick stone wall, sconces of glowing ice casting a blue haze onto her Father's lined face. She had done this to her sister. Glencora had wanted to turn back. Tears filled Reyna's eyes, hot and full of nettles. "I am so sorry, Father."

He clicked his tongue. "The Air Court is on the Rowan Road. When they arrive, they will reject our proposed alliance. There will be no betrothal. The future High Queen of the Air Court cannot be blind. It is against their laws."

Even now, in the depths of his grief, Father could not forget the political alliance with the Air Court. Reyna could not blame him, in a way. It would end the skirmishes, and help keep their people safe. Together, they would be far stronger against their common enemies, the Wood and Sea Courts. Together, they could perhaps beat the Ruin.

But Reyna did not want to think about that now. Not while Glencora roiled in her bed, her eyes burning from a powerful darkness that had somehow survived even after the Dagda had drained most magic out of Tir Na Nog.

"They will be angry," Reyna said.

"Only if we fail to provide them with an alternative," he said. "We have promised an alliance, a betrothal. We shall give them one."

Reyna's eyes widened as she stumbled back against the wall. If Father meant to fulfill their promise, then it would be Eislyn betrothed to the High King's only living son. He was not agreeable at all. Cunning, wicked, and revelrous, the rumours said. He'd fought in battles against the Ice Court, slicing his sword through ice fae necks. Reyna had fought against him herself. When Glencora had agreed to wed Prince Thane, it had turned Reyna's stomach, but she had known her sister would be strong enough to survive. Surely her father could not expect Eislyn to take up this quest, not in her current state. He must not be speaking of her younger sister at all.

Reyna shook her head. "But I formally withdrew myself from the line of succession. I am an unsworn Shieldmaiden, not a future High Queen."

"So then it will be your sister."

Eislyn. Reyna closed her eyes. Eislyn was still wounded from that night so long ago. Her father could not send her into the arms of a lethal prince, who had killed so many of their kind.

Reyna swallowed hard. "Eislyn is not the right choice for Thane."

Her father's jaw clenched. "No, she most certainly is not. Glencora is, but she is sick, blinded, and in excruciating pain. What would you have me do? Call off the alliance?"

A sharp pain went through Reyna's heart. So many of their people had died. If they did not make the alliance now, their ancient court might not survive. There were rumors of an impending invasion from the Wood Court. In addition to them, the Sea Court was always plotting, but no one knew quite what. Without the Air Court's numbers, Ice would surely fall.

"When will Prince Thane arrive?" Reyna asked.

"A moon ago, I received word they are approaching the Shard," her father replied. "Glencora has one week to recover from the Ruin."

2
LORCAN

Halfway down the long and windy road that stretched from the Air Court's capital city, Tairngire, to the northern ice city of Falias, news arrived on owl wings. Prince Thane's entourage slowed to a stop, horse hooves bumping against the rough, frozen ground. Lorcan rolled back his shoulders and sighed. Before magic had vanished from Tir Na Nog, he and the prince could have flown to the Ice Court instead of relying on the Rowan Road. It would have taken a day instead of weeks, and his body wouldn't have felt as though it had been pounded repeatedly by the blunt end of a sword.

A snow-white owl spun through the darkening sky and dropped a slice of parchment from outstretched talons. Prince Thane snatched the note into his gloved hands. The cluster of warriors began to mumble as they waited, the cold creeping in around them now that they were no longer moving forward. Lorcan agreed with their unease. He was not accustomed to these colder climates, and he felt every wisp of icy air in his bones.

Thane scowled and crumpled the note. "My spy inside the Ice Court reports that there is an issue with the betrothal. I may need to marry one of the younger sisters. Eislyn or Reyna, he says."

"Reyna?" Lorcan could not hide his surprise. There were many things said about Reyna Darragh, but *courtly* was not one of them. As he understood it, she had personally removed herself from the line of succession in order to become a Shieldmaiden. She rode horseback through the forests, her wild hair tangling in thorny, icy branches. She fought in battles with a sword as tall as she.

Surely the High King of the Ice Court—soon merely a king—did not expect Prince Thane to wed a female as rough and unruly as that.

Although…it could prove to be an interesting development. The hidden mark on Lorcan's right shoulder pulsed. He would have to get the news to the exiles immediately.

Thane tossed the parchment over his shoulder. It drifted onto the icy ground and was soon covered by falling snow. No evidence was left behind that the note had ever existed.

They resumed their trek toward the looming forests in the distance, a whistling wind whipping around their group. There were seven of them in total. Prince Thane always preferred to travel with six of his closest guards. They'd journeyed north for a week across the air fae lands before passing the border into the icy tundra. And they still had another week on the road before they reached Falias.

"This will not do," Thane said. "I agreed to marry the eldest. She is a great beauty and understands what is expected from her as my betrothed. I fear Reyna will run barefooted through the halls, the bottom of her dress stained with dirt. Eislyn might not be a much better option. I have heard she rarely leaves her chambers."

Lorcan raised his brow as he took in the prince of the Air Court. With long golden hair and matching eyes, he was the portrait of air fae nobility. His ears were as sharply-cut as his cheekbones, and an elaborate tattoo had been etched into his skin years ago, that of a leafless hawthorn tree, its naked branches stretching wide across his forehead. He lounged on his glistening black steed, his crown of twisting golden thorns askew. On official royal business, Thane wore a sleek set of leather armor dyed gold. However, he usually preferred a much more relaxed approach to daily dress.

"Your own garments are often stained with dirt, Thane. Particularly after a lively revel," Lorcan said with a smile as his horse cantered ever forward. These past years, he had grown close with the prince, and Thane didn't seem to mind when Lorcan spoke freely to him. What would cause offense from anyone else, Lorcan could get away with.

It put him in a perfect position to learn all of Thane's secrets.

"That may very well be true," Thane countered, "but what is expected of me is quite different to what is expected of a future High Queen."

Lorcan could not argue with that. Females in the nobility were not afforded the same freedoms as males, which was why most of Tir Na Nog had been shocked when the High King of the Ice Court had allowed his daughter to choose her own path.

Lorcan thought for a moment as they continued toward the forests ahead. Glencora Darragh had been a good match for Thane. The eldest daughter of a respected High King, she had been well-taught in the ways of courtly life. Together, she and Thane would create an imposing alliance against the sea and wood fae, two courts who were desperate for a chance to tear the Air Court apart.

Reyna Darragh, on the other hand, was unpredictable. Lorcan liked unpredictable.

"Reyna might not be the ideal match," Lorcan began, "but if you fulfill your promise and wed one of the Ice Court's daughters, you will have a new ally and one fewer enemies vying for your crown. And, if you do not…"

"The fighting will begin anew," Thane said with a frown. "And we cannot beat the Wood and Sea Courts alone, not with Ice battling us from the north."

Indeed, they could not. With Ice to the north, Wood to the south, and Sea to the east, the Air Court—and the great capital of Tairngire—was surrounded by enemies. The only relief came from the far southern regions where the Fire Court lay in ruins and the exiled Shadow Court was kept at bay by a stronghold that could never be breached.

Tir Na Nog had been at war for a century. Peace was a fickle thing, scarcely in their grasp. The alliance with the Ice Court held the potential for relief from bloodshed after all these years. If only Thane could marry Glencora Darragh instead of the wild creature who would no doubt bring more chaos into the Air Court. Of course, Lorcan should not care. The weaker the Air Court was, the stronger the exiles could become.

"Perhaps Reyna would be a good match," Lorcan replied with a hidden grimace. "Just because she has fought in battles does not mean she's as wild as the tales would suggest."

"The truth may be twisted but never false. Reyna will be everything we fear."

The truth may be twisted but never false. It was a particularly popular expression in the Air Court. Fae could not lie. It was some deep, honor-bound magic that had not vanished from the continent even with the Dagda's curse, at least for those fae who were still part of Tir Na Nog. Ice, Air, Sea, and Wood. Lorcan supposed those few remaining survivors that fed on soot and ash in the Fire Court could not lie either.

But the exiles could. When they had been banished from Tir Na Nog, all the ties that bound them to the lands had vanished, including the inability to lie.

They had lost the benefits of being a part of the continent, but they had also cast off the downsides.

"I believe it will be a great match," Lorcan said.

When Danu, one of their two moons, glowed high in the steel-colored sky, Lorcan spotted a bustling inn just off the Rowan Road. It backed up to the edge of a thick forest that rose up to scratch the clouds, evergreen limbs sagging from the heavy snow.

A large hanging sign was affixed to the wooden wall above the door, thick black paint spelling out the name, The Sapphire Axe. It swung in the icy breeze, the creak of the hinges drowned out by the cheering and pounding of drums that spilled from windows that glowed with blue light. There were stables to the left full of horses, along with several carts that dotted the snow-packed landscape around the inn. Even from a distance, Lorcan could feel a warmth seeping from the cheery building.

Thane sat up a little straighter on his horse. "We've been camping for days. I could use a night at an inn."

Indeed, the route from Tairngire to Falias had once been full of bright and bustling taverns and inns, but the war had left many too poor to continue on. No one travelled between the two cities anymore except for smugglers and thieves.

"I'm not sure that is wise, your grace," Vreis, a fellow guard, said from the head of the party. Lorcan had known Vreis almost as long as he'd known Thane. He'd joined the prince's personal guard around the same time ten years past. Vreis, unlike most fae, had short-cropped light brown hair and eyes that did not match: one dark brown, one golden. The short hair highlighted his wide jaw and pointed ears. Just like the rest of the guard, he wore dark leather armor with steel braces around his wrists. And he carried a bastard sword made from Tamaris steel, strapped to his back.

"Why ever not?" Thane asked. "It is cold in these lands. We should go inside and enjoy the warmth of the hearth."

"There will be many ice fae inside, your grace," Vreis replied. "Some may not be pleased to meet with the prince of the Air Court."

"I have come here to become their ally," Thane said with a frown.

"Yes, but Thane," Lorcan said, "we've been at war with them for a hundred years. It will take time for such deep-seated wounds to mend."

"Maybe so," Thane said. "However, we will never feel like our kingdoms have become joined if I avoid the ice fae. We will go inside."

Lorcan frowned, but there was little he could do. Once the prince made up his mind about something, he was as impossibly stubborn as anyone he'd ever met. With a sigh, he urged his horse forward and fell into step with Vreis, leaving the rest of the guards to keep an eye on Thane.

He lowered his voice as they approached the inn. "I have a bad feeling about this, Vreis."

"Aye," Vreis replied. "Do not leave the prince's side. Stay on high alert."

After dismounting the horses and leaving them in the stable, Lorcan and Vreis pushed inside the inn to scan for any threats. Thane had not been wrong. As soon as the door swung open before them, a soothing warmth flooded Lorcan's body. He glanced around.

The inn was packed, full of warriors donning Ice Court garb. They wore light armor beneath silver hoarfrost cloaks, the ice fae's sigil etched deeply into the undyed leather at their chest. Every one had a shade of silver hair, some lighter or darker than others, but silver all the same. These would be the warriors who stood guard at the border, rotating in shifts. They clustered around long wooden tables that held flickering blue candles and tankards of ale. The benches were covered in the fur skins of silverclaw bears, and a bard beat at a set of drums beside the roaring hearth. Several of the ice fae warriors turned to stare in their direction, eyes hardened.

They should not have come here.

Vreis momentarily cringed, but then he threw back his broad shoulders, lifted his chin, and stepped forward. Lorcan quickly shook his head and held out a hand to stop him. It was customary to announce the prince when he arrived, but Lorcan did not believe the ice fae would respond favorably to that.

For a moment, Vreis merely stood in the entrance of the inn. And then with a sigh, he turned and opened the door. Prince Thane strode in from the cold night, shining in his golden armor. Lorcan and his fellow guards might blend in, but Thane surely did not. The drumbeat stopped. The buzzing conversation transformed into silence.

Lorcan tensed.

A muscular fae, whose hoarfrost cloak had been tossed

onto the bench beside him, slammed his hands onto the table and stood. The contents of his tankard sloshed. "I know who you are. You're that prince." He spat the last word like a curse.

"You're right," Thane said easily. "Prince Thane of the Air Court. I've come to wed one of your princesses so that we may finally end the bloodshed between our two realms."

"Our princesses are too good for someone like you," the male said in a low growl. "You're not welcome here."

Lorcan cast an uneasy glance at Vreis. As much as Thane hoped for the alliance to solve their woes, there was far too much bad blood between the two kingdoms. In time, the ice fae might thaw to the prince, but it would take more than a day. Perhaps even decades.

But Lorcan also knew that Thane could not back down now that he had stepped foot inside the inn. He was a prince, the future High King. To leave would be to show weakness. And weakness in Tir Na Nog nobility was a death sentence.

Thane ignored the male glowering at him from his table and strode toward the bar maid, a slight female whose cheeks had gone white with fear. Her hands trembled as she reached for a tankard, but another loud slam stopped her short.

"I said you're not welcome here."

Thane turned to regard the fae behind him, face impassive. There were two of them now, both burly males who looked as though they could punch a hole through the very walls of the inn. One had drawn his sword, a glinting silver blade with a hilt carved into a pair of flared wings.

Lorcan ripped his sword from his back, and his fellow guards followed suit. And, as his stomach twisted, he watched as Thane pulled his own sword from its scabbard, twisting it sideways so that the sharp edge faced the argumentative fae.

The two ice warriors charged toward Thane who stayed rooted to the spot, waiting for the attack.

Lorcan cursed the prince beneath his breath. Thane was going to get himself killed. A flash of pain went through his mark, but he ignored it. He had to protect Thane, even if it went against his true liege's orders.

As the ice fae's glinting sword whistled through the air, Lorcan ground his teeth and charged. He got between the attacker and the prince a mere breath before the sword sliced right through Thane's head. He held up his own sword, blocking the blow. The steel rang in the dead silence of the pub, a clash that forced Lorcan to take a step back.

Instantly, his shoulder ached and pain lanced through his head. Gritting his teeth, Lorcan forced himself to fight through it, but the power of his mark was almost too much to bear.

He wanted to rip off his armor and dig the mark out of his skin. With his nails or his sword, he did not care, so long as it no longer plagued him. Stumbling to the side, he slashed again. He managed to knock the fae back, but a dozen more ice fae had joined the fight. Lorcan and his fellow guards were sorely outnumbered. Still, they fought on, throwing themselves in front of the prince to protect him from harm.

From behind Thane, a youthful fae wearing a cook's apron suddenly appeared with a small dagger in his hands.

"Thane, watch out!" Lorcan shouted.

Thane whirled. He stabbed blindly at the approaching boy, whipping his blade around just in time. Thane made contact, and his sword slid deep into the ice fae's body, blood blooming on the white apron.

Everything stopped.

Lorcan's heartbeat thundered loudly in his ears. Prince Thane of the Air Court, the supposed new ally of the ice fae, had just killed an innocent cook, even if the boy had been wielding a blade.

And all of these warriors loyal to their kingdom had witnessed it.

"Vreis," Lorcan grunted. The warrior gave a solemn nod. He shoved his sword into the chest of the nearest ice fae, downing him even as the fight had come to a terrible stop. Lorcan whirled to the next, and the fighting began anew. He sliced and parried, killing fae after fae until blood painted the walls of the inn.

After what felt like hours, the slaughter was over. They had lost two of their guards, but the Ice Court had lost dozens. Lorcan shuddered and wiped red spatter off his face as he strapped his sword onto his back, grimacing at the stench of blood and guts that hung in the once-cheery air.

"We will have to destroy the evidence of this fight," Vreis said quietly as the two of them watched the prince stumble out of the inn and into the night, his face full of shock and regret. "If the Ice Court discovers what happened here this night..."

"They will never ally with the Air Court," Lorcan murmured. "How will we hide it? It isn't as though Thane can lie."

"Their Ruin," Vreis said. "Tales say it looks as though it burns buildings to the ground. We will set fire to this inn. That will destroy all signs of battle. And then we will never again speak of this night."

Lorcan grimaced and turned away, his mark pulsing with pain. He followed Thane out of the inn and explained the plan. The prince looked dumbstruck, his eyes wide, his cheeks as white as clouds.

"This is not what I wanted, Lorcan. How did it come to this?"

"A century of war, my old friend," he muttered. "Death is far more familiar now than peace."

As the flames engulfed the pub, Lorcan stumbled away, insisting he needed to relieve himself in the forest. He stomped through the snow, holding tight to his shoulder. The mark's pain was so intense that he almost fell to his knees.

When he was out of earshot of the prince and his fellow guards, he pushed aside his tunic and hissed, "Begone. I am following orders. Nothing good will come out of my letting the prince get murdered on my watch. There were plenty of others to witness my actions. I would be banished from the Air Court, and your work is not finished as of yet."

He always felt strange speaking to his mark. It was not as though the maker of it could hear him or even see what Lorcan was doing. The mark had a mind of its own, and *it* decided when it thought he wasn't following orders. And, somehow, it could understand him.

Immediately, the sharp pain transformed into a dull ache. Satisfied, Lorcan shoved the sleeve of his tunic over his shoulder to hide the mark, crunching through the snow to rejoin Prince Thane, Vreis, and the others beside the burning pub. Orange light filled the night sky, great plumes of smoke joining the falling snow.

That had been far too close. If the fight had not been so chaotic, Thane would have noticed the sluggishness of Lorcan's swordplay. It could easily happen again. The further he got into his mission, the more his mark doubted his intentions. The more Lorcan doubted them himself. He would have to be more careful.

Otherwise, Thane would soon realize that Lorcan was not who he said he was. Or worse...the mark would finally make him do something he would forever regret.

3
THANE

Prince Thane had never visited the centuries-old city of Falias, and it was nothing as he'd expected. In the midst of so much ice, he had imagined a dark and dreary hulking mass of nondescript buildings sat amidst barren lands. But Starford Castle sat atop a majestic hill, surrounded by snow-blanketed evergreens, its six magnificent towers topped with ice-blue spires that glowed.

The city itself spilled out on the hills around the castle. Buildings were interspersed with the ancient trees, stone houses with thatched roofs that sagged with snow. Most of the buildings were simple structures, but every inch of the outside walls had been carved with designs—a pair of flared wings on some, a single eye on others, one that seemed to watch him as he moved down the snow-packed street. No smoke puffed out from chimneys. Fire wasn't needed here. The ice fae didn't feel the cold.

Still, the city teemed with life. Ice fae hurried through the bustling market streets, eyes alight, mouths turned up into smiles. They wore little, at least compared to Prince

Thane and his entourage, now down to five instead of the seven they'd once had. Because of the slaughter at the inn. Thane tried to push those thoughts into the deepest, darkest corners of his mind, but it was next to impossible. That night at The Sapphire Axe would haunt him to the very end of his days.

A crowd had gathered to watch Thane's procession up the hill to the gleaming castle that he could barely see through the snow and mist that swirled through the air. The further north they'd travelled, the thicker the falling snow had become. Thane could not help but be amazed. Falias was in one of the most southern regions of the realm. What would the ice be like on the northern shores? Perhaps one day he would journey across these strange lands, so long as the alliance went according to plan.

Several ice fae guards, donning armor that matched those of the fallen warriors he'd met at The Sapphire Axe, led the prince and his companions through the open castle gates. A large courtyard stretched out before him. Here, his boots still crunched on snow as the white flakes clung to the elaborate stonework that stretched high into the cloud-scudded sky. The castle here was not as expansive and imposing as the one back home, but it was impressive nonetheless. It looked as though it had been carved from the very ice beneath his feet, as if the ground and the stone had become one.

The royal family stood in the icy courtyard, save the eldest daughter. Their expressions were pinched and their eyes were hooded. Even Reyna, who he recognized at once, had a hollowed look about her. Something must have happened here. He had passed a village hit by the Ruin only two days past. The strange dark magic seemed to be clawing its way through these lands.

If Thane's mother had seen the extent of the damage,

she would have insisted they turn back. The Ice Court was a cursed place, she would say. Thane wasn't entirely certain she'd be wrong.

But she had decided to stay behind at the capital while he went to fetch his betrothed. The High Queen was not here, and Thane had made a promise. Despite his hesitance toward the two younger Darragh sisters, he would never break his word.

Thane regarded Reyna carefully. She was not exactly what Thane had imagined when he'd dreamt of his future queen. Her eyes were wild, along with her cascading silver hair. She was quite tall and awfully lean and toned, most likely due to her insistence on gallivanting around the countryside as if she were a Shieldmaiden. Her father seemed to allow it. Reyna would have to become accustomed to quite different expectations if she were to become his betrothed.

The High King of the Ice Court stepped forward. Cos Darragh towered over his daughters and the various lords and ladies that had come to meet Prince Thane. He wore his dark cloak just as well as he wore an air of superiority. A crown of thick silver branches perched on his head, the sigil of the Ice Court etched deeply into the front of it. Ice wings. A reminder of their magic, their heritage. But very few ice fae still had their owl familiars in a world that had fallen from magic.

Cos Darragh with his waist-length silver hair had long been the ruler of these lands. He was as old as the war. Older, in fact. Thane could see the age in the lines on his face, whiskers stretching out from his eyes. This king had fared far better than Thane's father. With the magic gone from Tir Na Nog, fae were beginning to grow old and die. The alchemists had been unable to find a way to reverse the decay.

"Prince Thane of the Air Court," Cos said, his voice ringing loud and clear in the hushed courtyard. "We welcome you to Falias. I trust you had a good journey."

"Long and cold," Thane said, choosing honesty rather than the mincing of words. "And I believe we passed some of your Ruin not two days past."

The High King nodded. "Yes, there have been several recent brushes with it, I am afraid."

Thane understood. "Princess Glencora. Is she..."

"She is recovering," the High King replied. "However, we fear she may be permanently scarred from the incident. I hope that in her stead you find Eislyn, my youngest daughter, agreeable."

Thane turned his attention on the two daughters who stood silently by their father. They were alike in many ways. Silver coloring, bright eyes, strongly tipped ears that sliced through their hair. He would not deny that there was a breathtaking, ethereal beauty about them.

The youngest sister appeared courtly enough. She wore a pleasant expression, and her hair was perfectly coiled on top of her head. Her cheeks were rosy, and her posture straight. Quite the opposite of her older sister. Reyna clearly held no regard for courtly customs, nor did she seem embarrassed by her unruly hair that flowed around her shoulders. Pride flickered in her eyes, as well as defiance. If Thane cast a too-long glance in her direction, he was certain she might transform him into molten metal with her very eyes.

But it was Eislyn who huffed. "This is ridiculous."

"Eislyn," Cos said, turning toward his daughter with a frown.

"No, I will not bite my tongue," Eislyn said before turning her wide eyes on Prince Thane. "You mean for me to marry this male, but he is our enemy. He has been for as long as I've been alive. He fought in the Battle for the Shard. So many of our people died that day. And he *killed* them. Go on and make this alliance if you must, but *I* will not be a part of it. I will never marry this air fae."

Her cheeks went pink after she'd shot out the words. Thane's spirits promptly darkened. Eislyn whirled on her feet and stomped out of the courtyard. Her silver hair sprung free of its bun, cascading down her slender back.

Cos let out a heavy sigh and pinched the bridge of his nose. "My apologies, Prince Thane. I—"

"Do not worry yourself. The change in circumstances has clearly caught her by surprise." Thane turned to the only sister left standing in the courtyard. Reyna gazed after Eislyn, her face lined with worry. "May I see your sister, Glencora? I would like to wish her well."

Reyna shot him a scorching look that could have melted his very armor. "Very well then. Come along if you must."

As she turned to march toward the nearest tower, Lorcan edged up to Thane and spoke quietly into his ear. "The tales are wrong. Reyna *is* a great beauty."

"Beauty does not a queen make," Thane said tightly.

Thane placed the back of his hand against Glencora's cheek. She was cold to the touch, though clearly breathing. Her eyes open wide, she stared up at him, unseeing. Lorcan had been right. Reyna was a great beauty, but Glencora had the composed, refined air of the nobility, even in her current state. Her smooth silver hair spread across the white pillow like long strands of glistening silk. She had an upturned, button nose, rosy cheeks, and plump lips.

"Can she hear me?" he asked, twisting to face Reyna who stood quietly in the center of Glencora's bedchambers. Blue light glowed from sconces on the stone walls, highlighting the neat and orderly state of the room. There were no extra touches, no added refinement. There was a coldness to these chambers that reflected the landscape outside.

"She is asleep," Reyna said quietly. "It is difficult to tell."

"And she is blind?" he asked.

"Yes. For now."

Thane sat heavily on the chair beside the bed. "I wish to marry Glencora. My mother will not be pleased, but—"

"She may be *permanently* blinded," she said, voice growing hoarse. "She is weak. She can hardly eat. Try as she might, she has not been able to leave that bed."

Thane glanced up to see Reyna giving him a very frank look. "Perhaps she will improve quickly."

"I wish for that more than anyone," Reyna said. "It is my fault she is in this state. However, we must be practical. She is unlikely to recover on her own accord. She needs a cure, one that has never been discovered. We may yet be able to find one. Eislyn is very determined to find the answer herself. But it may be months. Or years. The sun will turn around Tir Na Nog far sooner than Glencora's eyesight will return."

Thane let out a heavy sigh. Even if the strength returned to Glencora's bones, he could not wed her if she remained blind. The laws of the Dagda forbade it. *A king and queen must be whole and unblemished to be fit to rule.* He sometimes questioned his god's laws, even if only silently, within the safety of his own mind. If a ruler was good and strong, why should it matter if they were blemished?

"I aim to fulfill my promise to the Ice Court. I want nothing more than to end the fighting between our realms," Thane finally said after several moments of silence. He glanced up at Reyna, who had moved to stand over her sister, staring down at her with a pained, pinched expression on her face. "But how am I to do that with one princess ill, one defiantly opposed to marrying me, and one no longer a princess at all?"

Reyna lifted her eyes to meet Thane's. The anger had gone from them now, her mind too focused on her ailing sister. "You must understand my younger sister's situation. All she knows of you are the stories she has heard."

"Stories you yourself have told her, I suppose."

The former princess pressed her lips together and nodded. "You have been our enemy, Prince Thane. For a very long time. And I saw you kill those I loved with my own eyes."

Thane knew that better than anyone. He had fought on the battlefield against the ice fae during the bloodiest slaughter in their shared history: The Battle for the Shard —the small strip of land that separated their courts. He'd seen Reyna through the clashing of swords, wielding her own as if it weighed little more than a twig, her silver hair a tornado of power around her. The two had never come to blows, even if his father had ordered Thane to seek her out. It had been the first time he had ever refused to do his father's bidding.

So many souls had died that day. Hundreds of air and ice fae had been slaughtered. As Thane had stepped through the blood-drenched snow, corpses piled up waist-high, he had made a vow to himself. The war with the Ice Court had to end. He and his army had not tried to take the Shard ever again, though it had taken him six years to convince his mother of a full alliance. In the end, she had agreed. His father never had.

Even now, the High King of the Air Court sat on his

throne, angrily shouting about his son's decision to extend a hand to their northern neighbors.

And Thane had then risked it all—the time, the effort, the pleading, the safety of his people—by stepping foot inside that inn, The Sapphire Axe. His stomach twisted at the thought, memories churning through his mind. The blood and guts splattered on the cheery wooden walls. The moans of pain before the survivors had succumbed to the flames.

Thane had only been trying to prove a point at first. He was their new ally, and he would not run away, weak and afraid. And then, he'd only been trying to protect himself. That cook had appeared from nowhere. Thane hadn't meant to kill him.

With a sigh, he stood and turned his thoughts back onto the present. "We will never become allies if we cannot put the past behind us."

Reyna gave him an odd look. "Eislyn is special. She is unlike you and me. What kind of assurances can you give to me? The tales say that you are wicked, cruel, and revelrous even off the battlefield. And I have seen you fight."

Thane lifted a brow. "You speak like a father."

"I speak like an older sister."

He smiled. "I'm here so that our two realms can become one. No more killing. No more death. If that is my aim, why would I be cruel to my wife?"

"You haven't answered the question," Reyna said quietly.

The truth may be twisted but never false. With the inability to lie, fae were often clever with their words, and there were unspoken rules on what could and could not be asked. Yes and no questions were often refused. If one always responded to questions when the answer was a yes, then it became clear when the answer was a no. It was the only way to protect one's deepest secrets from a harsh world where lies were as uncommon as magic now was.

"I will not be cruel to Eislyn. You have my word."

Reyna sighed and closed her eyes. "I cannot lie. I do not want you to marry my sister, but my kingdom needs peace. I will speak with her and make her understand why this alliance is as important as it truly is. I'll have her sit next to you at your welcome feast this evening. Be charming. And kind. We may be able to salvage this yet."

Hope flared in Thane's chest. Rising from the chair, he smiled. "Thank you, Reyna."

She held up a finger to stop him. "But I must warn you, if you are ever cruel to my sister, *ever*, then I—"

"You'll be forced to put me in my place? I would expect nothing less," he said, still smiling.

"No. I will kill you."

4

REYNA

Thane Selkirk was everything that Reyna did not like about courtly life. He wore an air of superiority like a cloak, and he peered down his very sharp nose at everyone beneath him. The low fae who served his food were nothing more than objects who would scurry around, doing whatever he pleased.

Unfortunately, Reyna had been seated directly beside him at the head table when Eislyn had not appeared for the feast. Reyna had spent the afternoon urging her sister toward the betrothal, as much as the conversation had pained her. Her younger sister was not suited to this task, and she deserved far better than this enemy of a prince. But Eislyn was their only option.

And she had made her position very clear.

"What have you studied?" Thane tried as he took a long gulp of wine from a chalice that matched his sleek golden hair.

"I have studied horse riding, owlry, sword and arrow skills," she said crisply. That had not been what he'd wanted to know, but it was how she chose to answer all the same. Thane wanted to know what wifely, courtly skills she possessed. The answer to that was *none*.

Reyna did not know needlework, she could not play an instrument, and she certainly could not smile sweetly and listen to the dreary conversations between noble males.

Thane paused with his chalice halfway to his mouth, and then he eked out a very strained smile. "I see. Your father has certainly been lenient with you. Your sister, Eislyn...does she possess the same skills? What kind of training has she undergone? Similar to Glencora, I suspect."

Reyna gave him a sharp look. "Eislyn is not here."

Thane set down his chalice, sighing. "Reyna, I do not wish for conflict between us."

"Then, let us change the subject to something else," she said through gritted teeth. "I understand the importance of our alliance, but I do not wish to discuss my sister as if she is meat you wish to buy from the market."

Silence hung heavy between them even as the roar of the feast filled the air. It seemed as though the entire Ice Court had turned out for the feast. Some of the lords and ladies were eager to meet their new ally, but far more were curious to lay their eyes on the enemy who would steal one of their princesses away from the castle. There had been very little outright hostility, though their veiled words had been clear enough. The ice fae did not trust the prince.

From the head table, Reyna stared out at the lively Great Hall. Two long wooden tables stretched across the stone floor, silver cloths draped along the length of them. Dishes were placed at regular intervals. There was roasted rabbit, venison pie with a flaky crust, and piles of buttery potatoes. The Ice Court had even imported slabs of sharp cheese from the Empire of Fomor specifically for this occasion.

Six banners hung along the walls, the court's sigil proudly displayed in silver and blue. Before the war began a century ago, each banner in the Great Hall had been different, each highlighting one of the six courts of Tir Na Nog. Back before the realms had fallen apart.

"You care very deeply for your sister," Thane said, lifting his golden brows toward the hawthorn tree tattoo that stretched across his forehead. "Both sisters, I expect."

"I do," she said. "They are the warmth that beats through these frozen lands."

"Ah. Now I understand the words of your court." He gave Reyna a slight smile. "I never knew my older siblings, so it's difficult to imagine the protective instinct you must feel."

"I would do anything for them."

He turned and lifted his chalice once again. "Even marry a prince you do not like after formally removing yourself from the line of succession?"

Surprise flickered through Reyna's mind. "I…"

He emptied his drink and then motioned at the nearest servant. "Do not look so concerned. This was never what you had imagined for your life, and I will not hold your resistance against you."

"That's very kind," Reyna murmured, wondering if there was some kind of catch.

"I only ask that you remember what is expected of a princess, and of a future queen. It is quite different than what is expected of a warrior."

Reyna frowned. "Perhaps it shouldn't be."

Thane let out a light laugh. "You may be right in that, but there is little we can do to change that. Instead, we must fulfill the roles that the Dagda has given us. If he decides that you ought to be my High Queen, then so be it. But Reyna, you must do what is required of you."

Reyna grabbed her own chalice and drank deeply of the sweet wine. A mere second ago, she had forgotten how she felt about Thane and this entire alliance. He had almost seemed agreeable for a fleeting moment in time. Kind and understanding. But he was anything but.

"Unfortunately, I am not an option. I am no princess."

Reyna suddenly felt the weight of a pair of eyes. She turned from Thane's unyielding gaze and scanned the rousing crowd. The table that sat on the lefthand side of the hall did not hold the nobility. Instead, it had been packed with guards, warriors, druids, and stewards of the crown. One of them stared right at her.

She recognized the male as one of Thane's personal guards. He had introduced himself as Lorcan, she believed. With chin-length black hair that hung in loose waves around his rugged face, his expression was shielded, but there was no mistaking the piercing dark eyes. He wore leather armor that clung tightly to his muscular frame, and a glinting Tamaris steel bastard sword was strapped to his back. As she met his eyes, his gaze never faltered. And something strange twisted in her gut.

Reyna flushed, sat back, and frowned. Why was this male staring so intently at her?

"Ah, you have spotted Lorcan," Thane said from beside her. "He is my most trusted guard."

"Does he often stare holes into stranger's faces?" Reyna asked sharply. He was still watching her every move. It was unnerving.

Thane chuckled. "Oh, yes. He intimidates everyone he meets. But he has saved my life on more than one occasion. So, he can glower as much as he likes."

"Saved your life?" Reyna cut her eyes toward Thane. His face was impassive, but a darkness churned in his golden eyes. "There have been attempts made against you?"

"You sound surprised," Thane said. "We are at war. Many rightfully believe that my death would be a great blow to the Air Court. I have no living siblings. With my demise, there would be no heir."

Reyna sat back in her chair. "I had no idea the Sea Court had become so bold."

"Perhaps, but it could have just as easily been the Wood Court," Thane said.

"You do not know which court it was?" she asked.

"It was one or the other," he said. "This is why our alliance is so essential to the future of our people. Together, our might is stronger than theirs alone."

Reyna frowned. She now understood why Thane was eager to continue with the betrothal, even if he found Eislyn less appealing than Glencora. Thane needed them just as much as they needed him.

"I do not disagree with you," she said. "However, I am not the one you need to charm. I am a Shieldmaiden. Not a princess."

"Here you are, your grace." A serving girl appeared behind them with a jug of wine. She bowed low, pink dotting her cheeks. "Do you wish for some more wine?"

Thane frowned and held up his chalice, silently waiting while the serving girl poured his wine. As soon as she bustled away, he stood. "Excuse me for a moment, *Shieldmaiden*. There is something I need to attend to."

Reyna scowled up at him. "You're leaving during your own welcome feast?"

"I'll return soon enough." With that, Thane strode away from the table and headed toward the door that led out into the courtyard. An empty chair now sat beside her. On the other side of it, her father narrowed his eyes. He likely thought she had said something to run him off, but she'd only spoken the truth.

39

Frowning, she turned her gaze back onto the feast where the rest of the court appeared to be having a much more enjoyable night. Reyna watched Thane's warrior edge toward the door. He cast a furtive glance around the feast as he pressed a large hand against the warped wood. Setting her chalice down before her, Reyna could not help but lean forward, head cocked. Did he plan to follow the prince? Then, why was he moving so curiously?

Lorcan cast one last glance behind him, and then he pushed out into the night. She must follow him.

"I'll be back in a moment, Father." Reyna pushed up from the table, and those around her fell silent. She wished they would carry on with their conversations, paying her no mind. She had grown accustomed to being invisible these past years. With Prince Thane here at court and the question of the betrothal hanging in the air, the entire kingdom had grown far too interested in her every move.

Father dragged his gaze away from the feast and frowned up at her. "Do not tell me you are begging off from your duties already. I asked you for this one night, Reyna."

"I will return," she said with a tight smile. "I need some fresh air. It is stifling in here."

"Very well." Shaking his head, he turned back toward Lord Morcant, who sat on her father's other side. He was one of the more esteemed lords of the realm, their distant cousin who oversaw the trade route up north.

Reyna hurried toward the door. It had taken far too long to extract herself from the feast, and she hoped she would catch sight of Lorcan before he vanished into the night. He was up to something. She was certain of it. A loyal warrior he might be, but there was something else lurking beneath the surface. Reyna was rarely wrong in her instincts. So, she followed the warrior into the night.

5
EISLYN

Eislyn often felt as though she and her sister, Reyna, were opposites. Reyna adored the wilderness. She thrived in the thorns and the snow. Eislyn hated the outside world. She would rather curl up beside a blazing fire with a book in one hand and a goblet of wine in the other, even if she was immune to the cold.

And yet, Eislyn found herself agreeing with her sister for once. The gods be damned. She had no desire to play power games while her skirts swished against the gleaming, golden floors of the Air Court. She would not marry Thane, no matter how desperately her father begged her.

Thane was a cruel male, and she had far better things to attend to than transforming into his polite, quiet little bride who followed his every command. He was known to spend his nights in wicked revelry, and he'd slaughtered hundreds of ice fae in the Battle for the Shard.

"'Allo, Eislyn," her old, dear friend, Albin, said as she whispered into the library and shut the heavy door quietly behind her. He sat at the table in the very center of the carpeted floor, a pair of spectacles perched on his nose, his long hair white at the ends. Albin was an old fae, even older than her father, from a time before war had ripped the world to shreds. A time when magic filled the ruined lands. As it disappeared, so did he. He had aged a great deal, just as the humans did in the kingdoms beyond the Mag Mell Sea.

"Glad to see you, dear Albin." Eislyn crossed the room and sank into the high-backed wooden chair across from his. A familiar musty scent filled her nose. The stacks loomed high along the curving tower walls, reaching up toward the glass ceiling above. Some of the tomes here were ancient. Far more ancient than even Albin. They spoke of a time she wished she could have seen. Peace, tranquility, happiness. A world without Ruin.

"I cannot say I am surprised you have come here this night." He glanced up, slightly smiling. His pale blue eyes twinkled. "Avoiding that prince then, are you?"

"I have no wish to be wed to a prince who would rather feast on venison pie than seek to heal these lands," she said sharply.

"All princes and princesses must eat, my dear," he replied. "Even the most honorable of them."

As if in response, her own stomach growled.

"Well," she said. "If *you* are so interested in meats, then why are you here in the library rather than at the feast?"

He sighed and pressed his withered hands against the curling pages of the book spread out before him. "I suspect our reasons for being here are quite similar. Your sister is ill. We must find a cure immediately."

Hope flickered in Eislyn's troubled heart. "I am glad I am not the only one who sees the importance of finding a cure. Even Reyna has attended the feast."

"Your sister has a good heart. You know that better than most," Albin replied, giving her a steady look. "She believes the alliance with the Air Court will save these lands, which will in turn save our people. And there may be truth in that."

Eislyn sighed and glanced at the towering stacks. Somewhere in the pages of an ancient manuscript, she hoped to find the answer to her one and only question. Could the Ruin be destroyed? It had not come from nothing. She had been searching her entire life for a cure, but a new fire had been lit beneath her feet these past weeks. Her sister's life hung in the balance.

And nowhere in these many books had she ever found the answer.

Still, she would keep looking. It was the only thing she could do.

"If she believes in the alliance, then why doesn't Reyna marry the prince herself?" Eislyn asked.

"Because she cannot, my dear," Albin said. "She removed herself from the line of succession. Even if everyone around her considers her a princess, she isn't one anymore. The Air Court will not accept anything but a true royal blessed by our god."

"Father would return the title to her if she asked," Eislyn said. "You know he would. He wishes for it every twin moon."

"Aye." Albin nodded. "But she *must ask*."

With a frustrated sigh, Eislyn pushed up from the table and drifted toward the stacks that stretched along the curved walls. Over the years, this library had become her home far more than her chambers ever had. Set at the top of the tallest tower, the library's glass ceilings provided a view of the constellations on nights when the sky wasn't full of snow-thick clouds. The shelves were a jumble of multi-colored spines, books collected from all across the continent. At the very top of each stack, only accessible by a tall wooden ladder, curling scrolls were bunched together.

She wandered to the far left where they kept their many tomes of history, so many that they flowed from the shelves to form towering stacks on the floor. She gazed at the titles even though she knew every one. She had read all of these books. More than once. Eislyn did not quite know what she was looking for. Some kind of sign, a signal that would aim her in the right direction to find a cure.

The library door clicked open. Surprised, she whirled toward the sound and almost gasped out loud at the sight of Prince Thane's muscular form filling up the doorway. He wore a new set of gold-dyed leather armor, clean and polished rather than the dirt-stained set he'd worn when arriving in Falias. With his sleek hair topped with that golden crown, he looked very much the part of a powerful prince. She hated him for it, even as she stared in amazement at the elaborate hawthorn tree tattoo etched onto his forehead.

The prince gazed around the room until his eyes landed on Eislyn. She swallowed hard and grabbed a random book off the nearest shelf, just so she had something to hold tight to her chest.

"Hello, Princess Eislyn." He tipped his head forward in a slight bow, even if he did not need to do so. "I need to speak with you."

"If you have come here to change my mind, then you will be sorely disappointed. You should return to the feast. The celebration is for you, after all."

Thane ducked into the room, and the door slammed hard behind him. He glanced at Albin. "I would rather discuss this alone."

Eislyn frowned. "Albin is my dear friend, and he knows

everything in the world about me. I will not send him away based on your whims."

"Princess." Albin stood and gave a slight bow before turning toward the prince and doing the same. "Please excuse me. There is a task I must attend to for a moment. Eislyn, I will return momentarily."

Eislyn frowned, her heartbeat flickering in her chest. She did not want to be left alone with Prince Thane. "Albin, please."

"I will only be gone for a moment."

The old male bustled past Thane, pushed open the door, and disappeared into the dimly-lit corridor beyond, leaving Eislyn alone with one of her greatest enemies. It was the very opposite of how she had longed to spend her evening. Her absence from the feast must have taken his notice. An unfortunate development.

Prince Thane gazed around the library. There was no appreciation in his expression. He had probably never read a single book in his wicked life. "I see you are a reader then."

She clutched the book tighter to her chest. "How did you find me?"

A slight smile tugged at his curving lips. "Princesses cannot go anywhere without being seen."

"Maybe not in your court, but we allow our females far more freedom than you are accustomed to," she snapped. She could not help herself. She had come here to escape the prince, and he had followed her into her safe haven all the same.

"Yes, I see that," he replied. "Your Reyna has the freedom to do as she pleases."

"And have you come here to speak with me about Reyna?"

"I have come to apologize for my past actions. I cannot

change them now, but I can say I am sorry for any pain I have caused."

She stared at him. Based on what Reyna had told her about the Battle for the Shard, he had certainly meant it at the time. "Your apology has been heard. However, that does not mean I will agree to be your wife."

"Of course not," he answered, far more kindly than she expected. He turned his attention back onto the books, gazing around the library as if it were a strange curiosity he had never before seen. "The servants say you spend a great deal of time here. I expected to find these shelves packed full of fiction, but I see a number of historical tomes instead."

"Yes," she answered stiffly. "I am researching our past in order to save our future."

He cast her a strange glance. "How do you mean?"

She gestured at the walls of books. "Somewhere, there must be information that can provide answers about the Ruin. I maintain that this strange, destructive magic came from somewhere. If I can find the truth in these pages, perhaps I can save this kingdom."

"Ah." He gave her another kind smile. It unnerved her. "And you could save your sister."

"My sister has rejuvenated my search."

"How many of these books have you read so far?" he asked. "And have you found anything useful as of yet?"

She winced and turned away. "I have read them all, and I have not found a damn thing."

"All of them?" He strode further into the circular room, surprise in his golden eyes. "And you have found nothing?"

"Nothing that offers hope," she said with a sigh. She held out her book and scanned the words on the cover. *The Realm of Ashes by Juzeth Dubh.* It specifically spoke of the dark magic that had destroyed the Fire Court and left it in smoking ruins. Eislyn had been so thrilled when she had found this book in a market on the eastern shores of the Ice Court. She had been certain that whatever had destroyed the fiery kingdom had found its way into the Ice Court's lands. Ash and ruins, unseen flames and blackened husks.

But the tome had provided very few answers. The author had written it fifty years after the horror and did not know the truth of it either.

If she could somehow find a survivor…but she knew she couldn't. The Fire Court had been destroyed five hundred years ago, and fae no longer lived as long as they once had. Without magic to prevent ageing, their world was fading fast.

"I may be able to offer you some hope," Thane said, pulling Eislyn out of her troubled thoughts. He had wandered back over to the center of the library and had tipped back his head to gaze up at the glass ceiling. Overhead, the clouds had scuttled into the darkness and brilliant starlight cast a silvery glow onto Thane's upturned face.

"You?" She frowned. "Because you will pledge to send your armies here to tackle the problem? I do not think brute strength is the solution to destroying the Ruin. Its nature is of magical origin. We need our own magic to return to us. We do not need swords."

"I do not speak of swords," he countered. "Have you not heard of the great libraries of the Air Court? In our capital city alone, we have twelve."

Her eyes almost bugged out of her head. "Twelve libraries in a single city?"

"Yes, Eislyn. Twelve." He gave her a broad smile. "Each one five times larger than the one you have here. If it is answers you seek, then answers you shall find."

"In the Air Court," she said, frown deepening. "I suppose you are trying to dangle your libraries in front of me, hoping I will agree to become your betrothed."

"That is how matches are made," he replied. "There is something that you want, and I happen to have it."

She arched her brows. "Ah, but what is it that *you* want, Prince Thane?"

He cocked his head. "An alliance with your court."

"Yes, but why?" she probed further.

"To combine our strength, put an end to the war between all of the kingdoms, and rule over all of Tir Na Nog."

She drew herself back and lifted her chin. "That is what I suspected. You are everything I thought you were, Prince Thane."

"You do not approve of ambition?" He glanced around. "Tell me, do you not wish for your name to be written in books, celebrating your accomplishments when you rid the realm of the Ruin?"

"No," she said fiercely, curling her hands into fists. "I do not want to end the Ruin for my sake. Do your people mean nothing to you? Does peace not matter? Or is it all king, king, king? Power and status and wealth?"

He flinched and stepped back. "Of course I wish for peace."

"That is not the reason you gave me when I asked why you want this alliance." She closed the distance between them and pushed her finger into the very center of his armored chest where the sigil of his court—a golden crown—had been etched into the leather. "You did not even hesitate when I asked you. Your first thought was of power."

He glanced down at where her finger touched his golden armor, and then back up to her eyes. "Perhaps I am the monster you make me out to be, but that does not change the fact that we both have something the other wants. If you agree to the betrothal, you will have access to every library in my city. You may spend hours there, combing through the books and seeking your answers."

"Maybe so," she said in a harsh whisper, her heart racing. "But I will not marry you Prince Thane Selkirk of the Air Court. I will not help you claim the power you so desperately crave."

6

REYNA

When she pushed open the door, her low-cut, deep blue gown swishing around her slippered feet, a blast of frosty air hit her square in the face. She stepped out into the snow. As the door slammed shut behind her, the icy air cocooned her body. Being a fae born in the north, she did not feel the cold as the fae of other courts did. She was not certain she had ever shivered a day in her life. The snow felt like home. The ice warmed her feet. The bite of it made her feel alive. She wondered if this was how Thane felt when the harsh winds of his kingdom pummelled his face.

Unfortunately, as soothing as the chill felt along her bare arms, unease sunk deep into her bones. There was no sign of Thane's warrior in the courtyard. She cast a glance around the quiet square. During the day, this part of the castle was a bustle of activity. Every morning, her father welcomed the traders of the city through the gates. They would set up their stalls, hawking their wares to the low fae who made the trek into the city from the surrounding villages.

Reyna loved the market. She mingled with the villagers and paid visits to the traders as often as she could. Now that she was no longer an official member of the court, she had the freedom to go almost daily.

She turned left toward the path that led away from the square and deeper into the castle. There, she spotted a pair of large footprints in the snow. Narrowing her eyes in determination, she followed the trail. Her footsteps were quick. She was accustomed to the icy surface, and soon she had wound through the silent castle buildings before coming to a stop just outside the Roost Tower.

The footprints stopped just at the door, which had been left cracked. Blue light splashed onto the snow from the sconces that hung from the interior walls. Frowning, she pushed inside. There was only one reason to visit the Roost. Thane's warrior had come here to send a letter.

Reyna slowly made the long trek up the spiral stone stairs. The Roost was set at the top of the castle's second tallest tower with windows overlooking the northern forests that stretched as far as the eye could see. The Ice Court relied on their owls for most messages, delivered quickly throughout the realm. They had hundreds trained for this purpose, housed in the expansive space above. Wingallock and the few other familiars would sometimes join the other birds in the Roost, though Reyna preferred to keep him in her chambers. She did not like to be parted from him for long.

At the very top of the winding stairwell, Reyna pushed through the door and into the Roost. Inside, hundreds of wings fluttered against the icy air. The six round windows held no glass, allowing the birds to come and go as they pleased, and timber beams had been built into the walls, providing perches and corners for nests.

She glanced around. Lorcan wasn't here either. Disappointment churned through her gut. She had been certain she would catch him in the middle of...something. It was hardly a crime to send a letter, but he'd been acting so odd.

A snow white owl flew down from above and landed gently on her shoulder.

"Hello, Wingallock," she cooed to her owl familiar, stroking the pale feathers beneath his chin. "I do wish you could attend the feast, but Father is afraid you will scare the guests. They are not accustomed to animals like we are. Have you happened to see a grumbly-looking warrior up here recently?"

Wingallock cooed back, and then opened his sharp talons. Inside lay a curled parchment, tied together with blue string.

"What's this?" she asked, frowning.

She took the note and unrolled the parchment. It crackled beneath her touch. Her eyes tripped across the words, horror and anger building within her as each second passed by.

Dearest Reyna,

I understand you are no longer a member of the nobility, but there is no one else I trust with this truth. A week past, I was on the road to Tairngire, determined to smuggle some hoarfrost silk across the border. Please forgive me for that.

I planned to stop at our favorite inn, The Sapphire Axe. And I witnessed something terrible. The prince who has come to wed your sister stopped there for the night. A fight broke out. I cannot say who started it, but I can say who ended it.

Your new prince ally murdered young Zed, the boy we played with in the courtyard, the boy who learned to be a cook. The prince and his guards then killed every single ice fae in that inn, and then burned the place down.

He cannot be trusted. You must do something to stop him.

Return to your place in the court if you must.
 In sorrow,
 Aoiffe

Reyna's heart thundered in her ears as she crumpled the note in her fist. Her old friend, Aoiffe. They had grown up together. They had become Shieldmaidens together. And then they had fought in the Battle for the Shard side by side. Scarred from that blood-soaked field, Aoiffe had turned her back on her duties and then looked to smuggling to get by.

The last time Reyna had seen her, they had argued fiercely.

Reyna put her fist into her mouth and bit down hard to hold back the scream building in her throat. The note spoke of a horror she did not wish to believe, but Aoiffe could not lie, even on paper. The prince, the Ice Court's new ally, had murdered dozens of ice fae on his way to claim his bride.

He had killed Zed. Reyna's squeezed her eyes shut. She could picture the boy's face in her mind's eye, and memories of their time spent running barefoot through the castle grounds flickered across the back of her eyelids.

Anger and determination coiled in her gut, as venomous as a dragon. The call of her warrior soul was a drumbeat in her ears, urging her to battle. She would not stand for this.

❂

Reyna found her sister in the library.

"Eislyn." She was bent over a book, back curled like a coiled snake. Shadows clung to her form, dancing from the candles that dripped wax onto the library table. Unease whispered through Reyna. Her sister had been plagued so long by nightmares, they had started to cling to her like wraiths. Eislyn glanced up from the book, and the strange darkness vanished without a trace.

"Reyna?" Her sister dropped the book onto the table. "What are you doing here? Shouldn't you be at the feast?"

"I need to ask you something very important."

Eislyn frowned. "I refuse to speak of this bloody betrothal anymore. I have made my decision, and Thane should learn that 'no' is in someone else's vocabulary other than his."

"That is not what I came here to ask you."

Eislyn cocked her head, confusion rippling across her face. "Then, why are you here?"

Reyna ground her teeth together, forcing herself to say the words out loud. "Will you help me convince Father to return my titles to me?"

While reading the terror-stricken message from Aoiffe, Reyna had become certain of a horrible truth. There was only one way forward. Only one way to save her kingdom and find a cure for Glencora's illness. Reyna was not fit to be a queen. She knew it. Thane knew it. Even her father knew it. She had not prepared for that kind of role. While her sisters had been inside their chambers memorizing every royal's name and title, Reyna had been in the courtyard swinging a sword at potato sacks stuffed with hay.

But none of that mattered, not when their ally still murdered her people, on their own lands, in their own inns. Her kingdom was not safe so long as Prince Thane still lived. So, Reyna would have to marry him herself, biding her time until he sat on the throne.

And then she would kill him, taking control of his kingdom herself.

7

TARRAH

Tarrah Glas stood outside a short, squat castle made from the gleaming black stone that could only be found in the shadow fae realm. The hulking structure hid in the shadows of the Misty Wastes, but she was near enough to spot its square towers as she demanded to be seen by the exile king. Her head was thrown back, and her long raven hair swished against her armoured waist. The two guards who stood at the gates eyed her with a distinct air of wariness. She did not blame them. Even though she was a low fae of humble birth, they *should* be careful of her.

"What business do you have with the king?" the larger of the two demanded. Wearing grey scales and a thick helmet that shielded all of his face but a piercing set of silver eyes, he was a formidable presence. Indeed, he was almost as twice as tall as she. Clearly, he had ancient Unseelie blood running through his veins.

"Important information. He will wish to hear what I have to say."

The second guard gripped the elaborate hilt of his

longsword. The blade was made of shadowsteel, and the hilt had been carved into two black interwoven antlers, the infamous sigil of the Shadow Court, the very court that High King Sloane Selkirk had destroyed when he'd exiled them from Tir Na Nog fifty years past.

The guard peered down at her with narrowed eyes. "You are a commoner. A low fae. You cannot demand to see the king whenever you wish. If you have need of his assistance, you may bring your concerns to him on the first of the month, just like everyone else."

Tarrah let out an impatient huff. "My concerns are not mine to bear alone. They are important to the future of this exiled court. It has to do with the king's secretive war with the Air Court."

Both guards suddenly straightened. Now, that had gotten their attention.

"Where did you hear such a thing?" the taller asked with suspicion in his voice.

"As I stated, I have some information for the king."

The two guards turned away and bowed their heads as they spoke in quiet whispers. Tarrah watched, striving to hold back her eager hope. She had been trying to speak to the king for weeks. She had travelled across the Shadow Court's lands, across long stretches of scalding deserts with hills full of black shifting sand, with no one to keep her company but the visions churning through her mind.

Finally, the guards turned back toward her, and the taller of the two spoke in a low growl. "We will allow you to see the king. But be warned, low fae. If you make any move against our ruler, your life is forfeit."

Tarrah held back a smile. "I would not expect to survive such a thing."

The guards led Tarrah through the looming gates. The ancient castle rose through the mists, red light from the baking sun glinting across the black stone walls. She walked up the long and winding dirt-packed pathway, her feet struggling to find purchase on the crumbling rocks. Olc Fortress sat atop a dormant volcano, the stone walls looming out of jagged cliffs. Battlements glowed as they rose from pits of fire that flashed against the churning sky.

Olc Fortress only had two small towers, one on each side of the castle. It was an impressive and imposing structure, but it did not hold a candle to the true home of the Shadow Court, the one where their kings and queens had once lived, where rulers had been coronated in the sight of the Unseelie god, where the shadow fae's Seat of Power still sat waiting.

They had been driven out of that stronghold by the Air Court, the king and his entire family brutally slaughtered during the attack. Exiled from the rest of Tir Na Nog, the realm of the shadow fae had been plunged into chaos. In the end, the Lord of Olc Fortress had taken up the mantle of king, but he had never been coronated.

Not on the Seat of Power in the presence of their god.

And that made all the difference in the world, especially to Tarrah.

The two guards pushed opened the wooden doors of a large building that made up most of the castle's grounds. They led Tarrah down a long corridor before pausing at another set of doors. The taller of the two disappeared inside. Tarrah waited, hands clasped tightly in front of her. Now that she had made it through those walls, she knew the king would never turn her away.

Her visions had shown her that much, at least.

A moment later, the door opened once again, and the guard motioned for her to join him on the other side. With a deep breath, she squared her shoulders and stepped through the archway, her heart pounding hard at the thought of finally meeting her king.

Her footsteps echoed as she walked across the stone. The cavernous, empty room was large enough to hold thousands but only a handful stood inside. Four, Tarrah counted. The king himself and three others who were clustered around him.

Tarrah strode forward with the two guards on either side of her, their hands resting on the hilts of their swords. The only object in the entire room—the throne—sat beneath a circular window that glowed with the red light of the sun. It was a basic black chair that had little decoration. Not even antlers curved out of the top.

The king himself looked just as he had in her visions, though it was a shock to see him all the same. The most powerful fae in the entire kingdom was a small, hunched male with a large nose and small, shifting eyes. His brown hair barely reached his ears, and he wore simple black scales that did not stand out from the armor of his warriors.

There was a lot that Tarrah would need to do in order to transform him into the powerful ruler she knew he could be.

"King Bolg Rothach." Tarrah bowed before him, lowering herself to her knees, the stone floor cool and hard beneath her hands. "In the darkness, may I find you well."

"Rise." He appeared weak, but the king's voice was strong, commanding, and sure. Tarrah could understand how he had found himself rising to the throne. He had a power about him, a magnetic force. If given the proper ammunition, he could be a force to be reckoned with. She hoped.

Tarrah rose, but kept her eyes cast to the stone dais. Deference, she knew, was important here. He needed to see that she had no greater ambitions than coming to his aide.

Out of the corner of her eye, she could see the king's advisors frowning at her, though she did not raise her gaze to look their way. She would converse with them some other time. Her focus now was on the king.

"My guard has told me that you wish to speak with me. He said that you insist you have information that is of great value." He did not sound convinced.

"I do, my liege." Tarrah's words were a breath on her lips. She had worked so hard to get here. She had fought death and had won. Now, against all odds, she stood before her king, and the next stage in her plan had begun.

No, not my plan, she reminded herself. *My god's plan*.

"Well, go on then. Tell me what it is you came here to say. You do not have long. I have other...obligations to attend to this evening."

Tarrah knew what obligations he referred to. The king's many dalliances had not been kept a secret, not like his war with the Air Court.

"I know of your secret mission to upend the Air Court's status as the most powerful kingdom in Tir Na Nog." She lifted her eyes then to watch the king's face. Surprise, then concern, and then anger flickered in his dark eyes.

"Nonsense!" He slammed his fist on the arm of his throne. The entire floor beneath her feet shook in response. Just as Tarrah had expected. The king held some measure of power. "Whoever has threaded together these tales was only weaving lies."

"I saw it in my visions, my liege," she said, raising her

voice so that it echoed off the stone walls. "You have sent an instigator, a spy. You aim to use him to cause chaos and strife so that you may worm your way back into power. So that you may end our exile and become part of Tir Na Nog once again."

The guards beside her shifted uncomfortably on their feet. As for the king himself, he leaned forward, pure, unbridled anger flashing in his eyes.

"Where did you hear this? Your king demands you tell him right this instant, or you shall be thrown into the dungeons with the petty thieves and murderers."

"I have already told you, my king." Tarrah took a step closer to her liege. The guards on either side of her flinched, their fingers twisting around their antler hilts. "I have seen this in visions. I swear it is true. And it is not the only thing I have seen. Visions of the future. Ones I swear you will wish you knew."

"How can I be certain you are not lying to me?" He shook his head. "Visions? No one has seen any visions since Unseelie took the magic from these cursed lands."

"Because I believe it is Unseelie, the shadow fae god himself, who has given me these visions. And I believe he wishes for magic to return to us once again. If we fulfill the mission he has given us."

The king shifted on his black throne. After staring at her for a moment longer, he nodded. "Continue."

"The Air and Ice Courts have allied. They are heretics who believe in the wrong god. The Dagda, who was nothing more than a mere mortal that walked these lands. With their forces joined together, they have more strength than any other court can withstand. If we do not make a move against them, they will invade our lands and end the Shadow Court once and for all."

The king stiffened, and his lips were pulled down by a

heavy frown. "They have already exiled us. Why would they invade?"

"They will want our lands. They will want our people. Slaves, we will become, taken up north to mine the Ice Court's caves for ice glass."

"And this is what your visions have shown you?" He slammed his fist once again. "That all of us are doomed?"

"No," Tarrah said fiercely, a smile finally drawing up the corners of her lips. "I have seen us destroying them. I have seen us taking back the entire continent for ourselves."

※

The king decided to allow Tarrah to stay at the castle while he awaited word from his spy. He wanted confirmation that her visions were true before rushing headfirst toward the stronghold she insisted they take back. Until the king sat on his rightful throne, they wouldn't have the power to fight the full force of the Air Court's army. Still, she was willing to wait. She knew proof would come soon enough.

The taller of the two guards who had greeted her at the castle gates led her through gloomy corridors and into a part of the castle that looked rarely used. Cobwebs hung in the corners, and dust coated the floor. He stopped just outside of an open doorway that led to a cozy room overlooking the fire pits outside.

"The king would like you to stay here. Inside, you will find a bedchamber and a small room for hosting visitors. It is not much, I am afraid."

She smiled up at the guard. "It is far more than I have ever had before."

"What you spoke of to the king, how can you be certain these are visions and not merely dreams?" he asked, removing his helmet. He was as handsome as she had expected. His dark features were highlighted by a jutting chin and sharp cheekbones, and the pointed tips of his ears cut through his sleek black hair. Pure power radiated from his muscular body, so much so that Tarrah wanted to breathe him in.

Tarrah was always drawn to power.

She smiled, reached up, and pressed her fingers to his lips. Surprise flickered in his silver eyes, but he did not pull away. "Because I saw your face in my visions. And I saw you ask this very thing."

"So, then you could be lying instead," he murmured against her fingers.

"Perhaps." She dropped her hand. "But then how would I know your name to be Teutas, a loyal warrior pledged to the king? One day, you will kiss me. I have seen that, too."

With that, Tarrah smiled and strode into her new home.

8

REYNA

The Rowan Road was a long and winding rock-strewn path to Tairngire, the capital city of the Air Court. The party set off at sunrise a mere three days after the feast, the skies a clear blue that stretched on for miles. Thane was eager to return to his home. It did not seem he enjoyed the constant snowfall or the threat of the Ruin creeping in from every corner of the kingdom.

Reyna was also eager, but for entirely different reasons. It was time for her scheme to begin in earnest.

It had not taken much effort to convince her father. Indeed, it almost seemed as though he had been waiting for her to say she wished to return to court. He had hurriedly taken her into the throne room where he then bestowed her titles in the presence of Eislyn and Druid Aed. As she had never become a true sworn Shieldmaiden, the Dagda accepted her as part of the nobility once again. Thane had easily agreed to accept her hand. They were now betrothed.

As Reyna stood in the courtyard with Wingallock

perched on her shoulder, she watched the servants heft her leather suitcase into a cart that would follow along behind them. The entourage would travel ahead for the cart would take far longer to arrive in Tairngire. Father had offered to lend a carriage, but Reyna preferred to travel on horseback. Absentmindedly, she reached up and ran her finger along the smooth edges of her circlet—silver twisting bands that came together in the front to curl around the Ice Court sigil cast from silver ice glass. It had been so long since she had worn it, back before she had given up her royal title to become an unsworn Shieldmaiden. She was no longer accustomed to it squatting on her head and pinching her skin.

Reyna's heart ached. There was so much she was leaving behind. Starford Castle was the only home she had ever known. She would miss her sisters. She would even miss Father, despite their frequent disagreements. The frost and the ice, the orange sunsets streaking behind the snow-capped mountains. Reyna loved her kingdom fiercely.

And she must fight for it.

Snow crunched behind her, and she turned to find her sister stumbling toward her, suitcase in tow. She wore a pair of brown trousers and a tunic that matched, her hair weaved into a long single braid. Her leather boots were smooth and uncreased from little use. Her clothing matched Reyna's, minus the braid. Reyna preferred to wear her hair free, and her own boots were worn and faded. A servant hurried alongside Eislyn, wringing his hands, trying—and failing—to assist.

Reyna frowned. "What in the name of the Dagda do you think you are doing, Eislyn?"

Eislyn's eyes flashed. "I am coming with you."

"You most certainly are not." Reyna moved to stand

before Eislyn, blocking her sister's route to the cart. "Why would you even want to do such a thing? You made it more than clear that you are no fan of the Air Court."

She lifted her chin. "I can't very well let you walk into that viper nest alone, nor can I allow you to forget who you are and become *one of them*. Besides, as much as I dislike Thane, he was right. They have impressive libraries. Perhaps I can find something in them to help us stop the Ruin."

Reyna's annoyance softened. "Dear sister. I appreciate your wanting to protect me, but you don't need to worry about me."

She had still not told Eislyn of her plot, and she was not certain she ever would. It was far more dangerous for her sister if she knew the truth. Eislyn may have spent her years preparing for courtly life, but she had also rarely stepped foot outside of Starford Castle. She did not have experience in mincing the truth and twisting words. The viper nest would attack with fangs bared, sinking poison into her mind.

It was far better if she never found out.

"I know you are far stronger than I am, Reyna. On the battlefield. But how are you at court? You were never interested in learning about polite society. You will need my help there or else I fear you will stick your foot up your own arse." With a determined air, Eislyn lifted the suitcase from the ground and then stepped around her sister. Reyna continued to frown, but made no further attempt to stop her sister's progression toward the cart.

"Father will drag you back inside the castle when he gets wind of this. In fact, I will go tell him right this instant."

"I already asked Father. He agreed it was for the best." Eislyn smiled at Reyna's shock. "Do not worry. It won't be forever. This is only to ensure the betrothal does not fall apart. I'll return home as soon as you're married."

Her father had approved? Reyna should not be so surprised. He had been willing to send Eislyn into Thane's arms before Reyna had agreed to marry him. Of course he would want Reyna to have a chaperone. They all knew she had no training in intrigue.

"Eislyn," Reyna said, attempting a different tactic. "Part of the reason I agreed to the betrothal was to protect you from the Air Court."

"Yes, I know. And thank you for that." Eislyn reached out and squeezed Reyna's hand. "But it isn't as though I'm going to live there forever. You've saved me from a lifetime of unhappiness with the prince. And in exchange for that, I am going to help you."

There was a spark of determination in Eislyn's eyes that Reyna had not seen for quite some time. Her younger sister had spent so long being a hollow version of herself. Now, it seemed as though she'd found a purpose. And some hope. Not only for the end of the war but for an end to the Ruin.

The Air Court was not safe for Eislyn. Of that, Reyna was certain. Still, it wasn't as though she would be alone. Reyna would be right by her side. The idea of her sister going with her still turned her stomach, but she saw no way of getting around it, not if Father wanted her to go.

She would just have to make certain that her sister was long gone when the time came for Reyna to kill Thane.

The Rowan Road cut between the western edge of the Hoarfrost Forest and the eastern edge of the Sea of Fomor. Along some patches of the road, the right side of the path fell into jagged, icy cliffs that backed onto the sea. A light wind swirled around them, every so often bringing with it a spray of salty water as the waves bashed against the base of the cliffs.

Thane rode silently beside her. It had been a solid week since they'd left the castle, and he had spoken very little. At night, when they camped, their parties naturally split. Reyna and Eislyn sat with their five guards while Thane sat with his four. They exchanged very little conversation. Reyna liked it that way just fine. Knowing what he had done to her people at the inn, she knew her words would have bite.

But the time had come to broach the subject.

"We should make it to The Sapphire Axe by nightfall," Reyna said, watching Thane very carefully for a reaction. But it wasn't he who flinched at her words. It was his head guard, Lorcan. Reyna still did not know what he had done when he'd disappeared from the feast. She'd kept a close eye on him during their journey, but he had not vanished into the forests to send any more letters.

"We passed that inn on the way here." Thane held the reins loosely in his hands, his posture relaxed and unbothered. Even on a journey such as this, he still wore his gleaming golden armor as if to announce to the world his importance. "I assume you and your sister would prefer to stop there for the night rather than camping out in the cold."

Reyna bit her tongue. She so badly wanted to ask him a direct question, but if she did, he would be on to her.

"Is it cold?" Reyna smiled. She had not minded the

nights spent camping in the snowy forest. In fact, she had enjoyed it. They had not suffered bad weather. With the clear inky skies overhead, she had spread out her blanket on the soft ground and stared up at the glittering constellations, enjoying the feel of the frost on her skin. Thane still did not understand that the cold did not bother her in the least.

On Thane's other side, Lorcan frowned. "Perhaps we should press on. We will make it to The Sapphire Axe within a few hours, but nightfall is several hours past that. If we keep going, we could cross the border tonight and make it to the city that much faster."

"It is up to the princesses," Thane said firmly.

Reyna understood what the prince was doing. He was feigning nonchalance and ignorance of what lay ahead of them. If he did not pretend that stopping at the inn was an option, then there would be questions he could not answer for fear of giving the truth away. He was more clever than she had realized. But he was not the only one who could play the game.

Reyna smiled and turned to Eislyn by her side. "Lyn, what would you prefer?"

Eislyn exhaled a long breath. "While I do not mind the cold, I am unlike my sister. I am not accustomed to the hard ground and the skittering of shadows in the nighttime forest. If it would not slow us down a great deal, I would enjoy a night inside an inn." She perked up a little, straightening on the horse's smooth back. "Perhaps we could have an ale or two and hear some singing from a bard?"

Thane's eyes crinkled as he gave Reyna's sister a smile. "I wager there isn't a working inn in Tir Na Nog without a bard and some good ale."

Reyna could not help but note Thane's words. He was

COURT OF RUINS

so clever in the way he spoke. None of what he had said was a lie, but the implication was there all the same.

Dread tripped through Reyna's veins. She did not look forward to coming face-to-face with the destruction she knew awaited them on the path ahead. So many innocent souls had died that night. She hoped their bodies had been burned along with the walls. Their souls deserved far more than being left to rot.

"Then, it is settled then," Reyna said, squeezing Enbarr's reins with hands she forced to remain steady. "We will stop at The Sapphire Axe this night."

Several hours of companionable silence passed without incident. The southern end of the Hoarfrost Forest drew ever closer, along with the tall, ice glass gate that led to the Shard. The Shard was the only thing that had prevented the Air Court from invading Reyna's kingdom. It was a small strip of land that stretched between their kingdoms, almost like a bridge of sorts, fully made of ice. It took less than an hour to cross, but it was only wide enough for a handful of fae to stand side-by-side.

It was the only land that connected the Ice Court to the rest of Tir Na Nog. At many times over the past hundred years, the ice fae had considered destroying the Shard. Of course, there were other ways the Air Court could attack—and they had. By ship, by small bands of fighters that risked wading through the icy waters. Most of the battles between their realms had been nothing more than skirmishes, but those—along with the Battle for the Shard—had been enough to dwindle the ice fae's numbers. The Air Court had always had the superior army. Ice fae were meant for peace.

Thane stiffened as the blackened husk of The Sapphire Axe came into view. Reyna started, sucking in a sharp breath, even though she had been expecting the sight ahead. Eyes burning, she pressed a hand to her heart. There was barely anything left of the infamous inn. A charred pit was the only thing that remained. Anyone who had been inside when the fire had started would not have survived. Fury boiled in her gut.

Eislyn let out a sharp gasp. "What happened?"

Reyna did not answer. She did not know how she could speak about this without revealing how much she knew.

"A tragedy," Thane said quietly. Reyna could not bear to look at him, but she did so regardless, only to see the look on his treacherous face. There was a hint of remorse flickering in his golden eyes, but was it all an act? He had known what they would find when they passed the inn, and yet he insisted they come anyway. He was prepared. Perhaps he had even been practicing his frown.

"Reyna, is this the Ruin?" Eislyn asked, reaching out with trembling fingers to grasp her sister's arm.

Reyna closed her eyes. "It certainly does appear that way."

"Unfortunately, there is nothing we can do here," Lorcan spoke up with a quiet voice. "We should continue on and find a sheltered place to camp."

"Surely the inn was not in this state when you made the trek north?" Reyna could not help but ask.

Let us see if he can sweet speak his way out of this one...

"Quite the opposite in fact," Thane said smoothly with no trouble at all. "When we arrived, it was a very lively inn, wouldn't you say, Lorcan?"

Lorcan merely grunted.

"I cannot believe this," Eislyn said, voice wavering. "Why, one of our cooks left the castle to come work here only last year. Zed. You remember him, don't you, Reyna?"

"Of course I remember Zed."

The memory of Zed fuelled her vengeance. Thane

could not get away with what he had done. He could not be allowed to rule over the ice fae when he had murdered innocents the very same day he'd been proclaiming an alliance. *She* would not allow it.

"Come," she said with a sigh. "There is nothing we can do here. We should find somewhere to camp for the night, just as Lorcan suggested."

Lorcan's visible tension drifted into the wind. He gave Reyna a nod and flicked his reins, restarting their trek forward. As they left The Sapphire Axe behind them and approached the Shard, Reyna cast one last glance over her shoulder at the only lands she had ever known.

There were no trees or thorns or hoarfrost worms surrounding her, but she swore she heard those ancient voices that had been with her most of her life. She did not know for certain what they said, but she did know this: they were urging her forward.

※

When the party crossed the border between kingdoms, Reyna felt a sudden shift in the very fabric of her world. The snow still crunched beneath Enbarr's hooves, but it felt different somehow, almost as though it had been dulled. The orange colors in the sky were far less vibrant, and the scents in the air went weak.

She glanced around her. Ahead lay the lands of the air fae, but it did not look far different than the kingdom she had left behind. Fields of snow stretched out before them, disappearing far into the distance. Further south, she knew she would find the grasslands that covered most of the realm, but this far north, the ice had not yet left her. A light breeze pushed at the silver hair that framed her face, and for the first time in her entire life, she shivered. By her side, Eislyn's teeth began to chatter.

"Ah." Thane smiled. "I suppose you have not experienced the shifting of the elements before now, have you?"

"Neither of us have." Reyna did not point out that he and his court were the very reason that they had never left the safety of their icy lands. "Why is the ice a different color? And the sky?"

Thane frowned in confusion.

"By leaving your kingdom, you have allowed your senses to dim," Lorcan said. "You draw power from the ice of your lands but not from the ice here."

Reyna had heard tales of this before, but she was surprised it rang true, even now. "But the Dagda took our magic away."

"*Most* of the magic," Lorcan corrected. "You still have your familiar, do you not? You can still draw some strength from your element. The power of our magic is fading, but it is not yet fully gone."

At the thought of her familiar, she glanced up at where Wingallock circled their party, swooping through the skies.

Reyna had not realized she would weaken herself by leaving her kingdom. What would that mean for her fighting? Had she only ever been strong because of the ice beneath her feet? Could she still do what she needed to do without that extra strength?

I can, she thought. *I will*.

An hour south of the Shard, they found a small cluster of trees and rocks that would shelter them for the night. Reyna was still growing accustomed to her changed senses and still shivered beneath her cloak. It was not as if she were truly cold. It was different than that. There was something in the wind, something harsh and cruel that bit at her neck.

The fire proved difficult to light in the wind, and only their huddled bodies around it kept it flickering into the night. It was the first evening they had spent all together, and Reyna felt starkly uncomfortable at the closeness in which Thane sat beside her. Instead of sharing body heat, she wanted to stab him.

She supposed she would have to grow accustomed to that as well.

Thane seemed relaxed and comfortable, lounging against a stone while his guards stomped through the snow around them, securing the perimeter of their camp. Only Lorcan sat with the prince and princesses. Thane pulled out a flask, tipped the contents into his open mouth, and the scent of spiced wine spilled into the night.

"I suppose you're eager to get to the castle," Thane said with a lazy smile. "I daresay you will be impressed. Of all the castles I have seen in Tir Na Nog, it is by far the most spectacular."

Eislyn wrapped her arms around her knees and gazed into the fire. "Will it be dangerous?"

Reyna stiffened. So did Thane.

The Prince turned toward her. "Why would you ask if it will be dangerous?"

He didn't say no, Reyna noted.

"We are your sworn enemy," Eislyn said frankly. "Regardless of the alliance, there will be some who do not want us there."

Thane shifted uncomfortably, no longer as relaxed as he had been the moment before. "Princess Reyna is my betrothed, and you are her sister. You are under my protection."

He still did not say it wasn't dangerous.

"But enough of all this doom and gloom," Thane declared. "Lorcan, do give us a tale. The princesses were hoping to hear a bard tonight at the inn. Regale us with a story of one of your countryside antics instead."

Countryside antics? Reyna shifted slightly to get a better view of Lorcan in the orange glow of the fire. He was such a stark contrast to the prince. Where Thane was lean, Lorcan wore muscles as if they were a natural part of his leather armor. Where Thane lounged with relaxed superiority, Lorcan had an alert air about him that suggested he was prepared to jump onto his feet at any given moment.

Reyna had met many low fae who lived in the small villages dotted throughout the ice realm's countryside, and she had never met one quite like Lorcan. There was a hard edge to him, and his eyes held a glint that suggested he had seen far more than even she.

"Oh yes." Eislyn clapped. "Do you have any tales of monsters?"

"Lorcan has many tales of monsters." Thane turned to his head guard. "Do you not, old friend?"

Lorcan scowled but began to speak. "In the grasslands of the Air Court, there are whispers of a thing called the Wild Hunt."

Eislyn's eyes widened. She leaned forward, her face lit up by the glowing flames. "We've heard of the Wild Hunt. Is it real? Do they really carry a boar's head around and drop it at the feet of those they plan to kill?"

Thane grinned and leaned back against his rock, tipping another dose of wine into his open mouth.

"It is a thing that must be only spoken about in hushed voices," Lorcan pointed out before nodding at the trees that provided slim shelter from the wind. "As a child, I worked in the fields day and night. The more grain we produced, the richer our Beltane feasts would be each year."

Reyna nodded. It was the same for the ice fae. They mined for ice glass and spun silk from hoarfrost worms. The more they yielded each year, the better their celebrations. Reyna had often wondered if there could be a better way, one that didn't drive the low fae to utter exhaustion.

"Once," Lorcan continued, "I stayed far too late in the fields. The crops had been short that year. Wind and dust had stripped away far too many stalks during the continent-wide storm that hits our lands every six years. I was desperate to help my family." He shook his head. "I had paid no notice to the darkening sky when suddenly I was all alone with nothing but the whistling wind to keep me company. That is when I saw them."

Reyna shivered. The Wild Hunt was nothing more than a children's tale, she reminded herself. Most fae lore was. And, if the Wild Hunt had ever truly existed, it no longer would now. The wildest of the creatures and the most monstrous of the powers had vanished along with the fae's own magic. Lorcan could not lie, but he had only been a boy. An overactive imagination was the best explanation for his words.

"They were unlike anything I had ever seen," he said in a low voice.

Overhead, the sky cracked. Reyna glanced up, her eyes searching the sky above the trees. The brilliance of the stars had vanished. Now, nothing remained but a blanket of darkness. She shivered again, pressing up from the ground. A strange hum pulsed beneath her feet. Fear tumbled through her. Her guards were by her side in an instant.

"We need to ride," she said sharply. "Now."

"What in Dagda's name for?" Thane frowned up at her,

his eyes half-lidded from his drink. "Lorcan was just getting to the juicy part of his story."

She pointed at the sky, her hand trembling. "The Ruin is coming. I can feel it in my bones. We must leave now, or we will get hit by it."

Reyna's heart had begun to race as Thane made no effort to move from his spot. She turned toward Lorcan, pleading with her eyes. Thane might not understand the horrors of her world, but somehow, she knew Lorcan would.

Lorcan tipped back his head and frowned at the sky. "How can you be certain?"

"I've been in the middle of it, far more times than I wish to count," she said fiercely. "You must trust me. It is coming, and we need to leave."

Lorcan stared into her eyes. After a moment, he jumped to his feet.

Thane shook his head and laughed. "Surely you're not listening to the princess. The Ruin has never struck the Air Court. Why in Dagda's name would it choose to turn south now?"

Reyna had an inkling, but she did not wish to speak it.

"There is no time to worry about that now!" Reyna grabbed her sister's arm and hauled her to her feet. Eislyn did not object. Her cheeks had gone white, and that familiar haunted look had filled her eyes. If the prince wished to stay and get slaughtered by the Ruin, then so be it. But she would not allow her sister to undergo the same fate.

"Thane. We have to go. Now." Lorcan extended his hand.

Reyna was certain that Thane would continue to argue, but Lorcan's words seemed to knock some sense into his wine-addled brain. He grabbed the warrior's hand and leapt to his feet, collecting his strewn belongings. They had barely unpacked, and it did not take long before they had returned to their horses.

"How far does it reach?" Lorcan asked Reyna as they steered their horses in the direction of Tairngire. "How long must we ride to escape it?"

Reyna did not know. Or, rather, she had known once. The Ruin had never spread past the villages, and it never attacked twice. Not until Reyna and Glencora had discovered those children.

She stared at the endless sea of darkness overhead. "We ride until we see starlight."

9

MARIEL

"Oy! Mariel, where's my damn ale?"

Mariel Dalais bustled through the packed tavern, balancing four overflowing mugs in her petite hands. It was a lively evening, and Winter Solstice had only just passed. Every single fae of Drunkard's Pit, the slums of the city, seemed to be out celebrating the end of their coldest days. In the city of Tairngire, that meant dozens had tried to cram into The Bloody Dagger. It was no small feat to keep them all fed, watered, and entertained.

Mariel stopped at the nearest table where one of her regulars, Tomas Hardingale, had been shouting at her. He was tall with long black hair and sharp grey eyes, wearing sturdy clothing and pouches that hung from his leather belt. If she didn't already know and love the lad, she might have been tempted to give him a slap right on his rosy cheeks. At only sixteen, he was a good hundred years younger than she, and her protective instinct curled around him like a cocoon.

"Tomas." Wobbling, she plopped a mug of ale in front of

him. "Shout at me again, and you will get no more ale from me this night."

He grinned up at her with two rows of perfect, shiny white teeth. Mariel did not know how he managed to keep them clean. As the magic of the world had faded, so had the fae's resiliency to rot and disease. Most low fae couldn't afford to procure cleaning potions. In Tairngire, ale was cheaper than medicinal potions, and most alchemists, a new occupation only created since the Fall, were reserved for the nobility.

"You always say that," he countered. "And then you bring me more ale."

Doling out the remaining mugs to his companions at the table, Mariel leaned down and hissed into his ear. "Perhaps I will bring you an ale. And perhaps I will dump it on your head. Or worse."

Tomas stiffened. He cut his eyes toward her and nervously licked his lips. "I was only messing around, Mariel. I won't shout at you again."

Satisfied, Mariel stood tall and strode back toward her cache of ales, bitters, ciders, and wine. It had not been her words that had chilled him, but the threat of what lay beneath. Mariel was infamous, and for good reason. She would never hurt the lad, but she would gladly hurt anyone who threatened the lives of those who came to The Bloody Dagger.

Her tavern wasn't much to look at, but she loved it all the same. Located in the slum quarter, it was surrounded by dirty streets and makeshift tenements. A two-storey timber and brick building, it stood out from the dilapidated buildings around it. The leaded glass windows were many, and well-made wooden tables and chairs stretched across a rickety floor. And every single chair was taken this night.

A tall, willowy female with wide, deep brown eyes stood waiting for her at the wooden bar top. Mariel slid in behind it, wiped her hands on her ragged dress, and smiled at the girl. She was far too young to be in an establishment like this, but Mariel was not one to turn away a paying patron.

"What can I get you, love?" Mariel asked sweetly, wearing her kind tavern owner mask like a second skin. It was not at all who she was beneath the facade, but she did not like anyone to know. Until it was too late.

The girl wrung her hands; her eyes darted around the bustling tavern. "I am not certain here is the best place to entertain this conversation."

Mariel frowned. "You are not here for sustenance."

The girl shook her head, her eyes widening in fright.

"Very well." Mariel turned toward her brother who was squatting at a table in the corner, booming with laughter, along with his fellow blacksmith mates. She signalled at the bar, and then at the girl. His expression darkened.

The girl's wide eyes followed Mariel's gaze toward her brother. "Oh no. I thought I only had to deal with you."

"Do not worry, love." Mariel edged around the bar and took the girl's slim arm, gently leading her to the back of the tavern. "Mavis is my brother. He takes care of our patrons while I sort these things out in the back."

"You do this often then," the girl said quietly as they pushed through the throngs of celebrators.

"Far too often," Mariel replied grimly. "The streets of Drunkard's Pit are riddled with violent crime. The High King does not bother with us. He is far too busy sitting on his stolen throne to care one lick about us low fae."

Mariel led the fae through a burlap flap and into a chilly store room lined with shelves of ale and cured meats. Two wooden chairs sat waiting for them. Unfortunately, this was not the first time Mariel had held this type of meeting, nor would it be the last.

"Sit." Mariel turned toward the nearest shelf and poured a shot of her strongest spirit into a small mug. She handed it to the girl. "Drink. Tell."

The girl eagerly knocked back her head and tipped the liquid down her throat. She winced, but her cheeks immediately brightened. That was more like it.

Mariel sat and waited.

"I was out past curfew two evenings past," the girl said quickly.

Curfew. Mariel frowned at just hearing the word. It was a self-imposed rule amongst the fae who lived in Drunkard's Pit, one known only to the poor, unfortunate souls who were fated to be born in these streets. The wealthier fae of Tairngire did not have to worry about such things. But those of the slums had to be off the streets when Danu rose into the night sky. If they weren't safely inside their homes, they might find themselves on the wrong end of a dagger.

Wincing, Mariel held up a hand. "First, tell me your name."

"Nia." She swallowed hard. "Daughter of Linnon Todt. We live in the tenements several streets over. I have not married yet. Neither has my sister."

"I know of Linnon Todt. Good male. Strong in the Elemental Arts before the Fall, when our magic left us." Mariel gave a nod. "Continue."

"I was out past curfew." Her cheeks reddened. "Meeting a boy."

"Nothing to be embarrassed about, love. We have all of us done it, even those who wish to pretend otherwise."

Nia nodded, relief passing across her tense face. "It was late. The second moon, Brigantu, hung low in the sky.

When I reached the corner of Scarp Street and Muck Side, I..." She swallowed hard. "I saw something."

Mariel leaned forward. "What did you see?"

All the color drained from Nia's face. She flicked her eyes to the ale lining the walls and hunched over in the chair. "Can I have another spirit, please?"

Without a word, Mariel stood, poured the poor girl another drink, and pressed it into her shaking hands. After she tipped the contents into her mouth, she started talking.

"I saw someone else walking home. A boy, I think. I didn't recognize him, and he had a hood over his face. He was up ahead of me on the street." She cleared her throat, and tears filled her eyes. "Suddenly, two other fae jumped out of the shadows and attacked him. With daggers. He..."

Mariel placed a hand on Nia's shaking knee. "Go on."

"They killed him. They searched his body, stole his coins, and then wrapped him up in burlap before carrying him away." Her hands twisted together, knuckles going bone white. "I hid. I watched the whole thing. I did nothing to stop them. I just hid."

"As well you should have," Mariel hissed as she leaned closer to stare into the girl's tear-filled eyes.

Nia blinked and shook her head. "You don't think I should have tried to stop them? But..."

"Listen to me, Nia." Mariel's heart thumped. "If you had attempted to save this boy, you would have joined his soul in death. Are you skilled in combat? Has your father trained you to wield a sword?"

Nia frantically shook her head.

"Then, there you see," Mariel hissed. "This is not your fault. It's the fault of our hateful High King. If he kept proper patrols on these streets, if he ensured the laws were upheld in the low fae quarters, then and only then would the murdering stop."

Slowly, anger replaced the anguish in Nia's eyes. "He is not a very good king."

"No, my love. He isn't." Mariel had never meant anything more than she did when she said those words. For years, she had longed for the High King's untimely death, if only so his son could rise to his rule. Thane was not much better than his father, or so she had heard. But perhaps he could be reasoned with, unlike High King Sloane.

Nia took a long breath into her lungs. "I came here this night because I saw the murderers' faces. One, I did not recognize. But the other, I did."

Mariel pressed her lips firmly together. "Good. Tell me his name and everything you know about him. And he will never murder another ever again."

❦

After Mariel's meeting, she returned to her regular duties in the tavern. Her brother silently watched her from the corner, no longer booming with laughter along with his mates. She bustled through the maze of tables, doling out cider, ale, and rabbit pies. Her feet ached by the time the night ended. She had to shoo out a few of her regulars, but she would not keep the tavern open until sunrise this night.

There was other work to be done.

As she locked the door, her brother came up behind her, a steadying presence when the world around them felt as though it was slowly falling apart. Once, they had been part of a great kingdom. Once, they had wielded great forces. So much power had been in their grasp, and the capital had thrived because of it. Now, they were nothing more than tavern owners, barely getting by, living in a city devoid of magic and ruled by a pitiful king.

"I do not suppose I can talk you out of doing this again," Mavis said quietly.

She twisted to face him, fire flickering in her belly. Looking into his eyes was almost like looking into a mirror. They were both of slight height, their hair was a matching shade of blonde, and their copper eyes were lined with gold. They greatly resembled their parents, but the world had ceased searching for them so long ago that it no longer mattered.

"The innocents who live in these godforsaken streets need to be protected."

"Aye. But why do you need to be the one who protects them, Mar?" her brother asked.

A familiar question. And she always answered it the same. "Because I am the only one who can."

Mariel left her brother to finish clearing up the tables while she changed into a pair of black trousers and a matching black tunic. She armed herself as best she could. Hidden daggers in the folds of her clothes. She pulled her long golden hair into a high bun and slid another tiny dagger into the strands.

And then she took to the mud-slick streets.

The night was deep and quiet. Both moons were obscured by a blanket of dark clouds, and shadows hugged every corner of the claustrophobic streets. In the far distance, the golden spires of Dalais Castle rose above the dilapidated buildings of Drunkard's Pit. Up there, the nobles swished through their magnificent hallways, drenched in luxury. Down in the depths of the slums, innocents were murdered for pocket change.

Mariel had once been a high fae, second in line to the throne. When the war had begun, she'd been forced to flee and hide amongst the commoners. The Selkirks had stolen the crown, killing every member of her family. They'd pulled it off by slowly getting their own spies inside the castle. And then they'd signalled the attack at a feast by placing a severed boar's head in front of Mariel's father's seat. For a long time, Mariel had kept her head down, doing nothing more than existing amongst strangers, dying her hair brown. But she had been quiet long enough. The real Mariel had roared to life several years ago. If her mission to clean up these streets ended with her head on a pike, then so be it.

Mariel kept to the shadows as she edged down the street toward the sagging house at the nearest corner. The murderer was none other than the local smithy, a male called Dwynn. Mariel knew the lad well. She had bought from him. She had traded wine for steel. A pang went through her heart at the thought of what she must do, but she would not back down from the challenge, regardless of who he was.

The most dangerous criminals were the ones she thought she knew. They existed quietly, lulling everyone around them into a false sense of security. This would not be the first familiar face she saw in the dark night. And, as much as it pained her to admit, she knew it would not be the last.

As she inched closer to the smithy's door, a shadowy figure whispered out into the streets. Instantly, she went still. The form was large and muscular and drenched in black garb. Thick hands twisted into fists by his side. Mariel's heart thumped. It was the smithy.

He strode down the street, his boots sinking into the mud, and Mariel quickly followed after. When he came to a bend, he swerved to the left. Then, he suddenly stopped, cocked his head, and twisted toward her. She minced into the shadows of the building to her left, but it was too late.

"Someone is there," he said quietly, bright green eyes flashing in the dark. "Show yourself."

Mariel stepped out of the shadows.

The smithy did not look the slightest bit surprised. "So, it is true then. You work for the Bloody Dagger, the vigilante."

"That is not what I would call myself," she said simply, focusing on his dark tunic, searching for a weapon. So far, she could see none, but that did not mean he held no steel. It could be hidden elsewhere on his body just as hers was. "Although it must be true what I have heard about you. You prowl the streets at night, seeking easy prey. I have to admit I am surprised, Dwynn. I thought better of you. Your smithy runs well. Is thieving for airgead coins really necessary?"

"You do not know of what you speak."

"No?" She arched her brows. "Then it was not you who murdered a boy on Scarp Street several evenings past and stole the contents of his pouch?"

Dwynn sneered. "I admit to killing the boy, but I am no thief."

Mariel blinked, staring at the smithy. "You did not wish to steal his airgead? Then, why did you kill him?"

"Ask the High King," he said with a laugh, and then turned to stride away from her.

Confusion rippled through her. "Ask the king? What in the name of the Dagda does Sloane have to do with your murdering?"

He continued to walk with his back facing Mariel, clearly unconcerned about what she might do. "Like I said, ask the High King."

She narrowed her eyes, and a dagger flashed into her

hands. "You will not get away with murder that easily, Dwynn. Do not underestimate me."

Dwynn stopped and twisted toward her. He shook his head. "You do not want to do this, Mariel. Who will supply you with your endless stream of blades if not for me? Most smiths will not trade. Others will require coin. Coin you do not have."

"Perhaps not," she shot back. "But I will not stand idly by while the innocents of Drunkard's Pit are murdered, in the High King's name or not."

"You risk committing treason?" he asked, lifting his brows.

"My mere existence is treason." She hissed the words and stalked toward him. Whipping another dagger from her waistband, she shook off the sheath.

"Mariel…" Dwynn's eyes widened and he took a step back, as if he truly had not expected her attack. That was how she always got them. No one ever suspected the quiet, kindly tavern owner with curvy hips. Her infamy only extended so far. Many knew they could find the Bloody Dagger by speaking to her, but they did not truly believe she was the one who stabbed in the night. She was merely the go-between. The real wielder of vengeance had to be someone else, they always thought. Someone larger and stronger than she.

"Mariel, you do not want to do this." He grabbed his own weapon, a glistening sword with a much longer reach than her tiny silver blades. "You will not win against me. You have no training. Your strength will not match mine."

"Is that what you truly believe, Dwynn?" Her dagger flashed as she leapt toward him. Mariel had training aplenty. Her father had taught her himself when she'd been nothing more than a wee girl with a dream in her head: a kingdom full of peace with Mariel as High Queen. That dream had never come true, but she'd never forgotten her training.

She reached Dwynn before he even knew she was coming for him. Her blade sank deep into his fleshy neck, and red splattered the grime-soaked ground.

10

REYNA

The galloping hooves were thunderous. Reyna clung tightly to Enbarr's grey mane, breathing in the pungent scent of roots, dirt, and sweat. She didn't dare glance behind her, nor did the others in her party. They could all feel the Ruin bearing down on them like the encroaching mass of a heaving army.

They rode like that for hours, outrunning the ebony specks that fell from a sky that had been sapped of all light. At times, Reyna could not help but wonder if this was it. Had the world finally come to an end?

A single star appeared in the sky before them. And then another, quickly followed by dozens more. Hope speared Reyna's heart, and she pushed up from Enbarr's sweat-slick neck to guide the mare to a stop. Wingallock hooted, quickly landing on her shoulder, his talons piercing her cloak.

Reyna turned to glance behind them. The sky had cleared; no more ash drifted down from above. It was almost as though the Ruin had never even been there. Almost. There was a stretch of charred ground that disappeared into the distance. The snow and grass had melted away. A strange smoke curled from where the blackness had fallen.

She whistled a signal to the others who had kept charging ahead, too tired to notice that the terror had stopped.

In an instant, Lorcan was by her side, gazing in the direction they'd run. His chest and shoulders tall, he did not look at all the worse for wear, as if he were accustomed to fleeing for his life from an enemy that would never back down. "It has finally stopped."

"So it seems," Reyna said. "Although I do not trust it to remain that way."

He frowned. "Where did it even come from? Why did it follow us here?"

"If we had the answers to those questions, we might very well be able to stop it."

"Thane is exhausted." He twisted to where the prince barely clung to the back of his horse, his eyes half-lidded. A flicker of annoyance went through Reyna. As the future ruler of this realm, surely he should be the strongest of them all. "So are your sister and the horses. We should try to make camp nearby."

Reyna nodded toward the distant yellow glow on the horizon. "It is almost first light."

"Yes," Lorcan said, sounding troubled. "But it is near a week before we reach Tairngire. We should rest, if only for a few hours."

Reyna turned to gaze at the warrior. His muscular body seemed to hum with power even if that made little sense. He sat tall on his horse, the light wind rippling the dark hair around his face and the distant sun casting sharp lines onto his strong jaw. The scent of him drifted toward her, leather and smoke and steel. A strange sensation fluttered in her belly. Lorcan could not be trusted, but she could not deny that his unyielding strength was…impressive.

"For someone who's been awake all night, you don't seem at all tired," she noted.

Lorcan's body went tense. "Neither do you."

At that, he turned his horse around and trotted back to his prince's side. Reyna watched him go with slightly narrowed eyes. There was something odd about Lorcan, though she could not put her finger on what it was, something that drew her to him. Perhaps she was only imagining things. After all, he had been at the inn when Thane had attacked her people. He had likely participated in the assault himself.

She couldn't trust any of these air fae. And she could never let herself forget what they had done.

***

The Air Court's capital city, Tairngire, rose up before them in great, gleaming shades of gold. They were still half a day away, but they were close enough that the weariness began to melt from Reyna's body. She was tired of being on the road. The Ruin had not attacked them since their fearful race through the night, but they had still ridden hard for the city's gates. No one wanted to risk it happening again.

As they drew closer, Reyna could not help but stare in awe at the city that stretched out before them. Even with the concentric walls looming high, Reyna could still see the impressive expanse of buildings. Tairngire was thrice as large as Falias. Clusters of stone buildings with wooden shingles dyed gold climbed up a hill where Dalais Castle perched high above them all. The castle itself was breathtaking. With buttressed walls, it was hewn from polished white stone, and golden spires rose majestically into the darkening cerulean sky.

Set on the mouth of the Bay of Wind, Tairngire was a mercantile city full of bustling canals and booming trade. It had once been the wealthiest city on the continent, but as Reyna and the rest of the party continued down the path, she began to spot pockets of blight. Rot seemed to creep through the city, stretching across sagging buildings and muddy roads.

As they approached the open city gates, several guards stood waiting with a carriage that looked as though it had been spun from the very same gold that topped the castle spires.

From the front of their party, Lorcan jumped off his horse, his boots splashing into mud, and greeted the guards.

"This has been an exceedingly long journey," her sister whispered as they slowed. "Please do not tell me that we must stop again."

Thane glanced up from where he sat sipping on another flask of wine. He had started on it at first light, almost as though he were steeling himself for the return to his court, and dusk now darkened the skies. "A formality. The prince and his betrothed cannot very well waltz through the gates with zero fanfare."

Reyna's stomach twisted. She was not accustomed to hearing herself referred to as someone's "betrothed" as if she were Thane's mere property and nothing else. In truth, that was how most in this city were likely to view her.

"*Must* there be fanfare?" she asked. "As my sister said, this has been a long journey."

"There are certain things expected of us here," he said. "The low fae enjoy celebrating my return from such a lengthy absence. I have been away over a month, and I have brought with me my future wife." He glanced down at Reyna's clothing. "There is nothing to do about your trousers for now, but few fae will see them if you are inside the carriage."

Reyna pressed her lips together to prevent herself from arguing more. She enjoyed mingling with her people, but she did not enjoy being paraded in front of them. She supposed she did not have much choice in the matter, something she knew she must quickly grow accustomed to. From now on, her life would become a series of events of which she had next to no say.

At least, not until she killed the future king.

The guards opened the carriage doors and motioned toward Reyna. With a sigh, she swung her legs over the side of her horse and dropped onto the muddy ground. She climbed the steps of the carriage, settling in on the seat across from Thane. Eislyn joined her, hands tensely clasped in her lap.

The interior was just as elaborate as the outside. The seats themselves were made of gold and were covered in lush pillows dyed a brilliant orange that matched the sunset streaking across the sky. Two thin strips of white cloth hung over the windows, but they had been pushed away so that the nobles inside could be seen by those on the streets.

The carriage rumbled toward the gates, and Reyna steeled herself for the fanfare. She did not believe she should be cheered for her mere existence. She did not deserve adoration for sitting in a golden carriage whose wheels cost more than most of their homes. It turned her stomach, but she would endure it. One day, all of this would change.

As the carriage continued ever forward, Reyna whistled and called her familiar to her side. Wingallock flew into the open carriage window, and a few alarmed shouts peppered the air. She smiled as he settled onto her shoulder.

Thane frowned from the opposite seat. "I am not certain this is appropriate."

"Where I go, Wingallock follows. We are one and the same."

"And you, princess?" Thane asked, turning to Eislyn. "Have you never felt the call of a familiar?"

Eislyn flushed and glanced down at her muddy leather boots. "No, your grace. A familiar is a rare gift these days. Reyna is lucky to have one."

The trio fell silent as the looming gate passed overhead, the wheels of the carriage rolling into the city proper. Cheers erupted around them, and Reyna could not help but stare at the hundreds of low fae who stood waiting for them to pass. The streets were clogged, the crowd barely held back by armored warriors. Many of the fae waved golden banners, and others beat drums.

Eyebrows raised, Reyna turned toward Thane and rose her voice to be heard over the roaring crowd. "Is this standard?"

He gave her a slight smile. "The procession is standard when I return. The turn-out is not. These fae wish to get sight of their future queen."

A strange feeling twisted her gut. These fae had come out to celebrate her, but she did not plan to become the person they wanted her to be. Did they truly love their prince? They appeared happy enough. Glowing cheeks and wide smiles. Small children were held high in the air, the mothers hoping for a blessing from the nobility.

She gave them all a slight smile, but she could scarcely stomach her unease. This city would one day be hers. But only in the death of their beloved prince, their future High King.

Still, Reyna could not forget what he had done.

At long last, the carriage rolled onto the castle grounds, and the gates were shut tight against the cheering crowd. The carriage door swung wide, and the three of them clambered down the steps and into the courtyard. Everything was bright and gleaming and clean, even the white stones beneath her feet, save the splattering of mud she had dragged in on her boots. Reyna dropped back her head to look up. The golden spires seemed to stretch past the very sky itself.

"Welcome to your new home," Thane said from beside her. "What do you think?"

"I think..." Reyna's stomach fluttered. It might be an impressive sight, but that did not mean it would ever feel like home. "It is certainly very shiny."

Thane furrowed his brows and opened his mouth to speak, but he was interrupted by the clatter of hooves. A warrior rode up before them, holding leather reins in his gloved hands. "Prince Thane. There is an urgent matter I need to speak with you about. It involves your mother."

The High Queen? Reyna frowned as she watched the life drain out of Thane's eyes. His back stiffened, and his jaw clenched tight. He did not even glance in Reyna's direction when he shot his next words her way. "Lorcan will ensure you are seen to. I must go."

Eislyn and Reyna stood shoulder-to-shoulder, staring after Thane. He moved with fierce determination, as if the matter at hand was a fire that raged through the streets. It was curious.

"What do you reckon that is about?" Eislyn asked as they waited for the rest of the guards to leap down from their horses.

"I have a suspicion that the prince and his mother do not see eye-to-eye."

"Careful," a voice warned.

Reyna spun on her feet. Lorcan stood just behind them, his hands tucked behind his back. The stance made his chest look broad, particularly where the armor strained to contain his muscles. He was larger than most air fae. Now that they stood within the gleaming city itself, it was clearer than when they had been surrounded by the towering trees of the ice fae realm.

"I suppose you're going to tell us that we shouldn't gossip," Reyna snapped. "Not only are my actions to be monitored, but my words and thoughts are, too."

"Your words, yes. You cannot lie, so every spoken sentence means a great deal in this court," he said, nodding toward the crowd of low fae watching them through the gated castle entrance. "But you can think whatever you damn well please, just so long as you consider your words when sharing them. Now, princesses, I must beg your leave."

Lorcan nodded once more, and then took off across the courtyard after Thane.

Reyna and Eislyn exchanged a weighted glance. Wingallock let out a curious hoot.

A smiling female suddenly appeared before them, distracting the sisters from Thane's sudden disappearance. Short and slender, the fae wore servant's attire: a long linen skirt the color of mud, a pearl-white tunic, and a thin leather belt. She wore her curly hair loose around her shoulders and regarded them both with sharp amber eyes.

"Good evening, your highnesses. My name is Diccea, and I serve Prince Thane. Please come with me. I will show you to your chambers." The fae did not wait for their response. She scurried away, leading them toward another pair of gates set into the polished white stone walls.

Guards trailed behind them as they moved along, both those that Reyna had brought from the Ice Court and several more of the Air Court's own. It was quite the entourage.

Diccea opened the gate and motioned them inside. There, they found another courtyard, empty and silent. The castle gardens stretched out all around them, full of lush green shrubs and delicate winter flowers. An ancient square tower rose up before them, the tallest of the castle's many. By itself, it was almost as large as the entirety of Starford Castle.

"Is that where we will be living?" Eislyn asked with a gasp.

"No, your highnesses," Diccea said with a smirk. "That is Mistral Tower, home to the chambers of the High King and Queen. We have prepared chambers for you in White Stone Tower on the northern side of the castle, overlooking the Bay of Wind."

She resumed her journey across the courtyard. Reyna and Eislyn had no choice but to follow closely behind, Wingallock still clinging tight to Reyna's shoulder with his talons. They passed beneath the shadows of the looming towers, a biting wind whipping through their hair. Eislyn's silver strands had sprung free of her braid, and they curled around her flushed cheeks. Reyna could not help but wonder if her dear sister was regretting her decision now that she had firmly stepped foot inside the viper nest.

When they finally reached the northern walls, Diccea led the sisters into a small tower that seemed dwarfed in comparison to Mistral Tower. She led them up a small circular staircase and into a corridor lined with flickering torches. They used fire here, Reyna noted.

They came to a stop outside two doors that were set into the stone walls across from each other. Another servant stood waiting, her garb a replica of Diccea's. She stared at Wingallock with dull grey eyes that matched her fraying hair. Her round cheeks were devoid of any color, and her pouting lips were cracked. She shuffled on her feet, clearly unnerved by Reyna's familiar.

"Princess Reyna, this is Ula, your lady's maid." Diccea motioned at the servant who waited by the door. "Princess Eislyn, I will serve as yours. Please follow me."

With that, Diccea and Eislyn disappeared through one of the doors, leaving Reyna and Wingallock alone with the strange, haunting lady's maid.

"Your highness." The lady's maid gave a slight bow and then led Reyna into her chambers.

The rooms inside were far more expansive than Reyna was accustomed to. There were three of them in total. A small boudoir for bathing and dressing, a bedchamber that held a four-poster bed that could have swallowed her own bed whole. The gleaming golden sheets sparkled even in the dim lighting, and the pillows were plump and large.

The third room would serve as her private drawing room. It held several sofas, along with an elaborately-carved bookshelf, though no books sat there waiting to be read. Several plush pillows were dotted around the room, some large enough to be used as a footstool. Each had been embroidered with golden thread, forming the crown sigil of the Air Court. A lush circular carpet spread across the center of the timber floor beneath a small wooden table that held a multitude of candles. The scent of rowan blossoms filled the air.

Unlike her castle back home, these chambers held several arched windows with chevon carvings detailed around the edges. Each had a stone seat, complete with more plush pillows. A set of embroidery needles sat in one.

"These are your chambers," Ula said stiffly before shooting another nervous glance at the owl. "What else can I assist you with, milady?"

"At some point, I would like to visit the market. Where can I find that?" Reyna asked. "At the Ice Court, we have one daily in our courtyard."

Ula gave her a hard look. "We may have made an alliance with your kind, but we are not the same. There is no market inside the castle gates. That would not be at all safe for the nobility."

Reyna frowned and absently ran her fingers along Wingallock's feathers, where he still perched patiently on her shoulder. "Very well. I can visit the market in the city."

"I am afraid Prince Thane will not allow that."

"What ever do you mean? Why would he not allow it?"

"It is not safe for you to wander the city streets," Ula replied, her face impassive, those strange grey eyes hollow and glazed.

"I don't understand." Reyna waved at her beautiful chambers. "Surely I am not to stay inside these castle walls perpetually."

"You have no need to leave. Everything you could possibly require can be found here where it is safe." Ula moved toward the door. "If you have concerns, you ought to speak with your betrothed."

As the servant slipped out the door, Reyna spotted the armored arm of a warrior standing guard outside her quarters. Reyna's frowned deepened. The Air Court would claim he was there for her protection, no doubt. But Reyna had not been born yesterday. The guard was there to keep her inside these rooms, just as surely as he was there to keep an enemy out.

With a heavy sigh, she crossed the smooth timber floor and stared out the window. Wind battered against the tower, causing the glass to quake. Down below, she knew the teeming city stretched far. But she could not see it. Her window faced north, overlooking a steep cliff that plunged to the Bay of Wind. There was nothing but inky darkness for her to see.

"What have we gotten ourselves into, Wingallock?" Her owl, for once, stayed silent.

She was trapped inside a gilded cage, and she saw no way to escape.

11

IMOGEN

Imogen was tired of her plaything. Unfortunately, her plaything just so happened to be the High King of the Air Court. When they had first married, he had promised her the world, even the lands beyond Tir Na Nog, but he had given her nothing more than boring nights alone in her bedchamber.

That was, until she'd met the male standing before her now. He had come to them in the Great Hall while the rest of the court was distracted by her son's arrival with his new betrothed. Standing beside her husband's throne, Imogen gazed out at the empty space. Usually, the angular room was packed with tables and feasting guests. Now, the lofted ceilings with their white stone arches seemed steeped in shadows without the bustle of the court.

"Aengus," she said with a slight nod when he knelt before her and her unfortunate husband. "Why have you come to see the king?"

Her lover smiled, his narrow grey eyes twinkling with delight. His glossy ginger hair hung to his shoulders, the ends whispering against his leather armor. As always, his rapier hung on a belt around his waist, but Imogen was certain he'd never used it. A slight male, a warrior he was not. Cunning, on the other hand...

"My liege. I have come to you with some unfortunate news." Aengus spoke with an odd accent. No one quite knew where he originated. When asked, he refused to tell. At first, Imogen had worried that he was a shadow fae, but he had proven himself incapable of telling a fib. He cast an almost imperceptible glance her way, but she could do no more than merely press her lips tightly together.

He continued. "It seems there is a vile rumor spreading throughout the realm."

Imogen's husband leaned forward and frowned. He was a shell of the male he used to be. Once a powerful fae of brute strength and charm, he now sat withered in his Seat of Power, an imposing throne of black vines and thorns that grew from the very stone beneath their feet. He had cropped his hair short when it had transformed from golden into grey, and his once bright eyes were now dull and faded. Wrinkles stretched across his pockmarked skin. He was no longer immortal as he had once been.

He braced a forearm on his knee, his hand dangling limply to the side. It was his signature move, Imogen knew, intended to make him seem nonplussed and unconcerned. But she also knew that it meant the very opposite.

"What vile rumour?"

"One about you and...well, your power, my liege."

High King Sloane stayed silent and still, but his blood was no doubt boiling in his veins. He did not like his power being questioned, and Imogen knew why. His power was all a front. How he had managed for so long in a world without lies was remarkable.

"This sounds like a baseless rumor," he said with a

frown. "You should not have bothered me with it. I have much more important matters to attend to."

"My liege, I am certain it is the truth." Aengus's narrow eyes flicked toward Imogen again.

Sloane whirled toward her, his withered hands clutching the thorny arms of his throne. "You are not involved in this, are you? You wouldn't dare."

She merely smiled a toothless smile.

"This is treason," he said in a hiss, jerking his head back toward Aengus. The sudden movement caused his thick golden crown to go askance. It was a perfect symbol of the truth of the High King of the Air Court.

"There are letters waiting," Imogen's lover cut in before the king could call for his guards. "If anything happens to me, or to the High Queen, those letters will be sent immediately. All of the realm will then know."

Sloane sneered. "Perhaps I shall call your bluff and have my guards take you straight to the dungeons. You will need no trial, not when your crime is treason. I will see your head on a pike."

"Go on then," Imogen's lover replied with a slight smile. "Call the guards, if you dare for all of Tairngire to know your secret."

Imogen swore beneath her breath. Aengus was playing with the king, as he was wont to do when it came to his enemies. But she knew that Sloane would not bend if he were given too much time to consider the implications.

"Aengus," she said sharply. "There is something you wanted to suggest to my husband, I believe."

"Oh yes. Your liege, I have come here to suggest that you abdicate your throne. And to allow the High Queen to rule in your stead."

Sloane scoffed, and the loose skin beneath his chin wobbled. "You do not honestly expect me to bend to this baseless blackmail. I am High King Sloane of the Selkirks, the Conquerer of Tairngire."

"You are the bastard son of a human and Lady Moina Selkirk, not the son of Lord Piran Selkirk. You sit on a throne of lies. And you have no power to prove otherwise."

The king's face went as white as the snow on the ground outside of the city. She had long since suspected that Sloane was not a true ruler in the eyes of the Dagda. There had been rumors, of an age ago, of his mother lying with a human male. Lord Selkirk had forbidden anyone of ever speaking of it, calling it a crime deserving death. The rumors had vanished into the darkness of the night, but Imogen had never forgotten.

And when her husband's strength had faded in time and when his beauty had dimmed with age, she had known the truth of him. He had blamed it on the Fall, the day that every living fae in Tir Na Nog had collapsed onto the ground unconscious. When they had finally come to hours later, magic had vanished. But Sloane had aged so much faster than those around him. As High King, he should outlast them all. He had the power of his throne.

"The shadow fae must be behind this," Sloane hissed. "Liars, the lot of them. I will prove it."

"They are not behind this, Sloane," she said simply. "Mince your words to deny it if you must, but think of what your people will do when they hear these rumors. If they decide you are a false king, they will have you hanged. It is against the law of our god for a half-human male to become the High King of our great court. Unblemished and whole, you are not. And then Thane will never have a chance to rule."

That had finally got him, Imogen could see. Sloane cared little for her, but he loved his boy fiercely, same as she.

"You said you did not want him to rule," Sloane hissed.

"For now," she replied, having counted on this. It was a risk, but a calculated one. If everything fell into place, then she would rule long enough to bring all the courts together beneath her boot. And then she would step aside and allow Thane to rule, but only then. "He is not ready."

Sloane growled. "He is of age. For *years*, he has been of age."

"You have heard how he spends his nights. He is not fit to sit on that throne. One day he will be, but that day has not yet come."

"You are merely saying that so that you may sit your own arse on the throne."

"Perhaps." She shrugged a delicate shoulder. "But I am also not wrong."

"You care for him, even if you prefer to pretend you do not." Sloane narrowed his eyes. "This will destroy him, Imogen."

"He will get to rule his precious kingdom," she hissed. "But I get to rule it first."

Sloane let out a heavy sigh, slumped back into his throne, and closed his eyes. "Very well. I suppose I do not have another choice. I will abdicate my throne, and I will pass it on to you until he is ready to rule. But you must promise me that you will never reveal the truth, not even to Thane."

Excitement flickered in Imogen's heart. "I promise."

She could not lie, nor could she swear to a promise without binding herself to her words for eternity. The fae might have lost most of their powers and the lands might be drained of magic, but some things had not changed at all. Fae could never lie, not so long as they were a part of the great continent of Tir Na Nog. The only fae who could lie were the ones who had been exiled: the shadow fae. Luckily, they were no longer a concern.

Now that she had spoken the words aloud, Imogen would forever be unable to speak Sloane's truth to anyone. Aengus, however, had not made that vow. An oversight, on her husband's part.

Sloane heaved a heavy sigh and stood, relinquishing his Seat of Power. "It is done. Take my crown from me so that I may keep my son."

Imogen smiled. She could scarcely believe her luck. For years, she had been working toward her plan, plotting and scheming behind her husband's back. It had taken a long time to get the right pieces into place. She needed a lover so devoted to her that he would risk his own neck to put her on the throne. Of course, Imogen was not dimwitted. She knew that Aengus had not made his moves out of love. He did it because he himself wanted power.

And he would never get it.

"Mother." Thane stormed into the Great Hall, his hurried footsteps echoing in the empty space, his body visibly shaking with anger. His uncle, Lord Bowen Selkirk, followed closely behind, confusion rippling across his usually amiable face. Imogen stood tall and gazed down at the two Selkirk males. They were almost mirror images of each other. Golden hair and eyes, polished yet commanding presences. Lord Bowen was tall and well-built even as the lines around his eyes showed his age. He was what Sloane should have been.

Thane glared at the empty throne, at his father's resigned face, and then at Aengus grinning broadly. "I had hoped the guards were wrong, but it looks as though I thought too highly of you. This is a coup. This is treason, and I will not stand for it, Mother."

"Thane," Lord Bowen said in a calm voice, laying a

steady hand on Thane's arm. "Hold on now. Certainly there is an explanation that makes sense. Surely our dear High Queen would not steal my brother's throne from him?"

Imogen just ignored him.

"It is not your decision, Thane," she said crisply, though an ache filled her heart at the hatred churning through her son's eyes. He would never forgive her for this, but she was only doing what was best for both him and the realm at large. She was trying to *save* him, if only from himself. One day, he would see. "Your father has abdicated the throne."

"That is a lie," Thane said through gritted teeth. "Father would never abdicate. He loves this realm and our people."

Imogen fought back the urge to snort at that. Poor Thane. He always believed the best of people, but he had never been more wrong. Sloane did not care about the low fae. He was ready to end the war, sacrificing them all to the hands of the gruesome Wood Court and their monstrous High King who delved in dark things. She would never allow that to happen.

"I cannot lie," Imogen declared. "Ask him yourself."

Thane shook off Lord Bowen's hand and strode up the steps to the stone dais. He took his father's weathered hands in his. "Father. What are you doing? You cannot step down. The throne is yours until the day you die."

Sloane sighed and patted Thane's hands. "I am sorry, my son. The throne was never mine to have forever. It is your mother's now."

"What?" Shock flickered across Thane's face. "You do not wish for me to rule?"

"One day, Thane." Sloane shook his head. "One day. For now, we have a High Queen Mother. She has ruled by my side for a century, and this will keep the realm at peace while war threatens to kill us all."

"But..." Thane's eyes went wide, and he stumbled back. "You cannot do this. You *cannot*."

"I am sorry, my son." Sloane reached up, yanked off his crown, and dropped it onto the throne where it made a thump as heavy as Imogen's heart. "It is done."

12

REYNA

Reyna had spent time at court before. She had grown up a princess after all. However, she had never experienced it quite like this. The day began at first light. Here, much further south than Falias, the sun sneaked into the sky hours earlier than she was accustomed. Ula, her lady's maid bustled into her bedchamber without knocking and threw open the curtains to reveal a sodden, grey sky.

Frowning, Reyna pushed up from the lush sheets and felt the cool bite of the wind. Wingallock hooted from where he perched on a wooden bedpost above her. He would have spent the night hunting, returning through the open window just before dawn.

"Good morning, milady," Ula said, standing primly with her grey hair pulled back into a high bun. Her matching eyes were as distant and hollow as they had been the day before. "We must get you bathed and dressed."

"Dressed for what?" Reyna asked.

"For court, of course," Ula chirped. "You have much on your program. There is the daily morning mass to attend in the Adhradh, followed by your official introduction to the court in the Great Hall. After that, you may find some free time to visit the gardens, though I imagine there are many who wish to meet the prince's betrothed."

Reyna sighed. The entire thing sounded absolutely exhausting. Introductions at court meant hours of polite conversation—which meant *boring* conversation—particularly in the company of fae who could rarely say much of consequence. The inability to lie and the fear of offending the High King and Queen resulted in dreary, uninteresting babble.

But Reyna did not have a choice. It would not be appropriate for the prince's new betrothed to bow out of her official introduction to the court. Reyna had made the choice to come here, and she had to embrace her new role, including all it entailed. Besides, she needed to begin her scheme in earnest, which meant building relationships and finding allies.

When she finally took the throne, she needed to be certain she would have some measure of support. Otherwise, another power-hungry fae would make a claim.

After Reyna swung her legs over the side of the bed, Ula led her into the boudoir where her bath awaited her. She stepped inside the small thin strip of a room where the far end held another set of arched windows overlooking the bay. Now, with the sun climbing into the sky, Reyna could see the glistening blue sea stretching toward the horizon.

Reyna came to a stop beside the bathtub, a circular wooden bucket just large enough for her to fully immerse herself. Steam curled from the water, and the scent of sweet green herbs and rowan blossoms filled the air. There were several bronze ewers scattered around it, along with a couple of sponges, and three small wooden stools.

She pointed at the stools. "Who are those for?"

"Me, milady, and two other maidservants. They will enter as soon as you are undressed and in the tub."

"I prefer to bathe in private," Reyna said.

"In private, milady?" Ula asked with a frown.

"I do not need assistance in this," she said.

"Very well, milady," she murmured before scurrying out of the room. She pulled the door behind her but left it open a crack. Reyna could not help but feel bad for the female. She knew she was a difficult noble to serve, but she hated the preening and prodding that went along with a royal bath.

After shrugging off her sleeping garments, Reyna slipped into the water. It almost scalded her skin, and she had to grit her teeth to refrain from shrieking. Had they *boiled* the water before bringing it to her chambers? What in the name of the Dagda had driven them to that? Reyna had only ever taken cool baths with waters gathered from melted snow.

Shaking her head at the overwhelming heat, she grabbed a sponge and got to work, scrubbing her face and arms. It had been a long journey, and she'd taken a dip into the sea only once. The brine still clung to her skin, along with days worth of dirt. After she scrubbed herself clean, she took a moment to close her eyes and steel herself for the day ahead.

The door creaked open. Reyna frowned, eyes still closed. "I really do prefer to bathe in private, Ula."

"So that you can sneak in a few more moments of sleep, it appears," a deep voice replied, one that definitely did not belong to Ula.

Reyna's eyes flew wide and she twisted toward the door, and bath water sprayed over the edges of the tub. Lorcan stood tall just inside the boudoir, clad in a fresh set of leather armor that fit him so well that it should have been a sin. His dark hair had been pulled away from his face, highlighting the sharp tips of his ears and that jaw that cut like a knife.

Flushing, Reyna dipped lower in the tub, all too aware that the water was clear enough for him to see every single inch of her. "What are you doing in here? You can't just charge into a princess's chambers when she's taking a bath!"

A dangerous smile curved his lips. "Apologies. You were once a Shieldmaiden, so I did not take you for the modest type."

She narrowed her eyes. "You thought I enjoyed prancing around naked just because I learned how to wield a sword?"

"That is not what I said." His gaze dropped for just a moment, almost too quickly for Reyna to see, but it was enough for her entire body to feel engulfed by flames. This damn scalding water... "Regardless, I hardly call your bathing the same as prancing around naked."

"You can see everything," she said, eyes still narrowed.

"Indeed, I can."

Tension punctuated his words, and Reyna clung tightly to the wooden edges of the tub, scarcely daring to breathe. A roar had built inside of her, desperate to get out, but all she could do was stare at the warrior who stood before her, staring right back.

In a garbled voice, she finally said, "Did you just come here to gawk at me?"

His eyes flickered with heat. "The prince requested that I stop by this morning to ensure you reached your chambers safely."

Ensure her safety? What an odd request. Why would she be anything but safe inside these castle walls? At the feast, Thane had mentioned that there had been attempts on his life. Had there been another? Did it have anything to do with why he'd run off as soon as they'd arrived in Tairngire?

There were so many questions she wished to ask, but instead, she chose a different route.

"Well, you've ensured it now, haven't you?" she snapped. "You are free to stop gawking now."

"All right." He gave a slight bow and turned to go but paused just before he reached the door. "But if I were gawking, princess, you would know."

※

Reyna angrily stood still while her lady's maid dressed her for the day's activities. She had been able to shrug off assistance with the bath, but gowns were an entirely different matter. She glared at the wall as Ula cinched the material tight behind her back, going through the last few moments over and over again in her head.

Lorcan had gotten her flustered, and she didn't like it at all. Who did he think he was? He couldn't just storm in announced. Did he have no sense of decorum? And then pretending as though he hadn't been just as aware of her nakedness as she had been.

She had thought *Thane* would be the insufferable one. Turned out it was his warrior instead.

"What do you think, milady?" Ula stood back and motioned toward a mirror.

Reyna stared at her reflection. The sapphire gown was a respectful nod to her ice fae heritage while acknowledging that she had left that court—and its icy blues—behind. The material was much thicker than the hoarfrost silk she usually wore, a soft cotton that hung heavily on her frame. With long sleeves that flared at her wrists, her arms seemed to disappear into the fabric itself. Silver wings had been embroidered along the low-cut bodice, and a soft leather belt cinched her waist. The color brought out the silver of her eyes, and her hair hung around her shoulders in loose waves. Ula had even done something to her cheeks. They were rosier than usual, making it look as though she had just flushed from a particularly nice compliment.

She looked like a princess.

Reyna hated it.

"Milady?" Ula prodded.

"This will certainly make me fit into court well, I believe," Reyna said. "All I need now is my dagger. I'm certain we can find a spot to hide it in these sleeves."

Ula peered up at her, frowning. "Milady, your dagger has been taken to the armory. You have no need for it at court."

Reyna whirled toward her lady's maid, her heart pounding in her chest. *"What?"*

"Milady." Ula stumbled back, her eyes wide. "It was not my doing."

"Whose doing was it?"

"The High Queen."

Reyna's hands fisted. Not only had the High Queen taken away the one thing she had left to protect herself, but she'd stolen something that was of far greater value than she could ever comprehend. That dagger had belonged to Reyna's mother.

Seething, Reyna pulled her emotions tight into her chest so that they did not overflow in front of her maid. She could not appear too angry in front of the wrong person. She could not show just how much defiance churned inside her soul. The silent war had begun, and she had not even stepped foot inside the Great Hall yet.

※

Reyna had rarely attended mass back home. While the Air and Ice Courts worshipped the same god, the laws surrounding religion were nothing alike. High Kings and Queens of this strange new realm were required to attend daily mass unless extenuating circumstances demanded otherwise. Coronations took place in the sight of their god, and they were required to follow the Dagda's every law, according to how the air fae had translated them. Many Air Court rulers had been removed from power for not following the laws of the Dagda. Some had even been hanged.

Reyna had never been certain if she truly believed in the teachings of the Dagda. At times, she had looked to her god with hope and wonder, trusting everything her people believed. But if the Dagda had given the fae their magic, then why had he taken it away?

So, she was pleased when daily mass ended quickly and without incident, and soon found herself standing within the extravagant Great Hall with the rest of the courtiers. The expansive space had been decked out in a multitude of thick golden banners that hung along the white stone walls. The ceiling rose high overhead, and dozens of looming arches curved down to form pillars that dotted the room. Two long wooden tables took up a large portion of the space, even if it was not yet time to dine. Several courtiers sat together, heads bent as they no doubt shared the newest gossip of the day. The room was cold and dark, even with the overhead chandelier that held a hundred flickering candles.

Reyna gazed toward the far end where an impressive throne sat empty. It was made of twisting thorns and vines that looked like part of the stone itself, as if the chair had grown out of the ground just as it was. But the High King was nowhere to be seen. Neither was the High Queen. Prince Thane stood in the far corner, speaking to an elegant male who was a mirror image of her betrothed, if Thane were perhaps fifty years older.

She had sat with Eislyn at mass but had lost her on the walk to the Great Hall from the Adhradh, their place of worship. With a frown, she craned her head, searching the crowd.

"Welcome to the Air Court, Princess Reyna." A female appeared and provided her with a kind smile. "How are you enjoying our brisk winds?"

Internally, Reyna sighed. And so it began. She could not be truthful, but she could not offend. The courtier before her appeared nice enough. She was shorter than Reyna with the golden hair that was common in the nobility. Her gown was simple compared to those around her—a plain orange with no added decoration—and she gently rested a hand against a round belly. So, this was Lady Epona then. She hailed from a castle further south but had relocated to Tairngire when the war grew closer to her lands. The battles near her castle had ceased now, but she had not gone back.

"The winds truly are brisk," Reyna replied with a fake smile pasted onto her face. "Back home, they are much milder."

"Milder? In those icy lands? Surely not."

"There are brisk winds along the Rowan Road once you reach the cliffs, but most of the realm rarely suffers more than a light breeze."

"And you arrived just yesterday, did you not?"

Reyna nodded.

"Surely you must be tired from your journey."

Reyna smiled and nodded. "A good night's sleep in a real bed has provided me with plenty of rest..."

She trailed off and smiled as the conversation continued. It was so very dull. Weather and rest. Boring topics.

"I don't suppose you have heard what has happened?" Lady Epona asked. "Your prince did not arrive to a very welcoming court."

Reyna perked up a bit. "What do you mean?"

Epona glanced around and dropped her voice to a whisper. "His mother has taken over. It seems she somehow convinced the High King to step down and insist she rule in his stead, bypassing the standard line of succession. Our prince will still be High King one day, of course, but it will not be now."

Reyna's mind spun, and her palms went slick with sweat. How had this happened? With the High Queen on the throne...it changed everything. Thane had been set to take over his father's rule in only a few short years. The High King was visibly ageing, and he was growing tired, sick, and dull. Reyna had only agreed to come here thinking she would get her chance soon. But Thane's mother was nothing like Sloane. She was strong and powerful, according to the tales. It would be decades yet before her health failed.

To be stuck inside this court that long, surrounded by enemies...

"That is..." Reyna trailed off, unsure of what to say.

"Highly unusual?" Brows arched, Epona nodded. "It is within the bounds of the law, but that does not make it right. The last time a High Queen took over from an abdicated High King was almost three hundred years ago. And we all know how that turned out for the realm."

Reyna frowned. She did not know. Another thing she would need to brush up on. As a child, Glencora had taken her history studies extremely seriously. She had spent hours upon hours learning the background of not only the Ice Court but of the other five courts as well. Reyna had only ever been interested in the lore of the ice fae, nothing more.

She would need to remedy that, it seemed.

"Forgive me," Reyna said. "I don't know that particular story."

"Centuries ago, the Air Court was ruled by a High Queen named Andraste and a High King named Midir. The power was hers, it came through her bloodline. She chose a low fae to marry, despite her father's insistence she marry Lord Louarn. And she let him sit on the throne, even though it was hers." She shot a conspiratorial glance over her shoulder, as if she did not want any of the other courtiers to overhear the conversation. "No one knows quite why, but the High King abdicated his throne in the end. It caused chaos in the realm, and started a civil war between the warriors here in Tairngire and the southerners."

"The Andraste Strife?" Reyna asked. She knew about the Air Court's infamous war, of course, but she had not known the spark had been lit by an abdicated king.

"That's right," Epona said eagerly. "Obviously, there are theories. An affair is the most popular among them. Wars tend to happen when queens and kings share their beds and their hearts with the wrong person."

Reyna gave the fae a pleasant smile. She opened her mouth to ask another question, but the lady plunged ever forward, clearly happy to have a fresh ear to listen to her gossip.

"I suppose you don't know about our vigilante either, do you?" she asked eagerly.

Curiosity lit up Reyna's heart. A vigilante? This was far more like it. "I do not, but I certainly wish I did."

Epona grinned, her own golden eyes sparkling with enthusiasm. "Tales say that a strong, brutish fae stalks the streets of the slums, killing murderers and thieves, finding justice for the poor low fae who cannot find justice for themselves. He knows everything about everyone. He is called the Bloody Dagger."

A vigilante dispensing justice? Reyna liked the sound of that. Whoever he was, Reyna wanted to meet this fae. "Who is he?"

"No one knows. His face has never been seen. Some say that he is the stealthiest fae to have ever lived."

"How could one find him…hypothetically, of course?" Reyna could not help but ask.

Epona's eyes widened. "Oh, you don't want to find him. He's somewhere inside Drunkard's Pit. It is a hellhole and not safe for the likes of you and me. Oh! There is something else you ought to know. Have you heard about the tension between Prince Thane and his father—"

But Reyna's attention had begun to drift again, her mind too focused on the new information she'd gained about this bloody dagger. She did not want to rely on someone else to do her dirty work for her, but it was a good back-up plan now that her situation had become much more complicated than she'd imagined.

Reyna might be trapped inside a cage for now, but somehow, she would find a way out. And her first stop would be Drunkard's Pit.

13

LORCAN

Lorcan had grown so accustomed to seeing Reyna Darragh in a travel-worn tunic and dirt-stained trousers that he did not quite know what to think of her in a courtly gown. She was stunning, of course, in a way that most ladies and princesses were. Rosy cheeks, hips that swayed beneath the flattering cut of that sapphire material, and a demure smile intended to charm.

I still prefer the trousers, he thought.

The warrior stood guard beside one of the many Air Court banners hanging from the lofted ceiling, watching the courtiers whisper and scheme, smile and nod, laugh and scowl. It was all very tiresome, and he was glad he didn't have to be involved. Most of their smiles were false, even if their words could never be. Reyna had joined in with apparent enthusiasm and had made great friends with Lady Epona. She'd been at this for hours. Lorcan could not help but be surprised. He thought she'd look down her nose at these things.

The daily court gatherings were drearily boring. Thane never thought so, but it was the truth.

Suddenly, Reyna waltzed to his side, slumped against the wall, and sighed. "I have had enough."

Surprise flickered in his veins, but he kept his face a mask and continued to stare ahead. "That's surprising. You seem to be enjoying this endless gossip."

"Every single one of these fae are smiling," she said, "but I would wager that half are not enjoying themselves at all."

"Only half?"

"The other half are only enjoying themselves because this is the highlight of the day. It's all the gossip. The room is thick with it." She sighed. "And I have had enough for one day. I think I'll take a walk around the castle gardens before the sun goes down."

"I'll escort you," he said, pushing off the wall.

She frowned. "I meant alone. Privately. Just like I wanted my bath to be before you barged in."

He tried his best to bite back his smile. "You cannot do anything in this castle privately, princess."

Scowling, she whirled toward the door and strode away, her hands fisted by her sides. Lorcan fell into step beside her, giving a nod to each of the warriors they passed. The prince had tasked Lorcan with keeping a special eye on his new betrothed. That was the only reason he had decided to join her for the walk, of course.

"Honestly," Reyna said when they stepped into the quiet corridor just beyond the Great Hall's looming doors. "Why are you following me around?"

"I am merely offering my protection," he countered. "I am a guard. It is what I do."

"I thought you were the *prince's* guard." She stopped as they came to a set of doors that led out into the castle gardens. Before she could open it herself, he pushed at the wood and motioned her to go first. Narrowing her eyes, she shoved past him.

"I *am* the prince's guard," Lorcan said as they stepped out into the dimming sunlight. Orange streaked across the horizon, casting a brilliant glow on Reyna's face. "And you are his betrothed. So, guarding you is well within my task."

Reyna let out a low grumble beneath her breath and trailed over to the entrance of the castle gardens. Well, one of the many entrances. Set inside the interior castle walls, the gardens stretched between the six towers that surrounded Mistral Tower. Pathways led between the shrubbery in a maze of looping routes. In winter, there were few flowers, and much of the greenery had lost its leaves, but Reyna still seemed keen to look around. In fact, her entire body seemed to come alive now that she had escaped the stone walls of the Great Hall. He hadn't noticed it before when she mingled with the courtiers, and he was shocked that he had missed it.

It was almost as though she had been muted before. But she practically hummed with energy in the presence of nature. So much so that he could not help but stare.

"Fine," she finally said as they passed between two shrubs that rose as high as Lorcan's head. "If I cannot rid myself of you, then at least make yourself useful. What can you tell me about the Bloody Dagger?"

Lorcan shot her a sharp look. "The Bloody Dagger? Why would you ask about him?"

She gave a delicate shrug. "Lady Epona mentioned him, but she didn't know a great deal. I just find the idea of a Tairngire vigilante extremely interesting."

He frowned. He bet she did. "You best keep your curiosity of this topic to yourself."

"There you go again," she said, throwing up her hands. "Monitoring my words. Doesn't that get dull?"

"I'm only trying to protect you," he said. And, somehow, that was the truth. Lorcan did not know why he wanted to shield Princess Reyna from the worst of this court, but he did. His hidden mark hummed, warning him, but he ignored it. "If you ask the wrong person about this, he—or she—might come to the wrong conclusion. If that wrong conclusion then reached the High Queen..."

Reyna stopped short on the garden path and propped her hands on her belted waist. "And what then? Surely the High Queen allows curiosities. She is not a tyrant. At least, I've never heard she is, not like the Wood Court's king."

"She's not a tyrant, but she is fiercely protective of her son," Lorcan warned. "Do not give her reason to perceive you as a threat."

Lorcan's marked burned, and he grit his teeth through the pain. Twisting away from Reyna, he stared hard at the red winter berries that dotted the bush just before him. The pain passed quickly, but it left a dull throb behind. Why had it flared now? Surely it didn't want him to destroy Reyna, too.

"Lorcan?" Reyna asked, gently placing a hand on his arm. She peered up at him, concern flickering in her silver eyes. "What's the matter?"

His gaze landed on her fingers. He could feel the warmth of her touch, even through his thick leather.

"Lorcan?" she asked again, edging so close that he could see down the front of her gown. He swallowed thickly, remembering the sight of her in that bath. It had taken a lot of effort to hold back the desire he'd felt churning in his gut. He had seen *every* part of her, and not one bit had been unappealing, particularly the soft slopes of her breasts...

Lorcan's mind snapped back to the present. What was he doing? This was the prince's betrothed. He needed to remove himself from the situation and stop thinking about her breasts.

"Nothing is the matter," he growled out. "This conversation has become dreadfully boring. One day at court, and you have already become one of them. Go on with your walk. I'll stand guard from the edge of the gardens."

Confusion rippled across Reyna's face, and then she scowled. Quickly, she dropped her hand from his arm. "Good. I was hoping to get rid of you so I could enjoy my walk in peace."

With that, Reyna twisted on her heels and marched away. She barely glanced at the greenery she passed. Lorcan watched her go, his heart pounding. Her blue gown swished around her hips, and her silver hair trailed down her slender back. Everything about her screamed power, in a beautiful, terrifying way.

Reyna Darragh was going to bring trouble to this court.

14

REYNA

It turned out that plotting to murder the prince was a dreadfully uneventful scheme. Reyna stood outside of the Great Hall with Thane, waiting to enter. Apparently, the High Queen was finally holding court and she wanted to meet her son's new betrothed. It had been a weeks since she had arrived in Tairngire, and Reyna's days had been plagued by endless gossip. Every day had been more of the same. She woke at first light, she bathed and dressed, she attended mass, and then she spent hours inside the Great Hall listening to courtiers prattle on about the same thing they discussed the day before.

She might perish of boredom before the prince died from the sharp end of her blade.

Speaking of the prince, she had seen little of him in the past several days. He had been too busy dealing with the fall-out of the abdication. His mother had replaced the entire council and had requested an entirely new set of personal guards. It seemed she trusted no one the king had held close to him. High Queen Imogen was even more paranoid inside these castle walls than Reyna.

Quite the accomplishment, Reyna thought with a slight smile.

Thane finally spoke. "Apologies, princess, for not introducing you to the High Queen before now."

His posture was stiff, and his eyes were hard and distant. As always, he wore his gold-dyed leather armor, though there was something about it that appeared rough around the edges for once. And there was a puffiness around his eyes. Perhaps he hadn't been sleeping.

"It is all right," she said quietly, all too aware of the many guards that surrounded them. Eyes and ears for the queen, no doubt. "I understand that there were some...unexpected developments upon your return."

"Unexpected is right," he muttered before lifting his eyes to meet hers. "Tell me, Reyna. You readily relinquished your titles and your claim to your kingdom's throne, did you not?"

Reyna frowned. She did not know where Thane was taking this. "At the time, I thought it was the best course of action for myself. Glencora was first in line, regardless. It did not matter if I chose a different path. It was unlikely that I would ever sit on the Ice Court's throne."

"But it did end up mattering," he pointed out.

"No one could have foreseen what happened," she replied. "If I had known, I might never have become an unsworn Shieldmaiden."

Thane's golden eyes were unreadable, something Reyna did not like at all. She did not wish to discuss her choices about the crown. So far he had not questioned her decision to marry him. If she answered wrong now, her entire plot might vanish into the harsh Tairngire winds.

"Something tells me you would have made the same decision," he said quietly. "I know why you agreed to this betrothal, Reyna, and it isn't because you suddenly yearned for power."

Reyna's heart flipped once. What had she done to tip him off?

He continued. "I know you do not care for me. You wanted to see the alliance between our realms continue, but you did not wish to doom your younger sister by allowing her to take my hand."

"I..." Reyna blinked. That was certainly not something she had ever expected the prince to say, least of all out loud and in front of so many witnesses. The guards that surrounded them served the High Queen. Some were likely her spies. She would be silly not to trust some of them with eavesdropping. This entire conversation would make it back to her ears.

The prince held up a hand. "You do not need to speak. I won't force you to confess or spin your words in a way that will only confirm the truth. I respect your reasons. Unlike my traitor of a mother, you do not yearn for power, which means you will not scheme for it."

Again, he nodded, though it appeared as if it were more to himself than to her. Reyna merely stood with her hands clasped tightly together. She did not crave power over the realms and the kingdoms, no. But she did crave power over *him*.

He didn't deserve to sit on that throne, ruling over the ice fae. Neither did his scheming mother. Reyna did not know how she would get the High Queen off that throne, but Reyna would not rest until she did.

The massive oak doors cracked open, and Thane motioned her inside. With a deep breath, she squared her shoulders and strode forward. This day, the hall was not the bustle of activity it had been in the days before. The tables had been pushed to the side to create a single aisle down the center of the room, leading straight to the throne.

Where the High Queen sat tall.

Reyna sized up her opponent. Imogen Selkirk was not an air fae, and she did not look like one. Born in the Sea Court, she had an angular face, sapphire eyes, and blue hair that cascaded down her body, stopping at her waist. A small circlet of golden thorns sat atop her head, but she would have had a courtly bearing even without the crown. Her yellow gown dipped low between her breasts, forming the shape of a V that led straight down to her navel. Golden swirls were embroidered into the trim, highlighting her tanned skin. The arms of her gown were much like the ones that Reyna had worn so far, long and flaring at the ends.

The High Queen beckoned her forward.

Squaring her shoulders, Reyna took purposeful steps toward the thorny throne. Her slippered feet scuffed along the thin, golden carpet that stretched between a few rows of curious fae. There were about a dozen witnesses, and they all twisted to watch her, silence hanging heavily in the air. If she were a more timid fae, she might feel forced to cast her eyes to the carpet that passed beneath her feet. But Reyna would do no such thing.

Finally, she reached the end of the aisle where the dais rose up before her, the thorns of the throne curling up toward the white stone ceiling. Thane still stood by her side. Reyna waited. It was customary for a fae—low or otherwise—to defer to the High Queen in terms of conversation. She would not speak until Imogen addressed her.

"Reyna Darragh," the High Queen of the Air Court drawled. Her voice sounded quite different to what Reyna had expected. Instead of high-pitched and soft, it was deep, commanding, and rough. "Princess of the Ice Court. Or should I say Air Court, as your court will soon be part of mine. *If* you marry my son."

Anger roiled through Reyna's gut. That was the High Queen's intent. Thane had not said it outright, but it had been suggested all the same. There was a reason the High Queen had avoided her until now. Imogen was not happy about the alliance. Reyna was not sure why, but she would find out.

Until then, she would have to rein in her emotions and not rise to the High Queen's taunts. Reyna still did not know how she would get Imogen off that throne. She'd hoped to find some gossip to use against her, but she'd come up empty there. Killing her wouldn't work. She didn't even have a dagger anymore. So, for now, Reyna would play nice and ask for her assistance with something easy, make her think that they were friends. And part of the reason they had allied in the first place was so that the Air Court could help with the dark magic sweeping through the ice fae lands.

"Thank you for finally meeting with me." Reyna bowed her head. "I wonder if I could speak with you about something that plagues my kingdom."

"Not a fan of pleasantries, then, I surmise," Imogen said icily.

Reyna shifted on her feet. She had chosen the direct route, as that was how her father preferred it, but it seemed this queen was fond of games. How extraordinarily tiresome. By her side, Thane cleared his throat.

"Apologies. *Your Majesty*. I am so eager to help my homeland that I forgot my manners. Indeed, I hope you are well. I am sure the brisk wind aides your health."

Imogen waved her hand dismissively. "It is too late for all that now. Get on with it. You want something. What is it?"

Reyna steeled her nerves. Imogen was an interesting one. She was testing Reyna, seeing if she could knock her off balance. Reyna would not allow herself to fall. "As you know, my lands have been plagued by a cruel magic. We call it the Ruin. It destroys entire villages. It kills innocents within moments of its touch. And now it has blinded my sister."

"So I have heard," Imogen said, staring down her nose at Reyna. "That is why, is it not, that you chose to marry my son? Your far more capable sister is ill in her bed."

"It is true," Reyna agreed. "Glencora has spent her life learning the ways of the court, and I have not. However, I have much to offer the—"

"Much to offer?" Imogen spread her arms as wide as the thorns around her, and then she laughed. "Then, why are you here begging for your High Queen's help against an enemy you cannot banish yourself?"

Reyna's chest flushed, heat creeping into her neck. "It is not as simple as fighting an army. There is something magical in its nature. We need—"

"Enough," Imogen hissed. "I have heard enough. You are either clever with your words or you have gone mad. Magic vanished a hundred years ago. I wished to ally with your court when it was Glencora who would end up standing by my son, but I do not approve of this ridiculous betrothal. You removed yourself from the line of succession. You are no princess in my eyes."

Reyna drew herself up. A tense cough echoed from the courtiers standing witness.

"Imogen," a soft, soothing voice spoke up from Reyna's left. She turned to see the older version of Thane striding to stand beside her. The prince's uncle, Lord Bowen, she believed. His shoulders were thrown back in determination, but his smile was kind. "Perhaps you should reconsider. The girl is pleading for the safety of her people. If there is a dark magic plaguing her kingdom—"

"Oh, dear." Imogen tsked and shook her head. "You sound as though you believe her every word. The girl is clearly mad."

Reyna stiffened. "I am not mad."

Imogen leaned forward, baring her teeth. "If you are not mad, then your lands are cursed. Leave me. I wish to speak of this no longer."

Reyna opened her mouth to argue, but Thane placed a soft hand on her arm. She almost jerked from surprise, recoiling from his touch.

"Come, Reyna," he murmured. "You must go."

Heart pounding, she fought to control her emotions. Princess Reyna—Thane's betrothed—needed to behave herself as long as Imogen controlled the crown. As much as she wanted to scream and shout and wave her arms like windmills, she could not. All she could do was leave, the weight of the courtiers' piteous gazes on her back.

She had not assumed much of Imogen, but she had certainly expected far more than this. Fae were dying. Fae who would become the Air Court's responsibility. And yet, she'd insisted on doing nothing to help.

The fire inside Reyna roared to life. As long as the Selkirks controlled the Air Court, the ice fae would never receive help with the Ruin. Hundreds more could die. Dozens more villages could fall. If she did not have reason enough to take the throne before, she certainly did now.

When they reached the double doors, the prince led her into the corridor and then turned back toward the hall. "Apologies, but there are still many things I must attend to with my mother today."

Reyna ground her teeth but nodded. She couldn't very well insist he shirk his courtly duties just because she had been offended by his mother. Besides, she'd had enough of the Selkirk family for one day, except for Thane's uncle. He was the only one of them who seemed decent enough to care about her kingdom. She said her goodbyes to her betrothed and took off down the corridor, looking forward to an afternoon spent alone for the first time since she'd arrived in Tairngire. Time alone meant time to think about her next steps.

"I will escort you back to your chambers." Lorcan appeared out of nowhere and fell into step by her side, one hand lightly thumbing the hilt of the sword belted around his waist.

She huffed. It truly was impossible to find privacy inside this castle.

"That is hardly necessary. I know the way."

"After your little spat with the High Queen, I thought it best to ensure you return to your chambers safely."

"It was not a *spat*." She shot him a harsh look. "Has anyone ever told you that it is entirely unnerving the way you creep around in the background? Why are you always around?"

His lips curled into a wicked smile. "Oh, yes. Why do you think Thane is so fond of having me as his personal guard?"

"Guards should fight, should they not?" She slowed to a

stop to give him an appraising glance. "You act more like a spy than a warrior."

He stiffened, but then continued on beside her. "Perhaps guards should be skilled in more than just combat."

Reyna sighed. It was difficult to argue against that. She cut her eyes sideways. "And perhaps princesses should be skilled in more than just intrigue."

"I did not realize that needlework and manners were considered intrigue." Lorcan paused to open the door that led to the towers beyond the Great Hall. Reyna strode through, even if she did want to tell him her mind. She could open her own door, thank you very much.

"Being a princess is wrapped up in shiny things. Pretty gowns. Fancy feasts. Glittering golden castles such as this one."

"And yet…" Lorcan prodded.

"It is all about intrigue beneath the surface. Who can get on top. Who can smile at the right fae and then frown at the other. It's all about power. It is what everyone wants, whether they deserve it or not. We both witnessed it just now. The High Queen played her hand. She does not want a rogue princess from the Ice Court to have any power at all, so she turned me down. If a different fae had asked for her assistance with the Ruin, I am certain her answer would have been very different."

Lorcan did not reply. Reyna had likely said too much, but she did not care. There was nothing in it that she wanted to keep to herself. Several moments passed along in silence. They made their way through the maze of the castle, until they found the dark and winding stairwell that led to her chambers.

"The prince is a good male. He will serve the realm well, including yours," he finally said as they reached the door to her chambers.

She frowned up at the warrior. He was so odd. She was still certain that there was something not quite right about him. He did not look like the nobility of the air fae, but that did not mean anything. Most of the low fae didn't either. Still, she could not help but think it was something else, something beyond his dark, curling hair and those raven eyes. It was the certainty that he was hiding something.

And, maybe, just maybe, she could use that to her advantage.

Reyna turned her attention back to the topic at hand—the prince. "Maybe Thane would help with the Ruin, but he does not have the crown. His mother does. It will be years upon years before his reign begins."

Lorcan looked surprised. "You sound disappointed. And here I thought that you, of all fae, did not want to find herself perched on a throne wearing something on her head much heavier than that little circlet of yours."

Absentmindedly, Reyna reached up and fingered the ice sigil on her silver circlet. She had not been forced to wear a different one yet, at least. One with the sigil of the Air Court—a gleaming golden crown. It took a certain level of self-importance to fashion an entire realm's sigil after their own crown. When Reyna became High Queen, that would be one of the first things she would change.

"For a guard, you are curiously interested in my motives." She smiled, a move that she hoped put the warrior on edge.

But he smiled right back. "I see you did not deny it. Do not assume that because I am a warrior, I'm unaware of the courtly way of mincing words."

She sidled up to him, tipping back her head to smile even more brightly than she had before. "I did not assume anything of the sort. In fact, Lorcan of the grasslands, I think there is far more to you than meets the eye. You're hiding something, and I intend to find out exactly what it is."

A strange look flashed across his face so quickly that she might have missed it if she hadn't been watching for it. It might have been surprise or annoyance, but it might have been something far more interesting: panic. With one last glance in his direction, she pushed into her chambers, her own mind whirring. If Lorcan truly were hiding something, then she might be able to use it against him, to further her scheme. She would do anything to save her kingdom.

And she would certainly not hesitate to resort to blackmail.

15

EISLYN

Eislyn gazed out the window, tears rolling down her cheeks. She crumpled the letter in her hand, and the parchment scratched against her fingers. The late afternoon Tairngire skies were slate grey, devoid of all color and light. Just like her heart.

She whirled toward Reyna, who stood solemnly in the center of Eislyn's private drawing room, Wingallock perched on her shoulder. Despite the weeks spent in the company of air fae, Reyna had never looked more *Reyna* than she did now. Most of the air fae courtiers preferred to wear their hair up and away from their faces, to highlight their many jewels, but Reyna still let her strands be loose and wild around her shoulders. The silver mane even seemed defiant in the way it moved. She wore a gown, just as she did every day at court, but she had stuck to silver and blue hues instead of yellows, golds, and oranges.

"How has Glencora gotten worse?" Eislyn asked, indicating the letter they'd received from Father only moments before. "She survived the Ruin. If it didn't kill her, shouldn't she improve?"

"I do not know, Eislyn," Reyna said softly, her own eyes glassy from unshed tears. Eislyn knew her sister was trying to be strong, for her.

"What can we do?" she asked, her voice rising. "How can we stop this? We're stuck inside this castle, forced to carry on as if nothing is wrong!"

The two of them had been heavily monitored since the moment they had stepped foot inside of Dalais Castle. They were constantly surrounded by servants and guards and required to attend daily mass and court. Eislyn had managed to beg out of a few days spent inside the Great Hall with the rest of the courtiers, including the first morning when she'd felt far too overwhelmed, but there had been little relief.

"I don't know." Reyna scowled and absently reached up to ruffle Wingallock's feathers. "I asked the High Queen for assistance today. She denied me."

Eislyn bugged out her eyes. "She *denied* you? But...that was part of our agreement. They were to help us with the Ruin as part of the alliance."

"The prince was to be wed to Glencora as part of the alliance as well. It seems that while the High Queen approved of our perfect eldest sister, she does not approve of me."

Eislyn's heart dropped. "Please. Do not tell me that means…"

Her time spent on the Rowan Road had convinced her that Thane wasn't quite the monster she had once thought he was. A cruel, terrible male who wished to burn down the world he was not. But that didn't mean he was *good* either. And the idea of the betrothal transferring from Reyna to her gave her dread.

Reyna crossed the room and took Eislyn's trembling hands into hers. She was so calm and steady, like a patch of ice amidst a desert. Wingallock hooted and lifted into the air, settling comfortably on Eislyn's shoulder. The owl pushed his soft face against hers and rubbed her cheek with his feathers. Eislyn's racing heart immediately began to steady.

"Listen to me. We will make this work. I came here to marry the prince, regardless of his mother. And you came here to find answers about the Ruin. We can still do that. Have you begun your search of the castle library?"

Eislyn shook her head. "Our days are so full. Every time I mention it, my lady's maid bustles me off to another event. I have begged out of court on a few different occasions, but then they make me rest inside these chambers. If I'm too weary for court, then I am too weary to do anything else, according to them."

With a grim smile, Reyna nodded. "I have not wandered the castle freely either. Even in a walk through the castle gardens, I am watched."

"They don't trust us," she whispered.

Reyna cast a glance over her shoulder at the door. "We need to get you inside that library."

"Yes, but how?" Eislyn knew at least one guard stood outside. Perhaps even two, since Reyna had come.

Her sister smiled. "I will go into the corridor and create a distraction. You run in the opposite direction, quickly. They'll never know that you have gone."

"Reyna," Eislyn gasped. "You will get me thrown into the dungeons."

Her sister gave her a frank look. "They cannot throw you into the dungeons for exploring your new home. You will be searching for a library. That's hardly scandalous. Or illegal. In fact, it's so innocent that I wish we had thought of it before now."

"But I don't even know where the library is."

"My guess is that it is in one of these six interior towers. Not this one, as it appears to be exclusively private chambers. Perhaps the next one over. Aurelian Tower."

Eislyn's heart began to pound hard as she stared at her sister's calm and unaffected face. She truly was serious about this. What was worse, Eislyn was even considering it.

"Shouldn't you be the one to do this?" she asked. "Sneaking around, avoiding guards. This leans far more into your strengths."

"My dear sister, you are the one who has spent years in research. You will know where to look in the library and what to read far better than I would." Reyna held out her arm, and Wingallock flew to her side. And then her sister's smile turned wicked. "Come. There is no time to waste."

Eislyn watched her sister rush to the door, and her heart went wild inside her chest. Fear tumbled through her. A roar filled her ears. She did not do things like this. Distracting guards, rushing into danger. Eislyn preferred to stay inside, where it was safe, where the world couldn't tear her apart.

But she had left her home behind to come to this strange court. To get access to their libraries. For her people. For the fading life of her sister.

With a trembling breath, she nodded to herself and scrambled after Reyna. Her sister shot her a triumphant smile and flung open the door.

"Wait here," she whispered.

Eislyn nodded.

"Lorcan!" Reyna shouted as she charged out of the room. "I would say I'm surprised to see your annoying face again, but that would be a lie. Oh, Wingallock! What are you doing!"

The rush of wings filled the air.

Her entire body trembling with nerves, Eislyn pressed down the front of her emerald gown and rushed into the corridor. Chaos had exploded to her left, but she didn't stop to see what Reyna had done. Instead, she swerved to the right and minced, footsteps light on the stone ground. When she came to a bend in the corridor, she took the next right. She stopped just out of sight of the guards, pushed her back against the wall, and dragged the cool castle air into her lungs.

Her heart ran wild; her face felt hot. She had just *sneaked* out of her room. Quite successfully. Is this what Reyna had felt like when she'd trained? No wonder she had grown addicted to the pounding excitement and fear.

With a quick nod to herself, she pushed away from the wall and inched down the corridor. At the end, there was a door that led through the interior castle wall to the next tower over, Aurelian Tower. No one had ever mentioned what that tower was used for, so she thought it was a good place to begin her search.

She glanced over her shoulder and continued on. After safely making her way through the castle wall and into the next tower, Eislyn slowed her steps. These corridors looked much like the ones in White Stone Tower. Dark and silent with the occasional flickering sconce on the stone walls. Dust floated on the air. There were a few shut doors she passed. She didn't stop to inspect them. They looked as though they led to private chambers.

She twisted and turned through the castle, her footsteps quiet, her heartbeat loud. From somewhere up ahead, a voice rang out. Swallowing hard, she stopped short. Could it be the library?

"Take this blood and take this flesh," the low voice murmured in a strange melodic tune.

Eislyn's heartbeat quickened. That did *not* sound like it had anything to do with books. She took a step back. She shouldn't be here.

"May thine shadows bind me…"

She nibbled on her bottom lip. Truly, she should turn back and return to her chambers. There must be some other way to find the library. But her curiosity throbbed in time with her heart. What was the fae up ahead doing?

Gritting her teeth, she took slow and quiet steps forward until she reached the edge of the door. She held her breath and poked her head to the side, just enough so that one eye could see inside the room.

A small grey male knelt on the floor, his back hunched, his body trembling. A naked corpse lay before him, and blood spilled onto the stone floor from the deep wounds in his chest. Tears burned in Eislyn's eyes. Her hand flew to her mouth to hold back a gag.

"May thine power complete me. May I become unblemished and whole."

A deep, dark power pulsed in the room. The corpse lifted from the floor. Eislyn let out a shriek and stumbled back. She whirled on her feet and ran, her silver hair streaming out behind her. She didn't dare look back. All she could do was flee, throwing open door after door until she'd reached White Stone Tower once again.

Breath heaving, she slowed to a stop and placed a hand on the wall to steady herself. The guards were around the corner. She couldn't let them see her like this, wild and scared and confused.

What had she just seen? That had been magic. But how?

And why? Closing her eyes, she could not erase the image of the bloody corpse on the floor. That old man. The grey hair and hunched form. He'd appeared as ancient as time itself. And then Eislyn knew at once who she'd seen.

It had been Sloane, the former king.

16
REYNA

"You didn't find it?" Reyna strode toward one of the many windows in Eislyn's chambers that overlooked the castle gardens. Her sister sat on a bench beside the flickering hearth, leafing through a handful of books she'd managed to request from her lady's maid. "And since when did my dear sister require flames to keep warm?"

Eislyn shut the book with a sigh. "I do not require it. The servants offered, and I did not wish to disappoint."

"I do not like it," Reyna said. "There is a dark magic in those flames."

"Using fire does not mean we will meet the same fate as the Fire Court," Eislyn said.

"We do not even know the fate of the Fire Court." Reyna let out a sigh. "Just as we know nothing of the Ruin. What happened yesterday evening? Did you run into more guards?"

The color drained from Eislyn's face. "I couldn't find the library. Instead…I found the former king, Thane's father, chanting over a dead body. And the body...sort of... lurched into the air."

Eislyn sucked in a sharp breath, terror flickering across her face. Reyna pressed her lips together. She knew it had been a bad idea for Eislyn to come here. It was far too stressful on her sister's mind. It had been a long time since Eislyn had seen something that wasn't truly there. Reyna had hoped that her haunted thoughts were fully gone. Hopefully, they had not returned for good.

Reyna settled onto the bench beside Eislyn and wrapped her arm around her shoulder, pulling her sister close. Gently, she said, "That sounds like something unlikely to happen. Corpses don't move."

"Oh," Eislyn said, her eyes widening. "*Oh.*"

Taking a deep breath, she stood and decided to steer the conversation onto something less painful for her sister. Eislyn knew that she sometimes imagined things, and she did not like to dwell on it. It pained her. At times, it embarrassed her.

"Right. That settles it then. Come with me. We need to speak to Thane about the Ruin. His mother refuses to assist, and you can't research if you aren't shown the library."

Eislyn didn't move, instead frowning up at her sister. "*Must* we go and speak with the prince?"

"I know you aren't fond of him, but we have no other choice." Reyna held out a hand. "He has seen the Ruin himself. Perhaps he can be reasoned with."

A strange expression flickered across Eislyn's face, but then she took Reyna's hand and stood. Together, they gathered the small collection of books and pushed out into the corridor. Reyna expected to find Lorcan skulking in the shadows but was relieved to see he wasn't there.

"No guards," Eislyn said, cocking her head. "That is unusual."

"They will be somewhere nearby. Let's hurry before they spot us leaving," Reyna beckoned. "I know the way to Thane's chambers."

Eislyn fell into step beside her, raising her brows. "You know the way? I know you do not care for appearances, Reyna, but surely you have not…"

Reyna gave her a sharp look. "I have not been in bed with the prince, if that is what you are presuming. Surely, you know me better than that. I would do nothing to threaten the alliance."

And bedding the Prince surely would. They were to stay chaste until their wedding night, according to the laws of the Dagda. That was one part of the law that Reyna could surely get behind. She was safe from the prince's advances. For now.

"What will you ask him?" Eislyn said as they turned a corner. Reyna stopped and looked around, frowning. She had been certain this was the way, but the castle was a maze of twisting tunnels. This one looked much like the last. In fact, it almost felt as though they were walking in circles. Shaking her head, she resumed their journey.

"I will demand that he allow you time in the libraries, and I will ask him to pledge his armies to the cause," Reyna said. "And then I will suggest that his mother's rule is not legitimate. He is the heir to the throne. This entire coup has been entirely odd."

Eislyn frowned. "Odd how?"

"Thane was set to take the throne in a few years' time. Now, suddenly, Sloane has passed his rule to Imogen? There is something amiss in it."

Reyna stopped again and gazed around her. The

corridor was identical the one they had just gone past. This was not the way to Thane's chambers. They were surely lost.

"This castle is nothing like our home," Reyna said quietly. These halls were dark and dreary, and a harsh wind bit her face. She thought she might even be cold. At the Ice Court, glowing blue orbs lined every wall, casting pure white light onto the slick floors. She had never gotten lost in those halls. She knew Starford Castle better than she knew her own mind.

"It is not as foreign as I am certain the Fire Court would be," Eislyn said. "At least there is snow in Tairngire this time of year."

"Not that we ever see it," Reyna said with a frown. If only she could step outside and explore the thick woods surrounding the southern edge of the castle, she might feel more at ease in Tairngire.

That was certainly why the High Queen had not allowed it. Putting Reyna Darragh of the Ice Court at ease was surely the last thing she wanted.

"Come," Reyna said. "We will need to retrace our steps. This is not the way."

As they scurried back down the shadowy corridor, the echo of distant footsteps filled Reyna's ears. Heart lifting, she spun on her feet. A tall, hooded figure strode toward them, his boots scuffing the stone floor. His face was hidden by the dark folds of the cloth, but the certainty of his footsteps combined with the grace of his movements suggested that he was a highly trained royal guard.

"Ah," she said. "We were just on our way to visit the prince, but we seem to be lost. Are we in the wrong tower?"

The guard did not respond. Instead, his feet moved faster against the stone floor. Frowning, Reyna glanced at her sister. She was watching the approaching stranger with a heightened sense of panic flickering across her face. When Reyna turned back to the guard, she understood why. He had pulled a dagger from the depths of his black cloak, and the steel end flashed ominously in the darkness.

"Eislyn," Reyna warned in a low voice as she shifted her body in front of her sister's. "Stay behind me."

"Reyna," Eislyn whispered, clutching the back of Reyna's gown. "What is happening?"

Reyna did not reply. The male was closer now. Only a few more moments, and his steel would ring through the air. Reyna's hands clenched. She had no weapon herself. Her own dagger had been taken from her weeks ago.

This very much felt like a trap, one that Reyna had walked straight into. She had allowed the Air Court to disarm her, and now, they had sent an assassin when no guards or courtiers were around to witness it. The High Queen had made it clear how she felt about Reyna. How best to take care of a pesky, unwanted betrothal? Murder it.

But Reyna Darragh would not go down without a fight.

The hooded fae rushed forward, but Reyna was ready. She caught his wrist with her hand and shoved him back. Surprised flickered in his eyes as his hood slipped back. She quickly sized up her opponent. Male, as she'd suspected. Light brown hair that hung to his shoulders. Flashing dark green eyes. Thin but likely stronger than he looked.

Growling, he took another swing at Reyna's head. She ducked low, just in time to avoid the blade.

"Cease this," he said as he pulled himself tall. "You *will* die here tonight. I will make certain of it. Stop fighting. It will merely prolong your suffering."

"You do not know how very wrong you are." Reyna smiled. "Nor with whom you are dealing."

The assassin let out a bitter laugh. "You are a princess."

"You're right. An unarmed princess. This is clearly an unfair fight. You think I'm weak? Then provide me with one of those other daggers you have hidden somewhere inside that cloak." Reyna continued to smile. "Or are you too afraid to make it a fair fight?"

The assassin narrowed his eyes. "You're merely trying to distract me. These games will not save you, princess."

"This isn't a game," Reyna replied, holding up her hands. "Fight me fairly. If you win, then you can go boast about your accomplishments to the ladies at the House of Skin."

She had gotten him with that. Reyna could see it in his eyes. She just wished she wasn't wearing this stupid courtly gown. The long skirts would surely get in her way.

"Reyna," Eislyn hissed from behind her. "Please do not do this. We should call for the prince."

"The prince is nowhere to be seen, Eislyn. We must protect ourselves."

She felt her sister's hands unclench the back of Reyna's gown, and then heard as she took several steps back. "I will go fetch help."

"No!" the assassin shouted. "If you run for help, I will not give your sister a fair fight."

Eislyn froze.

The assassin pulled a second dagger from the depths of his cloak. "Here."

Reyna took the steel, her fingers sliding appreciably across the golden hilt. "What are your terms? When will you surrender?"

"At death," he replied gravely.

A shudder went through her, but she hid it well. Reyna

had duelled before. As a Shieldmaiden, she had often been forced to stop a brawl between warriors. Many had wished to duel her as a way to settle the fight. But the win always came at first blood, never at death.

She curled her fingers tight around the hilt, steadying her nerves. If she died, Eislyn would be next. She wasn't just fighting to save her own life. For the first time in a very long while, Reyna stared face-first into danger.

Her blood hummed in her veins. She focused, sharpening her senses. Every speck of dust in the air seemed to swirl around her as she lowered herself into a crouch.

Then, before the assassin could react, she charged, slamming her shoulder into his gut. Surprised, he stumbled back. With a grunt, she slammed into his stomach again. He dropped his blade, grabbed her shoulders, and pushed her back.

Reyna leapt toward him, her skirts swishing around her feet, her arms outstretched. Her feet left the ground. He grabbed her arms, knelt and threw her back over his head where she landed hard on the stone ground and rolled, her gown bunching up all around her. Pain lanced through her body, but she ignored it for now. Panting, she scrambled to her feet, narrowing her eyes.

He was a better fighter than she'd suspected. But she was certain the same could be said in reverse.

The assassin flashed her a wicked grin, and then twisted toward her sister. He charged. Reyna let out a guttural roar. She raced after him, her blade held high. Her feet tripped on her skirts, and she tumbled to the floor.

He reached Eislyn first. Her sister stumbled back, eyes wide, her face white as snow. Time seemed to slow as he threw his dagger toward her, and then the tip of the blade sunk deep into her gut. Blood sprayed from the wound, drenching Eislyn's silver gown.

Reyna roared, fear tripping through her veins. She jumped to her feet and lunged toward the assassin, her arms outstretched. With a fury she'd never felt, she thrust her dagger toward his head. The blade crunched as it hit bone. His body went limp and tumbled to the floor.

It fell with a sickening thump.

"Eislyn!" Reyna fell to her knees beside her sister. She bent over Eislyn's body and placed trembling hands over the wound in her stomach. But she couldn't stop the blood, and she couldn't remove the blade for fear of making the wound even worse. There was nothing she could do but find help. Through the haze of fear, she lifted Eislyn into her arms and rushed through the dark corridor, shouting for help.

She didn't know how long she ran or where she went, but soon, she was surrounded by dozens of air fae guards. Gold flooded the darkness. Lorcan's familiar face flashed before her, but she could barely see him. The fear of losing Eislyn was almost too much for her to bear.

"Reyna?" Thane appeared before her. His eyes went wide as he caught sight of the blood on Reyna's hands and face, the wound in Eislyn's gut. Instantly, he turned toward his guards and shouted orders. Reyna barely heard him, too overcome by the panic clutching her heart. Eislyn was dying in her arms.

Reyna had not been quick enough in her attack. She had failed Eislyn again, just as she had all those years ago.

Thane vanished, and an ageing male in alchemist robes appeared before Reyna. He murmured softly. "Please, princess. You must release her. We can save her, but you must give her to us."

Numbly, Reyna nodded and allowed the alchemist to collect Eislyn in his arms. Blood stained his robes immediately. The red burned through the gold.

Thane took Reyna's hands as she stared after her dying sister. "Tell me what happened."

Slowly, Reyna looked up and stared into Thane's concerned eyes, her heart roaring in her ears. "Your mother sent an assassin to murder me."

17

THANE

Thane stared at his betrothed. She stood before him, soaked in blood in the middle of the dreary Zephyr Tower corridor. Surely she had not just accused the High Queen of the Air Court of sending an assassin to murder her. Imogen was not the type of fae to take these kinds of accusations lightly. She could be vicious when threatened. Already, she did not approve of Reyna. This would merely make it worse.

Reyna Darragh had led such a sheltered life. She did not know the kind of queen she now served.

"You are not thinking straight. Your ordeal has been overwhelming, I know. I will pretend that I did not hear you say such a thing," Thane replied, clenching his hands. He strode from one wall of the corridor to the next, ignoring the line of leather-clad guards ready and waiting for further orders.

Reyna blinked, and her eyes cleared. "Love can make you blind to the truth."

He flinched. "Just tell me what has happened. And

unless you saw my mother herself, refrain from making accusations."

"Very well." Reyna lifted her chin and crossed her arms. Her hands were still soaked in blood, and her gown was covered in it, but she did not appear to even notice it. "We were on our way to speak with you about the Ruin and Eislyn's access to the libraries. We thought you might lend us an ear. Perhaps we were wrong in that assumption."

"I would have lent you an ear in regards to the Ruin." He shook his head. "However, I cannot hear you accuse my mother of attempted assassination."

Thane's feelings toward Reyna were growing impossibly complicated. She was not queenly in the least, and she often spoke out of turn. She had more than once insulted him. Still, he found himself growing fond of her. Perhaps not the type of fondness that a male ought to feel for his future bride, but he did not wish to see her harmed. And he would protect her as best he could. That included protecting her from his own mother.

No, Thane did not believe that his mother sent an assassin after Reyna, but the queen *would* retaliate if provoked.

Reyna pressed her lips together. "Regardless, we decided to speak with you about it. On our way, we found ourselves lost. That was when the assassin appeared."

Thane frowned. "And he was alone?"

"I saw no one else," Reyna said. "This castle is a strange maze, but it was almost as though he knew we would be there."

"Perhaps he had merely followed you from a distance," Thane said.

"He was not behind us," she said. "He was ahead."

It was curious, he had to admit, but Reyna herself had admitted to navigating the castle falsely. "You do not know

COURT OF RUINS

these towers. Some corridors connect in ways you would not have known. The attacker could have followed, and then used an alternate route to cut you off."

Reyna's frown deepened. "So, the assassin was someone who knows the castle well."

"Dammit, Reyna." With a growl, Thane strode toward her. "You cannot continue with this single-minded attack against my mother."

She scoffed. "You truly believe that *I* am the one attacking in this instance? While my sister is bleeding out in your alchemist's ward?" With a bitter chuckle, she shook her head. "I actually had begun to believe that you would help us."

She pushed past the row of guards, and then stormed down the corridor, her silver hair trailing wildly down her back. Thane stared after her, not knowing whether he should order his guards to bring her back or to let her go.

"Let her have some air, Thane. Just send a few guards after her to make certain she remains safe." Lorcan edged up to his side. "She may be of ice, but she is fiery. You will get burned if you go after her now."

Thane gave him a sharp look but waved at two of his guards to go. "You will forget what you have heard here this night."

Lorcan lifted a brow. "You're referring to the accusations. I would not speak of it to anyone, even if questioned sharply."

"You cannot lie," Thane pointed out. "Your refusal to speak of it would be answer enough, particularly for my mother."

"She would have to ask the right questions." Lorcan shrugged.

Thane sighed, staring down the dark corridor where his guards now followed Reyna. "You do not know her as I do. She and Reyna have had a public tiff, and she has made it clear that she does not approve of our betrothal. She will know that many will jump to the wrong conclusion, including Reyna herself."

"I will not speak of it, Thane," Lorcan replied. "You have my promise."

Promises were not given lightly in Tairngire. They could not be. And Lorcan had never given him anything but loyalty. With a heavy sigh, he nodded and clutched Lorcan's shoulder, squeezing it tight. "I appreciate your service to me, Lorcan. I will never forget it."

Lorcan gave him a tight smile.

"What should I do now?" Thane asked.

"Truth be told, I would not speak with anyone about this incident, save your mother." Lorcan shook his head. "The celebration feast is set to occur within the fortnight, to toast to the alliance. If anyone hears that there has been a threat against Reyna's life, I fear the response."

Thane gave a slow nod. "Anyone else who wishes to make a move against Reyna would feel emboldened. Anyone who wishes her well might be too afraid to provide their public support."

"Gaining the support of the courtiers is necessary if this alliance is to stand."

"It is settled then." Thane gave a nod. "I will go directly to my mother."

Lorcan held up a hand. "Wait. Before you do, I would suggest you make one visit first."

"What would that be?" he asked.

"Eislyn Darragh has been gravely wounded. I would visit the ward first. Make certain she does not die, Thane."

Thane understood Lorcan's words clearly enough. If Eislyn Darragh died, the war would begin anew. High King Cos of the Ice Court would bring the entire strength of his army against the Air Court once and for all. And the dream of peace would be brutally shattered.

※

He knocked on the door of Eislyn's healing room. He had spoken to the alchemists first, upon his arrival. They had already patched her up and had given her a soothing, pain-sapping ointment made from rowan berries, knit-bone, and willow bark after making her down a lukewarm mug of nettle tea. The wound had been deep, but it had not pierced any organs. Eislyn might be weak for a good while—the healing of the fae was not what it had once been—but she had survived.

The alchemists held several rooms in East Tower for healing the ill and injured. These rooms hadn't existed a hundred years ago, back before the Fall, when fae could still heal themselves. There were about a dozen in total, each with a window overlooking the bay. Eislyn's room held a lush, four-poster bed covered in golden, silky sheets, a fur rug that stretched across the timber floor, flickering candles, and pots of herbs that spilled across shelves.

Eislyn peered toward the door, sleepily. Head propped on soft, feather pillows, a heavy patchwork quilt in blues and oranges had been pulled up to her chin. Even in her state, she was a breathtaking sight, her silver hair cascading around her petite face. "Prince Thane. I did not anticipate your visit or I would have donned a much more impressive outfit. This is not my best gown."

She had made a joke. Thane let out a relieved sigh.

"You look very fetching." He smiled as he eased into the room. "Perhaps you should discuss this new style with the court. It could prove to be very popular."

Eislyn surprised him by letting out a light laugh. "And what shall we call it? It would need a name."

"Perhaps it should be your own namesake," he replied. "Every time someone walks through the corridors of the Air Court wearing a blanket as a gown, everyone will think of you."

Her cheeks flushed, and Thane suddenly checked himself. Perhaps he was being far too friendly with the girl. She was his betrothed's younger sister. He had merely come here to check on her health. If she mistook his attention for something it was not, it could cause even more disastrous complications in an already far too complicated situation.

He sat on the wooden chair beside her bed. "I came to ask if you're well, but I suppose that is a ridiculous question."

Fear flickered across her face. "The alchemists say my sister is fine, but I need to hear it from you. Did that bastard harm her?"

"He caused her no harm, but I fear she may cause harm to herself."

Eislyn pushed herself a little higher on her bed of pillows. "In what way?"

Thane paused, unsure if he should say. "She has made accusations."

"Oh, I see." Eislyn sighed. "I love my sister more than anything, but she is very hard work. She always has been. I suppose you haven't experienced the joyous pains of life with a sibling."

Thane winced, and Eislyn immediately gasped. Heat flooded her cheeks as she placed a trembling hand over her mouth.

"I am so sorry," she whispered. "I didn't mean that. Please. I forgot about what happened."

"It is all right," he said sadly. "I never had the chance to meet them."

Years ago, the shadow fae had murdered Thane's siblings in a quest to find a way to blend the air fae's magic with theirs. It had been long before Thane had been born, but he still felt the loss all the same.

"I really am sorry."

"Well, I think more than just siblings can cause those joyous pains," he replied, trying on a smile. "I imagine mothers and fathers can invoke a similar feeling."

Eislyn grinned. "You imagine it or you *know* it?"

"I know it," he admitted.

She continued to smile. There was something in the curve of her lips that drew Thane to sit a little closer. It was almost impossible to believe that she had been through such a terrible ordeal. There was something so alive about her. A ferocity hiding beneath her fear. She was not as weak as she thought she was.

Thane did not understand why he was being so frank with this female. He ought not be. His quarrels with his mother were his burden and his alone. The realm need not know that they didn't see eye-to-eye, particularly now that she had stolen his throne away from him. There were those out there he knew supported his claim. His uncle, Lord Bowen, for one. If he drew a line in the sand, they would follow. But it would end in civil war.

And they could not protect their kingdom from the Wood and Sea Courts if they were fighting amongst themselves.

"You look as though you just sentenced yourself to a hanging." Eislyn reached out and wrapped her fingers around his hand. Her touch was cool, even when her cheeks were flushed by the alchemist's herbs and tea. "Don't worry. I am not one to gossip."

"It is very difficult," he continued. "My situation. It feels as though this entire court is weakly tied together by unraveling string. There are knives all around us, ready to slice through. It would not take much. The knives are sharp, and the string is thin and ragged."

She gave a nod. "You're right to be concerned. I will not mince my words to try and suggest otherwise. We have all been warring for so long. It has weakened our kingdoms, every one."

"And here I thought you were the optimist," Thane said with a hollow laugh.

"I am an optimist. I think this can all be undone." She shrugged her shoulders against the pillows. "But I won't pretend as though we are strong when we are not. But just remember, if we are weak, then so are they. The Ice Court has been at war for a hundred years. The Air Court has been at war for a hundred years. And the Wood Court has also been at war for a hundred years."

"And the Sea Court?" he asked, leaning forward, still holding tight to her delicate hand. "You did not mention them."

She frowned. "I must admit I am concerned about the part they plan to play in the upcoming battles. They have done very little in the war these past years. One wonders what they are up to on their islands."

Thane shook his head. He'd had similar thoughts. His mother had assured him that they were not a problem. They were her family, and she had somehow managed to talk them out of invading the air fae's kingdom for the foreseeable future.

So, she was certain that the Air Court needed to focus their efforts on securing the Wood Court first. Then, it would be three kingdoms against one. The Sea Court would likely surrender soon after that.

"You seem well-versed in the war," Thane said. "I thought your interests lay elsewhere."

"My interest very much lay elsewhere," Eislyn said, sighing. Her brilliant eyes shone. "But between Father and Reyna, I could not avoid warcraft."

Thane shifted on the chair. Eislyn had proven exceedingly easy to speak with, even on topics he preferred to avoid with most everyone else. How very odd fate could be. "Speaking of your sister, do you believe she intends to press forward with her accusations or is she merely speaking in the heat of the moment?"

Eislyn laughed, a sound that was like music to Thane's ears. "I would answer your question with a question of my own. If your mother believed someone had orchestrated an assassination against her, how would she handle it?"

Thane sat back and let out a low whistle. "You would compare Reyna to my mother?"

"They are a lot alike, which most certainly irritates them both to no end." She looked at Thane, ice blue eyes glittering. "Stubborn and headstrong, untraditional in the way they approach things, and fiercely determined to get what they want. Yes, I would compare them."

"That has given me much to consider," Thane mused.

"Reyna can be reasoned with," Eislyn added. "She is not a wild horse you need to tame. In fact, it is best you do not try. Instead, I would offer her something in return. And, well, *me* in return. We need your assistance with the Ruin. When I am fully healed, I need you to give me access to the library."

Thane gave a nod. He should not have been surprised by Eislyn's request. She was as single-minded as her sister, after all.

"All right." He smiled. "As soon as you are healed, I will give you a tour of the library myself, and then I will ensure the guards know you are allowed access at any time. Day or night. During court hours or not."

Eislyn's smile was blinding in its brightness, and it filled Thane with a strange sense of hope.

"Thank you, my liege," she said.

"Please," he said. "No titles are needed. Just call me Thane."

"All right then. Thank you, Thane."

Standing, he bid Eislyn a good night and headed back to his chambers. In the back of his mind, he could not rid himself of the image of Eislyn's face. Happy and bright, thrilled that he had agreed to help with the Ruin. And she had given him hope in return.

If only his betrothed made him feel the same.

18

REYNA

Reyna stood in the shadow of the Dagda, watching the High Queen stride up the wide golden steps toward the Adhradh. Daily mass would not begin for another hour. She had been watching the queen for weeks and had noticed that she'd always been seated far before any of the other courtiers arrived. So, Reyna had decided to arrive early herself and see exactly how the High Queen spent her early mornings.

The bronze statue of the Dagda rose high, scraping the bottoms of the bulging grey clouds. He was at least five times larger than a Tir Na Nog fae. On his raised stone platform in front of the towering Adhradh, he stood tall, shoulders thrown back, his powerful fingers clutching a great gleaming staff. Bronze-cast wings flared behind him in an unseen wind.

The Adhradh, the holy building of the Dagda's worship, loomed even larger than the powerful god himself. It was a great stone building shaped like a battle axe's curved blade, with a yawning entrance so tall and so wide that the statue could have walked straight inside if it came alive. Even here, the Air Court had left its mark. On either side of the entrance, golden banners hung from the high arching roof, so long that the bottom edges touched the ground.

The High Queen continued up the numerous golden steps. Her deep blue hair had been pulled up into an elaborate bun, the twisting strands dotted with multicoloured jewels. The back of her teal gown cut low, and the long train trailed behind her as she moved.

"You know, I'm not certain the prince would approve of this," Lorcan said from beside her. The ever-present guard had caught her on her way out of her chambers and insisted on tagging along. At this point, she just considered him her shadow.

Today, the winds were brisk and the air cold. Far colder than it had been in the days past, even if they'd left Winter Solstice behind. Lorcan had donned a cape with bear fur on the shoulders, and it draped over the top of his standard leather armor. Reyna had noticed it the instant she had seen him. She'd made a joking insult, but inside, she thought it suited him quite well. He even looked slightly more handsome than usual. But she would keep that thought to herself.

So, she kept her gaze focused on the queen. "I think he would be pleased if his betrothed showed some interest in the teachings of his god."

"And that is what you are doing then, yes? Showing an interest in the Dagda?"

"You shouldn't ask me yes or no questions." She pressed her lips together. "You know I can't answer plainly."

He smiled. "No, you *can*, your highness. It would just be unwise."

She scowled. She always hated it when Lorcan used her title, and she was pretty certain he knew it annoyed her, too. There was always something mocking in his tone. That was why he did it.

At the top of the stairs, the High Queen disappeared through the looming entrance. It felt like it swallowed her whole. And then the doors swung shut behind her.

"We should go inside," she said.

"I don't think I can allow you to do that."

Her hands fisted. "What? Why ever not? Surely I am allowed into the Adhradh to worship our god whenever I please? In fact, I am certain his laws would forbid anyone from preventing my entry."

"You know very well that you are not entering to worship. You're spying on the High Queen, princess. Are you truly so stubborn that you cannot see how dangerous that is?"

She propped her fisted hands on her hips and turned on him. "Dangerous enough to get me stabbed by an assassin?"

"Reyna," he warned.

"What?" She threw up her hands. "It's been over a week, and not a single thing has been done to discover the culprit behind the attack. My sister could have died, you know. If we hadn't gotten her to the alchemists so quickly—"

She cut her words short as emotion churned within her. Tears threatened to spill from her eyes, but she refused to cry. Not here. Inside the enemy's castle. In front of a warrior who made her life a living hell.

She couldn't go anywhere without him skulking along behind her. She knew he was only doing his duty and what the prince had ordered him to do, but it felt like he enjoyed riling her up and stealing away her privacy. His little comments, tossed in whenever he thought she'd forgotten he was there.

But she was *always* aware of his presence.

His eyes softened. "I am sorry about your sister, but she is recovering well. The alchemists believe she will be fully healed in time for the celebration feast."

Her anger calmed, just slightly. "I know. And I'm glad. But that doesn't solve the very crux of the issue, Lorcan. Someone inside this castle sent an assassin after me. They could very well do it again. What if Eislyn is with me during the next attempt? What if, this time, she doesn't survive it?"

Lorcan shifted on his feet. He lifted an arm, almost as though he were going to take her hands in his, but then he lowered it just as quickly. Her heart beat a little faster. "They searched the body. Thane made some enquiries. He believes it was a low fae who somehow got past the guards at the interior castle gates."

"A low fae decided to sneak inside the castle to kill me, not prompted, not paid?" Reyna arched a brow. "Do you truly believe that?"

"I believe the prince cares for the safety of both you and your sister." Lorcan gently wrapped his hands around her arms and drew her away from the Dagda's statue. "Which is why I cannot allow you to spy on the queen."

She huffed but didn't pull away. He strode backward, his eyes on her face, and she moved in sync with him, letting him guide her. She swallowed hard as their gazes locked. He'd worn his hair down today, and it fell in soft curls around his sharp cheekbones. A light stubble peppered his strong jaw. She wanted to reach out and trace her fingers along it. Most male fae preferred to keep their faces clean-shaven. She wondered what it felt like.

"You know," she said, still walking forward while Lorcan strode backward, his hands locked on her arms, "I could pull away from you and make it inside the Adhradh before you could stop me."

He smirked. "If you truly believe that, then why don't you try it?"

Reyna grinned. She took one more step forward, and then twisted on her feet, yanking her arms to her sides as hard as she could. She ripped free of his grip and ran. The cold streamed past her, biting her face, her long gown whipping around her like a hurricane. She pounded her arms by her sides, throwing her feet forward as fast as she could.

Excitement tripped in her veins as she threw herself up the first set of steps. And then a strong pair of arms wrapped around her waist and pulled her to a stop. The scent of leather, smoke, and steel flooded her senses. Lorcan chuckled into her ear, his mouth so close that she could feel his hot breath on her skin.

Reyna twisted toward him, his arms still wrapped around her. Her hands splayed against his muscular chest. They had nowhere else to go. Heat flickered in his dark eyes. Her heart pulsed. The laughter died on her lips, and she could scarcely breathe.

Footsteps sounded in the distance. With a gasp, Reyna stepped back, and Lorcan dropped his arms. They both spun in unison to see Thane striding through the courtyard toward them. He wasn't looking their way, instead animatedly speaking with his uncle beside him. Several more courtiers trailed closely behind.

"Oh, look," she said in a strangled voice. "The others are arriving for mass. Perhaps I should go inside now."

"All right," Lorcan grunted.

With a deep breath, she pressed down the front of her now-rumpled gown, squared her shoulders, and turned away from Lorcan. She felt the heat of his gaze for the rest of the morning.

The days passed quickly. Eislyn continued to heal, and Reyna continued to make failed attempts at spying on the queen. The celebration feast was approaching fast, and Reyna had made no progress on finding out who had ordered her assassination. And she'd certainly made no progress on her plot to get the High Queen off the throne.

As she stood in her chambers watching yet another sunset across the Bay of Wind, she stroked Wingallock's feathers and considered her options. As long as she was being watched and as long as she had no weapon, there was little she could do.

She needed more freedom, but she knew she wouldn't get it. She needed to find someone who could go where she could not. Or someone who might know the truth. Someone who knew everything about everyone.

"What do you reckon, Wingallock?" she asked.

He twisted his head toward her and blinked. Wingallock had even attempted to spy himself, but all the queen's important conversations seemed to take place behind closed doors where owls could not go. Nor could he ask questions if he found someone who might have the answers they needed.

She sighed. On the horizon, the grey clouds parted, revealing brilliant hues of orange and gold. The colors shined on the glistening sea, painting a magnificent portrait of the moment just before twilight. For once, the winds were still, but Reyna still felt the bite of the air all the same.

She did not *truly* know who had been behind the attack —though her suspicions still laid firmly with the queen.

But she did know one thing with absolute certainty. The first attack had failed, and someone wanted Reyna dead.

That meant there would surely be another.

"Wingallock," she said softly. "I need you to go to Drunkard's Pit. See what you can discover about the Bloody Dagger."

19

LORCAN

Lorcan stood in the shadows, surveying the drunken fae. Despite the High Queen's hesitation, Thane had convinced her to go ahead with the feast to celebrate their new alliance with the Ice Court. In the past days, news of the attack on the princesses had spread throughout the court, regardless of Thane's hopes of keeping it contained. There were whispers circulating within the nobility, rumors that Imogen wanted the Darragh sisters killed.

This feast was meant to prove otherwise. Imogen might not approve of the betrothal, but she did not wish to lose the ice fae's support.

Lorcan had a hunch where the rumors had originated. Reyna was dead-set on proving the High Queen was involved. So far, Imogen was still unaware of Reyna's accusations, but he knew she would discover it eventually.

Rolling back his shoulders, Lorcan surveyed the feast. The Air Court had filled the Great Hall in a way it rarely did. Extra feasting tables had been packed into the white stone room, squatting between the thick pillars that supported the high ceiling. Thin strips of cloth dyed gold stretched across the center of each one, the ends draping over the sides and drifting to the floor. A head table had been erected just below the throne's stone dais to hold a dozen of the highest ranking nobles.

Chalices were full of wine and mugs were overflowing with ale as servants moved through the hall with endless jugs. Everyone was at least six or seven mugs into the night, save the High Queen. She was infamous throughout the realm for her sobriety, a display of her dedication to the Dagda. Dozens of dishes covered each table, from spit-roasted pig, peacock and spinach pie, and jellies dyed golden with saffron. Sweet pastries were mixed in with the savory dishes in luxurious chaos. Lorcan could only imagine how the buttery crust must taste. As a guard for the evening, he could not partake.

Movement at the head table caught his attention. Princess Reyna stood from her seat. Wearing a courtly gown in an ethereal shade of silver that matched her eyes, she was a sight to behold. The bodice's neckband, lined in sparkling ice glass jewels, dipped low between her breasts, before the delicate hoarfrost silk flared out behind her in a long and flowing train. Unlike the style of the Air Court's gowns, this one had no sleeves. Instead, there were two simple strips of fabric that covered her shoulders, embroidered with sapphire wings. Her abundant hair was loose around her shoulders, just as she always wore it, but the strands were somehow wavy this night. An Ice Court circlet perched on her head, and the flickering torchlight from nearby sconces reflected off the silver band.

Lorcan did his best not to stare.

She was now moving across the floor, her eyes locked on where Lorcan stood in the shadows, away from the bustle of activity.

COURT OF RUINS

Her eyes were ice blue and her hair long and silver, but the heart of her was fire. He could see it in the way she moved. Her little chin held high. The flush in her cheeks. The heaviness of her footfall as she stomped across the Great Hall to stand before him. She'd brought her bloody owl along with her, too. Wingallock perched on her shoulder, his wings tucked tightly to his sides, staring at Lorcan with piercing yellow eyes that saw right into his very soul.

"Evening, princess. Look what the dragon dragged in."

She narrowed her fierce little eyes. "Yes, it appears he aimed to chew you up but then he spit you out instead. You must be pretty revolting when a dragon refuses to eat you."

"Well, then. With that kind of attitude, you certainly aren't playing the part of a sweet, little betrothed thing, now are you?"

"And you're not playing the part of a guard," she said, lifting her chin ever so slightly higher. "You're always there. Watching. Listening. Spying."

He crossed his arms. "What do you want, princess?"

"There's something I need to speak with you about. In the castle gardens." Two pinpricks of red dotted her cheeks. "I'll go out first. Follow me after a moment."

Lorcan frowned but curiosity got the better of him. He nodded and watched her weave her way through the throng of revellers. Her hips sashayed beneath the silken material, and her hair trailed behind her, down the length of her backless gown. She was slim, but Lorcan could see the lines of muscles etched into her back. Not the sweet, little betrothed thing, indeed. She was so much more a warrior than a future High Queen.

Lorcan followed after her, but before he reached the door, Vreis stepped directly in front of him. He wore leather armor that matched Lorcan's own, his bastard sword strapped to his back. His mismatched eyes flickered with concern.

"What are you doing, Lorcan?"

"Standing guard over the princess, just as I have been tasked."

"Careful, Lorcan. You have become exceedingly friendly with the girl."

Lorcan frowned. "I'd hardly call us friendly. She spends half the time insulting me. Just now, she suggested that a hungry dragon would find me too distasteful to eat."

Vreis clasped Lorcan's shoulder and lowered his voice. "Just be careful, my old friend. The prince does not take kindly to those who try to play with his toys."

Lorcan frowned down at Vreis's hand. He knew his old friend only meant to help, but he didn't appreciate the suggestion. Surely Vreis knew him better than that. But...of course, he didn't. Vreis did not even know who Lorcan truly was.

"I wouldn't interfere with the alliance," Lorcan said.

But wouldn't he? Lorcan no longer knew. His mark had been strangely silent these past weeks while he'd been guarding Reyna. At times, it would throb or hum, but it rarely blinded him with pain. It was almost as though it finally approved of what he was doing. But protecting the alliance was surely at odds with his true liege's goals. The Air Court was stronger with the Ice Court by their side.

"Good. Just be certain you remember that." Vreis patted his shoulder and then drifted away. Lorcan pushed aside his fellow guard's words and strode toward the door that would lead him outside where Reyna was waiting for him in the castle gardens.

The misty, wind-battered night enveloped him as the clattering noise of the court dimmed. Both moons would be high in the sky at this hour, but they were hidden by thick, rolling clouds. Reyna stood waiting in the shadows of Mistral Tower, beside a thick shrub that had yellowed from the wintry sun, her arms wrapped around her body in an anxious hug. Wingallock still perched silently on her shoulder, watching him.

"Are you chilled?" Lorcan strode toward her.

"The wind is harsh, but I am fine." Her eyes flicked in the direction he'd come. "Did you tell anyone you were coming out here?"

He crossed his arms. "No."

"You answered a yes or no question plainly." She arched a brow. "Only those who can lie do that. Such as the shadow fae, or the wielder of Mochta's Axe."

How odd that she would mention Mochta's Axe. It had been lost somewhere inside of the fire fae lands, during what many believed was the end of the elemental powers of the fae. No one had seen or heard of it since. Lorcan believed that the axe had been destroyed, burnt to a crisp by its own wielder, who had used it to lie one too many times. But that was only lore.

"You're pretty feisty toward someone who is trying to help you," he merely said. "Wasn't there something you wanted to speak with me about? But if you would rather hurl insults, then I'll return to the feast."

"No, don't go," she said quickly, shivering as another gust of wind blasted her in the face. "I do need to ask you something. You...know more about this castle than you let on, yes?"

"I'm not certain what has given you that impression."

"You cannot expect me to believe you are lurking around for no reason."

"Lurking?" He smirked. "I would hardly call standing guard lurking."

"Don't act as though I haven't seen you," she argued.

"You're always watching. Even if you aren't a spy, I know you're listening to everything that goes on inside this castle. Find it intriguing, do you? The politically messy lives of the royals."

He lifted his eyebrows. "Don't you?"

"I…" She trailed off, and then huffed. "Do you know who sent the assassin after me?"

Lorcan stared at Reyna for a long moment before replying. "No. I wish that I did."

"All right. Then, I need to know if there's a way to get out of this castle without being seen."

"You want to flee the castle?" He frowned. "Careful. If the wrong fae got wind of this, the Air Court could get the very wrong idea, especially after your accusations against the queen."

Her shoulders slumped. "This was a mistake. I never should have come to you about this. I thought you might understand, but that was a ridiculous notion. Please, forget I said anything."

Reyna turned to go, and Lorcan found his hand closing around her arm. Alarm flickering across her face, she stared up at him. The silver of her eyes was so very light, they almost melted into the darkness of the night.

"Tell me what you need," he said in a low growl.

She stepped closer to him and dropped her voice to a whisper. The harsh wind blew her silver hair over her shoulders, and the scent of mulled wine and silk drifted toward him. "I just need a little time out in the city one night."

"Why?" he asked quietly.

"There's someone I need to speak with. Someone who might know who sent that assassin after me."

Lorcan frowned. "Reyna, you know how I feel about you spying on the—"

"This isn't spying on the High Queen." Her hands fisted. "This is getting answers. This is finding the truth regardless of who was behind it. Someone tried to have me killed, Lorcan. And my sister almost died because of it. They will try again. I know it in my gut. I *must* find out who it was and stop them from trying to murder me again."

"I am your guard," he said fiercely. "I will protect you."

"You will?" She cocked her head. "And where were you that night? Why weren't you protecting me then?"

"I'd been with you all day. I was told to take the evening off..."

No one had thought much of the princesses' solo trek to find Thane. But Lorcan saw now...she had made a very good point. He hadn't been standing guard, and no one else had either. That could not be a coincidence. Which meant...Reyna was not wrong. Someone inside the castle was involved in the attack, someone who could influence the guard rotation. Lorcan thought back. It had been Vreis who had told him to get some rest.

Vreis. Lorcan winced. Surely one of his oldest friends could not be involved with this. There would be another explanation, one that made sense.

"You see, don't you?" she asked softly, peering up at him with those ethereal eyes of silver. "The attacker wasn't merely some random low fae who sneaked his way inside."

Lorcan's mark flared to life. Pain whorled through his shoulder, threatening to bring him to his knees.

He ground his teeth, and then let go of her arm. "I cannot help you."

Lorcan was troubled when he returned to the feast. Nothing made sense to him anymore. How could the High Queen try to murder her own son's betrothed? And Vreis? Why would he be loyal to such a terrible cause? Vreis was Thane's man. He always had been. The two of them had served the prince for years.

And yet...Lorcan wasn't truly Thane's man either. Were the both of them nothing more than a bouquet of pretty lies tied together with string?

"Lorcan," Thane called out when he rejoined the revellers. The prince clapped him on the back, his hand heavy and strong. "Where have you been? I thought I'd find you in your usual corner."

"I needed some fresh air. This feast is thick with sweat and ale."

"Aye," Thane said with a laugh, wine on his breath. "Just how a party should be. Join me at the head table. Mother is telling some tall tales about the selkies and nathair in the seas around the Sea Court's many islands."

Lorcan wanted to do nothing of the sort. Imogen had welcomed far too many to her table this evening. Her lover, Aengus, was even there, seated in the former king's position by her side. And Sloane was nowhere to be seen.

But his interest had been irrationally piqued. Could Reyna be right? Could the High Queen have had something to do with the attack? It seemed treasonous to even think it. Imogen might be a great many thing that Lorcan did not like, but she was not this. Lorcan could remember the day he'd joined this court. She had been as welcoming as Thane.

"I will join you for one story," Lorcan said with a nod. "But then I must resume my post."

When Lorcan reached the head table, he was seated two

down from Reyna. As he pulled out his seat and settled amongst the nobles, he could feel her silver eyes watching his every move. His own eyes were drawn to her, even though he knew he shouldn't look her way. He could not help himself. She was unlike any female he'd ever met inside the Air Court. He could remember the way she'd taken charge on the Rowan Road, when they'd fled from the Ruin. Her shoulders thrown back. Her eyes sparking with fire. Her confidence as she leaned against her horse's neck, whispering words at her mare.

Faster. Faster. Faster.

He blinked, drawing his gaze away. Reyna Darragh was as much a Shieldmaiden as any trained warrior. There was nothing of a princess hidden in those silver eyes. She had questioned his motives, but what were hers? Why had she agreed to leave all that behind for *this* kind of life? Surely, she would state the alliance as her reason, but then why would she risk that very thing by accusing the High Queen?

The sound of hearty laughter drew his thoughts away from the princess. Imogen and her lover sat with their heads bowed, their lips curled up in identical smiles. He frowned at where her lover sat. In the former king's seat.

"Thane," Lorcan said, turning toward the prince who was taking a hearty bite of steaming peacock pie. "Where is your father?"

"Oh." The light in Thane's eyes dimmed. "As you can see, he did not come tonight. I do not know where he is."

Lorcan frowned. "A bit odd, is it not?"

"Not in the least," Thane grumbled. He stuck into his pie again, shovelling in another mouthful. "While my mother does have her objections against Reyna in particular, my father did not approve of this alliance with the Ice

Court at all. To him, this feast isn't a celebration. It's a death sentence for our realm."

"Don't be too hard on him, son," Lord Bowen said from Thane's other side, his golden eyes far more tired than they usually were. He held a chunk of soft bread in his hands, slathered in thick butter. "He has his opinions on what is best for this realm, as do you."

"And yet he couldn't put aside our differences enough to join this feast." Thane shook his head. "We've disagreed in the past but never like this. He's always supported me. First, he stepped down from his throne years before planned, and then he gave the rule to my mother instead of me. He isn't acting himself." He shook his head. "Apologies, Lorcan. I brought you to this table to hear my mother's tales, not listen to my woes."

"Lord Bowen," Lorcan said, waving aside a servant who swung by with a jug of mead. "Do you know where the prince's father is?"

"No one knows where he is. My brother's face has not been seen since the day he abdicated his throne. Some suspect he may be staying at my castle down south, though I have not received word myself."

Lorcan frowned. "Does that not strike you as odd?"

"It is very odd," Lord Bowen said with a sad smile, draping his hand limply across his knee. "But it is just as odd that he would abdicate. Whatever the High Queen told him, it must have been horrendous enough for the blackmail to be successful."

"Blackmail?" Thane glanced at his uncle with a frown.

"Aye," Lord Bowen replied. "Sloane Selkirk would not relinquish power easily." And then he smiled. "But, I believe that is enough heavy chat for this evening. This is to be a celebration. Should we get the minstrels to regale us with a song?"

Sighing, Thane nodded, and Lord Bowen waved over a minstrel to request a song. They returned to their feast, both lifting their chalices in a toast. But Lorcan continued to stew in his thoughts. Lord Bowen's words had left him uneasy. The former king had not been seen in weeks, and he may have been blackmailed off his throne. By the High Queen.

He did not know how all the pieces fit together. Had the High Queen had him murdered? Or had Aengus, her lover? And then, had they set their sights on Reyna Darragh? It made little sense, but it did not matter. It was clear that something bigger was at play and that lives were at risk, including Reyna's. If he did nothing, and she ended up dead...

Suddenly, Lorcan stood from the table.

"Excuse me, your grace," Lorcan said to Thane. "I really ought to return to my post."

On his way to the back corner where he would stand guard for the rest of the feast, Lorcan passed Reyna's chair. He leaned down to whisper in her ear, and he swore he noted a shiver go through her body in response. "I will help you. Be ready to leave your chambers tomorrow evening. At high moon."

20

TARRAH

"King Bolg wishes to see you."

Tarrah thought those were the most wonderful words she had ever heard. She pushed up from her seat beside the open window, her bare feet brushing the warm stone floor. Her long orange dress flowed around her, and her raven hair flared at her shoulders, blown from the southern wind.

She clasped her hands together and smiled up at the warrior. He had been paying her visits almost daily now, and she could tell he wished to take her to bed. "Oh, Teutas. That is wonderful news. Tell the king I will be with him at once."

Shifting on his feet, the scales of his armor rippled. He held his helmet beneath his arm and his sword on his back. Teutas was always ready for war, even if it had been decades since he had seen battle. A low hum settled in her chest as she gazed at him. It was Unseelie, she knew, telling her this male with his jet black hair and his eyes of steel was her future mate. His seed would become the king that would finally stomp down the Fomorians beyond the impassable sea, beneath her god's weighty boot. But not now. Not yet. The battles would come first.

Tir Na Nog must be conquered before she turned her gaze west.

"I am to escort you, Tarrah. Without delay."

"Oh," Tarrah said, taken aback. She had been certain the warrior was bringing her good news. Why else should the king wish to see her? Her stomach twisted. Tarrah knew her visions rang true. They had been proven right, time and time again. Had the king tired of waiting? It had been weeks since Tarrah's arrival at Olc Fortress, and she had been eager to press forward with battle.

The king, on the other hand, had not. He wanted proof.

"Do not worry," he said with a slight smile. "He was not in a foul mood when he sent me to fetch you."

With a steadying breath, she nodded and eased her feet into the soft ebony slippers that had been given to her by one of the castle's many servants. The Shadow Court had provided for her in every way, even if they did doubt her true intentions. She had been given beautiful new gowns and a variety of slippers to keep her feet off of the baking ground. She still preferred to go barefoot most of the time. The warm stones kept her grounded.

Teutas led her into a corridor lined with flickering torches. Even if they were not of the Fire Court, the shadow fae seemed fond of flames. She had noticed the element almost everywhere she went inside the castle. She had wanted to ask on more than one occasion if so much fire was wise—the fire fae had been destroyed by their own magic, after all—but she had kept her thoughts to herself.

When they reached the empty, quiet throne room, King Bolg was waiting for her. He lounged on his black throne, one diminished leg crossed over the other. He tapped his ringed fingers against the basic chair, twirling a small

COURT OF RUINS

dagger in his hands. As always, his shifting eyes darted around the room, never landing on anything or anyone for longer than a mere second.

Several of his closest advisors stood clustered around him. She had learned their names over the past weeks, gathering information as best she could. Heremon, the square-faced male in dark brown robes to the king's right, looked after the crown's airgead, ensuring the king had enough to finance his castle and keep the nearby lords in check.

On the king's left stood Segonax, the commander of the shadow fae army. He had black hair, large grey eyes, and a flat nose, and he wore grey scale armor over a thick muscular chest. According to the whispered conversation of servants, Segonax was a powerful, steadying presence amidst a slightly chaotic court.

The third member of King Bolg's council stood off to the side, in the shadows of the looming walls. Nollaig, a one-handed female, who no one knew much about. Beneath her hood, her hair was as dark as the night, as were her eyes, and her armor had been painted black to match. The only shadow fae Tarrah had ever met with an animal familiar, Nollaig kept a crow named Holas permanently attached to her left shoulder.

As the moments stretched on in silence, dread crept through Tarrah's veins. She waited quietly until the king finally set down his dagger.

He turned his attention to her. "Tarrah. It seems the time has come for you to be judged."

She shifted on her feet. "If you are concerned that we have not yet had word, then I would ask you for your patience. It is coming, my liege. I just do not know when."

The king did not answer. Instead, he flicked his fingers at Nollaig. She strode from the shadows, her face obscured by a black hood, a letter in her hands. Her voice was grating when she spoke. "We have received word, my liege. It would seem that your new toy was correct. The Air Court has made an alliance with the ice fae. Prince Thane will marry one of the Darragh sisters."

Relief swept through Tarrah. She had known it. Victory lifted her chin, but she held back the fierce smile that begged to bloom on her lips. "A dangerous development."

"Aye," King Bolg said, snatching the parchment. He read the words, and then crumpled the letter in his tiny hand. "They are far stronger together than apart. If magic still ruled these lands, they would be unstoppable. Their elemental powers combined are magnificent indeed."

Tarrah had not even considered that part. When Tir Na Nog fae still wielded their elemental magic, Sea, Air, and Ice could create a storm of magnificent proportions. But that had been before the Fall, far before the shadow fae had been ripped apart.

And they would never again become whole unless the Air Court was destroyed.

"It is good they do not wield those powers then," Tarrah replied. "They may be stronger together, but they are not unstoppable."

"Indeed," King Bolg mused. "Nor should we allow them to achieve even greater power. If this single vision of yours has become fulfilled, I shudder to imagine how many more will follow suit."

"Surely, this is nothing more than a coincidence," Segonax argued. "Why would our god choose to speak to this low fae from the deserts?"

Tarrah pressed her lips together. "I have not once had an untrue vision, my liege. If I have seen it, then it is coming."

The king leaned forward. "I know what you wish of me.

You believe we ought to make haste toward the border and tear the Air Court from their lands."

"*Our* lands." Her hands clenched into fists as her voice echoed through the empty throne room. "The Air Court took Findius from us and blocked us off from the rest of Tir Na Nog. I mean for us to take it back. And then you can have the coronation you so richly deserve."

The king before her would never become the true High King of the Shadow Court until he reached the Findius Stronghold. The very castle that had been stolen from them. Inside those gleaming black stone walls sat the true Seat of Power of the shadow fae, the seat that the Unseelie god himself had blessed. Any king who sat on that throne became stronger, wiser, and more powerful than any other fae alive.

If they wanted their court to return to full strength, they needed to get that throne back.

King Bolg rubbed a hand against his stubbled chin. "Very well. I will agree to move forward. But we will start small, with some of the border towns. The stronghold will prove difficult to take. We should secure every fort and camp between us and them first."

His council murmured amongst themselves.

"My liege, are you certain you wish to do this?" Segonax asked with a frown. "I do not believe our army is large enough to retake our castle from the Air Court. If I did, I would have made this suggestion myself. And then, even if we do manage to retake the stronghold, there is the Wood Court to consider. The air fae built a wall to prevent them from attacking, but I fear it will not hold. The Wood Court has never tried to enter Findius. They wanted us to remain exiled, even if their enemy court was the one keeping us in line."

"Yes, my liege," Heremon added in a nasally voice, his

hands tucked into the pockets of his dark robe. "If we attack and lose, I fear we will not have enough airgead to make it through the year."

"I know how to take care of the Wood Court situation, and I have made my decision," the king growled. "However, Tarrah must agree to one thing."

Tarrah frowned, but she gave a nod for the king to go ahead. This, she had not foreseen.

"To prove that you are truly dedicated to this cause and not merely a puppet master pulling strings, you will join us on the battlefield. You stated that you have trained in combat, yes?"

Her stomach twisted. Tarrah was not a fighter. She hated the scent of blood. "I know archery, my liege, but that is all."

The king gave a nod. "Then, it is done. We will begin our preparations. Our war with the Air Court has begun."

21

REYNA

Reyna opened the door at midnight. Lorcan stood in the corridor, leaning lazily against the wall, until he caught sight of her garments. He jerked, surprise flickering in his dark eyes. She smiled. That was the reaction she'd hoped to see.

For her adventure into the city, Reyna had pulled one of her old tricks out of the bag. A collection of garments she'd gathered from her time spent as a Shieldmaiden, randomly cobbled together. Her bodice was ragged from wear around the sleeves, and her simple linen trousers had a hole in one knee. Both were dirt tone in color, ideal for blending in with the surroundings. To hide her silver hair, she'd found an old brown neckerchief and tied it around the top of her head like a makeshift hood. She'd topped things off with a pair of well-worn leather boots that were snug around her feet.

"You, ah..."

She smiled. "Something the matter?"

"I was under the impression that I was meeting Princess Reyna here this night."

"Princess Reyna is busy," she said. "But Shieldmaiden Reyna is ready for her trip into the city."

"Something tells me that Shieldmaiden Reyna causes far more trouble than she's worth."

She arched a brow. "Well, if you're not brave enough to go through with the plan..."

Lorcan smiled wickedly. "Oh, that's not it at all. I was merely thinking how fun it would be for the High Queen and her courtiers to see you now. You would be the talk of Dalais Castle."

"You don't think I should save it for my wedding day?"

"Well, one thing is certain, your new husband would be eager to get those rags off of you, if only so he could burn them."

Reyna's face flushed, and Lorcan fell strangely quiet, almost as though he had only just realized the meaning of his words. Clearing his throat, he glanced down the corridor and then motioned for Reyna to join him. She shut the door quietly behind her and fell into step by his side. They strode quickly in the direction of Zephyr Tower. As they hurried along, Reyna risked a glance at Lorcan. He was tall and commanding, the shadows of the corridor hugging his muscular body like a cloak.

Her heartbeat quickened.

"I can only get you a couple of hours in the city," he murmured, keeping his gaze focused on the stone floor ahead. "Whoever you plan to see, you need to do it quickly."

"A couple of hours should be sufficient."

The silence of midnight rose up around them as they roamed the castle. Lorcan took her through one corridor after another, down curving stairwells, and back up again. After awhile, Reyna had absolutely no idea where in the castle they were. She had put all of her trust in Lorcan. A frightening thought. He could very easily be taking her to the prince. Or, even worse, the High Queen herself.

"Here," he said quietly when they finally came to a stop at the base of a stairwell. A long tunnel disappeared into the darkness. "When Dalais Castle was first built, hidden tunnels were carved out beneath it. This one leads into the city proper. We'll come out through a false grate in the merchant district, which should be quiet and empty this time of night."

Reyna gave him a look. "We?"

"If you believe I would allow you to wander through the streets of Tairngire, alone and unarmed at high moon, then you are not as quick-witted as I thought." He grunted and shook his head.

"No one will speak to me if I have a castle guard stuck to my side," she said, pointing down at her well-worn trousers. "This entire disguise will be rendered pointless."

"I didn't tell you to wear a costume, princess." He shifted closer and flicked the edge of the neckerchief tied around her head. "And *nothing* could ever hide that wild silver hair of yours."

Her breath quickened. "At least stay a safe distance away from me. There's no reason to do this if no one will speak to me."

Lorcan frowned. He flicked his gaze up and down her body, clearly considering whether or not he should haul her back to her chambers. But finally, he relented. "I'll stay hidden. No one will see me."

"All right." She nodded and squared her shoulders. "Let's go."

Reyna pushed the grate aside and scrambled out into the street. A steady breeze whistled through the buildings as she gazed around. This was the merchant district, where various traders came daily to hock their wares. The stalls were silent and shut now. Empty. Eerily so.

Two full moons were high in the sky, casting ominous shadows on the dirt-packed ground. With a deep breath, Reyna moved down the quiet street. Her footsteps were loud in her ears, echoing off the brick and timber buildings that rose up on either side of her. She had longed for weeks to see Tairngire, but not like this. Not when the city felt full of the dead.

She came to a crossroads where she found two street urchins with gaunt, dirt-stained cheeks squatting in the shadow of a run-down tavern.

Kneeling before them, she said, "I need some information."

They both blinked at her with twin moons of gold, but only one spoke. "Won't say no airing without tingle tangle."

Reyna blinked. It had been a long time since she'd heard street slang. The urchins in Falias rarely tended to use it. With a smile, she dipped her hand into her pocket and withdrew a fistful of airgead. It was at least a hundred coins.

"This is enough tingle tangle to buy you both hot meals for a month." She held it up. "Information first, and then I'll give you the airgead."

The boy frowned. "Tingle tangle halfing first."

With a sigh, she dropped half of the coins before them. They clinked against the ground. Eagerly, the boys grabbed the gold and stuffed it into their ragged pockets.

"What airing you need?" the boy asked as he chomped down on one of the airgeads.

"Tell me how to get to The Bloody Dagger in Drunkard's Pit. The tavern."

The boy stopped chomping, and he exchanged a wary glance with his fellow urchin. "Whereing you from? No local. I can eye you."

"That doesn't matter." She held up the other half of the airgead. "Can you tell me how to get there?"

With a shrug, the boy explained. Drunkard's Pit was two districts over. It wouldn't be difficult to find. She'd know it as soon as she stepped foot inside, as the buildings would transform from timber to little more than rotting logs. The Bloody Dagger would also be easy to spot. It was the only building that didn't look run down. With a nod, she gave them the rest of their payment and continued forward.

Wingallock had spent several days seeking out information on the city's vigilante. In the end, he'd overheard several of the low fae speaking in hushed tones about the Bloody Dagger having taken out two more criminals on the streets. And they had discussed exactly where to find him. At a tavern he owned. It seemed the Tairngire fae had chosen his name based on where they could go to him for help.

Reyna turned left, all too aware of Lorcan's eyes on her back. She hadn't seen or heard him since they'd left the tunnels behind, but she could *feel* him with every step she took. He was far better at stealth than she had realized.

She came to a sudden stop. Drunkard's Pit stretched out before her, a mess of dirt, grime, and dilapidated buildings that shook in the harsh wind. Windows were broken or boarded up with warped slabs of timber. Rickety carts had been abandoned in the middle of the streets, full of muck. Everything was grey and dark and rotting, even the clothes lines that stretched between buildings. The cloth that hung from the unravelling string looked like rags, garments in far worse wear than her own disguise. The stench of rot was overwhelming. It made her heart hurt. No fae should have to live in a place like this.

In the distance the golden spires of Dalais Castle scraped the sky. The towers were gleaming and proud. It was a stark reminder to those fae down here in the streets, barely scraping enough airgead together to fund their next hot meal. The nobility did not care.

Only one building glowed with light. There was a sign out front, creaking in the wind. The Bloody Dagger. Blinking back her unshed tears, she strode toward it with fisted hands, her boots slurping in mud.

She pushed into the tavern. It was packed, full to the brim with laughter and cheer. Everything outside of this haven might be falling apart, but inside, there was hope. All of the well-made tables were full, and the stone floor looked swept clean. A rounded bar squatted in the center of the room where a short, curvy, golden-haired female poured ale. Her clothes were clean and well-tailored. She wore a thick pair of brown trousers, laced together with slivers of leather, along with an emerald tunic that hung off her shoulders. She whistled as she worked, her long hair kept out of her face by a thick braid. Several wooden barrels were stacked up behind her, along with shelves holding a multitude of mugs and tankards.

Squaring her shoulders, Reyna went straight to the bar. The female didn't even glance up. "Welcome. Take a seat. There's a free chair in the corner there, but you'll have to use an empty barrel as a table. Busy night. As always."

"I'm not here for ale," Reyna said quietly.

The tavern wench finally glanced up, peering at Reyna

with a pair of copper eyes lined in gold. Reyna had never seen eyes quite like them before. "You don't look like you're from around here."

Was it that obvious?

"I'm looking for someone. The owner of this tavern. Is he here?"

The female set down the tankard and wiped her hands on her trousers. "I own this tavern."

Reyna frowned. "I...is there someone else?"

"Oy, Mariel!" a boy shouted through the hum of the bustling tavern. Mariel, Reyna presumed, waved her hand dismissively and turned those unreal eyes back on Reyna.

"Why are you here, love? Just spit it out."

She took a glance around her, and then dropped her voice into a whisper. "I'm looking for someone who goes by the name of the Bloody Dagger. I heard he owns this tavern."

"He?" Mariel arched a brow, and then let out a low chuckle. "Should have known they'd eventually start attributing my work to a bloody male."

"You." Excitement tripped through Reyna's veins. "You're the one."

"The one and only." Mariel raised an arm and waved toward the back corner of the tavern before moving out from behind the bar. "Come with me. We shouldn't speak out here."

Mariel led Reyna through a burlap flap and into a storeroom lined with, barrels, spirits, and cured meats. The buzz of the tavern outside raged ever onward, the sounds of song and laughter seeping through the cracks. She motioned toward a chair and grabbed a bottle of spirits off the wall. "Need a little pick-me-up?"

"Like I said, I'm not here for ale," Reyna said.

Mariel frowned and set down the bottle. "You are nothing like anyone who has ever come to me before."

"That's because I'm not." Reyna reached up and untied the neckerchief around her head. Her silver hair sprang free, cascading around her shoulders.

Mariel let out a slight gasp, but to her credit, her expression never changed. Calm, steady, unbothered. This was no simple tavern owner. "Right. So, I've finally caught the attention of the crown. Took you lot long enough. Does that mean there are guards outside, waiting to arrest me?"

"I'm not here as part of the crown. I'm here because I need your help."

Mariel cocked her head. "Why would Princess Reyna, the betrothed of the future High King, possibly need my help?"

"Because someone inside that castle tried to have me killed. They sent an assassin after me. I managed to protect myself, this time, but..."

Silence stretched between them. Mariel merely stared at Reyna, her gold-rimmed eyes flickering with a strange flurry of emotions. Finally, she turned back to the bottle, poured the clear liquid into a small mug, and then handed it to Reyna.

"I think you need that drink after all, love."

Reyna didn't argue. Instead, she took the wooden mug and tipped the harsh liquid down her throat, wincing as it burned.

"You seem surprised. That's not the reaction I'd been hoping for," Reyna admitted after she'd handed the mug back to Mariel.

"Don't mistake me, princess," Mariel said, taking a shot of the spirits herself. "I am fully aware the Selkirks are an awful lot, particularly that male who we once had to call king. But I never imagined they would attempt to murder you. Us low fae down here in the slums? Certainly. But you are important to them."

"You really ought to be important to them, too," Reyna muttered. "But the truth is, I'm disappointed because I had hoped you would know more than this. Someone once told me that the Bloody Dagger knows everything about everyone."

"Ah," Mariel said, pouring another shot. "You hoped I'd know who was behind the plot."

Reyna took another drink, followed by Mariel.

"I am sorry to disappoint you, princess," Mariel said. "You came all the way here to Drunkard's Pit, and I known nothing about that plot. Information on the intrigues inside Dalais Castle is hard to come by these days."

"That's all right," Reyna said, slumping back into her chair. "I knew it was a long shot."

"Perhaps..." Mariel tapped a finger against the wooden shelf. "I can help you some other way."

Reyna perked up a little, straightening in the chair. "How?"

"I know how to get inside that castle without being seen," she said slowly. "I will do some digging around, see what I can find out. I just need something from you in return."

With hope in her heart, she stood. "Anything, so long as it's in my power."

Mariel smiled. "You seem decent, which is more than I can say for the rest of those nobles up there in the castle. When you marry Prince Thane and you take your place by his side, help these fae down here. Help those who are stuck in these slums. They need someone to look after them, and they have no one."

"They have you."

"That's not enough."

Heart thumping, Reyna gave a solemn nod. "I will do everything in my power to make this city a better place. For everyone. Not just those with power and wealth."

"Good." Mariel held out a hand. "Then, we have a deal."

"You should be careful." Lorcan fell into step beside her as she withdrew from Drunkard's Pit. She was leaving the filth behind her, but she would never forget it. She would help these fae when she took the throne for herself. They deserved far more than this.

Reyna rolled her eyes at the warrior. "So you have told me. Many times. You need not tell me again."

"What are you doing, princess?" he growled.

"I told you," she replied, cutting her eyes toward his leather-clad frame. "Trying to find answers. I want to know who ordered to have me killed."

"Speaking with informants is one thing. Seeking out low fae vigilantes is another matter entirely. What did you ask her? To become your spy?"

"She's just going to see what she can find."

"By spying on those inside the castle." Lorcan shook his head. "Reyna Darragh, Warrior Princess, Future High Queen, and Spymaster."

"Well, when you put it like that, why not?" She gave him a wicked smile. "It certainly has a nice ring to it."

"You're playing with fire, princess. You may be one of the strongest fae I've ever met. And you may be far more clever than most. But you *will* get burned if you continue down this path."

"And what are you going to do about it?" She rounded

on him in the middle of the empty street, hands on her hips. "Lock me inside my chambers? Inform on me?"

"I should," he let out a low growl, his eyes flickering. "I should throw you over my shoulder, carry you back to your chambers, lock the door, and toss the key into the Bay of Wind."

"Go on then." She sidled up to him and pressed a finger into the center of his leathered chest. "But you won't. Because you're all talk, Lorcan. Never action."

A dangerous smile curved his lips. He knelt, wrapped strong arms around her body, and then tossed her into the air. She let out a shriek, the sharp sound echoing through the silent night. With a grunt, he grasped her tightly to his shoulder and pinned her legs to his chest, almost as though he were wearing her as a shield.

The world began to bounce upside-down in her vision as he walked. She fisted her hands. "Let me go. I didn't actually mean for you to do this."

"Too late." His voice held a hint of a smile. "Never suggest I won't do something, princess, because you will always be proven wrong."

"Honestly. Put me down." She squirmed in his arms, but his grip was far too strong. She could only manage a slight tremble.

"I'll put you down when you're back inside your chambers."

"I'm never going to forgive you for this."

"Fine."

"I'm serious. I mean it, Lorcan. If you do this, I will hate you for the rest of my life."

"I don't know why you think I should care," he said coolly. "I am your guard. Not your friend."

Reyna fell silent, scowling, and hating the way she felt assaulted by his scent of leather and steel.

The warrior carried her all the way back to the castle and through the twisting corridors. When they reached her chambers, he kicked open the door and deposited her onto her bed.

She crossed her arms and glared up at him. "You can't lock me in here forever. The prince won't allow it."

"No, but I can lock you in here for the night." He smiled wickedly, and then backed out the door. "Good night, princess."

22

EISLYN

The door of Eislyn's private drawing room swung wide, and a dark-haired servant scurried inside wearing the prince's emblem: a black crown with the ends tipped in gold. She stood quickly from her seat beside the hearth, placing her open book on Selkirk history on the cushion while she bowed low. When she glanced up, the servant was gone. In her place stood Prince Thane.

She held in a gasp. Instead of his standard armor, Thane wore a relaxed, tawny linen shirt beneath a doublet spun from warm golden silk. His dark linen trousers were belted by fine leather, and metallic buttons in the shape of crowns lined the sides. A small section of his hair had been braided on one side. His ear sliced between the braid and the rest of his gleaming hair.

"You look well," he said cheerfully. "It is as though you were not injured at all."

Eislyn pressed down the front of her rumpled gown. She had been reading for hours, and the silver hoarfrost silk was now covered in fine wrinkles, like those around an ancient fae's eyes. "You are right. There seems to be no evidence at all that anything happened that night."

Thane's smile died. "Do not tell me that Reyna's accusations have gotten to you, too."

"Of course I don't blame the High Queen for a rogue fae's actions." Flustered, Eislyn pushed a single strand of hair behind her sharp-tipped ear. "But I don't understand why there have been no enquiries. Don't you wish to find whoever's behind this?"

"There have been enquiries," Thane replied. "Quiet ones."

She sighed. "All right then. Thank you for checking on me. I am feeling much better now."

Confusion rippled across Thane's face. "Do you wish for me to go?"

"I...was there something else? I assumed you came to check on my health."

A flush crept up his neck, and he cleared his throat. "I vowed to help you with the Ruin once you were feeling better. As you've recovered now...I thought I would give you a tour of the castle library."

"Oh." Eislyn's own cheeks went hot. "That would be quite helpful."

"Good." Thane beamed. "It is settled then. Are you ready to go now or should I come collect you at a later time?"

"Now is good," she said quickly, gathering her shawl from the chair to protect her arms from the blustery wind. "I see no reason at all to delay. Unless, of course...you are unable to attend to this right now? I know you're very busy."

"From now on, I am never too busy to help you, Eislyn."

Thane led Eislyn into the gleaming castle library. Dropping back her head, she gaped. The domed glass ceiling seemed so high that it should touch the sky. Shelves rose up two storeys above, every one packed tightly with leather-bound books. Curving wooden stairs led to a carpeted walkway to access the tomes on the higher level, lit by flickering candlelight.

A vine-covered tree sprouted through the timber floor, reaching up toward a high, impassable level stored with bound scrolls.

In the center of the floor sat three small empty tables. Thane motioned to the closest one.

Vreis left them in the library after giving it a full sweep. She imagined he was searching for assassins that lurked in the shadows. It gave her a chill. As much as she had pretended otherwise, the attack had scared her half to death. She could not get the images out of her mind. Knives flashing in the darkness. The blade slicing deep into her skin. She could even still smell the blood in the air.

It had reminded her far too much of her mother.

"Eislyn," Thane said quietly. She glanced up to find him staring at her with concern flickering in his aurelian eyes. "Are you certain you feel ready for this? We can return to your chambers if you would rather rest. The Ruin will not be solved today, whether or not we search these stacks."

"No, I am fine." She shook her head, ridding her mind of her thoughts. "It may not be solved today, but it will not be solved at all if I stay locked inside my bedchamber. Tell me, where should we begin the search?"

Thane seemed hesitant to continue, but he motioned for her to follow him through the towering stacks to the very back wall of the library. Here, the light was dimmer. Gold did not gleam from every corner. Cobwebs hung in the corner, a clear sign that it had been a very long time since anyone had been here.

"These are the books on dark magic," Thane said, his voice dropping to a deep whisper. "It is generally frowned upon to read these tomes, but these are terrible times. The Ruin is from dark magic. I know it in my bones. This is a very good place to begin your search."

Eislyn's stomach flipped. She could scarcely believe there were actual books on dark magic in the Air Court's library. Not only that, but they were in the *castle's* library. That meant a High King or Queen had collected them, or at least some member of the nobility. What would they have wanted with dark magic?

It was an Unseelie power, sent down for those who worshipped the dark god. It was linked to none of the elemental arts that the fae had once had. It was something else entirely. Something dangerous. Eislyn shivered just thinking about it. There had been a reason the Shadow Court had been exiled, and she was staring straight at it.

She glanced up at Thane, who had been watching her all this time. "Are you certain this is safe?"

"If it required practicing dark magic, then my answer would be no." Thane smiled. "We are merely going to read the books, Eislyn. To find a way to stop the dark magic. Not wield it ourselves."

Eislyn let out a breath. "Then, let's begin."

Together, they pulled four of the heaviest tomes from the shelves and settled into a table nearby. Without a word, Thane shrugged off his doublet and cracked open one of the books, pushing up the sleeves of his linen shirt. He began reading pages, not even making a fuss about the time this must be taking out of his other courtly duties. Eislyn could not help but stare.

He was nothing like his mother.

With a sigh, Eislyn turned to the books. Hours passed as they sat together in the library, their heads bent over the table. Eislyn read and read, pouring through the lore about the Unseelie god. Page after page. Each tome followed by another.

After a time, she found her attention turning back to the prince across from her. His eyebrows were furrowed in concentration. It wrinkled the hawthorn tree tattoo on his forehead, bending the branches toward each other. His skin seemed to glow from within, as if reflecting the true heart of him. When Eislyn had first met Prince Thane, she'd assumed the worst of him. Her court had fought him on the battlefield, after all. He had wielded his sword against them all. But what choice had he had? He'd only been trying to protect his realm. Perhaps...perhaps she had misjudged him.

"Thane," she said quietly, reddening immediately. "Forgive me. *Prince* Thane, may I ask you a question?"

He gave her a kind smile. "I told you that you do not need to use my title, Eislyn. And of course you may ask me a question."

"There are rumors about you. I'm sure you have heard them," she said, taking a deep breath. "They say that you spend every night revelling until dawn."

He surprised her by letting out a chuckle. "The rumors are true. Well, mostly. I do not revel *every* night."

"They are?" She tried to hide her shock, but she could not. From everything she'd seen of the prince since arriving in Tairngire, she had begun to think the tales were based on nothing at all.

He flipped a page of the book, casting his gaze away from her and onto the words. "Why should they be anything other than the truth? Fae cannot lie."

Flustered, she tried to return to her own book but

found she could not focus. "But the revels are full of wicked deeds. That does not fit with the Thane I know at all."

He flipped another page. "Have you ever been to a revel, Eislyn?"

"Me?" Her eyes widened. "Of course not."

"Then, you do not know what they're like." Frowning, he peered down at the tome before him. "This is quite unpleasant. A follower of the Unseelie can gain great powers by sacrificing the severed hands and feet of a *human*."

Eislyn gasped and leaned forward. "Does that have something to do with the Ruin?"

"No, nor does it say what great powers they can gain." He frowned and ripped the page out of the book, crumpling it into a ball.

Eislyn gasped. "You cannot destroy *a book*!"

"This is dangerous," Thane replied. "If a follower of Unseelie found this page, I shudder to think what they might do."

Eislyn shook her head. "But his followers have been exiled from Tir Na Nog. They'll never read that book."

"You speak as though you believe every one of them to be gone."

Eislyn jerked back. "What do you mean? They *are* all gone, aren't they?"

"I suspect some have stuck around." Thane went back to his book. "The Shadow Court was always a tricky beast. I would not be surprised if it has buried some antlers in the dirt, waiting for just the right moment to dig them up. Besides, not every follower of Unseelie is a shadow fae."

Eislyn could not imagine what would happen if there were still shadow fae around. They had murdered the entire Air Court fifty years past, all in a sacrificial plot to their god. Only the the High King and Queen had survived, along with Lord Bowen, the king's brother. Imogen and Sloane had three children at the time—Thane hadn't been born yet. In their rage, they had used their last vestiges of failing power to cut off the shadow fae from the rest of the continent.

"Well, I hope you are wrong," Eislyn replied, heart thumping. "We have far too much to worry about as it is. The Ruin, the assassination, the Wood Court, and the Sea Court." *And your mother*, Eislyn added quietly to herself. High Queen Imogen Selkirk would not go quietly into the night, nor would she step off that throne willingly.

Thane arched a brow and grinned. "I might know of a thing that helps one forget one's every woe."

"You mean the revels." She gave him a flat look. "I'm not convinced they are not the wicked orgies that rumors speak of."

"I'll show you." He reached out and placed a hand on her arm. Eislyn stiffened, scarcely daring to breathe. "Come with me tonight. It will be fun. I swear to you that you will not be harmed."

"I don't know, Thane," she whispered, keeping her arm right where it was, beneath his fingers.

"If at any point, you decide you wish to leave, I will whisk you out of there and deposit you safely inside your chambers."

Eislyn's neck felt hot, and she swallowed hard. She could not do this. It was a terrible idea. Beyond that, it was scandalous. The prince should be attending this party with Reyna. His betrothed, not her. Not to mention that she was more than just some random girl. She was his betrothed's sister. If anyone found out, the whispers would swirl through the castle faster than wildfire.

"Do you trust me?" Thane asked in a low voice. She met

his eyes, asking herself that very thing. Could she trust Thane? Would this turn out to be a viciously terrible idea?

"Okay." She let out a slight gasp at her own words, shocked she had agreed to it. "I will go. For a few moments. And then we will leave."

That night, Thane appeared alone at her door just after the Danu and Brigantu had reached the highest point in the night sky. It signalled midnight, a time that Eislyn had rarely seen. She was not entirely certain she should be seeing it now either.

He had donned black trousers, a black tunic, and a long black cloak that brushed across the floor as he shut the door quietly behind him. Eislyn's heart thumped as he gave her an appraising glance. It turned out that she had done well to anticipate tonight's dress code. She wore her own black trousers, borrowed from Reyna's trunk. Her mother's brooch fastened at the clasp of her cloak. It was one of three. Each of the sisters had been gifted one at her death.

"Very good," Thane murmured as he crossed the floor. He came to a stop before her, reached out, and touched the brooch. "You should remove that."

"Why?" She reached up and fingered the ice glass. It was the only thing of her mother's she had requested to keep.

"It is expensive," he explained. "And while your silver hair can be explained away, a brooch with the ice fae sigil cannot."

She could not help but take a step back. "Is it not safe for ice fae at your revels?"

"I asked you to trust me." He held out a hand, palm up. "Either do or do not."

With a sigh, she unlatched the brooch and dropped it

into his hand. He whisked over to her hawthorn jewellery box and placed it gently inside.

"Good. Now, we are ready to go." He held out his hand again. This time, she slid her hand into his. To her surprise, his fingers were warm to the touch. He led her out into the corridor, placing a finger to his lips.

Her heart beat hard. None of his guards were anywhere to be seen. They were truly going to sneak away without protection, only weeks after she and her sister had been targeted by an assassin.

"Do not fear," Thane whispered with a smile as he led her down the corridor. "You are not alone. I will protect you."

Eislyn's heart beat hard. She wasn't certain which she feared most. An assassin jumping out of the shadows or her sister's betrothed protecting her with his life and body. She nibbled on her bottom lip as they swiftly rushed down the curving stone stairwell. Shadows clung to their skin as they descended into the underground depths of the castle.

Eislyn had not told Reyna about her plans. Her sister would have locked her in her room, and Eislyn wouldn't have blamed her. This entire adventure was a wild, terrifying thing, and yet she found she could not stop her feet from moving.

They reached the bottom step and rushed through another dimly-lit corridor. Thane gripped her hand tight, pulling her to a dead end. A stone wall loomed before them. There was no door in sight.

Thane pressed a palm against the stone and took a deep breath. "I need you to swear that you will never reveal what you are about to see to anyone."

Eislyn's heart banged against her ribcage. She did not like to swear—no fae did—and especially not for something that she had not even yet seen. Still, her curiosity had gotten the better of her, and this was the most alive she had felt in years. "I swear it."

Thane shot her a crooked smile and pushed against the wall. Eislyn watched, hands clenching and unclenching. At first, nothing happened, at least not that she could see. And then the wall began to move. Tremors shook through the stone. She stumbled back, eyes wide as the very wall before them vanished into nothing. Another corridor now stretched out before them, and at the very end of it, she could see the churning sea.

"How?" she whispered, eyes wide. "That is magic, Thane. How?"

He merely shook his head. "I do not know. I suppose it is like the last grasps of magic that your own kingdom has held onto. You have your familiars, do you not? We have this miserable escape route. There are other tunnels beneath the castle, but this is the only one hidden by magic."

"Not all of us have our familiars," she reminded him. "The fae who were alive before the Fall managed to hold on to theirs. Any fae born since then…"

"Ah, I see," he said with a kind smile. "Reyna has one. I merely assumed that others did."

"Reyna is different in more ways than one." She shrugged. "She is not the only one with a familiar, but they are few."

"Well, then we can comfort each other in our lack of magic." He held out a hand and grinned. "Although what you will see tonight will surely be just as good."

And so Eislyn took Prince Thane's hand and followed him to the sea.

The corridor led to the sea where several small boats were waiting. Thane and Eislyn climbed inside one, rowing their way to the opposite shore. There, the city of Tairngire came alive. On the docks that wove through the city's northern canals, several musicians sat playing their fiddles and their harps and their flutes, stomping along to a lilting, upbeat song. Thane pulled Eislyn out of the boat, his entire body transformed during the short journey from shore to shore.

He no longer stooped as if the weight of an entire realm squatted heavily on his back. With his chin tipped up and his eyes sparkling, he almost looked happy. Eislyn couldn't help but smile right back. *Who is this male?*

"Welcome." He spread his arms and jogged a few steps back. "To the wonderful district of Toilichte, named after the very first High King of the Air Court."

"How are you able to come here?" she asked, hurrying after him. "Don't they know your face? Your tattoo is very...distinctive."

"Oh, they know me well, but they are also loyal to a fault. Every night, I come here. We laugh, we dance, we drink. And then they whisper a word of it to no one."

"Well, someone surely has been talking, for your revels are the gossip of the entire continent."

He winked. "And yet, no one knows the truth."

Thane led her off the rickety docks and onto a dirt path lined with hundreds of thatched roof buildings. There were more fae here in this small district of Tairngire than there was in all of Falias. The sheer scope of it almost took her breath away. Eislyn had never seen anything like it before. She had never left her kingdom. The closest she had ever gotten to seeing something like this was by reading books, over and over until she had memorized their words.

"Come," Thane said, beckoning her toward a grand timber building at the edge of the river. "We will be revelling in The Silver Sword tonight."

Eislyn's heart thumped, even in the midst of so much laughter, dancing, and music. Never leaving the safety of her castle also meant never stepping foot inside a tavern. She did not know quite what to expect.

When they pushed through the door, a blast of warmth hit Eislyn from the roaring central hearth. She glanced around, spotting at least twenty long, wooden tables packed to the brim with low fae of every shape, size, and shade. With unusually high ceilings and deep orange tables and chairs built from the Alder Tree, only found within Wood Court lands, the tavern felt like a whole other world. The buzz of conversation rose up all around them, and not a single soul glanced their way.

"This is your revel?" Amused, Eislyn arched her brow and turned toward Thane. She had expected pure chaos, bodies whorling, half-naked.

He grinned. "Don't worry. Things liven up as the ale gets passed around. Come. Let's have a few drinks while the bards have their say."

Eislyn straightened up. "There are bards?"

"There are *many* bards," he said, gesturing to the nearest table.

When they settled into the table, two overflowing tankards of ale landed before them. A woman in simple garb sauntered up to the table—human, Eislyn could tell by the smooth curving ears that were shown off by her hairstyle—a braided updo. Eislyn couldn't hide her shock. Few humans lived in Tir Na Nog. Even fewer freely in the capital cities. The courts tended to seek out humans and bind them into service at the castles. There was little they could do about it. Stronger, faster, and longer living, the fae could easily control the mortals, though the differences between the two races had been levelling out over the past few decades. Since the Fall, fae had slowly been losing their upper hand.

"Evening, Thane," the woman said, shocking Eislyn even further. She had not heard a single soul call Thane by anything other than his title since they'd arrived in Tairngire. "Who is this lovely thing you have with you tonight?"

"Evening, Phely. This is Eislyn Darragh." Thane grinned. "She's my guest. Treat her well. And don't tell the bastards from Faladrast who she is. They don't like ice fae."

Phely cocked her head. "Eislyn? Not Reyna then?"

"This is Reyna's sister."

Eislyn shifted uncomfortably on her chair. She had hoped no one would point out the oddity of the prince spending the evening with his betrothed's sister. She had tried to push her worry down, but the thought was there all the same. Their shared company could start vicious rumors, ones that they could not afford right now.

"Maybe this is a bad idea," Eislyn murmured as the woman strode away to deliver tankards to the next table. "This is going to spread like wildfire."

"No, it won't. These fae are my friends. Everything that happens inside these four walls never leaves."

"Then, how do you explain all the rumors?"

"None of those rumors started here."

Thane raised his wooden tankard and nodded toward Eislyn's. He had a twinkle in his eye and a smile on his face. She had never seen him quite so relaxed. Usually, there was a tension in his shoulders, a tightening in his jaw. She had never really thought much about it until then. A tense prince was not an oddity.

A cheerful, relaxed one, on the other hand...

The light in his eyes had her lifting the tankard and clinking it against his. She brought it to her lips and took a sip, making a face instantly. Eislyn had never been fond of ale or even wine, and her sisters had never encouraged her to drink. They had always worried for her and rightfully so. Eislyn's mind was often a mess.

But not this night.

Thane chuckled and slammed his tankard onto the table. "Too bitter?"

"I'm not sure." She gingerly took another sip. The taste was not entirely unpleasant. Bitter, yes, but also infused with something sweet, like berries. Almost instantly, there was a pleasant fuzziness in her mind. The world seemed to be a bit lighter than it had been moments before. The crushing fear of the Ruin almost dulled. "What's in this?"

"Rowan berries," Thane said, eyes smiling.

Eislyn sat up a little straighter. "You have rowan this far south?"

"We aren't that far south, Eislyn." He took another sip of his ale. "In fact, to most of Tir Na Nog, we're pretty far north. You saw the mountains in the distance on our way here. They're covered in snow and ice, just like your lands. There are rowan trees growing there."

Eislyn nodded. It was true. Even if they had crossed the boundary between their kingdoms, the snow still fell and ice covered the tallest of the peaks. The Ice Court still had trees, even though they were not wood fae. They also had lakes and ponds—though often frozen—despite not being of the Sea Court. For not the first time, she wondered exactly how the six kingdoms had come to be. The history was fuzzy and mostly based on lore. The six kingdoms had no origin...they'd just...always been there.

Eislyn tried another sip. This time, she did not make a face. "You know, I think I might like it."

"Good." Thane grinned broadly. "Although that might be a side effect of the magic."

She nodded. The rowan trees were one of the few things on the continent that had managed to hold on to the full strength of their magic. Over the years, many had tried to somehow harness that magic for their own use, but it had proven pointless. The most rowan could do was make someone feel fuzzy and relaxed.

Two things that Eislyn most definitely felt.

In the far corner of the tavern, a bard jumped onto a low square of a stage. He was tall and lean with ears that were so pointed they looked like twin daggers carving out of his head. Donned in the deep teal hues of the Sea Court, he wore a simple tunic and a matching pair of trousers. His shoes were also simple and leather. Dozens of gold rings dotted thin fingers that held a lap harp carved from whale bones. His eyes were a bright, gleaming teal, and his skin had the illusion that he shimmered as he moved.

Eislyn sucked in a sharp breath. A sea fae. The High Queen was the only other sea fae she'd ever met.

Without an introduction, the bard began to play.

> All the lands above and all the lands below
> Created from the god's own hand
> Blessed by the seas and cursed by the snow
> Where the ash spreads far across the lands
> Ghaisgeach comes riding in on wings of old
> The savior of the realm, as foretold
> A dance with the beasts
> And a song with the kings
> Only Ghaisgeach can bring the peace

The song was a sad one, a melancholy tune that dug deep into Eislyn's heart. When the bard pulled his fingers away from the harp and jumped off the stage, Eislyn noticed her cheeks were wet with tears.

Thane leaned over and whispered. "The next one should be happier. Most bards know better than to sing sad songs at a revel."

She brushed away her tears. "I liked it. What was he singing about? Who is Ghaisgeach?"

"Ancient sea fae lore," he said quietly. "Stories say that thousands of years ago, the sea fae tamed a sea monster called Uilebheist. Over time, they were able to communicate with the creature. He foretold of a time when the Thousand Islands would drown beneath the Mag Mell Sea, when the northern snows melted. The savior, the one who would put the islands and the seas and the ice back where they belonged would be called Ghaisgeach. Like I said, ancient lore."

Eislyn wanted to know more, but the next bard was already up on stage and playing a much more upbeat tune on a pair of bagpipes. She glanced at Thane, who was now smiling and tapping his foot along to the music. With a slight smile, she began to tap as well. As much as she wanted to dwell on the melancholy lore that spoke of danger and death, she thought that perhaps just this once she would allow herself to enjoy this night.

Death could wait until tomorrow.

23

REYNA

Steel whistled through the air. Footsteps thudded on stone. Shouts peppered the night. Frowning, Reyna crossed the room and yanked open the door, her heart pounding. Lorcan stood in the corridor, breathing heavily, sweat on his brow. He clutched his bastard sword in his hands, and he glared into the darkness of the castle halls.

"What's going on?" she demanded.

"Another assassin," he said gravely. "He tried to attack us with a battle axe but then ran. Hawk and Elweg went after him. I stayed behind to make sure he doesn't double back and try again."

Reyna gaped. "Another assassin? What did he look like? What was he wearing?"

"He was hooded and cloaked. I didn't see his face." Lorcan pointed into her drawing room. "Inside. Now."

For once, Reyna didn't argue with the warrior. She backed into her chambers and waited while he bolted the door. Quietly, he stood facing away from her, his sword still held out before him.

"We need to check on my sister. What if he goes after her next?"

"Your sister is fine," Lorcan said quietly. "She's with Prince Thane."

Reyna jolted, and then frowned. "Why in the name of the Dagda is Eislyn with Thane?"

"He's assisting her with her project." Lorcan turned slightly to gaze over his shoulder at her. Ferocity rippled off his body in waves. He looked like an angel of death. One that stole her breath away. "They're in one of the libraries together. Vreis and several others are keeping close guard on them both."

Reyna audibly sighed, relaxing just slightly. She'd expected another attempt to murder her. That wasn't what had scared her. It was knowing that her sister's life might be in danger once again.

Though she hardly trusted Thane, she knew he would not murder Eislyn inside his own castle. In fact, he'd seemed surprisingly concerned about her well-being after the attack. If anything, he would protect her from harm. An odd thought, considering he was Reyna's sworn enemy.

She supposed the enemy could be a friend for a time. But it would never last.

"You know you don't need to worry about her. Your sister is under the protection of the crown, just as you are," he said, turning back to the door. "There are guards stationed around you day and night, keeping a close watch."

"Yes, I have noticed that," she said dryly, eyeing Lorcan. "There is one particular guard I can't seem to get rid of."

"Trust me. I would rather have any other assignment. Your daily routine is becoming a bore."

"Go and do something else then," she snapped.

"Very well." Lorcan slid his sword into the scabbard on

his back. A *click* resounded in the silence. Without another glance in her direction, he began to move toward the door. "I'll be seeing you around, princess."

"It was certainly far easier to get rid of you than I thought."

"You told me to go and do something else." He twisted on his feet, smiling. "That's unexpectedly helpful of you, really. There's another task I need to attend to this evening. A quite important one."

"Is that so?" She glared up at him, propping her fisted hands on her hips. Her heart trembled in her chest. No doubt due to the excitement of the second attack and nothing else. "And what would that be?"

His smile widened. "I was planning on setting a little trap. It turns out you were right. Whoever wants you dead won't stop until he succeeds, so I thought I might lure another assassin out into the open. Then, they can be questioned sharply about whoever gave them the order. In fact, I *was* going to ask if you would like to join me, but if the princess insists I go alone..."

"No, wait," she said quickly, before he could disappear into the corridor. She shifted sideways to stand before him. "Tell me about this trap of yours."

Lorcan's eyes danced with amusement. He had her, and they both knew it. She wanted to smack the smugness off his face, but she couldn't risk losing her only chance at finding this would-be murderer.

With a bemused smile, he crossed his arms. "Do you still believe the Selkirks had a hand in the attempted assassinations?"

Reyna widened her eyes and glanced at the doors.

"There is no one there," he said quietly.

"I truly do believe someone inside this court ordered the attack. But the question I have is, *do you?*"

He was silent for a long moment before turning toward her with a frustrated sigh. "It is not my place to become embroiled in political schemings. In fact, it is the very opposite. I stand. I watch. I protect against outright attacks. I shouldn't involve myself in this."

"If that's how you feel, then why are you standing before me speaking of this?" Reyna asked.

He frowned. "I worry that you are right. And I worry that this will only end one way. With the death of you or Eislyn or even the prince. Or all three. Whoever wants you dead wants it for one reason. For power. And there are other odd things happening that I cannot explain...I will be truthful, Reyna. I worry for Thane's life. Other than the prince, the only fae I trust inside this castle is me. And, perhaps you, oddly enough."

Reyna's heart pounded hard, and she was forced to look away. She stared out the window at the windswept clouds, barely able to breathe. There had been so much passion in Lorcan's words. He deeply cared for the prince. For some reason, it touched her far more than she wanted to admit.

And it surprised her. In the Ice Court, it was not unheard of for kings and princes to form brotherly bonds with their guards, but she had not expected it here in these cruel lands.

Despite her hardness toward Thane, she could not stop a sliver of guilt from creeping in. Could she knowingly take Lorcan's help when his missive was to keep his prince alive? When she planned to kill Thane in the end?

She saw no other way around it. Thane had killed innocent ice fae on his way to Falias. He had murdered poor Zed. He had killed her kin during the war. Hundreds had died by his hands. At the moment, he was only bearable because an even worse tyrant sat on the throne. But when it came time for his reign, he would surely become the monster Reyna knew he was deep down.

Reyna steadied herself, standing tall. A few weeks spent inside of a foreign court, and she was already beginning to doubt herself. She needed to steel her nerves and remember exactly what she was fighting for. Her people. The low fae she had to protect. Their blood would be on her hands if she didn't stop the prince.

"You may be right in that. The High Queen might set her sights on the prince next." Not a lie. That *might* happen, though it was doubtful. Reyna could not imagine the High Queen killing her own son, regardless of how desperately she wanted to retain control of the throne. Imogen felt disdain for her son's choice in a wife, but that did not mean she was willing to spill her own blood.

Lorcan arched a brow. "You must think this family mad if you believe a mother would kill her son. Why marry into it?"

He had asked her this question before. Reyna could not help but wonder if he noticed her the same way she noticed him. Did he suspect she hid the truth?

"For my people," she said honestly. "As for what the High Queen is willing to do...I'll admit, her killing Thane seems unlikely. That doesn't mean it's impossible."

Lorcan frowned and turned his gaze toward the window once again. "If the High Queen had anything to do with this, we must find out before anyone else does. The repercussions could be..."

"Kingdom shattering?" Reyna suggested.

"The low fae would riot if word got out," Lorcan said. "Supporters of the High Queen fighting followers of the prince." His strong jaw rippled as he clenched his teeth. "Word would soon reach the Wood Court. They would no doubt feel emboldened to attack while the city was in chaos. This assassination plot could very well end in so much needless death."

Reyna looked up at him curiously. "So, do you wish to find the culprit or not?"

Lorcan suddenly reached up and clutched his shoulder, wincing slightly.

"We *must* find him. Or her," he said quietly. "But we must also make an agreement here in this room, bound together by our words. We cannot speak of this with anyone else. Not until we know the truth."

Reyna almost smiled, but she held it back. "Agreed."

"Good." He nodded. "Now, here is what I have planned."

24

EISLYN

An hour had passed. Perhaps two or three. Eislyn could not be certain. She and Thane had downed two more tankards each, and the rowan berries had most certainly gone to her head. Bards had come and gone on the stage, each one picking up the pace from the previous one until the entire tavern had broken out into one big ridiculous party.

A revel, she supposed some might say, though it was nothing like the revels of her imagination.

There was nothing dark about this night. Every fae and human in the building was happy, laughing, dancing. Even she and Thane had joined the crowd up at the front, twirling in circles, holding tight to each other's arms as they spun.

As one song ended and another began, Eislyn motioned for Thane to join her at the back. Breath heaving and sweat glistening on her skin, she dropped onto an orange Alder Tree chair and sighed. Eislyn had spent most of her life in a fog. There were years of her childhood that she could not even remember. Her sisters had spoken of it occasionally but never her father. There wasn't much she knew about that time. Only that she had not spoken for years.

Even after the world had restarted around her and she had found her voice again, she had still struggled to feel normal. There was always a haze surrounding her. A heavy force pressing down on her head.

This night, she felt none of that. She supposed it had something to do with the magic of those berries.

"That was a lovely song. Quite an eye-opening one at that. To imagine that you, Prince Thane, warrior and future High King, once hid under your mother's skirts as a small child." She couldn't help but laugh. Another effect of the rowan berries, no doubt.

"You seem to be enjoying yourself. Mostly at my expense."

She might have worried that he had taken offense, but the sparkle in his golden eyes said otherwise.

"I am." She fanned herself with the back of her hand. The air felt thick and hot, squeezing tight around lungs that were already struggling to breathe. "Although, as an ice fae, I am not accustomed to this kind of warmth."

Thane stood. "Some fresh air then. We have revelled for hours."

With a smile, she nodded and followed him out the tavern door. Instantly, cool wind blasted her face. She closed her eyes and pulled the air into her lungs, sighing with contentment as it soothed away the heat. Eislyn had never thought much about the chill of the north. It had always been a part of her. She had not expected to miss it, but it was almost as if she could feel the ice calling to her from far away.

Which was, of course, ridiculous.

"Come. Let's go down to the docks."

Thane led the way. They strode along a dock that jutted

out over a canal, filled with barges transporting goods to and from the capital.

Eislyn sighed and dropped back her head to look at the sky. The clouds had cleared this night, and the stars were out. They were not as bright here as they were back home, but she could recognize their formations just as easily. The Dagda was the brightest and most luminous constellation. Their father, their maker. The one who took their magic away.

On a night like this, she had almost forgotten it was gone.

"An airgead for your thoughts," Thane spoke up from his quiet stroll beside her.

"I'm thinking of home," she said wistfully.

"Do you miss it?"

She considered his question. "Yes and no. The Ice Court is all I've ever known, and there is nothing like the mountains there. The snow, the ice, the frozen world. I know you get snowfall here, but it isn't the same. Even though magic is gone, there is a power in the snow and ice. I don't know how to explain it, but it's there."

Thane nodded. "I often feel that way about the winds."

She glanced at him, surprised. "You do?"

"Not often." He pointed up at the towering castle in the distance, golden spires looming high. "But when I am out on the Observatory, and the evening winds whip around me, it feels unlike anything else in the world. It is why I don't believe the Dagda has truly forsaken us."

She stopped suddenly, turning to face him. "Reyna isn't convinced the Dagda is even real. Although..." She widened her eyes. "Perhaps I shouldn't have said that."

Thane smiled, his eyes kind. "Whatever is said and done at a revel stays at the revel, remember? I won't tell a single soul what we speak of this night."

"We're not technically at the revel anymore..." Still, she smiled back. As much as she had disliked Thane in the beginning, he was regrettably beginning to grow on her a bit. Nothing was as it seemed, not when it came to him. The cruelty wasn't there. The anger and rebelliousness wasn't either.

"The revel isn't over until we step foot back inside the castle." He began to walk down the dock again, their footsteps thudding against the wooden planks. A light wind whipped through Eislyn's silver hair, a welcoming embrace.

"May I ask you a question then?" Eislyn asked, tucking her hands into the pockets of her dark trousers.

"Anything."

"You fought in the war," she said quickly before she could lose her courage. "In the Battle for the Shard, the fight that cut down half of both our armies."

Thane was quiet for a long moment. She wondered if she'd asked too much. The walls between them had begun to fall away, but that did not mean they were gone. War was a different subject entirely.

"I did," he finally said, voice hard. "It was the worst day of my life."

Eislyn's heart thumped. "You were in the front lines, were you not?"

"I was right there in the thick of it, Eislyn." He sighed and ran his fingers through his long golden hair. "And I know why you are asking. Are those rumors true since the others are not? Did I kill hundreds of fae in the fury of battle? I cannot lie. I will not speak in riddles. The truth is I gladly fought against the ice fae. I tore them down, just as they tore down the folk of the air. Our two armies destroyed each other. I wish it weren't so, but it is."

Eislyn did not quite know what to say. She twisted her

hands together, gazing at the rippling water of the canal. "It was the magic."

"The magic?"

She nodded. "The Fall. That's what started all of this, isn't it? Without the magic, fae got scared. Like cornered animals. We did the only thing we knew to do and that was to fight. But instead of fighting against whatever took our magic away, we turned on each other. That will be what is the end of us. Not the lack of our power."

"You might be right." Thane smiled. "You really do know a lot about our war."

"And what do you think it is I am reading in those books of mine?" She gave him a sly look. "Do you imagine me tucked away, reading about warriors saving princesses from towers?"

He shook his head and laughed. "I certainly don't now."

Music drifted along the river as they passed another cluster of buildings. Eislyn glanced toward them, smiling as several fae spilled out of the open doors of another tavern. They were singing and dancing along to the music, bare feet tapping the dirt ground.

"This city is nothing like I imagined," she said, turning back to Thane. "And neither are you."

A strange expression flickered across Thane's face. "It is a wonderful city, isn't it?"

"From what I have seen." She nodded. "Although, surely there are sections that are not so...welcoming."

"You're right." He shoved his hands into his trouser pockets and tipped back his head as they continued to stroll down the dock. "We have slums just as any city does. There are dangerous districts that are not safe to go at night. My father largely ignored them as king, which only made the criminal underbelly much worse. I have heard rumors of murders in Drunkard's Pit, but I cannot be sure those rumors are true. There is no official record of them in any case."

Eislyn shivered. "No official record?"

"Do not worry, Eislyn. You are safe with me."

Eislyn glanced back at the city with new eyes. The docks here were lively and lit up in the thickness of the night, but there were pockets further inside where only shadows pulsed across the buildings. She had thought nothing of it. Sleeping fae, she had assumed. But perhaps there was far more to it than that.

The king had been a wicked male. It was good he had been removed from the throne. But Eislyn was not certain that the High Queen was much better.

"Is anyone looking into these murders?" she asked softly as they reached the end of the dock.

"If you are asking if my mother cares for the low fae, the answer is...at times, she does. But only when it suits her goals."

Eislyn frowned. "What in the name of the Dagda does she care about then?"

"Power."

It shouldn't surprise her. The High Queen had clearly manuevered herself onto the throne somehow, bypassing the standard succession that would have put Thane there himself. But why? She shook her head at herself. None of this mattered. The politicking, the thrones. All that mattered was the Ruin, and how to stop it.

Eislyn sucked in a deep breath of the cool, misty air. Warmer than the air back home but cool enough to give clarity to her thoughts. "And what do you care about, Thane?"

He towered over her, even with her height. None of the Darragh princesses would have ever been called short. With a distant look, he gazed over her shoulder, staring at the canal that rippled past the edges of the docks. She didn't know why, but she felt desperate to know his answer. The Thane she'd met back home, she would have been certain he was as terrible as his mother. But after the past weeks, particularly this night, Eislyn knew that power was the last thing Thane wanted. He'd answered this question for her before, but she had to ask him again now. What did Thane truly want? How did he want to make his mark on this war-torn world?

"I want to bring peace to this troubled kingdom," he finally said, wood creaking beneath his feet. "*Both* our kingdoms."

She smiled up at him, her heart expanding within her chest. This male was...

With a slight gasp, she yanked her gaze away from him and turned toward the canal. Her heart raced; her mind spun. What was she doing? This was wrong. The prince was not her friend, nor did he mean anything to her. He couldn't. Reyna, her sister, was his betrothed. They were to marry and unite the kingdoms.

"Is something wrong, Eislyn?" Thane asked, voice concerned.

But she could not look at him for fear she would blurt out the truth. "We should get back to the castle. It is getting late."

Eislyn wanted nothing more than to remain out in the city with Thane until dawn, to return to the revel and dance the night away. She had not felt this alive in...months, years. Perhaps ever. Thane had brought her back to life in a way that Eislyn had not thought possible.

Which was exactly why she could not remain out with him any longer.

"Have I said something wrong? I thought you were enjoying yourself."

"I was enjoying myself," she said quickly. "I just...I need some rest."

"Very well." He held out an arm and she took it, tucking her hand into the crook of his elbow. She shouldn't have done that either, but just once wouldn't harm anything. Without any further questions, he led her away from the docks and back through the hidden tunnels of Dalais Castle. Neither of them spoke. Eislyn feared she had said more than enough.

They reached the door of her chambers without being spotted. After she let go of his arm, he lingered for a moment longer, frowning down at his leather boots. "You would tell me if I have offended you, I hope."

"You have not offended me, Thane. In fact, you have done the very opposite."

He looked relieved. "Good. I feel the same."

Eislyn held her breath tight in her throat. Everything about Thane glowed. His eyes, his hair, the very soul of him. "Good night, Thane."

With a sad smile, he gave her a nod. "Good night, Eislyn."

Before he could convince her to turn back, she pushed into her chambers and shut the door behind her. Her heart still thumped hard. It had the entire way back from the canals. Thane had sparked something in her that she could not allow. Perhaps she had been wrong in coming to the Air Court.

As she pushed away from the door, she noticed a book sitting on her bed. Frowning, she moved toward it. That had not been there when she'd sneaked out with Thane. Had her lady's maid dropped it by for some reason?

She lifted the book from the bed and flipped open the weathered cover. A pen had scratched a title in a looping, twisting scrawl.

The Histories and Lore of the Sea Court.

Heart thumping, she dropped the book on the bed and strode over to the window. Had someone seen her out in the city? Was this some kind of warning to stay away from Thane? She had paid no heed to any books on the Sea Court before this night. It had been the last thing to interest her. Her focus had been on the lore of the ice, the snow, the blue-tipped mountains in the furthest corners of the north. And the mysterious flames that had destroyed the Fire Court's lands.

Tonight had been the first time she had heard even a speck of ancient lore connected to the sea fae.

And there was no doubt in Eislyn's mind that this was no coincidence at all.

Someone had seen her in the tavern with Thane, and they had put this book here to tell her that hidden eyes were watching her every move.

Or worse, had a new assassin tracked her to the tavern and then placed this here to scare her? If so, it certainly had worked. Terror tripped through her veins like acid.

Eislyn had not been certain she would sleep after discovering the twisted feelings of her heart, but now she knew that she would meet dawn with open eyes.

25

TARRAH

The king, it seemed, was as eager to retake the Findius Stronghold as Tarrah was. Not a week after receiving news of the Ice and Air alliance, Tarrah stood beside him on a field of ash, staring at the distant horizon where a flickering glow indicated life. Mist swirled around them. They had been travelling for days but only made forward progress at night, far off the road. They did not wish to alert the Air Court army that they were on their way.

Up ahead lay the first camp that they would encounter on their mission to retake their lands from the air fae. The camp had once been a small village called Bilivik with a population of around two hundred. Before the Fall, it had been popular with travellers and merchants heading toward the capital. The infamous House of Cleas lay in the center of the small cluster of buildings, a large, stone-walled theatre where everything seen inside was nothing more than an illusion, a specialty of the shadow fae from a time when magic had been alive.

Now, it was nothing more than a hollow pit. Air fae stood watch, an outpost meant to alert Findius of an impending shadow fae attack.

And this was King Bolg's first target.

"They likely have not spotted us yet," Segonax, the commander, said. "They will have grown complacent with time, and they do not anticipate an attack. However, they will be using the roof of the House of Cleas as a tower. It is quite tall for a village building, providing an excellent view of the surrounding area. As we draw closer, we will no longer remain hidden in the mists."

"So, we charge then," King Bolg said in a grave voice. "Provide them as little time as possible to scramble for their weapons."

Tarrah glanced to her side. Teutas stood directly on her left, his longsword heavy in his hands. Warriors stretched far beyond him. The entire shadow fae army had gathered for this fight. They were numbered in the thousands. Only a few hundred would be inside the camp ahead. It would be a terrible slaughter.

But this was what Unseelie wanted from them. They could not show mercy toward the air fae, not when they had been shown no mercy in return. The Air Court had stolen their castle from them. They had exiled the shadow fae from the continent, cutting them off from the rest of their world.

They deserved to die.

"On Segonax's order," the king said, his voice drifting to the warriors in the distance.

Tarrah shifted in her black leather armor and withdrew her bow from her back with sweat-slick hands. Her heart pounded; her ears rang with dread. Even though she knew the truth—that they would be victorious this night—fear tumbled through her veins. Blood would paint her hands, and death would cling to her body like shadows.

Segonax lifted his sword. "Charge!"

26

REYNA

Exactly four moons passed before Lorcan knocked on Reyna's door for their adventure. She yanked it open, excitement tripping through her veins. Life at court had returned to its exceedingly dull routine, and she couldn't wait to be back to doing something other than wandering around corridors in a heavy gown.

Lorcan's eyes widened when he got a look at her. She had brought out the garb she'd worn during their travel days. Hoarfrost trousers and leather boots, complete with a tunic in a shade of grey that would blend in with most shadows. Eislyn had stopped by earlier to weave her long, silver hair into a braid that hung down the middle of her back.

"Princess," he murmured with a bemused smile. "Not another disguise. We need you to appear as yourself this night."

"If an assassin falls into our trap, we may need to fight him," she replied crisply. "I am much quicker on my feet this way. And this is not a disguise. The courtly gowns, on the other hand, are."

"Hmm." He pulled back, frowning. "You have a point. In that case, we'll need to prevent the rest of the nobility from getting a glimpse of you. No matter. We'll sneak out through the tunnels."

Reyna smiled. "We get to sneak out through tunnels again? But I didn't think we were heading into the city this time."

"There is a special route that heads to the sea and the woods nearby it. It is a highly-kept secret within the Air Court. Thane entrusted me with the knowledge. It's only meant to be used in dire situations, such as if the city is under attack. However, it will be useful this night."

"On one condition," she said. "I need my dagger."

Lorcan frowned. "The High Queen has insisted that princesses do not have need for weapons."

"I know," Reyna snapped. "She took it away from me the second I stepped foot inside this castle, and she's never given it back."

"It's been safely kept in the armory. Which is a long walk from this tower, I might add. We wouldn't have time to fetch it."

"Then, hand me your sword. Some princesses are skilled in intrigue. I only know how to stab things."

"I will be doing all the stabbing this night."

"Absolutely not."

His expression darkened. "You do not trust me."

"I don't trust anyone," she said honestly. "Other than my sister."

"Very well."

To her surprise, Lorcan reached beneath his thick, fur-lined cloak to withdraw a small packaged wrapped in black hoarfrost cloth. He handed it to her, a slight smile playing across his lips. Wingallock hooted from his perch on top of the bed. He recognized the cloth as readily as Reyna did.

"I thought you might ask for this," he said. "So, I came prepared."

She narrowed her eyes, torn between annoyance and glee. "You forced me to practically *beg* for my dagger when you had every intention of giving it to me the entire time!"

"It would have been far less enjoyable to simply hand it over."

She wanted to be annoyed, but it was difficult to focus on her negative emotions when her trusty dagger was back in her hands. She peeled back the soft corners of the silky hoarfrost, and her dagger winked as the candlelight flickered across the icy surface of it. Lightly, she traced her fingers along the elaborate hilt. Ages ago, the creator of the dagger had carved dozens of wings onto the silver surface. The weapon had been passed down through her mother's family for centuries, and now, it was back in her hands again.

"You seem oddly attached to something as simple as a dagger," Lorcan mused.

Reyna narrowed her eyes and slipped her trusty weapon into the leather belt around her waist. "Don't presume to know how attached I should or shouldn't be to something that is mine. This dagger belonged to my mother."

Lorcan's expression softened. Not much, but enough that Reyna noticed it. "Ah. I see. The tales of her fate...are they true?"

"Far more true than I would like," she said, half-wondering why she bothered to explain this to not only a stranger but an enemy. "She died in the Ruin. I saw it happen with my very own eyes."

"That must have affected you a great deal," he murmured.

Reyna frowned up at him, expecting to see a familiar pity in his eyes. The ice fae had always felt sorry for her, even now. She and her sisters had been forced to grow up without their mother. Most people she met looked at her with sadness in their eyes, particularly any time her loss was mentioned. Reyna had never cared for the pity. She wanted something more.

She was no longer sad. She was angry.

Lorcan, however, gazed at her with understanding. "I lost my mother, too. Not to the Ruin, of course, but to something just as terrible as that. Because of it, I was forced to become something else." Suddenly, he stiffened and turned toward the door. "Come. We shouldn't wait much longer. The woods await us."

Curiosity bloomed in Reyna's mind. It was clear that Lorcan had spoken far more than he'd intended. She pondered his words. He'd lost his mother in a similar way. But how? She wanted to ask, but she could tell by his stiff back and clenched jaw that he was done speaking of it this night.

Whatever had happened, it had made him become something else, the strong and brutal warrior before her now. That, at least, she could understand. Perhaps Reyna would have always become an unsworn Shieldmaiden, even if life had gone very differently for her, but she did not think so. Her mother's death had made her want to fight.

The Ruin had not killed her, but it had still twisted her into something dark and dangerous.

Lorcan paused just before they reached the door.

"Wait," he said. "There was something else in the armory I thought you might like back."

Reyna twisted to gaze at where he pointed. The black cloth she'd discarded on the floor, the hoarfrost he'd used to hide her dagger. Frowning, she strode back to the cloth and gathered it into her arms. She held it out before her and—

She gasped. It was a black hoarfrost cloak. Simple yet refined. Thin yet strong enough to protect her from the wind. It had a simple hood and a clasp in the front. An ice sigil brooch had been clipped there. Eyes wide, she stared at Lorcan.

"Where did you get this?" she whispered, heat flushing her neck.

He frowned. "It was beside your dagger. Reyna, you look as though you've seen a ghost."

Reyna had. This cloak looked identical to her mother's. The brooch was also one of her own. Reyna had tossed both onto the snowy ground in the Hoarfrost Forest when she'd fled from the Ruin. She'd seen them melt into the darkness, destroyed completely by the black flaky ash. It was impossible that they could be here now.

Impossible. Yes, it had to be impossible. Whatever this cloak was, it wasn't hers. Neither was the brooch. As strange as it was, Lorcan had somehow found a duplicate. How, she did not know. But it was a puzzle to solve some other time.

She shook her head, clearing her mind. "Nevermind. I am just being silly."

"Is there something the matter with the cloak?" he asked, taking a step toward her. Concern flickered in his dark eyes.

"It just looks like something my mother used to wear, that's all." Bracing herself, she slipped the soft cloak around her shoulders. It even felt the same. Soft and light and strong. Just like her mother.

"All right then." But Lorcan did not look convinced. He gave her a strange look. "If you are not up to this, princess..."

"I am fine," she snapped. "You do not need to tiptoe around me as if I'm some helpless princess who needs to be rescued from hobgoblins. Or perhaps you're merely stalling because you're scared yourself."

"Very well." His lips twitched.

Lorcan moved into the corridor first before motioning for her to join him. Her skin itched as they began their trek through the dark stone halls. The tower was quiet this late at night. Few courtiers would be out of their chambers, and Lorcan had managed to dismiss the other guards that usually stood like stone sentries at each end of the corridor. It was all part of the plan. One that Reyna found increasingly thrilling with every moment that passed.

She was finally doing something about these assassination attempts. *Thank the Dagda.* She wasn't entirely certain how much longer she would have been able to stand being holed up inside her chambers with nothing to do but gossip and preen.

When they reached the stairwell, Lorcan continued to lead the way. They passed the exit to the floor below, and then the next. Finally, they reached the base of the tower where Lorcan paused, taking a quick glance outside before turning to face her. They were pressed very tightly together at the small base of the stairs. In the rounded landing, there was only enough room for them to stand still.

"There are a few guards at the far end of the hall," Lorcan murmured quietly. "Keep your hood up and your eyes down, and do not glance their way. Keep pace with me and act as though you have nothing to fear."

Nothing to fear? Reyna could not help but feel a bit

startled. Yes, they were sneaking around the castle in hopes of catching a murderous bastard, and they did not want to tip him off. But...

"Why would I have anything to fear?" she hissed, trying her best to ignore the way his leather armor brushed against her chest. "If we get caught, it isn't as though something terrible will happen...right?"

Lorcan was silent for a long moment. "We have been ordered to keep you confined to your chambers unless the High Queen herself says otherwise."

Reyna blinked and stepped back, but she could not go far. The curved wall behind her stopped her retreat. She curled her hands into fists, an uncontrollable anger whipping through her. "So, I am a prisoner now? Is that it?"

"Prisoners are not allowed magnificent chambers, princess," Lorcan said, though she could tell he clearly felt uncomfortable. He had been ordered to keep her locked up inside the tower, never to leave unless the High Queen spoke it herself. And yet, he was helping her traipse through the castle and out into the woods where they would attempt to trap an enemy.

He hated her, didn't he? Why would he help her do this? She pressed her lips together. Thane, of course. Lorcan cared deeply for the prince. He wasn't doing this to save her life. *She* wasn't who mattered to him.

"Do you still wish to go through with our plan?" he asked.

Reyna narrowed her eyes and smiled. "More than ever."

27

LORCAN

Lorcan found Reyna's bullheaded determination far more thrilling than he liked to admit. Even with the threat of facing the wrath of the High Queen, she was eager to draw another would-be assassin into their web. She'd even donned those tight, flattering trousers again, enhancing the curves of her hips and toned thighs. He found it difficult not to stare.

"Stay close beside me," he said quietly.

Lorcan pushed through the archway and waved for Reyna to follow. She hurried behind him, her dark hood framing her face. It completely obscured her brilliant hair from view, along with her ridiculous trousers. When he had opened the door to find her in what amounted to little more than silken pajamas, his jaw had almost hid the floor.

He'd known that she was a far cry from the other members of the nobility. He'd said as much on the way to the Ice Court. Still, he had not expected such a vibrant display of rebellion so soon. Despite her supposed disinterest in courtly ways, she had done everything she could to ingratiate herself into the Air Court. She listened to gossip. She smiled when lords prattled on about their wheat stores. He had to admit he'd been slightly disappointed at first.

In truth, it seemed she was hiding herself as well as even Lorcan did. Beneath the gowns and the rosy cheeks, Reyna Darragh was something else, and he wasn't entirely certain he knew what that something else was just yet.

No matter. He would find out.

They moved across the hall. Reyna followed his instructions and kept her gaze focused on the floor before them. As the prince's personal guard, Lorcan was unlikely to be questioned by anyone else. Unless they thought he was stealing away the princess.

They continued on, and the guards scarcely glanced in their direction. Soon, they were past the danger and headed toward the tunnel. Lorcan knew the way well. He led them through winding corridors and down endless stairwells until they reached the magical wall that blocked the tunnel. He pressed his hand against the stone and waited, smirking when Reyna gasped as it fell away.

To set the trap, Lorcan had chosen the Witchlight Woods deep beneath the shadows of the mountainous Cyclone Peaks, hidden only a few steps east of Dalais Castle. The two attacks on Reyna had both occurred inside the castle, but Lorcan had a hunch the next culprit wouldn't try a similar approach. He would bide his time, waiting until Reyna was alone. Outside the castle, if possible.

He had started some rumors with the guards and servants, who he knew would tell the others, after asking Vreis about the strange orders he'd received. Vreis hadn't known where the orders had originated, and his despair at being used as a pawn felt real. They were still no closer to finding out who was behind this, but hopefully they would be, after this night.

From an outsider perspective, Lorcan could imagine how others saw Reyna. Her gowns were lush and hugged her curving frame. Her hair was smooth and scented. Reyna had killed one of her would-be assassins. She'd protected herself just fine. But there were no living witnesses to prove it, except Reyna's own sister. Indeed, even Lorcan found it difficult to imagine the princess taking down a trained male twice her size.

Still, he would not underestimate this princess. Despite her slight size and her beautiful gowns, he saw the truth in her eyes and her strength in the way she moved.

At the end of the tunnel, the Bay of Wind blinked under the waning light of Danu and Brigantu, their twin moons. There were several boats bobbing along the shifting surface like dancers weaving to a muted song. But that was not their destination this night. Lorcan pointed to his right where the Witchlight Woods hulked in the darkness of the night.

The woods were small compared to the great, looming forests he'd encountered in the Ice Court, but it was one of the only groves found in the air fae lands where grassland was far more common than trees. Small enough to walk from one side to the other in only a matter of days, but large enough to get lost in if one did not know the way.

Now, the hulking yew trees, drenched in snow, looked like sentinels ready to strike.

"This is the Witchlight Woods then." A hint of a smile played across Reyna's lips as they strode down a path slick with a recent snowfall. Wingallock soared overhead, white wings outstretched, having found them near the tunnel exit.

"Don't look so giddy," he said. "We're not here to play."

"Aren't we?" She arched a brow. "We get to trap an assassin."

He grunted. "Only you would consider play to be putting your life in danger."

"I thought you were my big, bad protector who would never let anything happen to me."

He grunted again, his boots crunching snow.

"Besides," she said, chirpily. "I have my dagger now."

"The delight in your voice is alarming." He cut her eyes toward her, lips twitching. "I have never met a princess who finds so much joy in stabbing things."

"Just wait until you see me with a sword."

They found a small clearing just off the path. Several trees had been downed in a recent winter storm, winds yanking the roots from the ground. It seemed as good a place as any to set a trap.

"Wait here," he said.

"Are you certain this will work?" she asked with a dubious expression on her face. "Who in their right mind would truly believe I would come to these woods alone in the middle of the night?"

"No one. The rumors I've spread suggest you will be here right at dawn. Being homesick, you wanted to go in search of hoarfrost worms." He strode over to a yew tree and snapped off a branch toward the bottom, one so low that its absence would not be noticed. Retracing his steps, he began to brush the bristles against the ground, obscuring his own set of footsteps but not hers.

"What in the name of the Dagda are you doing?" She watched him intently. "You might be brushing away your footsteps, but the snow still looks disturbed."

He stared at the ground. She wasn't wrong. Where they had not yet walked, the snow looked smooth and pristine, glistening even in the dead of night. On the other hand, he'd left behind a bumpy, flaky mess.

"If the assassin comes and sees a second set of footprints, he might not approach," Lorcan pointed out.

"Right," she said slowly, frowning. "But I am certain this little trick of yours will only arouse far more suspicion. If it looks as though we've hidden a set of footsteps, then it will clearly seem like a trap."

Lorcan frowned, wishing she were wrong, but he had to admit that she had a point. "What would you suggest instead?"

Reyna stared at him for a long moment, and then gave him a wicked smile.

The back of his neck prickled with alarm. "I don't like that look on your face, princess."

She opened her mouth, shut it, and then shook her head. Her cheeks even flushed. "I have an idea, but I don't think you'll like it."

"Princess," he said slowly.

"Well, it seems a bit silly for a princess to sneak out of the castle for worms. I mean, I do love them dearly, but would an assassin know that?" she said, face turning an even darker shade of red. "But a princess might sneak out for another reason, especially if she did not wish to be caught inside the castle."

Lorcan still wasn't following. He crossed his arms over his armored chest.

"It's possible those guards even saw us leave together," she continued, rushing forward. "Depending on who the assassin is working for, he might learn this information before he heads out of the castle. And then, he'll expect you to be here with me."

"I'm one of the strongest warriors in this kingdom," he

said with a frown. "He is far less likely to attack if he sees you here with me."

"He would if you weren't armed." That wicked smile stretched her lips again, the wind rustling the fabric of her hood. "We could make it seem as though we sneaked out of the castle together. So that we could come here to be alone...as lovers."

Shock hit Lorcan square in the gut. Of all the things for Reyna to suggest...though, the idea did have some merit. The hoarfrost worm excuse had always sounded ridiculous in his head, but he hadn't been able to invent another rumor that sounded any better. This, on the other hand, would explain Reyna's desire to escape the castle, and it would provide a non-threatening reason for his presence.

Although...

"And how exactly would you convince him of this?" he asked.

"Yes, well." Reyna shrugged, flushing again. "We'll have to take off some of our clothes."

Lorcan found it difficult to muster up much of a reply. When he had once told Thane that Reyna was unlike any other princess in Tir Na Nog, he hadn't even known the half of it.

"Really now, princess. First the bath, and now this. You seem to enjoy throwing off your clothes in my presence. One might begin to wonder why." He shot her a wicked smile that matched her own, but inside, his mind ran wild. It was difficult not to drop his gaze and stare right at her breasts. Now that the thought had popped into his head, he was finding it difficult to concentrate on much else.

She rolled her eyes. "Oh, please. As if would ever want to get naked for your pleasure. Obviously, we're not *really* going to be lovers, now are we?"

She laughed, though he could not help but notice how tense the sound came out.

Lorcan stared at the disturbed snow. Why was he even considering this? It was completely preposterous, and it went against every bit of training he'd ever had. Indeed, this entire thing went against the orders from his king, even if his mark was once again strangely silent this night.

He should not even *be* here, helping an enemy princess trap the fae who wanted her dead. In fact, Lorcan's orders would be much easier to carry out if she weren't around, distracting him.

She stood there, regarding him carefully, her cloaked form backlit by the brilliant snow-drenched woods. "You don't like the idea. I suppose you have a better one?"

"No," he said slowly before meeting her gaze again. "This could work. We need a way to explain my presence here without it being a threat." Slowly, he nodded, as if trying to convince himself of this ridiculous plan. "We'll pretend to be lovers, caught out in the woods."

Reyna gave him a nervous smile. "Then, I suppose that means we should settle in for a wait."

It would be a couple hours more before dawn pushed the sun into the sky. The assassin would likely press out into the woods before then, but they still had some time to spare. With Wingallock circling overhead, they would be alerted as soon as anyone stepped foot into the Witchlight Woods.

They found a fallen tree well off the path and sat quietly on the icy bark. Reyna sighed and pulled her knees up to her chest, breathing deeply. Lorcan watched her. She seemed...almost peaceful. They were out here, trying to trap someone who wanted to kill her, and she looked far more relaxed than she had in weeks.

"You like it here," Lorcan finally said. "Out here in the woods."

Reyna smiled. "The forests feel like home. Castles do not." She opened her eyes and turned to him. The silver of them glinted in the moonlight. "Do you feel that way about the grasslands?"

Reyna often asked him about his past. He sensed there were deeper reasons for her questions than simple curiosity.

"I never felt as though I fit in back home," he said honestly. "Though I can't say I fare any better inside that castle. Thane feels like a brother to me, but the rest of that family..."

Lorcan frowned to himself. For so long, he had tried to keep Thane at arm's length, but it had become difficult as time pressed on. He'd formed a kinship with the future High King of the Air Court. A dangerous kinship. One that made his mark burn.

And, one day, that brotherly bond would turn to dust in his mouth.

Reyna nodded, as if she understood. "Starford Castle never really felt like home for me either, even though I love my family fiercely. It's always been this. The trees, the snow, the ice, the stars in the sky. It's almost as if I can..." She flushed again and shook her head.

He cocked his head, curious. "Almost as if what?"

"It sounds ridiculous."

"Tell me," he pressed.

She looked up into his eyes, those pools of silver staring back at him. "It's almost as if I can feel it all. I can even hear it."

Lorcan's heart thumped. Did she know what she was saying? "You feel a connection with your element here? But you're no longer inside your kingdom."

Reyna stared at him for a moment longer before laughing and turning away. "I know. That's why I said it sounds ridiculous. I should feel no draw to the lands here. I am born of ice."

"And you felt this in the Ice Court as well?" he prodded. Reyna should not have been able to feel it even then. Before the Fall, the magic of the fae had been drawn from the lands. And that great power that had once lurked beneath the soil, in the trees, in the winds, and even in the very shadows themselves, it was gone...for the most part.

"Perhaps it's merely my imagination." She sighed and dropped her chin to her knees. "That's what Glencora has always said. My imagination must have come with me...we're sitting on ice, after all. It makes sense."

But it did not make sense. Reyna must have suspected it didn't because she fell silent, fingertips slipping along the icy bark as she stared into the depths of the woods. He could tell by the hunch of her shoulders that she doubted herself. Being the only person who saw and felt things had an unfortunate effect on the psyche. It made even the strongest worry they were no longer sane.

Lorcan wanted to tell her that she was not the only one who heard the whispers of the dirt and felt the pulsing of the world beneath her fingers. But he couldn't. Not without risking it all. Not when he did not even understand it himself.

He had searched for answers. The libraries of Tairngire were infamous throughout the continent. If there was a book that could tell him the truth about the power he felt, it would be in there. Unfortunately, as the prince's personal guard, he had little time for perusing books, and he could not bring much attention to his pursuit of knowledge. He did not want anyone to discover the truth about him.

"You look as though you're as troubled as I am," Reyna said, elbowing his side. "Where did your mind go just now? Wait. Sorry. You don't have to answer that."

He smiled. For a princess, she often forgot her words. There were unspoken rules in the world of the courts. One of those was to never ask a fae what they were thinking. As much as fae enjoyed trapping others with their inability to lie, there were constraints. No one wanted to be asked what they were thinking, so no one asked. In a world where wickedness often ruled, they could be surprisingly strict about questions.

"I was thinking that I may have misjudged you when we first met," he said. "Truth be told, I thought you would make a terrible High Queen."

Reyna sat up a little straighter, though she did not look the least bit offended. "That is surprisingly blunt. And you've changed your mind, have you? You think I am a great match for your prince?"

He chuckled. "I didn't say that."

"I don't disagree with you, you know," she countered. "Glencora would have been a wonderful High Queen of the Air Court. She would have ruled well by Thane's side. I wish things could have gone differently."

He did not doubt that.

Overhead, Wingallock's cry echoed through the hushed night. Reyna suddenly jumped to her feet, dagger in her hand. Lorcan hadn't even seen her reach for the weapon.

"He's here. An assassin has actually come," she hissed, closing her eyes so that she could better see through her familiar. It was a strange sight, watching a fae channel herself in this way. Pure magic. A power that so few had. "A hooded figure, coming quickly but quietly down the path. He will be here in a few moments."

They gave each other a long look before racing back to

the clearing. Lorcan pulled the sword from his back, dumping it onto the ground. Then, he pulled his tunic over his head and tossed it onto the patch of snow he had disturbed earlier. Cool wind whispered across his bare skin.

And then he looked at her. Reyna had thrown her cloak on top of her weapon, and she had shrugged off her trousers, exposing a pair of very long, smooth legs. Beneath, she wore hardly anything. A white silken undergarment that barely covered her hips.

She snapped her fingers in front of his eyes. "There you go gawking again. Stop staring and get down on the ground with me."

He looked at her incredulously. "On the snow?"

Impatiently, she threw up her hands. "Yes. Why the hell not?"

"Because it's as cold as a Fomorian's heart," he hissed.

"If you're going to pretend to be my lover, you must get on top of me and kiss me. Now."

Reyna wrapped her arms around his neck and pulled him down on top of her. Lorcan did little to resist. A little warning bell clanged in his head, and the mark on his shoulder pulsed, but nothing more. Still, this felt wrong somehow. Reyna was Thane's betrothed. They were to marry.

What did that even matter? Lorcan almost muttered to himself aloud. It wasn't as though they were actual lovers, he had to remind himself. This was all for show. None of it meant anything real. So, the objections in his mind meant nothing.

So, then why did he feel so...unsteadied by it all?

Her body shifted beneath his. He braced his arms on either side of her head and dropped his mouth onto hers. She felt surprisingly hot to the touch. For some reason, he had expected an ice fae to be cold, as cold as the very snow itself. Instead, the warmth of her burned his skin.

Relaxing just slightly, he gave into the feel of Reyna's body beneath his. He slid his hand up the curve of her hip, appreciating the way her waist dipped before flaring out toward her breasts. He could remember exactly what she looked like without the constrictions of her gowns, memories of her glistening body in the bathwater pouring through his mind.

Reyna squirmed beneath him, twisting her hands through his hair. Pressing himself harder against her, he let his hand drift up just enough to trace the bottom curve of her left breast. His length went hard, and a need pulsed through him.

This is all pretend, he had to remind himself. As much as she seemed to be enjoying herself, Lorcan had to remember that it was all for show, to convince the incoming assassin that they were distracted, that Lorcan was not a threat, that they were not expecting a knife stab in the back.

As if to echo his thoughts, Reyna suddenly pulled back, cheeks flushed, and whispered, "Now!"

With a grunt, he pushed up from the snow-packed ground and whirled, landing on his feet. Addled, he leaned down to grab his sword, but Reyna was already launching through the air, straight toward the cloaked figure, with her ice glass dagger raised.

The assassin's hood dropped back. A familiar face peered back at them, shock and fear flickering through her eyes. The petite, grey-haired female stumbled back. For a moment, Lorcan could do little more than stare. The would-be assassin was Ula, Reyna's grouchy lady's maid.

But the shock of it all did not seem to register with Reyna. As she leapt, her body slammed hard into Ula. The assassin tumbled to the snow-packed ground. Reyna pinned her easily, her dagger's blade glinting as she pressed it tightly against her neck. "Who do you work for?"

Ula narrowed her sharp, grey eyes. "I work for you, milady."

Reyna growled, a sound that sent a thrill through Lorcan.

But he also felt dread. If Reyna's own lady's maid had been sent to murder her, then there was only one logical conclusion he could find. Someone inside of the Air Court truly was behind these attacks.

He needed to handle this very carefully.

"Princess," he said quietly as he rested a hand on her tense shoulder. She flinched beneath his touch but her blade remained steady against the assassin's neck. "We should deliver Ula to the dungeons where she can be questioned thoroughly. We need to know who is behind this."

At that, Reyna twisted slightly to scowl up at him. "Or we could simply question her here and now, and then kill her."

Lorcan understood her anger well. He wished he could give her what she needed, but he could not. "This affects far more than just you, Reyna. I need to take this to Thane."

"And what if Thane is involved?"

"Thane is not involved. I can promise you that." He leaned down to whisper into her ear. "If his mother sent the assassins, then he needs to know about it, and he needs the chance to be involved in the questioning. It will affect the future of this kingdom. And it will affect who sits on that throne."

At that, Reyna sighed and pulled her knife away from the maid's throat. "You better not be wrong."

28

THANE

"Lorcan, what is the meaning of this?" Prince Thane stormed into his chambers and slammed the door behind him, glaring at the warrior he thought he knew and trusted. "Why were you traipsing around in the woods with Reyna at dawn? Why does this spy insist you two are lovers? Fae cannot lie, Lorcan, so be careful of your words. I will be listening for the mince in them."

Thane's morning had been one bad thing after another. Not only had one of the Air Court's servants attempted to kill his betrothed but Reyna had also been caught rolling around in the snow with his closest friend and personal guard. To top it all off, Eislyn had been avoiding him. No, he couldn't think about that right now. There were far more pressing matters.

"Thane," his uncle said, stepping up beside him and clasping him on the shoulder. "Calm yourself, my boy."

He met his uncle's golden eyes. He'd been the one to catch Lorcan and Reyna sneaking in with the bound assassin, and he'd taken charge of the matter instantly. Despite the horror of it all, Lord Bowen had stayed calm, measured, unruffled. Thane truly did not know what he would do without his uncle's steadying influence.

"Right." Thane gave a nod and steadied himself. "Lorcan, please explain yourself."

Lorcan pressed his lips together. He appeared as calm and unruffled as Thane's uncle, but there was a new glint in his eye. Thane did not wish to know what that meant.

"The princess and I attempted to trap the assassin," he said calmly. "We embraced, hoping to convince the assassin that we were distracted. It worked."

Thane shook his head. "When I brought Reyna into this court, I expected there might be shenanigans, though I hardly expected them to come from you, too. Did you not think to run this wild plot by me first? Did you not understand that I would not wish to put my betrothed in harm's way? There is also the small matter of my mother's orders. You completely defied them."

"With all due respect, Thane, fuck your mother's orders."

The prince blinked, and his uncle let out a sharp gasp. Thane stared at his old friend, who merely stared right back at him.

But then he couldn't help but laugh. Lorcan never was one to mince his words. Thane did not know why he'd expected him to do it now. With anyone else, he would not have allowed it, but Lorcan was different. The warrior was the brother he'd never had.

"You know how I feel about the High Queen," Lorcan continued. "She's taken the crown from your father and has plotted to keep it from you. Now, she's keeping your betrothed as a prisoner in her chambers. I'd never say this anywhere but in the safety of your private chambers, but Thane...If she's behind these attacks, she needs to be stopped."

Thane's laughter died on his lips. His warrior's words unsettled him. In truth, it was only because Thane had recently had very similar thoughts himself. The entire plot suggested something that he did not want to face. If someone had commanded Ula to kill Reyna, it would have come from inside the castle. If not the High Queen herself, then someone else very close.

Lord Bowen cleared his throat. "As much as it pains me to entertain these accusations against the High Queen, your guard here does have a point, son."

Thane sighed and dropped into the lush golden sofa beside his unlit hearth. Dull sunlight streamed in through the windows, warming the room. But Thane felt cold. "Did you really have to do this without asking me? And taking Reyna, Lorcan?"

Lorcan eased into the chair across from him, propping one ankle on his opposite knee, the leather of his armor creaking. "You would have been obligated to say no, and while I'm happy to defy the High Queen...I serve you first and foremost."

Thane nodded.

"And, as for Reyna...I think it's time you acknowledge that she's far more capable than you'd like to admit."

Thane looked up. "You saw her fight?"

Lorcan was silent for a long moment, as though he were carefully considering his words. "She's powerful, Thane. Don't turn her into a pretty object who sits by your side at Beltane."

Thane flinched, frowning. Only a few weeks guarding the girl and Lorcan had become someone who spoke in her defense and took her out before dawn to trap assassins. Perhaps he'd made a mistake in assigning Lorcan to her guard rotation. The warrior was clearly beginning to forget Reyna's purpose here.

Certainly she was powerful, but she had agreed to be his betrothed. With that came certain responsibilities and expectations. There was decorum, and it was there for a reason. The low fae looked up to the rulers of their realm. Not because of who they were but because of what they stood for.

"You think she isn't suitable ?" Lord Bowen asked with a frown.

"Yes, Lorcan," Thane said evenly. "What exactly are you suggesting here?"

"You're angry," Lorcan said. "You shouldn't be. There have been plenty of Shieldmaidens in this kingdom over the years."

"Shieldmaidens are shieldmaidens," Thane argued. "Not future High Queens. One cannot be both."

Lorcan cocked his head. "And why not?"

Sighing, Thane shook his head. As a warrior, Lorcan would never truly understand the burden that had been squatting on Thane's shoulders ever since the day he had been born. Expectations, rules, responsibility. The future of an entire kingdom depended upon the way he—and those around him—handled himself. And now, the alliance with the ice fae meant that *two* kingdoms depended on Thane. Just as soon as he got his throne from his mother.

Lorcan was a warrior. He only had to worry about the fight. At times, Thane did envy his old friend. What would it feel like to have a life so free of complications? To know exactly what needed to be done? To never find himself torn in two, knowing that a single decision could change everything?

That was why there were such strict rules. On what to say, how to act, what to wear, and when to smile. It made the bigger decisions all the more easier.

Bigger decisions such as what to do about a household servant attempting murder on his future wife.

Thane drummed his fingers on the arm of his chair. "We must hide Reyna's involvement in this. For her sake. And for yours."

He left the full weight of his words unsaid. Lorcan was a clever lad. He would understand.

"Is that truly wise, Thane?" his uncle asked. "It will be difficult to hide."

The truth may be twisted but never false.

Again, Thane drummed his fingers. "I do not want to give my mother further ammunition against Reyna."

Lorcan sighed. "Very well. Tell her that I set the trap, and do not mention the princess."

"And the three guards who spotted you on your way to the tunnel?"

Lorcan merely shrugged. "Tell them not to speak. Pay them if you must."

"If you wish to go this route, son," his uncle cut in quickly. "Then, might I make a suggestion?"

Thane glanced up at his uncle's calming eyes. "Of course."

"Go request the assistance of my spymaster. He will be able to determine if the High Queen was involved, quietly."

"Right." Thane gave a nod and pushed up from his chair. "I must go speak with him immediately then. Before word gets out."

"And what would you have me to do help?" Lorcan asked.

Thane gave him a cold look. While he considered Lorcan his brother, he would not hide his frustration. Lorcan should have come to him first. And he never should have involved Reyna in any of it.

"Return to your post outside of Reyna's door. And this time, do not let her leave."

※

Troubled, Thane moved through the castle quickly. It would not take long before the rumors would begin to swirl through court. The air fae adored gossip, particularly anything remotely scandalous. So far, Ula had not been allowed to speak to anyone. He imagined it would not take long for that to change. Regardless of the truth, the prince could not afford for Reyna's imagined dalliances to become public knowledge.

He truly wished Glencora had never fallen ill.

She would never have traipsed through the woods to lie in wait and then press a dagger against a servant's neck.

He came to a stop outside of a door on the lowest level of Zephyr Tower. It was early yet, but he knew the male inside would be awake. A scuffling sounded from within, and then the door cracked open. A kindly weathered face peered out at him—the oldest fae inside the entire kingdom, Kelwyn.

Lord Bowen's spymaster.

"My liege?" Kelwyn gave him a look of surprise before opening the door wider, and then ushering him inside.

Thane strode into a room that was dark and dank, lit only by a simple fire-lamp perched atop a wooden table. A small cot sat on the opposite wall, sheets rumpled and smattered with dirt. The stench of body odor swirled in the dusty space, but Thane kept a straight face. Offending Kelwyn would do little good.

Kelwyn shut the door quietly behind him and turned to the prince. With withered hands and whiskers that stretched down the very length of his face, Kelwyn looked as old as he truly was, almost two hundred years. He wore a simple tunic and trousers in the color of wheat with small, well-worn leather boots. His eyes were a deep gold, the only thing about him that had not faded over the years.

"I'm surprised to see you at such an early hour, what with your revelling. What can I do for you, my prince?"

It was a slight dig, but Thane ignored it. "We have a slight problem, Kelwyn, and I must request your secrecy on the matter."

"My secrecy?" Kelwyn drawled in his scratching, aged voice. "You would have me lie, boy?"

Kelwyn was the only fae Thane had ever met who could lie, and only few were aware that he could. No one quite knew where he got such power, not even Kelwyn, if he could be believed. He was not a shadow fae. He'd been born right inside this very room. It made him one of Thane's most powerful resources, though he only used Kelwyn's special ability in matters of extreme urgency. The prince knew that if he asked him to lie too often, then others would quickly become aware of his gift, too.

Some secrets should stay hidden in the mists.

"I'm not certain," Thane said. "We have caught another assassin attempting to murder my betrothed, and her identity suggests that she may be working for someone inside of this castle."

"Ah." Kelwyn nodded.

"I need to find out who it was, but I need you to be discreet. Only a few even know the assassin was captured."

"I know why you've come to me. You believe it to be your mother."

Thane flinched. "I don't believe it. I need you to confirm that it wasn't her."

Kelwyn was silent for a moment before nodding. "And if it was your mother? What then?"

"Come to me immediately. Do not breathe a word about it to anyone else." Thane paused. "Lie if you have to."

He turned to go, but the spymaster cleared his throat before Thane could pull open the door. "And the payment. It will be the same as always?"

Thane stiffened and gave a curt nod. "You'll have your payment as soon as I have an answer. My uncle will see to it."

※

Thane didn't like using the spymaster. He was not a good male. Although, Thane thought, *he* hardly was either. A good male would not have gotten himself into this predicament. He would have seen the folly in agreeing to marry a female who cared more about her dagger than her future crown.

Sighing, he found himself drifting toward the library. He had not seen Eislyn in days. He doubted she would be rifling through the books this early, but there was no harm in checking before he returned to his chambers.

He pushed inside the grand double doors. Morning light speared through the glass ceiling, shooting a warm glow across the endless shelves of books. In the very center of the room, Eislyn sat at a table surrounded by dozens of leather-bound tomes. Her hair fell into her face as she curled over a piece of parchment covered in her scribbled notes.

With a fond smile, Thane approached her quietly. She must have found something interesting indeed to be this absorbed in her studies. Suddenly, she started and glanced up at him with those wide eyes that were pools of churning silver. When she saw him, she relaxed.

"Sorry. You surprised me." She gave him a small smile. "I've never seen you up quite so early. Not out revelling last night then?"

Thane frowned. He himself had helped craft the image. A boy prince, enamored with devilish revelry. He'd done it to make it seem as if he did not care about his father's atrocities. It had worked. Perhaps too well.

"You know I don't always stay out until dawn." He settled onto the seat across the table, watching her spin her feather quill in her fingers.

"No?" She looked genuinely surprised. "That is what the rumors say."

"I thought you realized that not all those rumors are true."

"Rumors must be based in truth, or they wouldn't exist at all. Maybe across the Mag Mell Sea, but not in our world."

Thane's frown deepened. Princess Eislyn seemed different somehow. She had grown colder toward him in the days since they'd spent the night out in the city together. Indeed, she almost acted as she had when they'd first met. It puzzled him. She had softened toward him, or so he had thought.

"Have I done something to anger you?" he asked.

Eislyn's cheeks flushed. "No, of course not. I'm just engrossed in my studies. There are some interesting passages in these books, and I'm trying to make sense of them. I've scarcely been able to think about much else."

He found himself smiling. While Thane was distracted by petty squabbles, courtly intrigue, and disobedient princesses, Eislyn had been tucked away in these stacks, searching for information on how to save her kingdom from further ruin. She was trying to save lives. He was merely trying to save his future crown.

"Tell me what you've found. I might be able to help."

She hesitated for a moment, but then nodded, twisting her parchment around to face him. "First, I started by going through the recent books on the Fall, searching for any mention of the Ruin. I didn't find much."

After pointing at the top two lines, she waited while Thane read what she'd written. There were two references here to the Ruin, found in books around sixty years old.

The Ruin will kill us all.

And then...

They control the Ruin.

Thane snapped up his head. "This is it. You've actually found something, Eislyn. Where did you read these two notes?"

She gave him a sad smile. "I was excited, too. It spurred me on, thinking that this was the answer to everything we needed. These books. The words found inside of them."

Confused, Thane nodded. "Of course it is. You've found references to the very thing that plagues your lands."

"Except, this is all I have found, Thane."

He stared at her for a long moment.

"I have been reading day and night all week. I've been through every book along that wall. These are the only two references to the Ruin. All I've done is confirm that whatever this thing is, it's been around since the Fall. There are no answers here on how to defeat it."

"Ah." Thane sighed and glanced around. There were books stacked all along the table, some piled precariously on top of each other. He turned his gaze back on Eislyn. Now that he knew how hard she'd been working, he could see the evidence on her face. Her eyes were tired, and her skin pale. How long had it been since she'd had a good night's sleep?

Reyna had warned that her sister was troubled.

"Eislyn." He reached out and took her hand. She gasped but didn't pull away. "This is just one library. There are more books to read, more references to check. But I don't want to see you drop from exhaustion because of this."

Pain flickered in her eyes. "Why should I not push myself as hard as I can? There are people dying, Thane. My sister...word came from my father again. She is still very, very ill."

He nodded. "I understand. But let me help you."

Thane ignored the voice of warning in his head. Now was not the time to get engrossed in books. There were assassins to worry about. Princesses running through the woods. His mother.

Still, he knew the Ruin was important, if only because Eislyn was certain it was. He could spare a few moments to take some of the weight off her shoulders.

"Were you up all night?" he asked gently.

She nodded.

"Right. You give me the books where you found these references to the Ruin and go get some sleep. While you rest, I'll make some notes and see what else I can find."

Cocking her head, she peered into his eyes. He still had not gotten used to those endless pools of silver. "You think you'll be able to find some meaning that I haven't?"

"Actually, no." He motioned for the first book, and she handed it over. It was a slick, red tome covered in smooth leather. It had been written sixty years before, back when battles still raged daily in their lands.

"Then, what do you plan to do?"

"I'm going to read it, note any important names or places, and then the two of us are going to search another library for these same subjects. We'll find the answer to the Ruin, Eislyn."

He meant his promise. He could not say it if he didn't. But what he didn't tell the princess was that it might take years for them to comb through every single book in every library in the city. The Air Court had collected so much knowledge over the centuries. The problem, of course, was finding it.

Eislyn stood, her light blue dress rumpled from where she'd sat in that chair for hours on end. Her silver hair curtained her face, drawing attention to the low-cut bodice that accentuated her small breasts. Thane swallowed hard and scolded himself. Regardless of her beauty, he should not look.

And yet, he could do nothing else.

He opened his mouth to say something that would no doubt get him into even more trouble, but the library doors suddenly swung inward. He jumped, startled, turning toward the sound. Lorcan stood with Vreis in the doorway, both scowling.

Slowly, Thane stood.

"Reyna did not return to her chambers," Lorcan said. "She's gone."

29

REYNA

Reyna had waited in the dungeons. Thane, Lorcan, and Lord Bowen had headed to the prince's chambers after depositing the would-be assassin in her cell. He'd ordered the princess to return to her own chambers while he determined how to handle this. But when had she ever followed orders?

Reyna had to take matters into her own hands.

The dungeons were full of shadows and mist. Even beneath the castle, a harsh wind whipped through the dank tunnels. A heavy chill settled into her bones as she pulled her cloak tightly around her shoulders. After the footsteps died away, she stood from her hiding place and went for the assassin.

She found Ula in a cell in a back corner, far from the other prisoners. They'd placed her here so that they could question her in privacy, no doubt. If the High Queen had made the order to have Reyna killed, Thane would want to control the information as tightly as he could.

And she didn't trust him to do the right thing with it.

Ula peered up at her with a scowl, her grey hair plastered to her face. Her cloak was soaked through with melted snow, and she shivered from the chill of it. The cell was small and cramped. There was a ragged blanket stretched across the floor and a wooden bucket in the corner. No windows, no light other than the flickering sconces along the corridor walls. The hard stone ground was covered in dirt and grime, and it reeked of filth and body odor. It reminded Reyna of Drunkard's Pit.

"I expected you would return." The assassin pushed up from the floor and strode over to the thick iron bars. Fae didn't like to use iron. It burned them by touch. Sometimes, they would use it in their blades, as long as the hilts were made of another strong metal. But dungeon cells were the perfect place for it.

Reyna crossed her arms. "You have information I need."

Ula smiled out at Reyna. "The prince ordered you to go. You don't follow orders. You aren't like the others."

"You're right about that, even if you're wrong about everything else." Reyna slid her ice dagger from her belt and twirled it in her hand, stopping it suddenly so that it pointed right at the devious fae. "Who do you work for?"

She laughed. "You truly expect me to answer that question?"

Reyna shrugged. "Willingly or not, you will answer."

"Torture?" She laughed again, glancing at Reyna's dagger. "You can't get inside this cell. You don't have the key. I'm not answering the question."

Reyna smiled and jangled the keys.

Shock registered in the assassin's eyes, followed quickly by suspicion. "How did you get those?"

"I ask the questions. Who do you work for? Is it Prince Thane?"

Reyna did not truly believe that Thane had ordered the assassination, but she'd seen her father work on prisoners before. There was an art to questioning when it came to fae. Humans were much easier. First, ask a series of yes or no questions where the answer is clearly a no. Lull them into a false sense of security. Allow them to get cocky. And then, when they have relaxed, lob your real question. If they refuse to answer it, then you have your truth.

"Is that what you think?" Ula asked, arching a grey-tinted brow.

"If not, Thane, then who?" Reyna asked. "Was it Lorcan?"

Ula shook her head. "I know what you're trying to do. I've been questioned before, and I know how you nobles handle things. I will not answer your questions."

Reyna jangled the keys again.

"I won't tell you," Ula hissed. "You can do whatever you want to me, but I will never spill the words. Because I know that no matter what I do, I'll end up dead in the end."

Reyna narrowed her eyes. The assassin was, unfortunately, right. Ula had been ordered to murder Reyna. She had likely promised to fulfill her quest to whoever controlled her. That meant she would never stop. And, even if she did, Tir Na Nog was not the kind of world where assassins were allowed to live. If Reyna didn't kill her, someone else would.

"You ought not to protect your master," Reyna said. "She or he will have no loyalty to you. You know that. If you tell me, then I'll...well, I'll let you out."

Ula snorted. "You mean for me to believe that you'll let me go free? That I'll live if I answer you honestly? Look at my eyes and my hair, milady. I was not born yesterday."

"I can't promise you'll live, but you'll get a head start. You might just make it out of this castle alive." Reyna strode closer, dropping her dagger to her side. "Imagine the alternative. You stay. You are questioned sharply. Eventually, whoever gave you this order will come here and kill you to prevent you from speaking. Or, the crown kills you first for treason. Either way, you have no chance if you stay inside this cell. But if you tell me now, you'll at least have something."

Ula blinked at her with those eerie eyes. Reyna hated to let the assassin go, but her need for truth was far stronger than her fury. If she had to do this to get answers, then so be it.

Ula sucked in a long breath, and then exhaled. She stared at Reyna with hateful eyes. "I am a coward."

"Does that mean you agree?"

"I'll tell you who sent me," Ula said slowly. "But you must at least unlock the door first. Otherwise, what assurance do I have that you'll allow me to flee?"

Reyna frowned. "My word. I cannot lie."

"That isn't enough for me," Ula whispered.

The princess continued to frown. Surely Ula didn't believe that Reyna could lie. Why would she insist on evidence of Reyna's words? A drumbeat pounded in her mind. She could walk away from this and return to her chambers. She could leave Thane to question her lady's maid turned assassin.

But Reyna could not trust Thane. He'd already proven that to her.

"All right," Reyna finally said, twirling her dagger once again. "But if you make a move to leave before you give me that name, then I will personally carve your skull out of your head."

Ula nodded and wet her lips.

With narrowed eyes, Reyna shoved the key into the lock and twisted sideways. A resounding click echoed through the dark dungeons. Ula let out a long, slow exhale, and then she smiled.

Reyna's heart twisted. "Time for your end of the bargain, Ula. Who was it?"

"I don't work for who you think," she hissed.

The rush of footsteps ripped Reyna's attention away from the cell. A figure hurtled out of the darkness. His arm was outstretched, his gloved fingers curled around the long hilt of a two-handed sword. The blade glinted as it whistled toward her head.

With a shout, Reyna jumped back, heart hammering. The figure swung again with a strength that caught Reyna off-guard. In fact, everything about this new arrival made her unsteady. He wore the dark leather armor of the prince's guard. His emblem had even been etched into the front. A thick golden helmet hid his face from view, but he was clearly someone loyal to the Air Court.

She ducked low, placing a hand on the stone floor to steady herself. She needed a moment to think. While she had plenty of training with the blade, a small dagger was all she had. His reach would far exceed hers, and his thick armor would help protect him from her blade.

But she was quick and she was smart and she had fought far worse than this.

More footsteps filled the air, only these came from directly behind Reyna.

"I appreciate the escape route, princess," Ula shouted on her way past.

Reyna ground her teeth. Out of the corner of her eye, a blur of grey streaked past. There was nothing she could do. Not when the prince's guard loomed over her with a sword.

The guard raised his sword high, the sharp end held right over her head. And then he threw all of his weight behind his blow. Reyna threw herself sideways, rolling on the floor. She shot out an arm as she moved, her blade slicing through his right leg.

She smiled when he screamed.

Jumping to her feet, she threw another blow toward his left side. The tip of her blade deflected off his armor. Frowning, she jumped a few steps back, just as he swung his sword wide.

She rushed him half a second later, holding the end of her hilt tight against her stomach with the end of the dagger sticking outward. With a roar, she slammed into the guard, chest against chest, her blade pointed up halfway toward the ceiling. It slid through his armor and into his gut with a horrible, squelching crunch.

His sword clattered to the ground as his eyes went wide. Gritting her teeth, she twisted the blade sideways, cutting through his flesh. And then she ripped it from his gut, pushing back his body with her boot.

He fell hard, blood splattering the stone walls.

"Princess Reyna?" Thane's shocked voice echoed all around her.

She glanced up to see him standing halfway down the corridor, the flickering sconces highlighting the horror on his face. Now, her betrothed finally saw her for who she really was.

She smiled. "Sorry. He tried to kill me."

30

IMOGEN

"Explain yourself," the High Queen of the Air Court demanded. She perched on her throne, narrowing her eyes at the cluster of idiots before her. The past few hours had been a flurry of activity that had beaten away the more pressing matters on her agenda. The bloody ice fae girl had caused trouble again. It did not surprise her in the least.

Reyna stood below the dais, her silver eyes flashing with determination. The rest of the courtiers were busy at morning mass, all except Prince Thane, Lord Bowen, Princess Eislyn, and that warrior who was always lurking around. They all stood around Reyna, clearly uncomfortable. Court had yet to begin for the day. The tables were empty. The banners had not yet been replaced with a clean set. Still, it was a shock to see a princess standing inside the Great Hall wearing nothing more than blood-soaked silken trousers.

This one is far too fiery. Much like me.

"I was attacked and I defended myself," the princess replied.

"A prisoner has escaped, and one of my guards is dead."

A strange look passed across Reyna's face. "Your guard tried to kill me. And that prisoner plotted to assassinate me."

"Aye." The High Queen leaned forward. "And your actions resulted in her escape."

Imogen had heard all about the night's activities. It seemed her son and his precious warrior friend had been particularly busy at dawn. The Lorcan lad had set a trap, luring the assassin into the Witchlight Woods. In the end, he had caught the culprit, and then he'd thrown her into the dungeons just as he should.

And then Reyna ruined it all.

"What did you hope to accomplish?" Imogen asked.

Reyna lifted her chin. "I wanted to find out who gave her the order to kill me."

A hush fell across the Great Hall. With pursed lips, Imogen sat back in the chair of twisting vines. She heard the implication beneath Reyna's words, even if she did not say it outright. Everyone in the entire castle knew by now what the girl thought, that Imogen wanted her dead.

It was clever, voicing the truth here in front of several witnesses. If the others did not have questions before, they certainly would now. Ula had been Reyna's lady's maid. She never left the castle. If someone had hired her, it would not be a great leap to conclude it had been Imogen herself.

"I see." Imogen smiled. "And did you get your answer?"

Reyna frowned. "She would not give up the name."

"Instead, you let her escape, and we will never know the truth. We had the opportunity to find the truth, to save lives. You could be targeted again. Or your sister."

Or my son, Imogen thought, though she did not speak that aloud. If anyone ever threatened his life, Imogen would tear down the very castle itself to save him. She'd lost her children once. She would not lose the only one she had left.

"You're right. I could be targeted again," Reyna said. "That is the very reason I questioned her. That's been three attempts to murder me so far."

"Aye. Did you not think I had my own plan, Reyna Darragh? One to find the truth? In time, I would have caught the assassin myself." Imogen wound her fingers around the arms of the throne and squeezed tight. "I had you confined to your chambers for a reason, and yet you defied me. At the expense of the safety of everyone in this court."

Lord Bowen murmured, and Imogen smiled. For a moment, she had sat on a knife edge. But she had made the right choice. Focus on Reyna's failings. She'd given her enough to work with, after all.

"You are dismissed. Return to your chambers and stay there until I say otherwise."

Reyna's eyes went wide. "You cannot do this."

"Oh, but I can, Reyna. Be glad I am not punishing you further."

Imogen stood and strode out of the room, her deep orange gown swishing around her feet. She went straight for the Council Room at the back of the Great Hall where matters of great urgency would be waiting for her.

It was a room only the quarter of the size of the Great Hall, yet Imogen found herself spending far more time inside these four walls than she did on the throne. Thick carpet in shades of gold stretched across the timber floor. An oak table sat on top, in the very center of the space. A dozen windows lined one wall, letting in the vibrant morning light.

Aengus sat at the table, moving carved wooden pieces

around a map of Tir Na Nog. His glossy ginger hair curtained his face as he peered down in concentration. He had begun to do this far more than he had in the past. He tried out strategy after strategy, pondering moves for hours. This time, he had put all of their forces into the Wood Court's forest-covered lands, leaving none at the castle for protection against anyone else.

Shaking her head, she swept her hand across the pieces and smiled as they tumbled like fallen warriors. "That would never work. Another court would merely attack us while all our armies are gone."

Aengus scowled, glaring up at her with narrow grey eyes. "Who? The Ice Court? I thought that wretched son of yours took care of that lot."

Imogen pursed her lips as she dropped into the wooden chair across from his. "They are cowed for a time, but I do not trust them. There is also the Sea Court to consider."

"Your family?" He snorted. "We would see them coming far before they ever got past the border. The Blade's Pass makes for a slow trek, followed by the low Summer Hills."

"Yes, which is why it's easy to protect ourselves against them. As long as we have troops in our own kingdom. Try something else Aengus. And this time, be sure it makes sense. And do not forget to consider the bloody Shadow Court. I've had word that they've now attacked three of our forts near Findius. I don't know what they think they're doing, but it's the most activity we've seen from them in years."

"They'll never breach the Findius Stronghold, and they'll have the Wood Court to contend with far before they ever reach us." Aengus narrowed his eyes. "But, I think, Your Majesty, that I will pass on my next attempt at our war strategy."

Imogen recognized that look in his eye. He was a

cunning, cruel fae, who rarely settled for what he had. Always seeking the next rung in his ladder. Always watching for weakness in those around him. She had allowed him that, encouraged him even, but she did not wish to entertain his grand delusions much longer.

"What is it that you want now, Aengus?" she asked icily.

"I want what you promised me. Divorce your husband, marry me, and make me the High King of this realm."

A chill went through Imogen. She had wondered how long it would take her lover to bring this up again. At first, it had been easy to put him off, but as time stretched on...

"I cannot divorce my husband, and I certainly never told you that I would."

"It was implied."

She stared at him evenly. "The laws of the Dagda do not allow a High Queen to divorce her husband."

"The law says that a High Queen cannot divorce the *High King*. It does not say *husband*. That is merely implied. And no one has seen Sloane for weeks. He scarcely matters anymore."

Imogen was silent for a moment. The technicality did exist.

"I believe the druids would translate the text to mean that I cannot divorce at all. There has never before been a case of a High Queen married to someone who is not also the reigning High King."

Aengus flashed her a wicked smile. "I know."

Damn him, Imogen cursed. He had foreseen this, had planned it even. Imogen had always known that he wanted the throne, but she'd always imagined that he would attempt to kill her for it. Instead, he had been moving his own pieces on his own board without her knowing.

"I cannot promise you this, Aengus. If there truly is a

way for us to marry, I cannot do it now just after having taken the crown from Sloane. It is too soon."

Slowly, he gave a nod. "Then, you must give me something else."

"Aengus, I said that I will—"

"Your son." He stood and thumbed the rapier at his belt. "He is the only threat."

Startled, Imogen sat a little straighter in her chair. "I think not. He might not be pleased with my decision, but he has not even hinted at challenging me."

"I've seen the look in his eyes. He wants the throne for himself. And if not him, then his future wife."

Imogen narrowed her eyes. Thane had been insufferable as a boy, and she was not fond of his reputation for revelry. He still had much to learn. Choosing the Darragh girl as his betrothed had only highlighted his inexperience. Imogen truly believed that the kingdom was better off in her hands for the time being, but that did not mean she did not care for the boy.

He was her son. He was blood.

"Aengus, I warn you..."

Aengus let out a low laugh. "Now, see, you have given yourself away. You act as though you are as hard as the white stone that surrounds us. That nothing can make you break. Watching you all these years, I've learned how very wrong that is. He is your weakness. Prince Thane."

Imogen's hands clenched in her lap. "You leave my son out of this."

"I've also spent years watching the lad. I know where he revels. I know where he goes alone and unguarded." Aengus braced his hands on the table and leaned toward her. "I'll accept that we cannot get married now, but I need something else. A position of great importance. One with power."

Imogen seethed. He could not get away with this.

"It's been you, hasn't it? You're the one sending the assassins after the girl."

He laughed. "Unfortunately, I cannot take credit for that. I don't care who the prince marries so long as I get what I want."

Imogen stared at her former lover. Because yes, after this, she would never allow him to touch her again. Grinding her teeth, she stared into his eyes. He had played her in a way that no one else ever had. He would do anything for power, and she knew it. He would rip her world apart.

He would kill her son.

"Fine." She punched the table, scattering the pieces once again. "You can have power. A place on the council."

"I need better than that."

"What then?"

But Imogen knew the answer to her question before she even asked it. Aengus wanted more than just a seat on her council. He wanted real power, the kind that he could taste. He wanted to be her right hand. The Grand Alderman. The second most powerful person in the entire realm. And then, if anything ever happened to her—and it would—he would be in the position to take her place. He'd found a way to sit on the throne himself, and this was it. And she would not be able to turn him down, for fear of what he would do to her only living child. Her son's life was at risk, all because she'd welcomed the wrong male into her bed.

Aengus shot her a wicked smile. "Make me your Grand Alderman."

31

MARIEL

Mariel perched in the snow-sodden tree. She was halfway up its thick branches, and the sharp green leaves pierced her bare hands. To others, the yew was poisonous, but it had never done anything more than pierce her skin. A couple of droplets of blood fell, plonking onto the snow far beneath her.

No matter. The hooded figure scurrying through the Witchlight Woods was far enough ahead that she did not notice the splotches of red. Mariel squinted, watching the female's hurried footsteps with keen eyes. She was heading further south, away from Tairngire and its surrounding mountains.

With a deep breath, Mariel leapt from her branch. Sun speared the trees, highlighting her route. She flew through the air, the icy air stinging her cheeks, the harsh wind whipping at her thick trousers. Her booted feet found surface on the next tree's branch, and her fingers curled around a new set of sharp leaves.

Mariel had been keeping a very close eye on the happenings at Dalais Castle. The past few days had been a bustle of frenetic energy. Princess Reyna and that broody warrior had attempted to trap another would-be assassin. And she had smiled when Reyna had demonstrated enough competence for her plot to work.

Unfortunately, it seemed the would-be assassin was on the run now.

With another breath, Mariel pushed off the branch and jumped toward the next. She easily closed the distance and continued along the next branch at a run, leaping once again when the next tree came within touching distance. Mariel smiled to herself, keeping up her pace as if she had raced through the trees a hundred times before.

Because she had.

Once, the castle that loomed to her right had been her home, and she had spent many days traipsing around the woods, climbing trees, and brushing the bottom of her gown against the dirt. She knew every trunk by heart. Now, the nobles who lived in the castle avoided the woods as if they were something to be feared.

As if responding to her very thoughts, the branch creaked beneath her boots. Breath puffing, cheeks warm, she grabbed onto the tree and came to a sudden stop. Mariel cocked her head, listening. Despite her pursuit of the assassin, she took a moment to regard her surroundings, watching and waiting for anything out of the ordinary.

Mariel had learned long ago that the Witchlight Woods were alive. Many believed that Tir Na Nog had been completely drained of magic during the Fall. This just wasn't the case. There were still pockets of power hidden throughout the realms, if one only knew where to look. The Witchlight Woods had always been a great source of power, and it continued to live on even while ancient fae began to wither and die.

As Mariel clung to the branches, the tree rumbled beneath her and wind swept through the brittle leaves. She closed her eyes and breathed in the magic that surrounded her body, scenting the rustling leaves and the pristine snow that doused everything in brilliant white. When she reopened her eyes, a small hole had appeared in the trunk of the tree. Inside, a small blob of sap glistened in the dappled sunlight. Greedily, Mariel pressed her finger against the sap and then brought the honey-like liquid to her tongue. As soon as she tasted the sweet sap, strength and power swirled through her veins.

The sap was one of Mariel's greatest secrets. She was well over a hundred years old, and she was as spritely as a twenty-five-year-old. Her eyesight was keen, her hearing amplified, and she could move with a speed and dexterity that most fae could scarcely remember.

Most fae her age were either dead or growing old as humans did.

Not Mariel.

When she had been nothing more than a wee child, the trees had revealed their secrets to her. Even now, they provided her with their strength. She did not know why they had not given their sap to the nobles who now ruled over these lands. Mariel often wondered if the trees somehow knew how the Selkirks had taken the throne.

With a new, electric magic surging through her veins, Mariel turned her attention back on the pursuit. The would-be assassin was now nothing more than a black speck amongst the towering trees, but it would not take long for Mariel to match her pace.

She leapt, arcing through the air at an almost-impossible speed. Landing on the next branch, she barely took two steps before she soared to the next tree and then the next. The ground far beneath her became a blur. The stinging in her palms from the sharp leaves faded into nothing more than a distant, dull ache.

Mariel felt like the very thing she was: a fae. For many of the inhabitants of this city, that was an impossible feat. She had tried to secure the sap for others, but the trees refused to yield it to anyone but Mariel. If she tried to leave the forest with it, the sap formed a hard lump, which then promptly shattered.

She continued to run through the uppermost branches of the woods, exhilaration pumping through her.

If only the sap could bring back her wings.

The assassin's hooded form became clear through the thick branches, and Mariel began to slow. The fae who had tried to kill Reyna, and then had somehow escaped, might not have Mariel's enhanced hearing, but Mariel did not want to take that chance.

She slowed, quietly stepping from one branch to the next as the fleeing assassin reached the edge of the woods.

Mariel ducked beneath a thick branch, falling into a crouch as she watched the assassin step out from the woods and scan the horizon. What was she searching for? The High Queen? Reyna had suspected that Imogen might be behind these attacks, but it made little sense for the High Queen to be this far into the woods. They had come to where the trees backed onto rolling hills, where thieves were becoming much more abundant. The war brought out the worst in most, especially so in the lands surrounding the castle. Anyone who came or went from Tairngire was at risk, so most never left the safety—or the lack thereof—of those walls.

Very curious indeed.

A lone figure appeared on the horizon, just beyond the slope of the nearest hill. Tall grass poked up from the ground beneath a dusting of untouched snow. The assassin stiffened when she saw the figure, but then she quickly relaxed. Mariel squinted, trying to make out the features of the new arrival even at the distance.

It took a few moments for his face to come into view. He strode forward on an ebony horse whose long dark mane rippled in the harsh breeze. He wore a dark green cap that matched his tunic. Beneath his cap, Mariel could just make out a head of moss-colored hair.

Mariel shifted on the branch, taken by surprise. It should not come as a shock that the Wood Court was involved in a conspiracy to murder Prince Thane's betrothed, but it shocked her all the same. It was a bold move, one that would no doubt have brutal consequences if the High Queen discovered it. She might not be Reyna Darragh's greatest admirer, but this type of assault would not go unpunished.

She frowned, mind whirring. The Air Court was already at war with the wood fae, but it had been almost a decade since an all-out battle had been waged between them. The fighting had died down, almost as though both realms were taking in a deep breath. Mariel could only see this escalating the tension once again, She did not wish to see things return to the near-constant struggles of her people, to the death and the blood and the fear.

Tairngire itself had never come under attack. If it did, thousands upon thousands would die.

Steadying herself on the branch, she waited while the wood fae approached. The assassin stepped toward him, her body tense and uncertain.

"You should not have come here," he said sharply, his hooded eyes flicking toward the woods behind the assassin. "Are you certain you weren't followed?"

"No one followed me." The assassin shook her head,

taking another step toward him. "I have been found out. I need somewhere to go. If I stay here, they will kill me."

"You were found out? How?"

"In my attempt to kill Princess Reyna, I...well, I misjudged her. She is the Shieldmaiden the rumors claim. I stood no chance against her. She caught me in the act, and then she had me taken into the dungeons where I was to be thoroughly questioned. Another tried to stop her. One of the guards you must have turned. But I believe she killed him, too."

Mariel smiled.

"I see," the wood fae said quietly. "That makes three of our spies that she has felled."

"Three?" the assassin asked. "She killed the original assassin, and then the guard who tried to stop her outside of the dungeon. No others."

Mariel cocked her head, listening closer.

"Perhaps we should have focused more on her sister. She needs to die as well if we wish to wed Princess Etaine to the Thane boy."

Interesting. Mariel pursed her lips, understanding at once the plot. The wood fae wanted the Darragh family out of the picture completely. Glencora, the eldest, was no longer a concern. Apparently, she had come down with a terrible illness. The other two girls were a problem though, at least according to the wood fae. Either could easily sit on the throne beside the future High King, confirming an alliance between their Air and Ice courts indefinitely.

But the wood fae did not want that alliance to proceed. They wanted a princess of the Wood Court to wed Prince Thane instead.

And they were willing to kill for it.

"If Thane had never turned down our proposal in the

first place, none of this would have been necessary," the wood fae muttered to himself.

Even more interesting. Mariel had not heard that there were discussions between the Air and Wood Courts. That information had been kept tightly under wraps. Knowing how the High Queen felt about Thane's betrothal to Reyna, Mariel could not help but wonder why Imogen had chosen that route.

It did not make a great deal of sense.

The Wood Court had greater resources, a larger army, and a direct southern trade link with the Empire of Fomor. The wood fae also sat directly between the air fae lands and Findius, the former capital of the exiles, which the Air Court currently controlled. From a purely objective standpoint, the air fae would be in a much better position if they allied with the Wood Court.

The only possible downside to their joined courts was the Wood Court's current ruler, High King Ulaid Molt. He ruled the wood fae as a tyrant, terrible and wicked and cruel. But the Selkirks were not much better themselves.

"You will need to focus your efforts on the younger sister," the assassin said. "She is far more vulnerable than Reyna. A threat could do the trick. If Reyna believes Eislyn is in danger…"

The wood fae's sharp gaze rested on the assassin's face. "Have you spoken to anyone about this? Is anyone inside that castle aware that you are our spy?"

The assassin shook her head quickly, and Mariel's stomach turned over on itself. The assassin clearly did not see what was coming, but Mariel did. And she had no desire to stop it. This fae had tried to kill Reyna, and she had suggested to target Eislyn next. The younger Darragh sister was an innocent, swept up in the intrigue. She did not deserve to die.

The wood fae smiled, lifted his sword, and sliced through the assassin's neck without even a moment's warning. Her head fell clean off and thumped onto the ground, droplets of blood mingling with the dusting of snow. Mariel pressed her lips together and watched as the wood fae wrapped her body in a cloak and then tied it to the back of his horse. A moment later, he took off toward the hills, dragging the dead assassin's body behind him.

Mariel watched him go with fire in her heart. The Wood Court wanted to destroy her city, her world, her fae. She might not sit on that throne, but the people were hers all the same.

But she didn't know how to stop them without bringing the war through the city gates.

32

REYNA

A hooded form dropped through her open window. Reyna jumped to her feet, whisking her blade out from beneath her pillow. She had managed to keep it, even after the incidents. No one had tried to take it from her. Yet. She knew it would only be a matter of time.

The hood dropped back, revealing Mariel's ethereal face. This night, she looked far younger than she had the last time Reyna had seen her, though the shadows pulsing through the darkened bedchamber could be playing with Reyna's eyes.

Mariel's gaze flicked toward the dagger. "I did not come here to murder you in your sleep, though I doubt I even could, if that was my objective. I hear you are quite accomplished with your blade there."

Reyna sighed and lowered her hand. "You gave me quite the fright. Why are you leaping into my window in the middle of the night? And, more to the point, how did you even get up here? Only my owl can get in and out this way. That's why the window is open. He's out hunting."

Reyna's chambers were near the top of the tower. The only thing below her was the bay. Mariel should not have been able to reach the window unless…no, she could not have wings. That was impossible. She regarded the tavern owner carefully. There was something…different about this low fae. Her movements were smooth and graceful, her eyes were sharp and keen. In fact, her entire presence exuded strength.

"Nevermind how I got here." Mariel dropped back her hood and began to pace the length of the room. She twisted her hands together, deeply frowning. "Your assassin escaped."

Shocked, Reyna stood a little taller and grabbed her cloak from the bedpost to wrap around her shoulders. Not for warmth, but because she was quickly realizing that she should be wearing more than her thin white nightclothes for this conversation. "I know. I was there when it happened. I went into the dungeons to question her, but another showed up to fight. In the end, she got away while I was busy fighting."

Mariel gave her an appraising glance. "A guard?"

"It seems that way."

"I have been doing my own spying, as you requested." Mariel suddenly stopped pacing to stand before Reyna. Her eyes sparked, her chin held high. She almost looked afraid but defiantly so. "I saw her fleeing the castle and decided to follow her."

Reyna's ears pricked up. This was far more than she could have hoped for. Desperate to discover who Ula had been working for, Reyna would have trailed her, but that pesky guard had gotten in her way. She had realized that had been the intention. The guard had only appeared the moment Reyna had unlocked Ula's cell door.

"Please tell me that she didn't manage to lose you in the chase," Reyna replied.

Mariel smiled. "She did not even know I was there."

Excitement tripped through her veins. This was it. The moment she would have confirmation that the High Queen was behind these attacks, providing her with the very hammer she needed to knock her off the throne. Thane would not stand for it. The High Queen would be forced to step down. And then the prince would take her place, marry Reyna, and then...

And then Reyna would have to kill him.

She frowned. "Well? Where did she go? To the High Queen?"

Mariel pursed her lips, that same strange combination of fear and defiance swirling through her sun-warmed eyes. "Before I tell you, I would like some assurances."

Reyna narrowed her eyes. "Assurances of what?"

"A promise."

"A promise?" Reyna took a step back. "I don't make promises."

Promises were deadly things. Few fae were willing to touch them. Even as the magic had vanished from the kingdoms, the power of a fae's word remained as true and as strong as ever. She would make bargains or deals, but she never spoke the word *promise* aloud when she did. Because she would be forever bound to it. It was why her father had never allowed her to become a true sworn Shieldmaiden. And now, she saw why. He had always hoped she would return to courtly life.

"If you don't make the promise, then I cannot tell you," Mariel said quietly.

Reyna frowned at the low fae. A desperation to fight against her words rose within her, but as she stared into those fierce eyes, she came to an understanding. Mariel would not back down. Whatever she had discovered had truly disturbed her, and she would take the information to her grave if she must.

"What is the promise?" Reyna asked.

"You must promise me that you will not tell the High Queen or Prince Thane."

"I…" Reyna furrowed her brows. "But—"

Mariel held up a hand. "It was neither of them."

A strange sensation prickled on the back of Reyna's neck. She had been so certain that the High Queen was involved. Who else would want Reyna and Eislyn dead? And, if she could not tell Prince Thane, then how could she use that information to her advantage?

She flicked her eyes toward the door. Outside, she knew Lorcan stood guard, protecting her from would-be assassins and keeping her from sneaking off into the woods. Mariel had said nothing about the warrior.

"Fine. I promise I will not tell Prince Thane or the High Queen."

Instantly, a strange sensation washed over Reyna. A flicker of magic, filling up her blood.

Mariel gave her a grim smile. "Good choice, though I must warn you, you are not going to enjoy hearing this. The wood fae are behind the attacks. They want to murder you and put their own Princess Etaine in your place."

Reyna could only stand and stare at Mariel in shock. The Wood Court? It was a plot that had never occurred to her. "Why in the name of the Dagda would they believe that Thane would even agree to that?"

"Apparently, the Air Court originally considered an alliance with them, far before they considered an alliance with the Ice Court." Mariel paused and gave her a meaningful look. "The two were to join forces against you instead."

Reyna curled her hands into fists. "They are mortal enemies. The battles between them have been far worse than anything encountered on ice fae soil."

Mariel shrugged. "The Wood Court has a far larger army and trade routes with the Empire of Fomor."

"So do we," Reyna argued. The trade route between the Empire of Fomor and the Ice Court had been well-established far before the beginning of the war. In fact, they had traded for centuries, using one of the only safe passages between the two continents. The Fomorians were a secretive lot, and they refused to allow Tir Na Nog fae to sail to their shores. Instead, they traded solely through two islands that stood between the continents. Up north, through Tuath Isle, and down south, through Deas Isle. It left the Ice and Wood Courts in control of very important land.

"Your trade route in the far north goes through icy waters, which is far less effective than the smooth sailing from the Wood Court's ports. They were the ideal option, Reyna. We both know it. And yet, for some reason, they chose you."

Reyna frowned. It certainly was curious, but that was a puzzle to decipher at a later time. The important thing was, the High Queen was not in fact trying to murder Reyna. Instead, the wood fae were. That changed everything. She could now see why Mariel had insisted on the promise. If Reyna went to either Thane or Imogen about these discoveries, they would no doubt restart the battles with the Wood Court in earnest. Hundreds of fae would die in the battles, and cities would surely fall. Perhaps even Tairngire. She could not fault Mariel for wanting to keep the people safe.

"And you are certain of this?" Reyna asked quietly, absently fingering her ice ring.

Mariel gave her a fierce look. "I would not reveal this type of information unless I knew with absolute certainty it were true."

Reyna nodded, gazing out the open window at the dark waters below. She could not see the city from this side of the castle, but she could imagine it in her mind's eye. Miles of buildings lit up from inside, smoke puffing up from stonework chimneys. So many lives.

Suddenly, a thought occurred to her. "You say you saw her go to the Wood Court. How did you manage that? The border is weeks away."

Mariel pressed her lips together into a thin line. "I can't be sure, but it sounds as if there is a small contingent of them hiding out in the hills just south of the Witchlight Woods. I do not know how many. I didn't risk being seen."

Alarmed, Reyna paced to the window and stared out, steeling herself as the wind blasted her face. "How would a group of wood fae avoid being spotted by the patrol? Though...the king controlled those, I believe. Did those warriors stop patrolling after he abdicated?"

"I have told you all I know."

She pushed away from the window, turning to face Mariel once again. "All right. Thank you for this. You have given me much to think about."

"What will you do?" Mariel asked, taking a step toward her, eyes hard. "They will not give up, you know. Your sister is in danger, too."

Reyna's hands fisted. "I know. They will need to be certain no Darragh will marry Thane. It's the only way they can ensure their princess will end up as his bride. I do not know what I will do, but I must stop them."

Mariel nodded, moved toward the window, but then hesitated. "May I make just one request, Your Highness?"

Reyna nodded. "Of course."

"Please make your choices carefully. We have been at war for a century. These people need peace." And, with that, Mariel hopped onto the ledge and disappeared into the night. Reyna watched her go, her mind whirling from the information she had just learned.

But before she could gather her thoughts, a click sounded from her drawing room. Footsteps thudded on the floor. And then a dark form filled her open bedchamber door.

"One might wonder about your sanity," Lorcan said, hand resting on the hilt of his sword. He leaned against the doorframe, sizing her up. Her cheeks flushed. She wore only her thin, white linen nightclothes beneath her cloak. They were fairly see-through, and the wind was cool, blasting into her bedroom through the open window.

She swallowed hard, memories of his hands and lips rushing through her like churning waves, threatening to pull her under. Their moments together had been nothing more than illusion, like dark magic. But she had felt something from his touch. She couldn't deny it, even if she tried. Her skin had come alive beneath his breath, his hands, his lips.

Of course, the last thing she wanted was for Lorcan to know how he'd made her feel.

Reyna glared at him. "Don't you ever sleep? No, don't answer that. I can tell you don't. Some might say you look dreadful."

But Reyna didn't think he looked dreadful at all. As always, he exuded power and strength, his well-muscled chest enhanced by his fitted leather armor.

"Rarely. And do you often have conversations with yourself?" His dark eyes flicked across her body, noting her cloak, and then lingered a moment on her peaked nipples clearly visible through her whisper-thin garments.

"I often have conversations with my owl."

He glanced at the open window. "Why are you out of bed and wearing a cloak? Going somewhere?"

"Are you asking me these questions because you hope to get me alone in the woods again? That was just a trap, Lorcan. It was nothing real."

A wicked smile curled his lips. "Interesting that your mind would go there."

"Do your guard duties now include harassing me in the middle of the night?"

"They do if I hear you speaking to someone."

"Go away."

"Tell me why you're awake, and I will." He smirked and crossed his arms. Rolling her eyes, she let out a frustrated sigh. Clearly, he wasn't going away until she gave him something.

"I'm having trouble sleeping."

An honest remark. Reyna had been fitfully flailing in her bed before Mariel's sudden arrival through the window. She could not get her mind to calm down, which meant her body was wound as tightly as a coiled dragon. Ula's escape had rubbed her nerves raw. She'd been so close to answers, and they had fallen through her fingers like shifting sand.

In the end, she had been right. Just not in the way she had expected.

Lorcan's face softened, but only slightly. "Perhaps if you didn't go rushing into danger headfirst, then you would not be so prone to sleepless nights."

"I appreciate the advice," she said with an eye roll. "Now, can you please go back to your post? I'm definitely not going to sleep with you lurking in the doorway like that."

He shifted into the room and settled into a chair beside

the bed, smiling all the while. "I think I will wait right here where I can keep an eye on you."

Frustration bloomed in Reyna's gut. "That is ridiculous. You can keep an eye on me just fine *outside*."

"Apparently not. Because you were just speaking to someone *in here*."

Reyna's mouth fell open. "That would require someone else to be here. Go ahead and check beneath the bed if you must."

The chair creaked beneath him as he leaned back, clearly getting comfortable. "Whoever it was is long gone by now."

"You came through the only door in this room."

He gestured at the window.

"The window?" She arched her brows. "You don't honestly believe that someone managed to scale the walls and come through the window, do you?"

"Why don't you tell me?" He smiled. "Did someone come through that window?"

Reyna's mouth snapped shut. And then she opened it again. Whirling toward the window, she stomped over to it and poked her head outside. There were no hidden ladders, no hooks jutting out of the stone. It was a sheer drop down to the cliffs where churning water splashed against the jagged rocks.

Heart thumping, she could not imagine how Mariel had scaled the thing but she had. She pulled her head back inside and twisted toward Lorcan. "Just look outside if you must. How would anyone have done such a thing?"

He made no move toward the window. "Just answer yes or no, Reyna. Did someone come through the window?"

She glared at him, fisted hands trembling by her sides. "In polite society, one never demands the answer to a yes or no question."

"And one never provides yes or no to such a question." He stood and stalked toward her, still smiling. "Because then one can never hide her deepest secrets."

Her heart thumped hard. Lorcan stared deeply into her eyes, darkness swirling through his irises. She itched to back away from him, to turn and flee from his inspection. But she couldn't even if she truly wanted to—and she wasn't entirely certain she did. It almost felt as though he could read her very soul, as if he could see every secret that she kept hidden from everyone else. The truth about why she had come here. Her fears that she would be found out, and that Eislyn would take a share of the blame.

Fear that the lands of Tir Na Nog would one day be covered in endless darkness.

Suddenly, he pulled back. She gasped, and hated herself for it.

"I will not answer your question, Lorcan," she whispered.

"In polite society, fae dismiss yes or no questions because they know that one day they will be asked something that would reveal a deep, dark secret," he said almost too softly for her to hear. "For you to refuse to answer, to play that game of words, tells me one important thing, Reyna Darragh. You have a secret. A terrible one. Just like the rest of us."

33

THANE

"Mother."

The High Queen glanced up from where she sat swirling a golden chalice of wine on her throne. Even in one of her magnificent gowns, she slumped sideways, one leg propped up on the vine seat's arm. Her eyes were half-lidded. Her cheeks were a blazing pink. Clearly, she was drunk. Thane frowned.

"I thought you did not believe in revelry, Mother." He had not seen her drink a drop in years. In fact, he was not certain he *ever* had. She liked others to believe it was in dedication to the Dagda, but Thane knew that it was tactical. She believed drinking would make her mind too slow, too prone to making errors, too likely to mistake hidden lies for the truth.

"I don't," she said, voice strangely clear. "I am not revelling. That would suggest some amount of good cheer."

He sighed and strode up the dais, gently taking the half-empty chalice from her drooping hand. Settling it onto the floor, he remembered why he had come here, and it was not to take care of a drunken queen.

He glanced at his uncle, who stood by his side, an encouraging presence. Lord Bowen gave a nod.

"Mother," he said again. And this time, his voice was firmer. "Uncle and I have just gone into the Council Room and found your lover sitting in the head seat."

"Oh, that." She waved dismissively, drawling her words like a drunken bard. "I named him my Grand Alderman."

Thane glanced at his uncle, and a meaningful glance passed between them.

He had been worried it was something like that. Lord Bowen had been the Grand Alderman during the High King's reign. When Thane's father had abdicated, Imogen had replaced the entire council, and had kicked Lord Bowen out of his seat. But she had not yet named a new Grand Alderman. She did not trust anyone with the title. Except, it appeared, the lover that helped her steal the throne.

"And did you have the wine before or after you put a scheming bastard in the second most powerful position in this kingdom?" Thane asked.

"Empire," she slurred. "You should start calling it an empire."

"I cannot start calling it an empire, Mother. We have an alliance with the Ice Court, yes, but our two kingdoms will not fully join together until I marry Princess Reyna and become the High King," he said through clenched teeth. "Which, as I'm sure you'll recall, has been put on pause. *Because of you.*"

She let out a heavy sigh, slumping further into the mess of vines. "You sound so agitated, my son. Why don't you join me for a drink? I know you love your wine."

"Imogen," his uncle said, frowning. "This is quite irregular. Aengus has no titles. He's had no experience in ruling a kingdom. No one even knows where he comes from. For all we know, he could be a shadow fae."

Imogen laughed, a cackling, high-pitched sound that echoed through the desolate Great Hall. "He isn't clever enough to be a shadow fae."

"He was clever enough to worm his way into the seat of the Grand Alderman," Lord Bowen argued.

She turned to Thane's uncle with piercing eyes. "And so were you."

"As Sloane's brother and a lord, that was an ideal choice," Lord Bowen said with a sad sigh. "And, speaking of Sloane, no one has seen him for weeks. What have you done with him, Imogen?"

"Oh, please," she said with an eye roll. "You know as well as I do that he scurried off to your castle down south to hide from his shame. Feurach Fortress is dreary enough for my tiresome husband to find enticing."

Thane closed his eyes, desperately calling upon patience he was not certain he had. "Mother. You cannot allow Aengus to be our Grand Alderman. There is no telling what he will do. If you thought Father's atrocities were bad—"

"I know exactly what he will do." She sat up a little straighter, her eyes suddenly clear. "He will scheme and plot, gaining himself more power. Eventually, he will best us all."

Thane regarded her carefully. "You're the one who put him in that position."

"Yes. Because I had no other choice."

"And so now your solution is to drink it all away instead of doing something about it?"

What frustrated Thane the most was not that Aengus had somehow weaselled his way into the position. It was that his mother was sitting back and allowing it to happen.

That was unlike her. For better or worse, Imogen was a force to be reckoned with. No one, not even her own son, had challenged her move to take the throne. She had that kind of power.

What in the name of the Dagda did Aengus hold over her?

Her long sigh whistled through the room. "Do not worry, my son. I will handle it."

"How?" he demanded.

"I do not know," she whispered.

He turned to his uncle. They had discussed this. It was the last thing either of them wanted, but neither of them saw another way. Lord Bowen gave him a kind smile, nodding gently for Thane to go ahead with their plan.

"All right." Thane squared his shoulders, lifting his chin. He had not wanted it to come to this, but she had forced his hand. "I am no longer going to sit by and allow this to happen. The throne is mine. I am the true heir and the High King of the Air Court. I challenge your rule."

Imogen stared at him for so long that Thane thought she might have fallen asleep with her eyes open. After a long while, she began to laugh. "My dear, idiot son. You have made your challenge, but you need witnesses. Go back to your chambers and think on it. Or go revel for hours. Get drunk. Do as you always do. If you still feel the same the next time you see me, then make your challenge then."

"I witnessed it." Lord Bowen crossed his arms over his golden tunic. "And I will inform the courtiers and the druids alike of Thane's challenge."

Imogen narrowed her eyes and stood shakily from the throne. "You are not ready to rule this kingdom. Do not make this mistake."

"I have made my decision, Mother. And I'll have my coronation by month's end."

"There are those in this court who are loyal to me," she said with a hiss. "I could bring my armies against you."

"Just step down, Imogen," Lord Bowen said quietly. "There's no need for bloodshed. Your son is the rightful ruler. Let him rule."

Imogen gave one last hiss, snatched her chalice from the floor, and stormed out of the Great Hall, leaving Thane to stare into the face of his future. The throne of vines and thorns. The Seat of Power for the air fae lands. He would finally become what he was always meant to be. A High King.

※

"I cannot believe I did that," Thane said quietly to his uncle as they strode down the corridor. His heart still raced from his conversation with the High Queen. All his life, he had always bowed before her. She was his mother. They might rarely agree, but he had always loved her.

"You did well, my son." Lord Bowen clasped his shoulder and squeezed tight.

Pride filled Thane's chest. "Thank you for your support. I do not know if I could have done it without you."

"Of course you could have. You just needed a little encouragement."

"I hope I didn't make a mistake."

"You did the right thing," his uncle said. "For yourself and for your people."

Thane glanced up at him. "Do you believe she ordered those attacks on Reyna?"

Lord Bowen sighed as they continued down the corridor, lit only by flickering sconces along the white stone walls. "Have you heard her deny it?"

"She has never denied it." Thane frowned. "She feels she shouldn't have to answer accusations."

"And the spymaster? What has he found?"

"Nothing conclusive, but he did find that Ula, the lady's maid, visited my mother in her chambers not a week past."

Lord Bowen winced. "That is hardly proof, but it is suggestive."

Thane sighed. "Regardless, I must go to Reyna now and tell her of my challenge for the throne. We will need to be wed soon after the coronation. It will strengthen my position within the kingdom, and bring our courts fully together."

Lord Bowen frowned, which caught Thane off guard. That was not the reaction he had been expecting from his uncle.

"What is it, Uncle?" Thane asked.

"The princess." Lord Bowen shook his head, his expression troubled. "After what she did, are you certain she is a good match? A good choice for the future High Queen of the Air Court?"

Thane frowned. He wanted nothing more than to protect his kingdom. Part of that protection included presenting a very solid, very secure ruling family. A marriage to a high-ranking noble, preferably a princess, would assist with that. And wedding a Darragh sister was essential to the alliance with the Ice Court.

Still, his relationship with Reyna had not progressed as he had hoped. Arranged marriages often resulted in two unhappy parties, but he did not think it had to be that way. He had been willing to try to love her, but she had barely even spoken with him since coming to court.

But the true issue was her rebelliousness, her wildness.

COURT OF RUINS

She had sneaked into the dungeons, allowed a prisoner to escape, and then had killed a guard. What else would she do? Could he trust her in the position of High Queen?

"She is an odd one, but I do not believe she's anything more than that. She means well, I think." Thane patted his uncle on the back. "I appreciate your concern. I will make sure to keep a close eye on her. In the meantime...I need to tell her about the coronation."

Lord Bowen frowned but did not argue. Instead, he trailed after the prince as he strode through the corridors and arrived at Reyna's chambers where Lorcan stood guard just outside her door. For a moment, Thane could not help but worry he would walk in and find she'd gone off on another one of her wild adventures. She did not seem to be overly fond of sitting still for very long.

Lorcan arched a brow, as if surprised to see the prince visiting his betrothed. He cast a glance toward Lord Bowen before meeting Thane's eyes again. "Evening, Thane. Everything all right?"

"I need to see Reyna. I assume she's here."

"Unless she's flown out the window, then yes." Lorcan gave a knock on the door, and then pushed it open. Inside, Reyna sat in a pair of silken silver trousers and a matching tunic, glaring out the open window at the Bay of Wind. Her owl sat beside her, flaring his wings against the wind. She started when the door opened, and then pushed to her bare feet. Even in her private chambers, she truly ought to be wearing a gown in case any courtiers came to visit her. There was much she needed to learn. No matter. He would ensure she was taught quickly.

"Prince Thane. Lord Bowen." She glanced at Lorcan but didn't greet him.

"I need to speak with you about something," he said in a strong, kingly voice, one that sounded far more like his father than he ever thought possible. He motioned for his uncle to join him in the room. Lorcan followed close behind, shutting the door behind them.

Reyna frowned, glancing from Lorcan to Lord Bowen and then to Thane.

"Is something the matter?" she asked.

Why did everyone keep asking him that? Was it truly that odd that he would visit his betrothed?

"I've decided to challenge my mother for the throne. She will step aside and allow me to become the rightful king, or I will be forced to turn my warriors against her. We will marry soon after."

"You're going to do what?" Lorcan asked sharply.

"Take the throne, Lorcan. Just like I should have as soon as my father stepped down."

Reyna stared at him, clearly shocked. She clutched at the bottom of her tunic, squeezing the material in her fist. Her eyes trailed over to Lorcan, and she shifted on her feet. "That…is surprising. I didn't think you wanted to do that. Why have you had a change of heart?"

He clenched his hands. "I fear my mother has been poorly counselled. She has made some discouraging mistakes, particularly in regards to a male whose name I refuse to utter. Add in the strange business with the assassins, and I truly do not know what to think. The court will be far better off if I just take the throne myself."

Twin pink dots appeared on Reyna's cheeks. "You're doing this because you believe she may have had a hand in the assassination attempts?"

"Partially." He nodded. "I did not want to think so, but I'm beginning to realize that she would go to great lengths in order to get what she wants."

Reyna pressed her lips together and turned back toward the window. Wingallock pushed up from the stone seat and flew to her side, settling onto her shoulder. Frowning, Thane stayed where he was, waiting for a reply. Reyna Darragh had been wildly unpredictable from the moment they'd met, but he thought she would be happy about this news.

This melancholy response was…confusing. Females often were.

"Is something the matter, Princess Reyna?" he asked after several moments passed in silence. "I thought you would be pleased. I know you've been concerned about the current atmosphere here."

Reyna twisted toward him with a pinched smile. "Apologies. I just want what is best for both of our kingdoms. And for my sister's safety."

"Ah, I see. You're worried my mother will make an attempt on Eislyn's life, even if I take the throne. Retaliation, perhaps?" He frowned. "She never does anything without purpose. Harming your sister does not help her in the least."

For a moment, Reyna's eyes went sharp. "It might if she wanted to ensure that you couldn't marry any Darragh sister at all. I believe you were considering another princess for a time. Etaine, from the Wood Court."

Lorcan let out an awkward cough, and Thane paused for a moment. How had she learned about that old scheme? It hadn't even been his. It had been his father's. One of the courtiers must have mentioned it to her. Gossips, the lot of them.

"My mother never wanted me to marry Princess Etaine. My father did," he admitted. "When I chose to ally our court with yours, he was none too pleased."

Reyna gave him a frank look. She did not look the least bit surprised. "Why did you make a different choice?"

"I refuse to ally myself with that king." He ground out

the words, but then shook his head. "But none of that matters. It had nothing to do with my mother. You and your sister are both safe here."

"I am not certain I agree with that," she said softly. "I can take care of myself. But Eislyn..."

Thane frowned as the meaning of her words sank in. "You wish to send her away."

He thought of the small silver-haired fae with her strangely haunting eyes and that laughter that sounded like music on the wind. He had visited her in the library as often as possible in the past days, pouring through books while she searched for a way to save her people. He knew that Eislyn was troubled, sad, and often scared, but she was kinder than anyone he had ever met. She was a pure soul.

A soul that he did not want to see corrupted by this wicked place.

Thane didn't want to send her away. But he'd do whatever he had to in order to keep her safe.

"Very well," he said, clenching his jaw. "If that is what you think is best, then we can have her returned home this week."

Reyna let out an audible sigh of relief, smiling now, even as her eyes were glazed with tears. She truly must have been worried about her sister. All because his mother had wanted to send a sharp and brutal message.

Message received, Thane thought bitterly.

34
REYNA

Reyna paced. Her heart pounded, and her palms were slick with sweat. She didn't understand why she was so on edge, as if she were standing on the crumbling rocks of a cliff with nothing to hold onto but an unravelling rope tied to a broken tree. This was everything she wanted. Thane would take over and sit on the throne. Eislyn would return home, far away from the danger of the Air Court.

She would marry the new king. She would kill him.

And then the kingdom would become hers. She would rule it without the wicked influence of the Selkirk family, bringing the air fae and the ice fae together as one. They would make a formidable alliance. A real one. Not one where half of the alliance murdered the other.

Still, she could not stop herself from trembling as Wingallock swooped nervously through the drawing room, knocking unlit candles off the chandelier. The situation was far more complicated than it had seemed at first. A band of wood fae were hiding out in the hills not far from the castle, plotting against the Air Court. There were spies lurking everywhere. Reyna was certain there were even more fae inside the castle, working for the Wood Court.

What would they do next? Who would they target?

She strode into her bedchamber and grabbed the knife from beneath her mattress. Then, she grabbed her cloak and pulled it tightly around her shoulders. There was no time to waste. Reyna must do something about the wood fae. She had to confront them before someone else found out they were there, before the war brought bloodshed to these city walls.

But what would she say? And how could she stop them from trying to kill her the moment she stepped foot on those hills? The wood fae clearly wanted something, and they would not stop until they had it.

They wanted their own princess on the throne.

Reyna could not give them that, but perhaps she could help them in another way. It would be a bit of a risk, but no great plans were ever easy. And she had no other choice. She knew they would keep coming for her, even if she married Thane. The only solution was to offer them something else instead. Something better.

Princess Etaine had two brothers, both older than she. Reyna would be free to marry either one after Thane's death. And, in Tir Na Nog, kings had more power than queens. Her kingdoms would become her husband's. If they allied, he would get two rather than just the one. Of course, she knew very little about these two princes. Were they kind? Were they honorable? Would either of them be any better than Thane?

Things were getting very complicated.

It was a dangerous plot, one that required her to play her hand. She would have to tell the Wood Court how she planned to seize control of the Air Court. But it was the only choice she had. The alternative was to tell Lorcan, who would no doubt tell Thane, who would then be forced to send his armies against his enemy. The Ice Court would get wrapped up in it all. So many of her people would die.

So, it was settled then.

"Wingallock," she whispered. Her owl flew down from the ceiling and curled his talons around her shoulder. He blinked at her, his tormented soul matching hers. "I need you to create a distraction so I can sneak out of here. But please, distraction only. And then return here where it's safe."

He hooted, displeased. He did not like Reyna rushing into danger alone.

But she would not risk her familiar's life.

With another agitated hoot, Wingallock took off through the window. A moment later, a heavy thud echoed in the corridor outside her chambers. Lorcan let out a shout. Footsteps pounded on the stone floor. She pressed an ear to the wood, listening. As soon as the footsteps faded into the distance, she threw the door open and ran.

She raced through the castle, retracing her steps. The towers and connecting walls were a maze of identical corridors. Fire flickered on the walls, a blur as she ran past. Dust swirled around her as her boots scuffed the ground.

Soon, she found the hidden tunnel. The wall that led out to the sea. She pressed a hand against the stone and closed her eyes, smiling when the pulse of magic responded to her touch. The hidden wall fell away, and she raced into the night.

Outside, bulbous clouds hid the moons from view, and a heavy rumble threatened rain. The temperature had warmed these past weeks, and the snow had already begun to melt. Patches of grass could be seen through the white. A strange longing filled Reyna's heart.

But no matter. Now was not the time to be thinking of ice.

She ran down the dirt path that led deep into the Witchlight Woods, boots slurping on the melted snow. It would not take long for Lorcan to realize she'd gone. Reyna needed to find the wood fae fast, before guards were sent out to track her down.

A sharp *crack* rang out behind her, the breaking of a branch. She whirled toward the sound, and a tall, muscular figure loomed from the shadows of the woods.

"Evening, princess."

35

LORCAN

Reyna stared at him, unblinking. Her cheeks were flushed as the wild wind tossed her hair around her shoulders. With the flutter of her cloak, the rustle of her silver tunic, and the dagger clutched in her hand, Reyna Darragh was no princess. She was a warrior. Fierce, strong, courageous.

Of course, this wasn't going to make Thane happy. What could she possibly be doing out here this time?

"Mind telling me why you're stomping around the woods with a dagger?"

"Go back to the castle, Lorcan," she said, stalking away from him.

He laughed, easily matching her stride, even though she made no attempt to mask her hurry. "You can't get rid of me that easily."

"Why not?" she asked, continuing her determined trek forward. "Shouldn't you have more pressing matters to attend to?"

"Such as?" he asked.

He didn't fail to notice that she'd avoided his question.

She clearly didn't want him to know what she was doing in the woods, her boots churning up clumps of wet snow. He had only known her for a short while, but he already understood her far better than he understood most. She had a spark in her eye and a determined set to her jaw. Whatever she was up to, she felt it was important.

"Getting my sister out of the city, for instance," she said as they passed the clearing where they'd trapped the assassin. And rolled around in the snow together, arms twined.

"Well, for one, it's the middle of the night. Two, you only just decided to send her home. We cannot just cart her out of the city with no warning."

"Perhaps you should," she said with a frown, still hurriedly rushing down the path.

"If you're so worried for her safety, then why are you out here traipsing in the woods instead of standing watch outside her chambers?"

She stopped suddenly and pointed her dagger at him. "And I suppose you would allow me to do that?"

"No," he said with a smile. "But when has that ever stopped you?"

Reyna rolled her eyes and resumed her rush down the wooded path. With a sigh, he followed suit. She moved quickly through the thick trees, ducking beneath snow-laden branches. Even against the slushy ground, she moved easily, her feet finding purchase against the slick surface.

He followed just behind, watching her movement. Her head swivelled from left to right. Occasionally, she stopped to examine a branch. She was clearly in search of something, though what she expected to find in these woods, he could hardly wager a guess.

He grabbed her arm. "Reyna, if you do not tell me what you're doing out here, I will be forced to carry you back to the castle. Thane's orders."

She yanked her arm away and whirled to face him. "I believe Ula came through here when she escaped. So, I'm following her trail."

He arched a brow. "Thane made it clear that he doesn't like you chasing after assassins in the woods."

She mumbled something beneath her breath.

"What was that?" he asked.

She sighed. "I said I do not care if he likes it or not."

"That is deliciously blunt." He smiled. "You have not fallen for his charms then?"

She gave him a piercing look. "What *charms*?"

"The charms that every female at court sees, other than you."

"No, I can't say I've noticed these charms," she said hotly. "But I've been fairly distracted by the repeated assassination attempts against me and my sister."

Lorcan frowned, though secretly, he felt pleased. Reyna and Thane clearly made a terrible match. He'd thought that from the moment he'd discovered that Glencora was ill. Thane would be far better off with someone else. Reyna would, too. She needed someone just as rebellious as herself. Someone who didn't care about court, or fashionable clothes, or simpering lords and ladies.

Someone who appreciated her for exactly who she was. Someone who never wanted that spark to fizzle out.

"I'm sure Thane will be displeased to hear that," Lorcan said, rather than voicing his thoughts aloud. Even if Reyna had not fallen for Thane's charms, she was still very much his betrothed. And she would remain that way, as long as he didn't let her run off into the woods to chase down assassins.

"I am entirely certain that Thane is aware our marriage is simply for the alliance." She shook her head and spun back toward the branch she had been inspecting. "Now, let me be. I can't track when I'm talking."

He inched up beside her and peered down at the branch. At the very end, where the bark narrowed into a sharp point, the branch had broken, as if someone had rushed by.

"A female of many talents," he murmured. "You can track as well as fight."

She shot him an odd look. "It's strange that you think those are talents. Most don't, particularly not my father."

"Why wouldn't I? You are fire with a dagger. I can only imagine what you can do with a sword. And the ability to track? Most fae are never taught that."

"I'm a princess. I'm not supposed to have the skills of a warrior."

With that, she pushed away from the tree and continued forward. Lorcan fell into step beside her, keeping an ear out for any sign of an approaching enemy, just in case any thieves lurked in the woods. He knew that he should stop her, even if that meant tossing her over his shoulder and returning her to the castle, kicking and screaming. But, in truth, he was intrigued. If the assassin truly had escaped this way, and they could find her, then they still had a hope of discovering who she had been working for.

And Thane needed to know if it had been his mother. He'd become certain that she'd been involved, but there was no proof. He needed to know the facts, one way or another.

A little voice in the back of his mind whispered to him, reminding him that he needed to focus on his mission. His mark even flickered a warning. All of this prancing around and seeking assassins was nothing more than a distraction, a diversion from his true goal. But

Lorcan's goal had become so muddied over the years. He had spent so long by Thane's side that he could no longer remember why he'd been so fuelled by vengeance all this time.

He no longer thought of Thane as his enemy.

It was a truth he'd tried so hard to ignore, but he couldn't anymore. Reyna's arrival at the Air Court had brought out something strange in him, a realization of who he'd become. No longer was he a male who hid in the shadows. He was part of the Air Court now. Suddenly, pain shot through his arm where his mark blazed to life. Gritting his teeth, he stumbled.

I didn't mean it, he told the mark. *Thane is my enemy.*

Immediately, the pain vanished.

Reyna had stopped and turned when he'd stumbled, and now, she was watching him with hawkish eyes. "What's the matter?"

"Nothing," he said. "I just tripped on some snow."

"You were wincing and clutching your shoulder. You've done that before. Is it a wound?"

"I said I'm fine," he growled.

The ice fae continued to regard him carefully, but then she shrugged and kept moving through the trees. Lorcan did not know what he was going to do. Clearly, the mark would never let him forget his mission. It would kill him if he ever broke away from it completely. He knew he'd been pushing it as far as he could for far too long. Eventually, his past vows would come back to force his hand.

In the meantime, he needed to keep Reyna safe. That, at least, was not against his orders.

Suddenly, Reyna stopped. She frowned, peering through the thick yew trees. "I can't see ahead. Can you?"

But he could see nothing more than darkness and snow-blanketed leaves, twisting together to form a harsh painting of shadows and light. "Not a thing. Where's your owl?"

"I left him back at the castle. For his safety."

Lorcan narrowed his eyes. "Safety against a fleeing assassin who doesn't stand a chance against your warrior skills? What aren't you telling me, Reyna?"

"I'll tell you soon." She glanced up, and then unclasped her cloak. The whisper-thin material flapped idly as it drifted onto the ground. "I'm going to climb this tree and see what's ahead."

Before Lorcan could argue against it, Reyna was halfway up the trunk of the tree. He shifted a little closer just in case she lost her grip and tumbled back down to the ground. But he knew that she would have no trouble, even though the trunk was slick with ice and the lowest branch rose high above them.

As suspected, she reached the branch with ease. Perching on top of it, she gazed into the distance. Lorcan watched.

What was he even doing out here? Better yet, what was *she* doing? Thane would be angry when he discovered that Lorcan had gone along with this ridiculous adventure, but Lorcan just could not seem to convince himself to turn back to the castle.

After a moment, Reyna leapt from the branch and dropped onto the snow before him, spraying up icy mist. Her cheeks were flushed with color but her steady breath suggested that she hadn't struggled at all to make the climb.

Lorcan lifted a brow. "Make that three talents."

She propped her hands on her hips. "Well, thanks for your help. I think it's time you turned back."

"Not happening."

Pursing her lips, her eyes darted to the side. Lorcan frowned. What was going on?

"I don't need your help," she said quickly. "In fact, her trail seems to stop here."

"I see. So, we should return to the castle then."

"I want to check up ahead anyway. But you go ahead and start back. I'll catch up with you."

"You're not going to get rid of me." Slowly, he crossed his arms over his chest. "What aren't you telling me? You said you'd explain. And now I think it's time for that explanation."

From the thick trees just ahead, a branch snapped. And then another.

Reyna grimaced. "I was afraid of that."

"Afraid of what?" Lorcan asked with narrowed eyes as he reached for the weapon at his back. Just as his fingers touched the tip of the hilt, an arrow whistled by his head. It slammed into the trunk just behind him, its sharp silver tip sinking deep into the wood.

Lorcan froze, and then slowly lowered his hand to his side. "Now would *really* be the time to fill me in, Reyna."

But it was too late. Dozens of fae swarmed the woods, surrounding them in an instant. They must have been lying in wait, watching the two of them trek through the woods. Reyna looked not the least bit surprised. She held up her hands, calmly waiting for the fae to strap their bonds around her. She didn't even try to fight, though it would have been pointless if she had. They were outnumbered twenty to one.

Lorcan held up his hands as the green-skinned fae moved toward him. He waited for them to wrap their bonds around his wrists. But then something sharp stung his cheek, followed by another sharp stab to his neck.

Instantly, his mind slowed and a strange buzz filled his veins.

"Poison darts," he tried to grumble.

And then all went black.

※

When he awoke, night had fallen. His head throbbed, and his throat felt like a dozen knives had been dragged into his gut. With a grunt, he pushed up onto his elbows and took in his surroundings. Iron bars blurred into his vision.

Reyna sat across from him, propped up against the bars of a cage, her cloak protecting her from the iron. Frowning, he glanced up, noting that the bars obscured most of the sky from view, including the sparkling stars that formed the constellations of their god. They were far from the woods and the castle, and instead sat in a rolling field of wheat. They were in the grasslands that covered much of the Air Court's land. In the distance, a fire roared, highlighting a small group of warriors, along with their tents, their horses, and their supplies.

"Welcome back," Reyna said.

He dragged his gaze back to her face. She looked good, even caged. Scowling, he said, "You got us caught by a rogue band of wood fae."

"I don't think they're rogues."

"Where the hell are we?"

"I'm not sure. I only just woke up." She glanced over at the camp. "We can't be too far from the castle though. About an hour's ride south maybe."

Lorcan frowned. "That's impossibly stupid of them. Our scouts will find them and send out a company to take them down."

"I don't think so. These wood fae have been camped here for a few days, at least."

That was odd. Scouts constantly patrolled the land that surrounded Dalais Castle for this very reason. The crown could not risk the enemy getting this close. If there were more of them, if they'd been forming an army...why hadn't anyone in Tairngire noticed this yet?

Suddenly, Lorcan realized exactly why Reyna had been out in the woods. And it wasn't to track down her assassin. It was to find these fae. She hadn't been at all surprised when they'd jumped out of the woods to surround them.

"You lied to me," he said, narrowing his eyes. "How?"

"I never lied. I was tracking the assassin. She came here."

"She was working for the wood fae? Not for the High Queen?" He moved to stand but remembered, just in time, that his head would smash the top of the cage if he did. It was only large enough for them to sit comfortably, but no larger than that. And he couldn't risk touching the iron bars. "Why didn't you tell Thane?"

"Because I don't think that conversation would have ended well."

"And *this* is ending things well?" He gestured around them.

"Admittedly, I didn't think they would put me in a cage. But I wasn't counting on you being with me. That may have made things worse."

He scowled. "You're blaming this on me."

"You have a very growly, angry presence about you. They probably feel threatened. A compliment, really."

"Reyna..." he said slowly. "I need you to tell me exactly what is going on here. No mincing words."

She pressed her lips together, silent for a moment before she replied. The wind rustled the tall grassy stalks around them, a rush of sound. "If the High Queen found out that the wood fae sent an assassin after someone inside of her court, what do you think she would do?"

"Attack," he said. "She would send out her guards to kill these fae."

"Exactly. And then what would the Wood Court do in response to that?"

"I see what you're getting at. But this wouldn't start a war. We're already in one."

"The battles have died down," she whispered. "This would just stir things up all over again."

"Reyna. They sent *assassins* after you."

"Because they feel threatened by the alliance." She sighed. "Truth be told, I would love to fight every last one of them. I'd love to wage war and take them down, to show them that they cannot threaten Reyna Darragh. But my vengeance is not what will keep our realms alive. My desire for justice will not save the lives of the low fae who must fight in the battles. We made one alliance. Perhaps we can make another. I came here to try and deal with them."

Lorcan stared at her from across the cage. Her eyes flashed, and dirt stained her cheeks. The passion running through her veins was unlike any he'd seen before. After so much war and so much death, so many of the low fae wore despair like a familiar cloak. They had all but given up, even the safest among them. The ones who could sit inside the castle, protected by ancient walls that had never fallen.

And yet here Reyna was, rushing headfirst into danger, all for a hope that things could change.

Out of the corner of Lorcan's eye, movement caught his attention. He turned to see two wood fae slowly stomping across the field toward them, the ends of their bows jutting up behind their heads, backlit by the Brigantu moon hanging low in the sky. Reyna sucked in a breath and straightened up a bit. This was her chance. The only one she had to make this right.

Lorcan did not have the heart to tell her that she was going to find herself sorely disappointed. Thane would never ally with the Wood Court.

"All right, you two," one of the incoming warriors said while the other waited at a safe distance. He was a slight and spritely thing, all long limbs and tree-like features. Like many wood fae, his hair was long and green, just like the color of his leather armor. "We have our orders. You'll be executed at first light."

"What?" Reyna asked with a gasp, half-standing. "I came here to make a deal. Your High King doesn't even want to hear me out?"

"No deal you can make will give us a better advantage than if you were dead." The warrior shrugged. "Sorry. Not my call. We'll give you tonight to pray to your god and say goodbye."

The warrior turned to go. Lorcan cleared his throat. Slowly, the warrior paused and glanced over his shoulder.

"No deal for you either, I'm afraid. As an Air Court castle guard, you can't really do much for us."

"You're making a big mistake," Lorcan said in a low growl. "I know why your High King wants Reyna dead. It's so that you can marry your own princess off to Prince Thane. And it might be a good plan, but only under different circumstances."

The wood fae frowned, inching closer to the bars of the cage. "What do you mean?"

Lorcan hesitated. To pull this off, he would have to lie. Reyna would likely guess he was fibbing. It was a risk, playing his hand before her so blatantly. But it might be the only way to save her life.

"Prince Thane will never marry your princess if you

murder Reyna. He'll be far too distressed by her death to consider marrying for a very long time." Lorcan could not help but shift his gaze to Reyna, who was watching him with a very odd expression on her face. One of disbelief. He turned back toward the wood fae. "Thane Selkirk has fallen in love with Reyna Darragh. He will be devastated by her death."

The wood fae frowned. "And what would you suggest we do instead? The king refuses to make a deal with Princess Reyna. Her word means nothing to him. She has no power as of yet. She's only the prince's betrothed. He isn't a king, and she isn't his wife."

"Send a note to Prince Thane telling him that you have his betrothed. He will come and make whatever deal you desire, in order to keep Reyna alive."

The wood fae nodded slowly. "Interesting. I will take this up with my king."

At that, he and his fellow warrior strode back to the camp. Reyna still stared at him with disbelieving eyes, but she did not comment on his lies. Perhaps she even believed him, though he doubted she would. She knew just as well as he did that Thane Selkirk was not in love with her, nor would he mourn her death for years.

Still, he had risked revealing himself for one reason and one reason only: to keep her alive.

And he had. For now.

36

THANE

"My liege."

Thane glanced up from his desk. Candlelight flickered throughout the study, and he noticed that the sky outside had become thick with darkness. How long had he sat here reading? Hours. So long that the morning sun had quickly vanished into the night. He had yet to press forward with his challenge for the throne, but he had been so engrossed in his research that he hadn't even thought to step away from his desk.

A boy messenger in simple brown garb stood in his open doorway, clutching a rolled-up parchment in trembling hands. Thane motioned him forward.

The messenger scurried to Thane's desk and dropped the letter, and then turned to rush back out into the corridor. The prince frowned as he shut the door behind him. That had been very odd indeed. Mother's choices for servants were becoming tedious. She had swapped out every one after the abdication, paranoid that spies were lurking amongst them. Or had she merely wished to install her own spies?

Shaking his head, he unrolled the parchment and read the words. Instantly, he dropped the letter as if he'd been burned. He leapt up from his chair, his entire body shaking with a rush of fear and adrenaline.

It was a letter from the wood fae. They'd captured Princess Reyna and Lorcan. And they demanded a meeting. If he refused, the wood fae would execute their captives the following night at high moon. His entire body burned.

The Wood Court had done this. *They* were the ones trying to have Reyna killed. It wasn't his mother, after all. He could not believe he ever suspected she would do such a thing.

Sucking deep breaths into his lungs, he braced his palms on his desk, his mind whirring. How had this happened? How had they captured them both? Had they sneaked inside the castle? No, that was impossible.

He ground his teeth together. His closest friend. His betrothed. If he did not do something, they would both die the next day.

I need to speak with Eislyn.

Crumpling the letter with shaking fingers, he pushed out into the corridor. He ran down the stone tunnels, ignoring the startled looks of everyone he passed, including his guards. Choosing the stairwell, he raced down the tower and into the library where he found Eislyn. Wearing a deep blue gown, she perched halfway up a ladder on one of the middle stacks. She looked so serene. So happy. He had yet to tell her that they were sending her away, and now he had far worse news than that.

"Eislyn," he said, breath puffing.

She twisted to face him, smiling, but then she saw the look in his eyes. Her smile dimmed. Understanding passed between them without a single word spoken aloud, as if

Eislyn could see the truth in the depths of his very soul. Tears filled her eyes, and she dropped the book she'd been holding. It fell with a loud thump that echoed in the lofted space.

"What's happened to my sister?" she whispered.

"It is not as bad as you may think," he said, though he had to stop himself mid-sentence. It might perhaps be that bad. He didn't know. The letter had demanded Thane's presence or Reyna would die. At least they had not killed her outright.

"Then, what is it?" Her voice was so soft that he could barely hear the words.

Quickly, Thane filled her in on the contents of the letter. As he spoke, his words sucked all the color from her cheeks. Her eyes were as wide as the twin moons in the sky, and her knuckles went white from where she clasped the ladder.

"Have you come here to tell me you are going to let her die?"

"What?" Thane straightened, frowning. "Of course not. You truly believe I would let your sister die?"

She closed her eyes. "I know how you feel about the Wood Court and its ruler. If you meet with them, they will make demands of you. Demands I am certain you will not bend to, knowing your opinion on High King Ulaid Molt."

Thane stood very still. The truth was, Eislyn was not wrong. He imagined he knew exactly what the Wood Court would ask of him. For him to cast off Reyna as his betrothed and take Princess Etaine's hand instead. Why they had decided not to kill Reyna outright, he could not guess. It would have been far easier for them to get what they wanted that way.

Because Thane did not wish to ally himself with the Wood Court. For the very same reason that his mother had been against it. The Wood Court was ruled by a wicked, cruel king. To ally himself with that court would put his own subjects at risk of his tyrannical rule. Thane knew it would only be a matter of time before the king's knife turned his way.

But staring up into Eislyn's silver eyes, Thane could not see any way out of it. He'd done everything in his power to avoid this very fate, but it had chased him down like a Fomorian during Beltane. He could not let Reyna die at their hands. It would destroy Eislyn. She would never be the same again.

"I will meet with them. And I will do whatever it takes to free your sister. Even if it means agreeing to wed Princess Etaine."

"And what of *our* alliance? Will it be over then?" she asked quietly. "If you marry their princess instead of ours, then what is to stop you from waging war against our court once again?"

Thane reached up, took her hand, and then led her down the ladder so that she now stood before him. But she still kept one hand firmly clasped to the ladder. Her fingers were cold to the touch, though Eislyn was not shivering. "No more war between us. I won't allow it."

"High King Ulaid will certainly want it."

"Eislyn." He twisted his fingers around hers and brought her hand to his chest. "Are you trying to convince me to leave your sister to die at the hands of the wood fae?"

"No," she whispered, staring up at him. "I am trying to decide if I need to send an owl to my father."

Thane's eyes went wide, and he dropped Eislyn's hand. If she sent an owl to her father, it would be to call him into battle. He would push into the Air Court lands to rescue Reyna from the wood fae. That move alone would send

Thane's mother into a frenzy. She would take the invasion as a call to arms, as a formal breaking of their alliance.

Thane was not the High King in the eyes of his people. Not yet. He had challenged his mother for the throne, but he had yet to make the formal announcement to the rest of the court. If the ice fae invaded now, their armies would listen to her instead of him. The transfer of power could be a tricky thing, and far trickier during active war.

"Eislyn, please. You cannot do that," he said quietly.

"I do not want to, Thane," she whispered back fiercely. "But I will if it is the only thing that will save my sister. I would do *anything* to protect her. *Anything*. Even if that means we..."

Thane stepped forward instinctively, almost as if her words had called him near. What had she been about to say just then? Before she had stopped herself? Probably nothing important.

"It is not the only thing that will save her," he finally said. "I will go meet with them. I promise. And I do not make promises lightly."

She trembled, and a tear slipped down her cheek. "Do you truly mean that?"

He nodded.

Eislyn let go of the ladder and launched into his arms. She wrapped herself so tightly around him that he almost lost his breath. The scent of rowan and snow enveloped him, burning him up with a sensation he had never felt. Her arms tightened around his neck, her hair tickled his nose. Closing his eyes, he held her close, his heart beating faster than Beltane drums.

"What in the name of the Dagda do you think you are doing, Thane?" His mother, clad in a deep purple gown that flared out behind her, stood glaring at where Thane had gathered twenty warriors in the inner courtyard just beside the entrance to the castle gardens. A bright morning sun flared overhead, reflecting off the white stone of the six looming towers that surrounded them.

Just behind his mother, Aengus lurked, her ever-present shadow.

Thane had refrained from telling his mother about the letter, Reyna's capture, and his subsequent plans to parley with the enemy. It was not the sort of thing that the High Queen of the Air Court would approve of. In fact, Thane distinctly remembered her reaction when his father had proposed an alliance with the wood fae. There had been a lot of shouting and throwing of slippers. His mother despised High King Ulaid and for good reason. He was a terrible male and an even worse king.

The leather-clad warriors shifted nervously on their feet as Thane turned toward his mother, holding his sword loosely by his side. He pasted on a pleasant smile. "I am speaking with my fellow warriors. This is the same company I fought with during the Battle of the Shard."

"And why would you be doing that, my son?" she asked icily.

"You've never fought on the battlefield, Mother. You wouldn't understand. Warriors create bonds that last a lifetime when they are knee-deep in blood and guts, their swords protecting each other from death."

She waved dismissively, her rings glinting beneath the sun. "So very dramatic. And while your words may be true, you are mincing them. You are not the only one inside this castle with spies. I know all about your betrothed's current situation. I am pleased to see that you are sending some warriors to take care of these intruders, but you should have brought this to my attention immediately."

Thane bristled and glanced at his company with a frown. He had told no one but these warriors of their mission. He trusted each of them with his life, and their loyalty. It was impossible to imagine their betrayal, but clearly his mother had dug her talons into the court far more than he had realized. Her spies were growing more numerous by the day.

"I do not need to bring it to your attention, Mother. For I am the rightful king," he replied, shoving his sword into the scabbard by his side.

Aengus frowned, and then leaned forward to whisper something into her ear. Thane took note of that action. He knew that Aengus was behind his mother's recent schemes, and he would no doubt attempt to stop Thane's coronation from taking place. The prince would have to keep an eye on this one.

"I have no intention of preventing you from taking the throne. But you have not informed the court, you have not had a coronation, and you do not have the crown. It still sits on my head," she said. "So, for now, I am still the ruler of this realm and control our armies. Tell me what you have planned for this attack."

Thane frowned. "I'm not attacking."

His mother hissed and took several long strides across the courtyard, the bottom of her dress swishing against the white stone. "Of course you are attacking. Why else would you have gathered your company here?"

"Attacking will only result in the death of Princess Reyna and Lorcan. I will go meet with the Wood Court and hear their demands."

Silence dropped like a stone. The warriors behind him cast uneasy glances at each other while Aengus smiled strangely in his mother's shadow. As for his mother herself, she did not need to speak for Thane to know her mind. Her eyes were alight with pure, unbridled anger. He had seen that expression on her face only a few times before. Once, when she had discovered that his father had been visiting brothels in secrecy. Second, when she had learned that High King Ulaid had risen to the throne in the wood fae lands. And third, when she had once recalled to him the events that led to the shadow fae's exile.

And now, when her only son wished to parley with their biggest enemy.

An enemy who had captured a member of their court.

"You cannot meet with them," she said, her voice loud and commanding. "I forbid it."

"You cannot forbid it, Mother. I am the king of this realm."

They stood face to face, son and mother, rightful king and taker of the crown. Two sides of the same coin, opposite in spirit but the same in aim. They both wanted to save their realm and keep their people safe. The only difference was, Thane was not willing to risk Reyna's life.

His mother was.

Aengus leaned forward again and whispered. Thane twisted his head toward the side, trying to catch a whiff of his words, but he had not been alive before the Fall, and he had never been blessed with the enhanced senses of the fae.

"Very well," the High Queen said with a smile. "I suppose I shall leave you to your preparations."

Thane frowned. That was it? She was giving up? He doubted it.

With one last smile, she turned and strode out of the

courtyard, leaving Thane staring dumbfounded at her retreating back. His warriors began to whisper worried words of unease. His gut twisting, he turned back toward his company.

"Let us put my mother's words out of our minds and return to what is important." He nodded, steadying his nerves, keeping an image of Eislyn's eyes in his mind. His mother had only been trying to intimidate him, to try and force him to back down. It was a show of power, one that he had seen her do many times. Her tricks would not work on Thane. "Here is how we are going to save our future queen."

37

IMOGEN

"You cannot allow Thane to take this meeting. It will only strengthen his position if they make some sort of agreement," the annoying buzzing insect whispered in her ear. That was how she had begun to view her lover—ex-lover, in fact. They had not made love in weeks. Imogen hoped they never did again. Unfortunately, he had a tendency to initiate an embrace on an almost-daily basis, particularly after he had made a courtier squirm.

She suddenly stopped in the corridor, whirling to face him. "My dear Grand Alderman. I can allow whatever I like. Or is that not my prerogative as High Queen of this realm?"

A flash of irritation on Aengus's face betrayed his true emotions. He tried to pretend as though he did not mind deferring to Imogen's power as High Queen, but she was not a fool. He wished to take her place on the throne, just as she wished she could discard him in a gutter somewhere.

"It is not wise. You agree or you would not have argued with your son in front of his warriors."

"Perhaps." She continued striding down the corridor. Instead of taking the path toward the Great Hall, she spun toward the right, aiming her feet in the direction of Curaidh Tower, where the crown's warriors lived and trained. "However, I am surprised by your reaction. You never seemed particularly opposed to High King Ulaid in the past. If Thane were to make some sort of agreement with him, would you disagree?"

"We do not need to be making agreements with these courts," Aengus said in that strange, hitched accent of his. "These alliances still leave us with kings and queens. Conquering is the way forward. It is the only way to create a true empire."

Imogen was not surprised to hear Aengus's views. She had heard a similar expression from her husband until he had decided that allying with the Wood Court was the way forward. She'd never quite understood why he had suddenly changed his mind, only a year past.

But Aengus was wrong. Under the proposed alliance, if Thane ever did marry the Darragh girl, he would become High King over both the Air and Ice Courts. Cos Darragh, Reyna's father, would retain the title of King, though he could no longer be called a High King. If they united with Wood and Sea beneath the Air Court's banner, there would be two more Kings beneath Thane's rule. In theory, Imogen would be pleased with the arrangement. From it, they could still create an empire.

But she would *not* ally her people with the Wood Court's ruler, Ulaid Molt.

She found herself in the unfortunate position of agreeing with her former lover but for entirely different reasons.

Aengus glanced around, and seeing where they were going, hurried his footsteps along in eager excitement. "So, the High Queen agrees with her Grand Alderman."

"The High Queen agrees with herself," she snapped.

Another flash of irritation crossed Aengus's face, but he quickly hid it with a smile. "And what of your son? How will you prevent him from sending his troops?"

"I won't. I overheard his plan. He will wait for nightfall so as to best hide his warriors in the darkness, in case the discussions go wrong. That gives my own troops plenty of time to track down these invaders and destroy them."

"And the princess?" he asked with a wicked smile. "This would be a grand opportunity to rid yourself of her. Your warriors could allow her to die in the fighting. It would not seem your fault if she were unable to escape alive."

Imogen pursed her lips and came to a sudden stop in the corridor. "Thank you for your advice, Grand Alderman. However, for this plot to work, I need your assistance with something. There is every chance that my son could change his plans. Go speak to Lord Bowen's spymaster. Have him watch the prince. If Thane decides to leave early, have the spymaster stall him. He may use whatever excuse he deems necessary."

Aengus's narrow grey eyes narrowed even more. He stood there for a moment, his mind clearly churning. Imogen wondered if he would defy her. She knew that he wanted nothing more than to see the troops off himself, likely to ensure that she followed through with the plan. And, she knew that he would no doubt make suggestions to the troops. About leaving Princess Reyna behind to be brutally murdered by the wood fae.

Imogen was not fond of the girl, but like it or not, Princess Reyna was one of her people now. And Imogen would *always* protect her own. She would have her warriors rescue the girl. Aengus would not.

And she did not want him poisoning the warriors' minds.

After a moment, he gave a slight nod. "I will deliver the message."

She watched him go, his tall, slight form disappearing down the long stretch of shadowy stonework, his rapier shifting with his every step. For now, she still held some amount of power over the Grand Alderman, but she knew it would not last. He would push, gently at first. But over time, his gentle prods would be as strong as a mountain weighing down the very dirt. If only she could kill him and remove his threat once and for all.

But she could not. He was the only other person who knew the truth about Sloane's humanity. She had vowed to never speak of it. If Aengus died, the truth died with him.

But perhaps that did not matter. Sloane had vanished down south to his brother's castle. His body was weak, his mind was old. He likely spent his days sitting by a window, reading a tome, and staring out at the Mag Mell Sea. He was no longer a threat to her.

She let out a heavy sigh and resumed her trek toward Curaidh Tower. Aengus would need to be taken care of, eventually. But right now, she had to destroy the wood fae.

38

REYNA

Reyna's vision swam. Hours of captivity were beginning to wear her thin. The wood fae had brought her and Lorcan bread and water, just barely enough to sustain them for another day. A slight wind rustled through the tall grass stalks that surrounded their cage, creating a sea of gold. It would have been beautiful, if she wasn't surrounded by thick iron bars that would burn her skin if they made contact.

"Snap out of it," Lorcan said. "You're an unsworn Shieldmaiden. I know your constitution is stronger than this. We have only been in captivity for two days, and they have fed us well."

"It's not the food," she said in a whisper. "It's Wingallock."

"Your owl?"

"My familiar," she said. "We're linked, he and I. Spending this amount of time apart is difficult on us both."

Lorcan was quiet for a moment. She knew that he was still annoyed at her for not explaining why she'd raced into the woods. In truth, she could not really blame him. Her mission had gotten them captured, after all. Even though it had not been her plan, she hadn't expected the Wood Court to be so opposed to letting her speak. They were more stubborn than she had realized.

"Is it painful to be away from your bird?" he asked.

"In a way. It mostly leaves me feeling tired, dizzy, and just…wrong."

"Can you call him to you?"

She shook her head. "I told him to remain in my bedchamber, and he is too far away for me to feel him through our bond."

"So, you came into this thing knowing that you might die," he said, tone turning sharp once again. "Alone and without telling a single person. Reyna, you cannot do these kinds of things."

"Why not?" She lifted her chin, eyes flashing. "I think it's fairly clear that no one in your court actually wants me here. The High Queen certainly doesn't, and Thane's had to settle with his third—and last—choice. The other courtiers have been either distantly polite or cruelly passive aggressive. The only person that has been even remotely kind to me is…"

She pressed her lips together, pulled her cloak tighter around her shoulders, and turned her head sharply toward the side, looking away from Lorcan. For a moment there, she had been terrifyingly close to telling Lorcan that he had been kind to her. It might have felt like the truth, but she knew it was far from it. Thane had assigned Lorcan to keep an eye on her, more to prevent her doing something that would embarrass him rather than because Lorcan himself wanted to protect her. That was not kindness. It was just his position as a guard.

"You may feel that way, but right now, Prince Thane will be making preparations to come speak with the

COURT OF RUINS

wood fae. In order to save you from captivity. And death."

She turned back toward him, eyeing him warily. There it was again. That strange suggestion that Thane was *in love with her*. Compared to the lifespans of ancient fae before the Fall, Reyna had not lived very long, but she certainly hadn't been born yesterday either. Prince Thane tolerated her, if even that. They had scarcely spent any time together since her arrival at his court.

In fact, he spent far more time with her sister, pouring over books to find answers about the Ruin.

She had not succeeded in seducing him, though she hadn't even tried. With assassins and vicious High Queens and spies jumping through her window, she had been distracted from her original intent. To marry the prince, get him on the throne, and then kill him so that she could take his kingdom as her own.

"I'm not certain if you truly believe that he cares for me or if you've found some way to lie," she said.

"Lie? Fae cannot lie, princess."

The truth may be twisted but never false.

His face was unreadable. A mask of indifference hidden in the shadows. It annoyed her. Reyna shifted against the hard ground and searched his ebony eyes for any indication of the truth. If he *were* a liar, then he certainly wouldn't tell her he was. But there was only one way he could avoid speaking the truth. And that was if he was a shadow fae.

That was impossible. The Shadow Court had been exiled so long ago that there wasn't a single trace of their kingdom left in Tir Na Nog. They'd been banished, cut off from the rest of the continent. At the time, it had been almost a death sentence. Their lands struggled to yield crops beneath the constant darkness of their skies, and they could no longer count on the trade routes. Tir Na Nog had been at war, but smugglers still crossed the borders before the exile. Shadow fae were willing to pay a great deal for food, and merchants did not care where that coin came from. But no more. Smugglers wouldn't risk it these days. Anyone who crossed that border was shot dead.

The Air Court had even taken control of the shadow fae's castle in the capital city of Findius. It sat just on the border between the Shadow Court and the Wood Court. Taking the castle prevented any shadow fae king from ever sitting on his true source of power: the coronation seat. Even now, those thrones held magic, bestowing the realm's blessing on any king or queen who sat there. Each court had a Seat of Power. And the Shadow Court's seat had been stolen from them, as retaliation for their brutal actions.

For years, there had been no sign of shadow fae in the other five kingdoms of Tir Na Nog. They had not approached Findius or tried to take it back. Reyna doubted there were even any alive. Bu if there were any shadow fae left, they would be living on the scraps of what the land could provide.

"A lie or not, you're wrong," she said, turning to gaze at the campsite where a new fire blazed. From this distance, it was impossible to hear anything the wood fae said. She pressed her fingers against the tiny patches of ice that were left on the ground and breathed in deep. A slight tingle of magic whispered across her skin but nothing more.

Lorcan crossed his arms over his leather-armored chest. "Thane will come."

She took in his strong jaw, his hard eyes, and his immovable strength. There was something he was hiding. Reyna was certain of it. "You never finished telling me

COURT OF RUINS

about the Wild Hunt. Back in your grasslands village. Tell me the story now. It will help pass the time."

"You're right. We got interrupted by your Ruin. It almost seemed like it was following you."

She frowned. "*My* Ruin? You speak as if you believe I had something to do with it." And then she realized what he had done. He had distracted her from her question. Typical fae nonsense. "Nice try. Tell me about the Wild Hunt. Or is there some reason you don't wish to discuss it?"

"It was fairly tramautizing to be chased down by Fomorians. I was only a boy. I don't enjoy recounting it."

She gave him a look. "You truly expect me to believe that Fomorians actually came over from their empire simply to chase after a small fae boy?"

No one had ever seen a Fomorian. No one alive, at least. There were stories, of course, just as there were stories of dragons once soaring through the skies. The tales would have one believe that every year Fomorians flew across their churning sea on wings spun from gold. They would steal horses from village stables, and then ride through the night, killing every soul they met along the way. And then, at dawn, they would slaughter the horses and eat their hearts before returning to their empire across the sea.

But those were just tales told to children to keep them from running through the fields or woods at night. The Empire of Fomor traded with the courts of Tir Na Nog. If the Fomorians enjoyed brutally slaughtering the fae, then why would they sell their wares to them?

"They do so every year," Lorcan said quietly, his dark eyes flashing. "At Beltane."

"Then, why has no one ever seen this? Except for you, of course."

"Because they kill every single soul who sets eyes on

them."

She shook her head and laughed. "Except for a small boy who somehow outran him."

"I am not lying," he said, grinding his teeth together.

She regarded him carefully. When a moment before his face had been a blank slate, his eyes held a darkness now. "No, I don't believe you are. You may, however, be mistaken. A dream or a nightmare, perhaps. Or someone was playing a trick. You were young, you might not have understood what you truly saw."

"I know what I saw, and I know what they were." His intense gaze locked with hers. "I stayed out late. Far too late. It was Beltane, and I should have known better, but I enjoyed being out in the fields. The Fomorians appeared, moon casting a yellow glow behind their shadowy forms. They came for me. I ran, faster than I have ever run, even since then, even on small legs that trembled with every step. At some point, they vanished from behind me. They let me live. I do not know why, but they did."

Reyna shivered. There was so much truth and conviction in his words. Before, she thought he had only been playing around, inventing some grand adventure to entertain her and Eislyn around the fire. But this was no fun story, sung by a bard.

It felt real and dark. And terrifying.

"But why?" she whispered. "They trade with us. And they've never sent their armies to our shores."

Lorcan merely shook his head. "If I knew the answers to those questions, Reyna, I would be telling them to the entire world. But do you not think it is odd how extreme they are in their dealings with us? How secretive they are about their own world?"

"They're a different culture," she whispered, though Reyna had always thought it odd. The Fomorians allowed trade between the continents, but they only did so under the strict agreement that the Tir Na Nog fae would never step foot on Fomorian land. Their ships, manned by humans, met the ships of the courts on the islands between. Anyone who ever tried to go further was never seen again.

Reyna considered Lorcan in a new light. Did this explain the hardness in his eyes, the strict set of his jaw? He held his well-muscled frame in such a way that made him seem closed off and cold at times. He had seen something that no other living fae had ever seen. Something dark and cruel and terrible. Reyna could relate. Perhaps they were far more alike than she had realized.

"The Ruin attacked a village when I was young. Fifteen years ago, my mother, Eislyn, and I went to visit our people. There had been a blight on the crops, during the continent-wide dust storm that happens every six years. We went to offer some hope." Reyna's breath shuddered as she exhaled, images of that fateful night flashing through her mind. "Wingallock soared in, screeching. I have never heard him make that sound, not before then or after. It was the first time he or I had ever seen the Ruin, and he was terrified."

Reyna lifted her eyes. Lorcan was staring at her, his face softening as she spoke.

"Before any of us knew what was happening, the Ruin attacked. Big black flakes that fell from the sky. Like snow, but…heavier, darker, and full of a pulsing kind of evil that made even the strongest warriors fall. Eislyn and I were standing right beside my mother when the flakes hit her."

She stopped, shutting her eyes tight. Several hot tears slipped through her lids and trailed down her cheeks.

"I am sorry," Lorcan said, his tone earnest and much less guarded than it had been seconds before. "It was a terrible thing that happened to you. But it has made you the fighter that you are."

Reyna opened her eyes, and understanding passed between them. He had stared darkness in the face and so had she. Somehow, they had both survived even when everyone else around them had fallen. It had made them hard. It had made fury fill their souls. Reyna felt as if she now stared into a mirror. He understood her, something that no one else had done in a very long while.

Lorcan suddenly cleared his throat and shifted on the cold ground. He glanced away, jaw clenching. "Prince Thane should be here any moment. It is almost nightfall."

Reyna blinked and wiped the tears from her cheeks. Why was she being so foolish? She hadn't cried in years. And her thoughts had betrayed her. Lorcan, the warrior, understanding her? Even if that were the case, she needed to rid herself of those thoughts. She had come here to marry Prince Thane and take the throne from the Air Court. If the prince suspected that she felt even a stirring toward his own personal guard, he'd send her right back home again.

Not that those stirrings meant anything. She had only gotten caught up in the moment. They were trapped inside a cage together, held captive by an enemy court. It had meant nothing. Anyone would feel a connection in that scenario.

Still, she could not stop her mind from drifting back to that moment in the woods when she had kissed him. That had been a charade, of course, but there had been a brief moment when she'd forgotten everything but how his mouth felt against her skin. She had wanted to get lost in the moment, to forget about the assassin tracking her down.

She needed to get out of this cage.

39

EISLYN

Eislyn padded through the castle halls, as quiet as a mouse. She did not know where she was or where she was going, but she did know that danger lurked in every corner.

A quiet voice drifted toward her. An ancient voice, one whose every word rattled like parchment in the wind. She crept ever closer to the voice. She was drawn to it. Whoever it was needed her.

She found him inside a cramped room. A small, hunched man whose patchy hair had gone grey. Wrinkles covered every inch of his arms. Was he a thousand years old? Or was he human? She could not tell. His back was to her. He knelt on the cold stone ground, bent over a yellowed corpse. There were six deep cuts on the body's chest.

"What are you doing?" Eislyn asked.

He turned to her then, smiling. Blood stained his teeth and drenched his curving lips. Bits of flesh stuck to his cheek. A severed boar's head sat discarded in the corner, leaking gore.

"Feasting," he hissed. "And you are next."

※

She awoke screaming. Sweat clung to her brow, and her entire body shook as if it had been taken over by an groundquake. Images of blood and gore flickered in her mind. She pressed her hands tight against her ears, murmuring to herself to block it all out.

The door flew open wide and footsteps pounded on the ground. Vreis, her guard, peered at her with concern, followed quickly by Thane. His familiar face soothed her, that swirling tattoo providing her with a root to ground her capsized mind.

"Open the curtains," Thane ordered to his guard. "The darkness is too much for her."

A moment later, light speared Eislyn's face as the setting sun shone through her window, but it did little to clear the cobwebs in her mind. It had only been a dream, but it had felt so real. Her fear was making her see and hear things once again.

Thane wrapped his strong arms around her and pulled her to his chest. "Eislyn, you are safe. I'm here. You are safe."

She sighed and breathed him in, relishing in the scent of his leather armor. Her panic began to fade, but the images in her mind still looped, over and over and over again. Ancient face, blood-stained lips, corpse riddled with wounds. A severed boar's head, a symbol of impending death.

After a time, he pulled back. "What is the matter? Why are you in bed in the middle of the day? Why have you been screaming?"

Eislyn had needed to lie down as soon as she had heard about her sister. The fear and panic had been too much for her to bear. She'd felt ten years old again. It had taken her back to a time she could scarcely recall. Shadowy visions in her mind of an Eislyn who had barely been able to function.

"I am terrified that something is going to happen to my sister," she whispered. "First Glencora, now Reyna..."

Thane brought her to his chest again and sighed. "I made a promise to you, Eislyn. I will rescue your sister. We've made the preparations. We go after nightfall."

"I worry about you, too, Thane," she said quietly.

"Life here at court has been difficult on you," he said, sadness creeping into his voice.

"At times," she admitted. "But it has not all been bad."

"Princess Reyna believes you might be safer and happier back home," he said. "I'm inclined to agree with her."

"What?" With a frown, Eislyn pulled back. Her heart twinged at the serious look in his golden eyes. "But what about my research? I need these libraries to stop the Ruin."

He pushed a strand of her silver hair behind her ear. "We can send a cartload of books back with you. And I can send more once you finish with those. And I can continue to read here as well, aiding your search for answers."

A new pain curled around her heart. "You are serious about this. You've even been thinking it through."

"I will be taking my throne very soon," he said. "The wedding will follow soon after. After that, I think it is best if you go."

She ground her teeth together and glanced away, her eyes burning with unshed tears. The books weren't the issue. She needed to research, but there were other ways. Her pain came from something else. And that something else was Thane.

It was ridiculous for her to feel this way. Eislyn hadn't even wanted to marry the prince. He'd come to her, asking for her hand. And she had refused him. She knew he and Reyna did not love each other, but how could she tell him she'd changed her mind now? After everything?

He clearly still wanted to go through with the betrothal. If Thane felt anything for Eislyn, would he not ask her to consider taking her sister's place? Instead, he wanted her far away from him.

Thane gently tucked a finger beneath her chin and tipped back her head. His eyes speared hers. "You're upset. I did not think you wanted to come to the Air Court, Eislyn."

"I didn't," she whispered. "But it is not as bad here as I feared."

He gave her a slight smile. "Does this mean you do not dislike me anymore?"

She pressed her lips together. How could she tell him the truth?

"It means that I do not wish to leave this place." It was all she could admit.

His eyes moved back and forth, as if searching her soul for an answer to a question he had not voiced. She could scarcely breathe. His head had lowered to hers and his lips were dangerously close. Her fingers ached to reach up and trace the very shape of them.

"Thane," she whispered.

From behind them, Vreis cleared his throat. Heat engulfed Eislyn's face. She had forgotten the guard was standing there.

"I do hate to interrupt, my liege, but I've just received word from one of the warriors inside of Curaidh Tower. It appears your mother has made her own plan. And it may be too late to stop her."

40

MARIEL

The streets outside of the castle were thick with bodies. As the sun dropped lower, the merchants and tradesmen began shouting from their stalls. They had only moments left in their trading day, and the throngs were out in full force. It had been a pleasant day in Tairngire. Spring was on the horizon, bringing with it the milder temperatures that were preferred by the air fae. The citizens had been out to celebrate. Beltane was drawing ever nearer.

Mariel perched on a thatched rooftop, clinging tight to one of the few timber beams that stretched across the top of the building. She stared down at the fae coming and going from the marketplace. Some entered the outer castle courtyard. Guards and courtiers, mostly. She had been waiting all day.

One benefit to being ancient compared to everyone else was that Mariel had the kind of patience that the younger set did not understand. What was one day when she had lived thousands of them?

A soft breeze blew across Mariel's face. She closed her

eyes and breathed in the wind. It no longer powered her as it once had. The days of drawing magic from the elements had long since passed, but she still felt the soothing embrace of it all the same, as if it curled around her, protecting her, urging her toward her aims.

And her aim was to find out what the king—the former king now—was up to. While she had been distracted by Reyna's plots, four more low fae had ended up murdered in Drunkard's Pit. One for each week that had passed. She did not think the timing of the deaths was a coincidence. Every week, a fae was murdered. And the king was involved in it somehow.

She smiled when two figures appeared in the outer courtyard. One was the ancient spymaster employed by Lord Bowen and Prince Thane. Or, at least, that was what Prince Thane thought. In truth, his father had been pulling the strings of the secretive spy far before his son ever had. If there was someone inside that castle that knew what was happening to the low fae of Tairngire, it would be him.

In the shadows of the castle walls, he spoke quietly with another male. This one she did not recognize, for he was not of the nobility. He wore standard woollen trousers and a matching tunic in the color of drab brown. The arms were frayed at the edges, and the leather belt around his waist had faded with time. Tawny hair framed an angular, sunken face, and his weathered skin covered slim, bony arms.

He was a low fae. What, pray tell, was a low fae doing lurking inside the castle walls with the spymaster?

Mariel's keen eyes followed the suspicious male as he left the courtyard and ducked through the open gates to mingle with the rest of the fae scurrying through the marketplace. The warriors stationed outside the castle paid him no heed. With a frown, Mariel edged to the corner of the roof.

He merged with the throngs before ducking into a side street. Mariel followed quickly after, leaping from roof to roof to stay out of sight. No one looked up. They didn't think to. No longer did the skies fill with wings. The fae had fallen to the ground forever, and the world above was no interest to them now.

Except for Mariel. The rooftops had become her home just as surely as the tallest trees of the woods had.

She jumped across another gap in the rooftops, her feet landing lightly on the thick beam. As the male slowed in the street below, she fell into a crouch, fingers gripping the rough wood.

During her pursuit, the remaining light in the sky had vanished. Ominous shadows danced in the street below where the male lurked outside of a cluster of doors. They were in a district called Ironless Ward, one that bordered Drunkard's Pit. The lack of riches was reflected even here. There were several rows of tenements pushed up together, each new level more lopsided than the one below.

Her heart beat hard as she considered what that meant. The male below no doubt intended to murder another "inconsequential" low fae. She gripped tighter to the beam and waited. Long moments stretched by. The darkness deepened. The warmer day that had come with the sun now faded into a chilly night. Mariel had not brought a cloak, but she did not shiver.

One of the doors cracked open, and the light from within splashed onto the muddy ground. Mariel's breath froze in her throat, and she leaned forward, her shoulders jutting out beyond the building in which she clung.

A young fae stepped outside, or young in Mariel's estimation. He was tall and lanky and looked to be perhaps twenty or twenty-five years of age. Just a baby. So new to this world. And then the knife flashed.

Mariel leapt with a soundless shriek. Wind whipped around her, her loose tunic flapping around her stomach. The ground rushed up to meet her, and she pulled her own two daggers out from their sheaths. She landed in a crouch just in front of the attacker, putting her body between his and the boy.

Shock flashing across the attacker's face, he stumbled back. "What…?"

"Run," she hissed to the boy behind her. "Get out of here now."

His breath caught. His footsteps pounded on the ground, fading into the distance. All the while, Mariel stared up at the attacker, eyes narrowed, body ready to pounce. To his credit, he did not turn and run, though he likely assumed that Mariel would shove her daggers into his back if he did.

He was right.

"How did you do that?" he finally asked, knife still held before him. "That drop should have killed you."

"But it didn't, and now you have to answer to me." Slowly, she stood, careful to keep the blades twisted in his direction. "Sloane or someone working for Sloane commanded you to kill this boy. Yes or no."

He shook his head and took a step back. "We're not supposed to answer yes or no questions."

The truth may be twisted but never false.

"I will stab you in the heart if you do not," she hissed, anger rattling her heart. "The murder you were about to commit was Sloane's doing. Yes or no."

His Dagda's Apple bobbed as he swallowed. Fear flickered through his yellow eyes. "He'll kill me."

"No. *I'll* kill you."

"All right. Yes." The attacker's eyelids fluttered shut, and he whispered something to himself. Likely a prayer to the Dagda. But the Dagda did not hear the needful calls of murderers.

"And why did Sloane want you to kill this boy?"

He shook his head. "I don't know. I didn't even speak to him. Someone inside the castle passed it along and told me what to do. It didn't even matter who it was. I just picked the first person to step through that door."

Mariel ground her teeth together. It was as she'd suspected. For some reason, the former king was behind these attacks, but there was no rhyme or reason to it. He did not pick specific targets. The low fae were likely indistinguishable to him. Any of them would do. The question was, why?

Mariel could tell she wouldn't get the answers to those question from this fae. He didn't know. He was blindly following the orders of a king who was no longer even his king, serving most likely out of a deep-seated fear that if he didn't make the kill, someone might murder him instead.

With a heavy sigh, she lowered her daggers. "I just have one more question for you."

He nodded eagerly, fingers trembling around his blade.

"If I let you go, you'll still kill an innocent low fae. Yes or no."

His face blanched, and he whispered, "We're not supposed to answer yes or no—"

Mariel loosed her dagger. It soared through the tiny alley and sunk into the attacker's throat. Blood spurted down his neck, large droplets mixing with the mud at his feet. His eyes rolled back in his head, and he slumped to the right, falling heavily onto his side.

Sliding her second dagger back into her waistband, she

strode over to the corpse. "I'm sorry, but I can't let you kill someone."

She leaned over him, shoved her boot against his chest, and yanked her dagger out of his throat. Then, she wiped his blood on his own tunic, leaving him in the middle of the street for someone else to find. There was no time to hide the body nor would it matter if it somehow traced it back to her. She was the Bloody Dagger.

Mariel did not know why the former king was having the Tairngire low fae murdered. She did not need to know why. All that mattered was that he was still at it even though his reign had come to an end.

There was only one thing she had to do now.

Murder the king.

As soon as she stepped foot inside the Witchlight Woods so she could use the castle's hidden entrance, she knew something was wrong. Air Court warriors rushed past her. Dozens of them. They were decked in full gold-dyed armor, their Tamaris steel swords glinting beneath the bright glow of the moon. With a frown, she stepped up beside one as they passed her by. He flinched for a moment, reaching for his sword, before he saw that she was nothing more than a low fae.

"What is happening?" she asked quickly. "Where are you going?"

He glanced behind him as more warriors rushed by. "I shouldn't say."

"Why? Is there something to fear?"

With another glance over his shoulder, he lowered his voice. "Do not speak of this to anyone."

She nodded eagerly.

"Princess Reyna has been captured by some wood fae hiding out in the hills beyond the woods. They sent a ransom note. A meeting with the prince in exchange for her life." He pressed his lips firmly together. "The High Queen has decided to attack. Get out of these woods at once. It isn't safe."

At that, he turned and joined the rest of the warriors rushing toward the hills. Mariel stared after him, heart thumping. She understood at once what must have happened. In an attempt to avoid a renewed war, Reyna had gone in search of the wood fae to make some sort of deal. That plan had backfired on her.

Mariel felt partially responsible. Indeed, she had begged Reyna not to tell Prince Thane.

She stared after the retreating warriors, torn. Her vengeance drove her toward the castle, but her heart strived to go help Reyna escape the clutches of the wood fae.

But there was little she could do. The air fae warriors would reach the hills far before she could. The battle would begin. The first of many more to come. She sighed and closed her eyes. In an attempt to prevent another battle, she had somehow only caused it to happen.

For a moment, she wondered if she was going about this all wrong. Would killing the former king help the low fae of Tairngire? Or would it only make the situation even worse? All she wanted was to protect her people. Years ago, that ability had been taken away from her. She'd been cast out, replaced by a vicious king who murdered his subjects.

Tairngire would never be safe as long as he was alive.

Nodding to herself, she set off toward the castle, renewed determination churning through her veins. She would figure out what to do about the wood fae later. For now, she had a king to kill.

She pushed into the hidden entrance and crept through the tunnels, breathing in the musty scent of dust that swirled through the darkness. When she reached the end and pushed on the wall, someone was waiting for her on the other side.

It was the spymaster.

"Ah." He gave her a kind smile that was just as much a lie as his words. "Just who I was waiting for."

Mariel reached for her daggers, but the spymaster held up a hand as a dozen warriors whispered out of the darkened corridor behind him. Half of them held glinting steel swords while the other half held nocked arrows. She froze, fingers halfway to her own weapons.

"What is this about?" Mariel whispered.

"The High Queen wishes to speak with you."

She tried to rein in her surprise. That was the last thing Mariel had expected the spymaster to say. What in the name of the Dagda would the High Queen want from Mariel? Did she know the truth about who she was? Or worse, did she know that she had come here to kill her husband?

Mariel itched to turn tail and run, but she had been well and truly surrounded. She wasn't certain she had much of a choice.

***

The High Queen lounged on her throne, a large goblet of wine sloshing in her hand. Mariel eyed it with a frown. The High Queen's sobriety was well-known and celebrated throughout the realm. A demonstration of her dedication to the Dagda and her faith. And it was not just that. Her eyes were lined in purple. Her deep crimson gown was disheveled, and her blue hair poked out from the side of a messy bun. Her golden circlet was even askew.

No one else was in the Great Hall. Even the tables had been carried out. It was eerie and so unlike the joyous, buzz-filled room that Mariel had once known.

"Thank you, Kelwyn," the High Queen said to the spymaster. "You and your warriors may go."

"But, Your Majesty. Your safety is our utmost—"

"I said you may go," the queen said icily.

With a frown, the spymaster motioned the warriors out of the Great Hall. The door shut heavily behind them, entombing Mariel with the queen. She kept her mouth shut tight, waiting for whatever had brought her here. This was *entirely* odd. She thought she ought to be afraid, but...she was merely curious.

"You may think I do not know what happens in my court," the High Queen finally said.

"I think nothing of the sort." Mariel's voice echoed against the looming stone ceiling, a sound that might be intimidating to some but was music to her own ears. It had been a long time since she had heard that echo.

"So, I am to believe that you thought your conversation with Reyna Darragh had gone unnoticed?"

Which conversation?

"What ever do you mean?"

Imogen arched her brow. "You have been sneaking around, asking questions of the servants. Did you think you would not be seen?"

"I merely wanted to assist the princess in finding whoever was responsible for the attempted murder against her," Mariel said quietly.

"And did you?"

Mariel thought for a moment but saw no reason to play games. "The wood fae."

Imogen let out a strangled sigh, and then slumped further into her throne of twisting vines. "Impressive, I have to say. You discovered it far sooner than I."

Surprised, Mariel stayed silent. She certainly hadn't expected the High Queen to commend her snooping around and causing mischief within her own court. When she had exited the hidden tunnels, she had been surrounded by armed warriors. And yet...there was no hostility in Imogen's expression.

How very curious.

"May I ask why you have brought me here?" she asked, and then added, "Your Majesty."

Imogen took a long drink of her wine and then dropped the empty goblet to the stone floor where it fell with a heavy *clunk*. She sat up a little straighter, brushing the remnants of the drink from her lips with the back of her hand.

"When I was informed of your conversation with Reyna, I had our spymaster look into you," Imogen began. "He painted quite the interesting portrait of you. A pub owner in Drunkard's Pit, but one with a reputation for justice. Vengeance, really. I know who you are, and I know what you can do. And I know why you have come here this night."

Mariel's feet were like pure lead, rooted to the spot. She held the air tight in her lungs, not daring to breathe.

"You believe my husband to be involved in the deaths of those innocent low fae. You wish to see him dead, and I do not blame you for that in the slightest."

"I..." Mariel could not form words.

"Unfortunately, the spymaster does not truly work for me. He is my husband's creature. He suspected you would come here this night. The former king is well-guarded and has squirrelled himself away."

For a moment, neither female spoke. They stared at each other, considering. There was a lot that Mariel thought she knew about the High Queen, but she could not have prepared herself for this. She wasn't even entirely certain what *this* was.

"Why have you brought me here?" Mariel finally asked. "It's not to imprison me or you already would have."

"No." Imogen pushed up from her slouch and smiled, flashing Mariel her wine-stained teeth. "I have called you here to give you a warning and some advice. The spymaster will expect me to either throw you in the dungeons or have you beheaded. I will do neither, but it does mean that your life is forfeit if he ever finds you again. I would not return to your pub if I were you, not so long as he lives."

Mariel's heart thumped hard. "Is that the warning or the advice?"

"That was the warning." Imogen's smile grew wide. "My son has decided to take this throne from me. He will demand his coronation soon, and his father has no choice but to make an appearance. It might be the only chance for someone to get close enough to…take care of the problem."

Imogen continued. "Sloane was a vicious king and is a cruel man. I cannot kill him myself. The Dagda would never forgive me. But if someone else were to turn their daggers toward his heart…I would make no move to stop her."

Mariel's hands fisted. "This is truly what you want, Your Majesty?"

It was as close to a yes or no question that one could get, and Mariel should not have asked it.

But Imogen gave a nod. "Yes. However, I believe I am

doing you a favor by delivering you my husband and making certain my spymaster does not chop off your head. I only make one request."

"Go on then. What do you want?"

Imogen's smile grew wide. "During the coronation, I'll give you a signal, when the right time comes. When it does, make certain you take out my former lover as well. Grand Alderman Aengus. Ginger hair, grey eyes."

"I know who he is," Mariel said quietly.

"Good. Now, go. You can escape through that door there and go out the window. Something tells me you are well-versed in scaling castle walls."

That was the only encouragement she needed. Mariel gave the High Queen one last nod, and then fled the castle, knowing that the warriors would not be far behind.

41
LORCAN

Full dark had arrived, and there had been no sign of Thane. Perhaps Lorcan had been wrong to trust that his oldest friend would come. He might have lied about the prince's love for Reyna, but Lorcan had been certain of their impending rescue regardless of his feelings.

Reyna was looking weaker by the moment. Her cheeks, which were normally full of blazing life, had gone white. She had also stopped arguing with him, which alarmed him far more than the glassiness of her silver eyes. She had mentioned something about her owl, about how her soul was linked to his. If only he knew how to call the creature to her aide, he would.

"Thane's not coming," she said softly from where she had propped herself up against the bars, bundling her cloak into a pillow to protect herself from the iron. At first, they had sat across from each other, but as they had shared tales of their past, he had moved to her side. She struggled to stay upright, and well, he did not wish to see her fall face-first against the hard ground, even if she did annoy him far more than seemed possible.

Lorcan frowned. Perhaps it was time to consider the alternative. Now that it was dark, Lorcan thought he might be able to get out of this cage. He had waited, certain that the prince would come along. But also because he did not want Reyna to witness his abilities. It would fully reveal the truth about who he was.

With no sign of Thane, he didn't have any more time to waste. The wood fae had been clear. If Thane did not show, then they would kill Reyna on the spot. He wouldn't be able to protect her if he kept waiting for the prince to come for them.

The enemy had bows and arrows. Most wood fae were excellent shots.

Reyna's eyelids had fallen shut at some point during their conversation. She looked peaceful, her face turned up toward the rising moon. While she wasn't watching him, Lorcan called upon the darkness that surrounded them both. The shadows pulsed around him, whispering across his skin. And then he did what he always did—he did not know how it happened, he just did it. Closing his eyes, he pulled the night into him, and magic filled his pulsing veins. He *moved* through the shadows, passing from one side of the cage to the other.

When he opened his eyes, he stood outside of the iron bars, peering in at Reyna. Her own eyes were still shut. She had not noticed.

Their belongings were propped up against a rock a short distance away. His sword and her dagger. Rustling through the tall grass, he inched toward the rock and grabbed their weapons. The wood fae never noticed, too busy stomping around their campfire in the distance, likely planning for Thane's arrival that had not yet come.

Back at the cage, he considered his options. He didn't

have the key, nor did he think he could work his sword in the lock. If he had time, perhaps.

They did not have time.

Drawing the shadows into his body once again, he leaned down and wrapped his hands around the bottom bars. The iron burned his skin, as if lava had been poured across his fingers. Pain lanced through his entire body. Gritting his teeth, he pulled. He strained against the heavy cage. It weighed thrice as heavy as him, and the iron burned deeper into his palms. But the cage moved.

Reyna suddenly awoke and was on her feet in an instant. She stared at him open-mouthed, clearly dumbfounded by his strength. And perhaps the fact he now stood outside of the cage rather than within it.

"Come on," he said through gritted teeth. "Do not make me hold this any longer. The iron burns."

She blinked the shock out of her eyes and ducked beneath the bars, joining him on the other side.

That was about the time that the night rang with steel.

Lorcan tossed the ice dagger to Reyna and whirled toward the sound, flicking his wrists to rid himself of the blinding pain left behind by the iron. Shadows whorled around him. They seeped into his skin, his body still tuned into them. They soothed the pain.

The campsite was ablaze with activity. Warriors donned in gold-dyed armor waved a banner and rushed toward the wood fae tents, their swords raised in the air. Shouts filled the quiet night, roars of bloodlust. The sigil on the banner was unmistakable. A golden crown. The air fae had arrived but not in the way Lorcan had imagined. He knew Thane hated their High King, but he had still believed he'd agree to attempt a resolution. But this was no resolution. It was war.

"How did you..." Reyna still stared at him, seemingly

oblivious to the battle waging only a short distance away from them.

"The Air Court has arrived," he said grimly. "But instead of bringing diplomacy, they have brought swords. Come. We should run from here while the wood fae are distracted."

"No," she said fiercely, dagger in hand. "They came here to save us. We should join in the fight."

"Reyna, you're not well."

Indeed, she swayed a bit on her feet.

He was not surprised that she wished to fight. It was in her blood and her bones and her soul. Something had happened to her as a child that had forever changed her. It would always be with her, whispering in her mind. Reyna was a warrior just as surely as any he had ever met, maybe even more so. She might have been born a princess but she had grown to be a wielder of blades.

"You're right. I'm not. But I do not think we have much of a choice in the matter." She pointed toward the campsite with the end of her dagger. Several of the wood fae had noticed that they were no longer locked up tight in their cage. They were on their way, angry faces lit up by the blazing fire. Two had a sword while only one held a bow. However, that bow had an arrow nocked, and it was aimed right at them.

Lorcan dropped his singeing hand on Reyna's shoulder, pushing her to the ground. "Duck into the grass. Stay low."

Reyna crouched into the grass beside him. They sat together, shoulders brushing as the grassy stalks whispered in the night like a field of swaying golden worms. Their breath mingled in the cold air, fogging before them.

Suddenly, an arrow punched the ground only a few feet from where they crouched. Reyna did not flinch. She didn't even blink. Instead, she kept her gaze locked on the blades just before her as if she were focused on something far beyond. She was listening.

Suddenly, Reyna leapt up from her crouch with a roar, her dagger outstretched before her. Lorcan half-stood, watching as she sank her icy blade deep into the wood fae's heart. Reyna yanked her dagger out of his limp body and ducked again, just in time to miss the next volley of arrows.

Lorcan tried not to stare. Even as drained as she was, she had come alive in the fight. Her cheeks were flushed once again, and her silver eyes sparkled in the moonlight. She looked like an agent of death.

No. A *goddess* of death.

Shaking his head, he turned his attention back to the task at hand just in time to pull her back to his side, yanking her out of the path of the next arrow.

She mumbled something to him. He thought it might have been a thanks.

Smiling, he heard the soft steps of the second wood fae. He pushed up from the ground and swung wide. His sword connected with the wood fae's neck, slicing clean through. Blood filled the air as his body fell, the head tumbling away into the distance.

That only left one wood fae. The one with the bow and arrow.

He had vanished somewhere in the fight. No doubt he was keeping out of the range of their blades. Frowning, Lorcan cast his eyes to the campsite. Bodies littered the ground. Most of them wore the colors of the Air Court. Gold mixed with the crimson of blood. His stomach dropped as he watched a wood fae slice down what looked to be the last air fae standing.

The air fae fell.

The Wood Court had won this fight.

"Reyna." Lorcan grabbed her hand and pulled her toward him. She fell against him, her fingers splayed against his chest. He tried to ignore the thrill that went through his gut. "We've lost this fight. All our warriors are dead. The archer has likely run back to camp to tell the others that we've escaped. We'll be surrounded within moments, and we cannot fight them all. We have to run now."

He expected her to argue. She liked to do that where he was concerned. But when she glanced back at the camp, her jaw set and that flood of life in her cheeks vanished.

"Okay," she answered. "Whatever hope we had for a treaty is gone now. I won't stick around here just to die."

Simultaneously, they dropped back their heads to examine the skies above. Lorcan had long ago memorized the constellations and the position of the twin moons for each month of the year. He surely knew north from south and east from west as if it had been etched into his very skin like the mark he kept hidden from the world.

The mark that had been strangely silent this night.

"This way," they both said as one, turning left from the campsite and pointing due north. Their voices rang like two steel blades that had crashed together. Lorcan's lips twitched. How could they be so in sync? Why did it feel as though he stared at the other half of himself? A slight smile crested Reyna's lips, an expression that matched Lorcan's own.

A roar sounded in the distance as the wood fae turned their attention on their fleeing captives. Lorcan held out a hand. Reyna took it.

And then they ran.

42

REYNA

"Where in Dagda's name are we?"

Reyna and Lorcan had stopped to rest in the swaying stalks as they had fled from the wood fae's campsite. Their blazing fire was now only an orange speck on the distant horizon, but somewhere out there, the wood fae pursued them as doggedly as a dragon after lamb.

Regrettably, they were somewhat lost. When they had fled captivity, Reyna had assumed that they would quickly stumble upon the woods that backed up against the castle. She had been very wrong. The camp was deep in the hills. It would explain why it had taken so long for the Air Court warriors to find it.

The two of them had followed the constellations until a thick cloud cover obscured the stars from view. Now, they seemed no closer to Tairngire than they had when they'd first fled.

Lorcan knelt on one knee, his arm braced on his other. His face was flushed from the exertion but he was not winded in the least. His breathing was steady, and his eyes were clear. He was demonstrably stronger than most fae Reyna had ever met. There was also the matter of how he had escaped the cage and then lifted it as if it weighed nothing more than a small wagon. The iron burns on his palms no longer seemed to bother him.

Suddenly, the skies opened up. Rain poured down from above, soaking them instantly. Water ran down Reyna's face, dropping into her eyes. Her palm soon became slick around the hilt of her ice dagger. If the wood fae tracked them down and forced an attack, she knew it would not take much for her grip on the slippery surface to fail.

"We need to take shelter until the skies clear," Lorcan shouted over the roar of the downpour. "If we keep moving forward at this rate, we might very well end up further away from the castle than before."

"Where?" she shouted back, pushing her wet strands out of her face.

He pointed to the right. "Before the rain began, I spotted a small outcropping of rocks. We won't be able to start a fire for fear of being spotted, but at least we can remain dry."

Reyna shivered as a sudden bout of wind blasted her in the face. They were not sea fae, accustomed to the slashing rain and pounding waves of the sea. Lorcan stood and motioned for her to follow. As they crept through the slick darkness, she could not help but cast her gaze his way, wondering at the secrets contained inside that mind of his.

There was so much she wanted to ask. Where had he found that strength? And why had he not used it before? Most importantly, *who was he*? She no longer believed his tales. Lorcan was not a village boy who had stumbled into the Air Court's castle accidentally. There was far more to his story than that. She knew it in her very bones.

They reached the outcropping of rocks just as the rain

thickened, hurtling down with a force that felt like punches against Reyna's skin. It wasn't a particularly large rock formation. Most in the grasslands wouldn't be, as it made little sense for them to even be there. She knew the Dagda religion taught that these random formations were some sort of sign from their god. Something left behind from his days spent walking these lands.

There were five large stones that joined together before them. They curved toward each other, coming together at the top of Reyna's waist. Just enough room to create a cave of sorts. Reyna ducked inside, and Lorcan quickly followed.

Instantly, her skin whispered in relief, now shielded from the pounding rain and the brutal winds. As she settled onto the dirt-packed ground, Lorcan slid his fingers into his dark, wavy hair and shook out the water. Reyna could not help but stare. And then her body began to shiver uncontrollably.

Suddenly, the weariness that had begun to plague her from Wingallock's absence came crashing down upon her like an avalanche. Her entire body ached. She had pushed it to its limits, forcing it to fight and flee when half of her soul was missing.

"Reyna?" Lorcan knelt beside her and pressed the back of his hand against her cheek. His touch was like fire. "You're freezing." A beat passed. "Is this an ice fae kind of cold or is something wrong?"

She slumped against the stone and let out a very long, tired exhale. "I am not sure. I think I might be cold, but it's hard to say since I normally don't experience that sensation. Ice doesn't bother me, but…Wingallock is so far away. His presence always strengthens me." She shivered.

His face furrowed in concern. "You are cold then. Your owl has been protecting you from feeling the ice. With these harsh winds and the slashing rain, the chill has sunk into your skin."

"Are you cold?"

"I am," he replied. "Though not like you. We need a fire, but we can't risk the wood fae spotting it. There's only one solution. You're going to need to undress."

Clarity rushed back into Reyna's mind as she bolted upright. "Am I truly that delirious that I just heard you telling me to undress?"

"You're not delirious, Reyna." He unclasped his sword and let the scabbard drop onto the ground behind him. Reyna followed his every move, breath catching. He was all hard lines and sharp angles except for the long dark hair that curled around his pointed ears. "The water has soaked through our clothes, and the winds will keep battering us until this storm lets up. We will fall ill unless we keep ourselves warm, and we do not know how far we are from the castle and the alchemists who can heal us."

"Surely you don't truly expect me to undress before you," she said, her voice coming out far strangled than she intended.

His dark eyes sparkled in the darkness. "You better believe I do. Or I could do it for you instead."

Her face flushed. Suddenly, she did not feel quite so cold anymore. With shaking fingers, she pulled on the strings that kept her tunic tied together at her throat. Lorcan watched her, silent and still. She untucked the shirt from her trousers and pulled it over her head. Beneath, she wore simple undergarments. When wearing gowns, the garments beneath were much more complicated, but tunics and trousers required very little. And, unfortunately, they were very much see-through.

Before she could lose her nerve, she kicked off her boots and pushed down her trousers. But instead of finding warmth from the freedom of her damp clothes, Reyna shivered, and her teeth began to chatter.

As she had undressed, Lorcan had quickly followed, tossing his leather armor into the corner of the make-shift cave. He now knelt before her, completely naked save for a small strip of brown quilted cloth belted around his waist. His well-muscled chest glistened from the rain that had soaked through his garments. His arms rippled with strength. And, she could not help but notice, a significant bulge hid behind that belted cloth.

She felt warm all over.

Lorcan reached out and traced a finger along the undergarments that were plastered to her damp skin. "You should remove those. They are soaked through as well."

She glanced down, noting the peaked nipples poking through the thin, white material. Heart racing, she held still as Lorcan's hands drifted south, pulling at the bottom hem of her garments. She held her arms over her head and let him pull the cloth off her body. A cold wind from outside of the cave pushed into the rocks and whipped across Reyna's bare breasts.

Lorcan stared into her eyes, and she stared right back. She could barely breathe. What was he thinking? And what was she doing? In the back of her mind, she knew she was breaking so many rules just by being alone with this male, let alone naked with him. He wasn't touching her, but he didn't need to. The desire coiling through her was treason enough. If the High Queen found out about this...

Her teeth chattered even more.

"Your lips are blue," Lorcan said in a low voice that sent a different kind of shivers across her body.

"Is this what it's like to be cold?"

"I'm afraid it is." He frowned. "We need to share our body heat."

Reyna's heart thumped hard. She did not know why she was finding this entire situation thrilling and terrifying all at once. During her Shieldmaiden training, she had learned what to do in emergency situations such as this. Stranded in the elements with little warmth, the sharing of body heat was essential to staying warm. Reyna had always dismissed these lessons. She was an ice fae. The cool air and the ice beneath her feet had never bothered her.

But without her owl familiar nearby, everything had changed.

And now, here she was, with a muscular, naked warrior fae kneeling before her, offering to warm her body with his. She could barely think straight.

So, with a nod, she turned her back toward him and lay down on the cold dirt. She heard him shift against the ground, lowering his body behind hers. Strong arms wrapped around her and pulled her close. The scent of him was almost overwhelming: leather and steel and smoke. Warmth pulsed from his body, soothing her trembling skin. Her heart still raced as fast as a dragon through the skies, but the feel of him burned away her fear.

She finally let go of all her pent-up tension, giving in to the cocoon of warmth, sighing, letting her mind drift away.

※

She awoke to darkness. A pocket of warmth surrounded her as the wind whistled through the rocks like a high-pitched bird's cry, and suddenly, she remembered where she was. Lorcan's arms still enveloped her, and his face was pressed against the back of her neck. She could feel his hot breath on her skin, and traitorous desire stirred in her core.

"You're awake," he murmured, lips moving against her

skin. She trembled, though this time, it was not from the chill. "Are you feeling any better?"

"I am," she admitted. "I suppose you were right about the body heat."

"Of course I was." She could feel the smile on his lips. "Maybe now you will stop fighting with me every time I make a suggestion. Though, I doubt it."

With a slight hitch in her breath, she twisted on the ground to face him. He remained where he was, face close, arms draped across her body. Their noses were scarcely an inch apart.

"Thank you," she said slowly, her cheeks burning. "And I'm sorry. I fear my resistance to cold has left me."

"You will get it back," he said. "As soon as your owl returns to your side, your resistance to the cold will return. He is part of your soul. You need each other to survive."

"You speak with longing."

His eyes darkened. "I have never had a bond like that."

For a moment, Reyna could do nothing but stare into his eyes. The wind still roared around the rocks as rain pummelled the ground just outside their enclosure. She did not know how long they had been in their shelter, nor did she care. Right now, it felt as if the world was very far away. All the courtly politics she hated so much, all the battles and the wars. She wanted to forget it all for just a little longer as her heartbeat drummed in her ears.

"I have never been naked with a male before," she whispered.

Lorcan reached up and traced his finger down the length of her face. She shivered. "I feel very fortunate to be the only one."

His mouth was suddenly on hers. With a gasp, she curled toward him and opened her lips to invite his tongue inside. He kissed her hard and fiercely, as if a sudden hunger had taken over his mind. A hunger that she felt herself. The weariness of the past two days no longer plagued her. Body lit up by his touch, she dug her fingernails into his back and pulled herself so close that her peaked nipples pressed into his chest.

In truth, she did not know what she was doing, nor did she care to think much about it, lest logic took over and put a stop to it. She had felt a connection to this warrior from the moment she had seen him, and he saw her in a way that no one else ever had. She saw him, too, even if he still kept his secrets hidden away from her.

Back at the castle, she would never again have the chance to give in to her desires, and one day, Lorcan would likely be torn from her side. He was Thane's warrior. Thane's confidante. If he ever discovered what she had planned...

His hot mouth on her throat pushed all those thoughts out of her mind. Sparks lit up on her still-damp skin. She moaned as his strong hand slid down the side of her body and then ran along her back to cup her arse. Need curled through her core like fire. The cold of the rain-soaked night was nothing more than a distant memory.

Scratching her fingernails down the length of his muscular back, she shifted her thigh sideways and slid her leg around his waist. He moaned, his hard length now pressing against the very core of her. She was slick with need, and her desire pulsed out a drumbeat between her thighs.

Everything about this male called to her. The way he stood tall and strong when the rest of the world was falling apart. The way he moved with vicious grace as he swung his sword. His dark eyes. The way they saw so much, how they stared right into the very depths of her soul. His sharp cheekbones, his cutting jaw, the mound of delicious dark curls on his head. And the way his body felt against hers.

As his mouth dipped even lower, his lips melting against her aching nipples, she wanted to scream. But she couldn't. The enemy was close by. Even with the pounding drums of the rain, she couldn't risk her explosive screams reaching the ears of the wood fae.

All she could do was writhe in the dirt.

He flipped her onto her back and peered down at her. His eyes were hot with need; her desire was reflected in his burning gaze. With a guttural growl, he pinned her wrists against the dirt, and then penetrated her with his massive length. Stars lit up in her vision.

A soft moan slipped from her parted lips as his cock throbbed against her slick walls. A million tiny tremors shook her body. Her breath was stuck in her throat. He pushed in deeper, and her back arched. This was unlike anything she had ever felt in her life.

"You are amazing, Reyna Darragh," he groaned as he pulled back and then pounded deep inside of her with one intense stroke. She cried out, unable to keep her pleasure hidden any longer.

Again, he slowly pulled back and then slammed hard into her core. She was a mess beneath him. Every single part of her felt alive, but her body could do nothing but shake from the intensity of the sensations pouring through her. She stared up at his dark eyes, and he smiled. Her heart flipped.

Leaning down, he dragged his tongue across her nipple. Heat flooded her veins even as she trembled uncontrollably. An impossible ache had formed between her thighs, a need so great that she could barely think around it. She needed more. More or she would burst into flames.

Lorcan sucked on her nipple as he stroked her aching

insides with his hardness. She panted beneath him, and hooked her leg behind the back of him, yanking him toward her, desperate for more. His pace quickened. The whirlwind of sensations threatened to pull her under, drowning her in the thick of it.

And then, suddenly, it was if everything popped. Pleasure throbbed through her core, and her back arched. She shuddered around him, her entire body transforming into a trembling mass of pure delight. Clinging onto Lorcan's muscular arms as if they were a lifeline, she let go of everything, giving in to her deepest, darkest need for him. It nearly pulled her under.

His moans mingled with hers as his length throbbed hard between her thighs, emptying his seed inside of her.

A moment later, they lay together in the dirt, arms and legs wrapped around each other, sweat glistening on their once-cold bodies. Reyna could barely comprehend what had just happened. She had imagined what sex would be like, of course, but this had far surpassed her imagination. It had felt as if they had shared something far greater than just their bodies. Even if they had not spoken a word through it all.

As the rain continued to thunder down outside, Lorcan shifted to face her and pushed her damp air out of her face, smiling. "I hope you are pleasantly warm now."

Her face flushed, even after what they had just shared. "I'm certainly not cold."

The wind caressed her thigh. She frowned. No, that couldn't be the wind. It still raged through the grasslands, bitter and harsh and terrible. This had felt more like a slight breeze, a whisper of something else.

She glanced down, gasping at the black shape curling around their bodies. It looked like black smoke, drifting through the cave. It looked like...shadows.

Reyna pulled back, heart hammering hard. Lorcan's face had darkened, and his expression was as unreadable as it ever was. Suddenly, she understood everything. She knew what he had been hiding. He had always seemed different, and now she knew why.

Lorcan was not from these lands. She had guessed it before, but she hadn't thought it possible. But now she stared the truth in the face.

He was a shadow fae.

43

LORCAN

Lorcan stayed very still as he watched the truth churn through Reyna's silver eyes. Her mouth had parted. She looked as though she had seen a Fomorian, charging at her across the fields. Everything within him wanted to jump to his feet, explain it all, and force her to understand that he was not the monster she thought he was.

But he truly was that monster.

Lorcan was a shadow fae. His kind had been exiled from Tir Na Nog fifty years past when their High King had brutally slaughtered dozens of air fae nobility. He had never meant to drop his guard and allow the shadows of his skin to seep out in front of someone else. He'd always been in control. He'd never allowed his mask to drop, not even in front of Prince Thane.

He hadn't even realized he'd done it this night. Not until he saw the look of horror pass across his lover's face.

Reyna sat up, breaking the cocoon of warmth that had formed around them. She looked absolutely breathtaking, even when she looked as though she might strangle him. In fact, her anger brought out her characteristic fierceness, one of the things that had drawn him toward her in the first place.

His taste in females was going to get him killed someday.

"I suppose half of the things you've said to me have been lies," she finally said, her voice as icy as the winter winds of the north. "If not more."

"I am careful with my words, same as every other fae alive. But most of what I have suggested to you has been the truth."

"And Thane?" She pulled her knees up to her chest and wrapped her arms around them. "Does he know what you are?"

"He does."

She looked at him hotly. "Is that another one of your lies? Because I find it impossible to believe that the prince of the Air Court would choose a shadow fae to be his closest guard."

"You may ask him yourself when we return to the castle. Thane and I have known each other for a very long time. He knows what I am, and he has accepted it."

Of course, that was not the full truth. Lorcan had been born on Air Court lands, son to an air fae female and a shadow fae male. According to the magic of the realms, that would officially make Lorcan an air fae, one who had no shadow fae powers. A fae could never be both. It was impossible. The son or daughter always took after the mother. Never the father.

That would mean Lorcan couldn't lie. But he could.

And that would mean he couldn't draw power from shadows. But even in a world post-Fall, he could that, too.

In truth, a part of him ached to tell Reyna everything. Logically, he knew that was a terrible idea. She was betrothed to marry the prince. One day, not long from now, she would become the High Queen of the Air Court herself. If the war went the way they hoped, she might even become an Empress.

If Lorcan told her everything, not only would he lose that spark he saw in her eyes but he would likely forfeit his life.

His mark burned even as he contemplated it.

Frowning, she dropped her chin to her knees and stared out at the grasslands. The rain had begun to die down, and a pinkish light filled the horizon. Soon, they would no longer have an excuse for hiding out in these rocks. She would be free of him just in time to run straight back into Thane's arms.

"So, you are a shadow fae." She lifted her eyes and twisted to face him.

"Not entirely. My father is a shadow fae, but my mother wasn't."

That was the truth, at least. His father had bedded many females over the years from every corner of the continent. He had hoped to create a hybrid, a fae skilled in two elements instead of just one, believing that was the way to take back the realm.

But he had been wrong. His father's blood was strong.

Lorcan had warned him to cease his actions, but his father never listened to his bastard son. Another shadow fae had once tried to create hybrids. And it had resulted in the deaths of dozens. It was a magic not to be trifled with, but these males were convinced Unseelie wanted them to do it.

"And you have some magic," Reyna said softly. "I saw it. Tendrils of shadows pulsing around you. And that's how you were able to get out of the cage."

He nodded. "It hasn't always been the case. My power

came to me about fifteen years ago. It isn't always perfect or strong, but I can draw upon the shadows at times. For strength, for hearing, for sight. Sometimes, to shift through them."

He probably shouldn't have shared that with her. That was one thing Thane didn't know. The prince believed that Lorcan had no shadow fae powers at all, that he had inherited his mother's element instead of his father's.

Her arms dropped away from her chest as she shifted toward him. He tried—and failed—to keep his gaze on her face. "How does it feel? The magic?"

Lorcan thought for a moment. "It just feels...right. Like the blood in my veins and the air in my lungs. In truth, it's hard to remember how it felt to live so long without it."

She nodded. "You could have told me, you know. It was a shock, but it isn't as though I don't understand what it feels like to be apart from everyone else."

"I couldn't have, Reyna," he said. "It was too big of a risk. Prince Thane does know where I came from, but no one else does, especially not the High Queen. She wouldn't be as understanding as her son. She is venomous toward shadow fae, and for good reason. The courtiers would call for my head, and Sloane, that old bastard..." He shook his head. "He's the worst of them."

"The worst of them?" Reyna arched her brow. "Don't tell me the esteemed warrior despises the entire court."

He chuckled. "There are many terrible people inside of the Air Court. There are just as many good. Thane, for one..."

He fell silent, frowning. His mark burned at his words. Thane was not vicious, evil, or cruel. He sometimes made poor choices, but didn't they all? Fae were no better than humans in most regards. They liked to think they were, but they were wrong.

COURT OF RUINS

A strange expression flickered across Reyna's face at the mention of the prince. He could not blame her. She was to marry Thane, someday very soon. In several months' time, she would be a wedded female. And she had just given herself to another male.

Lorcan had tried to hold himself back, but his need for her had been too great. When she'd stared into his soul with her silvery eyes, he'd had no chance. He had caved to his carnal desires, thrusting himself deep inside of her. She had felt like hot silk around his cock. If he could turn back time and undo it all, he wouldn't.

"The rains have let up," she whispered. "We should probably return before the Air Court sends out another band of fighters to get slaughtered."

Damn the rains. Only a light drizzle that was more like a mist had settled over the grasslands, creating a thick fog that blocked the distant hills from view. It would be difficult to find their way back, but Reyna was right. They needed to return to the castle to warn the others, before the wood fae knocked down the city gates for war.

Reyna slipped back into her damp clothes, and Lorcan followed suit. They had dried slightly in the night, but only just. The cold material clung to his skin, sending a chill deep into his bones. What he would give to toss them off again, and hide away in this tiny cave with Reyna for as long as they could live.

"I won't tell anyone," she said just as Lorcan turned to duck out of the cave. "Everyone has secrets, and it isn't my place to reveal yours to the world."

That caused Lorcan to pause, just for a moment. Guilt clouded his mind. Should he tell her everything? He hated hiding the worst of it from her. Maybe she would hate him forever, but...

He opened his mouth to try to find the words but was

stopped short by her sudden gasp. Lips parted, she pushed out of the cave and gazed around the grasslands. He followed suit, following the line of her eyes.

A new chill swept across his body. All around them, the wheat had charred. Where the golden stalks had swayed beneath an ever-present breeze, there was nothing but piles of black ash. He glanced at Reyna. Her hand was at her throat, and her face had gone grey. No longer did the scent of wheat curl around them. It had been replaced by the pungent aroma of soot.

"The Ruin," she whispered. "It was here."

44
THANE

Lorcan and Reyna stood before him, looking very much the worse for wear. Reyna's silver hair was soaked through and plastered to her ashen face. Her clothes were damp, as were Lorcan's. Water splattered onto his chamber's stone floor. Black soot clung to their matching leather boots. Reyna's owl had flown in through his window moments after her arrival, and the poor thing now perched on her shoulder, rubbing his curved orange beak against Reyna's cheek.

Reyna and Lorcan had come in through the hidden tunnels beneath the castle to find Thane stewing in his study. As he had prepared the day before to parley with the Wood Court, his own mother had sent troops first. Every warrior she sent had died in the fight, save one, who had reported back to the castle. He had told Thane that his betrothed and his warrior had somehow escaped from their cage, but they could not be found.

Now, they stood before him, with matching chagrined expressions.

"Well, first, I am glad to see you are both alive." He

sucked a deep breath in through flared nostrils. "However, I must ask. Whose idea was it to run off to confront the wood fae without informing me first?"

"Mine," Reyna said quietly, eyes downcast. "Lorcan attempted to stop me."

"He must not have attempted very hard," he said in a snap, pounding a fist against his desk as he stood. "Lorcan is larger than you and far stronger. If he had followed orders properly, he would have dragged you back to the castle, kicking and screaming if he had to."

Reyna lifted her gaze, her eyes flashing. "It isn't his fault. I didn't tell him what I was doing until after we got captured."

Of course she hadn't.

"I see." His gaze turned toward his warrior, the one he had trusted above all else, the one who had failed him this time. While he normally appeared strong, firm, and unruffled, Lorcan now looked as though he'd been rolling around in the dirt. "What is your response, Lorcan?"

"You are right, of course. I should have dragged her back as soon as I saw her sneaking out of the castle. I did not. And, for that, the fault lies with me."

With a frown, Thane regarded them both. Each taking the blame for the other's actions. He could distinctly remember a time when they hated each other. They could scarcely get through a day without hurling insults. How quickly things could change. However, despite his annoyance, he could not help but soften, just a bit. He was glad they had finally formed a friendship. They both meant a great deal to him.

Sighing, Thane sank into the wooden chair behind his desk. The both of them remained standing, water forming puddles around their feet. He would not keep them much longer. Surely they were cold, tired, and hungry after their ordeal. But there were some important things to attend to first, things that could no longer wait.

"Regardless of how I feel about your actions, I can agree with you on one thing. We need to handle this wood fae situation very carefully. My mother's actions have only antagonized our biggest enemy, and there will no doubt be repercussions to that."

Reyna frowned. "Your mother?"

"I didn't send those warriors. The High Queen did."

Anger flashed in Reyna's eyes. "Attacking the wood fae like that...so many innocents are going to die as a result. Doesn't she realize that? They're not just going to sit back and let that go."

"No. No, they are not." He pinched the bridge of his nose. "But she believes that they cannot get away with what they have done. I understand her position. They sent multiple assassins against my future wife. Then, they captured her, all the while hiding a secret band of warriors in our realm. They are the ones who have agitated us, not the other way around. And then there is High King Ulaid, of course..."

"You agree with the High Queen's decision?" Lorcan asked, clearly shocked by his old friend's words. Thane knew the letter must have been his warrior's idea, a hope for peace, not war. But he hadn't counted on the letter falling into the wrong hands.

"I don't agree with it, but I do understand it." Bracing his fisted hand on the desk, he stood once more. "My mother's actions have given me no other choice. I do not trust her to lead even a moment longer. Her personal vendetta against the wood king has made her blind to reason. I have made my announcement to the court, and I have called for an immediate coronation. It will take place at the week's end, just long enough to call every member of the nobility to Tairngire." He paused. "After which, I will wait no longer to wed. Another week will pass, and then I will take my wife, securing the alliance with the Ice Court."

He stood tall, chin raised. For so long, Thane had cowed to the whims of everyone else. He had never stood strong on his own. So many voices whispered in his ears, pulling on puppet strings he had not even realized he had. But now he was the rightful king, and he would take that crown and that throne. And he would no longer wait around for any of it to happen.

Reyna stared at him, her cheeks flushed, her hands fisted by her sides. She did not look like a female who had just been told she would become the High Queen of an ancient, powerful court. And he knew why. Reyna Darragh did not want to marry him, and she never would.

In truth, he did not want to marry her either.

"What is the matter, Reyna?" he asked calmly.

"I..." She glanced at Lorcan, and then back at Thane. "This is happening sooner than I expected. We will need a little time to prepare."

He nodded. "You're right, of course. However, some of the finest servants in all of Tir Na Nog work inside of this castle. They are up to the task. In fact, I wager they will enjoy it. It has been a very long time since we had a royal wedding in this kingdom."

"Very well," she said, clearing her throat. She glanced at Lorcan once more. "I suppose I should start the preparations today."

"That will be unnecessary," he said coolly.

She frowned at him, confused. "What do you mean?"

"You see, I have learned something very important through all this. My mother has made some terrible mistakes that could end up costing us this realm. But Reyna, so have you. Your intentions were pure. That I do not doubt. But you are not fit to rule. You're a Shield-maiden, not a future High Queen."

"Thane, what are you doing?" Lorcan asked, inching closer to the desk.

Reyna clutched the wet fabric at her throat. "I don't understand."

Thane smiled. He did not know why he hadn't seen this as an option earlier. There was no reason why he shouldn't change his mind. He'd been afraid, perhaps. Worried that his feelings were one-sided. But now he knew that they were not.

"I am going to free you from your agreement to marry me, Reyna, and make the decision I should have made in the first place." He shifted on his feet, nodding to himself. "I will wed your sister, Eislyn Darragh, instead."

45

LORCAN

Reyna looked as though she had been punched in the gut. Lorcan, however, wanted to smile. He held it back, as difficult as it was.

"My sister?" With wild eyes, she threw her hands in the air. "You can't do that."

"Why ever not?" Thane snapped back.

This was a very interesting development, one that Lorcan himself had not seen coming, even though it made perfect sense now that he'd heard it. Thane and Reyna had never been a good match. They were so very different in so many ways. And where they were alike, it was in the worst way possible. Where she was fire, Thane was ice. Where she was wild, he was calm. He revelled, certainly, and enjoyed a jolly party, but he always expressed incredible restraint, even with the ale surging through his veins. Reyna just liked to charge in, daggers flashing. Thane could be calculating and cruel. Reyna could be, too. The combination, in theory, might have created something that sizzled. Instead, it was a dud.

Inside the very depths of his soul, Lorcan smiled.

"Because..." she sputtered. "We have an agreement. We're betrothed."

"Courtly betrothals can change in an instant." Thane frowned and cocked his head. "I know things are different up north, but our two courts are alike enough that you should understand that much at least. Our betrothal has been secure solely because of the alliance. Neither of us want to see it fail. However, as your sister is here, we can call off our ridiculous charade of a betrothal and form an alliance that will not make both of us miserable."

Reyna's fisted hands trembled. Lorcan watched her reaction, frowning. He had understood their affair to be nothing more than a flighting fancy. One that drifted away on the wind as easily as it had come. However, her pain and frustration at Thane's decision made little sense. She clearly had no love for the prince. The only reason Reyna had agreed to the betrothal in the first place was because Eislyn had turned him down. And now her younger sister had warmed to Thane, very much so. Reyna should be happy.

"There was a reason I volunteered," she said. "That reason has not changed. I fear for my younger sister to marry a prince who once killed our people on the battlefield."

He arched a brow. "Oh, I remember very clearly. You agreed because you were worried that I would act cruel and vicious toward your sister. And you still believe that, even now? You know me, Reyna. Do you not? Have you not seen how well I treat her?"

Reyna glared at him. "However kind you have been to Eislyn, that does not change the past. It doesn't change what you have done. I know what happened on your way to see us. I know the truth about The Sapphire Axe."

Shock flickered through Lorcan. He stared at Reyna,

seeing the vengeance in her eyes for the first time. No wonder she had tossed aside her Shieldmaiden duties to marry the prince. She hadn't done it to protect the alliance. She'd done it to protect her sister from Thane. He'd always wondered at the distance she'd kept between herself and the prince since arriving at court. Now, he knew why.

His mark pulsed happily.

This wasn't good. This wasn't good at all.

Thane braced his hands on the desk and leaned across it. "I am sorry for that, Reyna. I truly am. It was a terrible mistake, one I wish I could take back. But I have made my decision, and it isn't going to change. Do not mistake me, Reyna. I care for you. But you will not be my queen. Your sister will."

46

REYNA

Reyna stood before the mirror, scowling at herself. Her plan to take control of the Air Court had been up and ruined, and it was entirely her fault. She had intended to play the part of the betrothed princess: dignified, calm, and measured. Dutiful. Happy.

Normal.

Unfortunately for Reyna, those personality traits were in total opposition to her true nature. She had blown it, and it hadn't even taken a year. By being brash and reckless, she had convinced the prince that she would be the worst possible Darragh to sit on the throne beside him. She knew that she wasn't perfect. Many of his complaints were founded. That didn't mean that she would not be better at ruling than he. At least she wouldn't go around killing innocent allies.

Reyna pressed down the front of her long and flowing black gown. Today, Thane would be crowned. He would finally sit on the Seat of Power and take his rightful place as the High King. A week later, he would wed her sister. And there was little Reyna could do to stop it.

Thane had not yet told Eislyn of his plans. Reyna had requested for him to wait until after the coronation to inform her. Her sister had been a mess of emotions when Reyna had returned from the wood fae. She'd even mentioned having strange visions again. Eislyn needed time to breathe before the next issue came hurtling straight toward her.

And Reyna needed time to think.

There might still be a way to turn things around, but...she didn't know how just yet.

With a heavy sigh, she turned to the side. Her hair had been pulled up into a curling mass of silver that cascaded in a single line down her back. The ebony gown dipped low to her hips, the trim elaborately embroidered with silver-spun hoarfrost. On the gown itself, she had requested an embroidered pattern of dark wings trapped within spinning circles, and a pair of silver hip pads that looked like armor. Her waist had been further cinched with a silver belt made from linked chains. The sleeves were long and flared out at the ends. Inside one, she'd hidden her ice dagger.

And, of course, she had topped off the look with her mother's ice ring, and the silver circlet that she had begun to forget was even there. It almost felt like a part of her now.

A light knock sounded on the outer door of her chambers.

"Come in," she called out, turning away from the mirror.

The door cracked open, and Lorcan strode inside. He had exchanged his worn leather armor for a much more refined set. He wore a glinting hand-beaten metal breastplate adorned with the Air Court's crown sigil, right above his heart. His hair had been pulled back away from his face, highlighting the sharp point of his ears and the strong line of his jaw. Reyna flushed and swallowed hard, finding it impossible to think of anything but the way his lips had felt trailing across her skin.

"Hello," she said quietly.

"Princess Reyna." He lowered his head slightly before raising his eyes to hers. That same strange darkness flickered inside of them. Now, she knew what that was. His shadow magic pulsing deep inside of his soul.

"I..." She stumbled on her words. "What are you doing here?"

"Our new High King has requested that I escort you to the coronation."

"Oh. I see." Her heart sank, just a little. In the days following their return to the castle, Lorcan had not sought her out, nor had he taken up his usual post outside of her chamber doors. It had disappointed her far more than she had wanted to admit. After everything they'd shared, she hadn't expected him to avoid her.

"Are you ready? The coronation will begin soon."

"Lorcan," she said, taking a step toward him. "Tell me about The Sapphire Axe."

His jaw clenched. "That is Thane's story to tell. Not mine."

"No." Determined, she took another step. "You were there, too. I need to know what happened. I need to know what he did. I need..." She closed her eyes. "I need to know what kind of king my sister will marry."

"You want to know if he is a good male." He let out a heavy sigh. "Tell me, princess. What have you seen with your own eyes? Is he terrible and cruel? Or is he trying to do the right thing by his people?"

Reyna's heart clenched. She did not truly know Thane, but she had watched him all these days inside the castle. He had shown a great deal of care toward her younger sister. He had spent hours inside the library, searching for an answer to the Ruin. And he had put aside his own personal views on the wood fae in hope of saving her from certain death. He was not all bad. She knew it in her gut. But she still needed to know the truth about that night.

"Please just tell me." She opened her eyes to stare up at Lorcan, her heart thumping. "Why did he slaughter all of those ice fae?"

"You won't stop asking until I tell you, will you?" Lorcan turned away from her and strode over to the open window. It was midday, and the sun beamed down from a spring sky. "He wanted to stop at The Sapphire Axe to rest for the night. It had been a long journey. The ice fae...they didn't want us there. Thane felt he couldn't leave, for fear of showing weakness. A fight broke out. Several fae rushed him with blades. Thane was merely protecting himself, and then his guards, including me, were forced to jump into the fight to protect him, too. Both parties were at fault. It was a terrible thing to have happened, and Thane wished it never had."

Reyna stared at him, her heart thumping. "You could be lying."

He sighed and turned to face her. And there was conviction in his eyes. "I'm not lying, Reyna. I know what you want to believe. That Thane is terrible and brutal. That you need to save your sister from him. You've seen each other on the battlefield. You've considered him your enemy for so long that hatred toward him feels as natural as breathing. It's easy to continue believing what you always have, even when challenged. It's a hell of a lot harder to admit that you may have been wrong."

Her eyes burned as frustrated tears threatened to spill down her cheeks. Fisting her hands, she turned away, trying to still the rapid beating of her heart. Lorcan was right, of course, and she hated him for it. Reyna did not want to let go of her vengeance. It had buried itself so deep inside her bones that it was part of her now. If she extracted it, she would lose a part of herself.

Who was she if she was not the enemy of the Air Court? What was her purpose if she no longer had that?

The wind whistled through the open window, and she breathed in the cool air. A small voice whispered in the back of her mind.

You do not need vengeance to protect your realm.

"Reyna," Lorcan said, breaking through her thoughts. "There's something else I ought to share with you. It's not about Thane. It's about me. But I—"

A trumpet blared and echoed through the stone corridors of the castle. Lorcan snapped his mouth shut, and gave her a tight smile. She twisted toward the sound, desperate to wind back time.

"What is it, Lorcan?" she asked, knowing his answer before he even spoke it. "What do you want to tell me?"

"We don't want to be late to the coronation." He motioned toward the door. "We will speak after."

With a sigh, she nodded and pushed out into the corridor. To celebrate the occasion, every wall of the castle had been lined with flickering golden lights rather than the standard fire sconces. It cast a yellow haze across everything, filling up the gloomy tunnels with the glow of the Air Court's brilliant, luminous color.

Lorcan closed her chamber door behind them and motioned her toward the stairwell. They fell into step as they made their way to the Great Hall, silent and tense. She ached to ask him what he'd been about to tell her, or to speak of the night they'd shared, but she couldn't. Not with the walls around them, ever listening.

At long last, they pushed into the Great Hall. It was packed to the brim with tittering fae in rows of wooden seats. Every member of the court had come. Many from far beyond the walls of Tairngire. The lords and ladies of the court would want to witness the coronation of their new king, and enjoy the hearty feasting that came after. She spotted Lady Epona and Lady Arabella, dressed in full courtly garb. She recognized several other courtiers from her days spent gossiping in this very hall, but many more she had never seen.

With a warm hand on her elbow, Lorcan led her through the crowd and deposited her into a row just behind Imogen and her Grand Alderman, Aengus. She sat beside her sister, who smiled up at the empty throne. Eislyn had been decked out in even a grander gown than Reyna's. The silky dress had been dyed a deep gold, the perfect match to the court's own color. Her silver hair cascaded around her petite shoulders, and her eyes had been outlined by thick black kohl.

She looked the perfect portrait of a princess, and the elaborately embroidered gold gave her away as someone quite special indeed. Reyna wondered if her sister had even noticed.

Likely not. Otherwise, she doubted she would be beaming as she was.

In fact, why was she even beaming at all? Eislyn *hated* Prince Thane.

High King Thane Selkirk, Reyna corrected herself. It would take some time to become accustomed to that.

"Isn't this exciting?" Eislyn whispered as lilting harp music began to soar through the grand, lofted room. "I've never been to a coronation before."

Reyna frowned. "I did not realize you were this interested in coronations."

Eislyn flushed. "Yes, well. I suppose this one is different."

"Different how?"

"Well, because it is Thane, of course." She flushed further. "As you know, he's been helping me with my research into the Ruin."

At once, Reyna understood. Eislyn's flushed cheeks, her smile. Thane's insistence that they wed. Heart pounding, she turned her gaze toward the throne of vines where the Elder Druid waited for Thane to join him for the coronation. Thane had not lied, but he had obscured the truth. He had not changed his mind about Reyna *solely* because of her actions.

He had fallen for Eislyn.

Reyna twisted her hands together in her lap. Eislyn clearly felt the same about him. In fact, Reyna was not certain she had ever seen her sister blush until now. Did she love him?

The music built to a crescendo, and suddenly, the door behind the throne swung wide. Thane strode through, clad in refined coronation garb. He wore a long tunic in gold brocade, and a full matching cape that had been fastened by ornate golden clasps, the sigil embossed onto the surface. He strode forward in tall leather boots, his head free of a crown for once. His long golden hair shone, and his ornate tattoo seemed to swirl across his forehead as he moved.

He was the picture of royalty, chin high, eyes firm and unyielding. The entire court fell into a hush. No one dared speak.

Thane knelt at the feet of the druid. It would be the

only time that the High King would ever kneel before anyone but his god.

The Elder Druid smiled down at Thane. He was a contrast to the new High King. He wore the standard uniform of the druids, a simple brown leather robe that wrapped around his entire body. He had no hair atop his head, nor did he wear the sigil of any kingdom. His loyalty was to the Dagda and the Dagda only. Instead, he wore a simple silver necklace on a string of leather. It held the Dagda's symbol—a maze of squares.

"Thane Selkirk, of the Air Court. Son of Sloane Selkirk and Imogen Selkirk. Father of none. You stand before the fae of your kingdom, to confirm your place on the Seat of Power. The Dagda has judged you worthy. Your court has judged you strong. Arise and take your place as the High King of this ancient realm."

He placed the golden crown on the High King's head. And Thane stood. The entire court watched in awe as he strode to the throne, stood before it, and lowered himself onto the Seat of Power. Everyone gasped as he sat tall and grasped the twisting vine arms. Power hummed beneath Reyna's feet, and then cheers filled the air.

Reyna forced herself to smile along. This was the day she had been waiting for, but it had not happened as all as she had hoped. A new High King sat on the Air Court's throne, ready to rule over two kingdoms, one that would become his as soon as he married Eislyn.

Her stomach twisted, unease churning through her. Could she let go of her vengeance? Could she watch him marry her sister and claim the ice fae realm as his?

Thane rose and vanished through the door from whence he'd come. While Thane made his prayers to the Dagda, the rest of the court would file out of the room and head to the Banquet Hall, a smaller version of the Great

Hall reserved specifically for coronation and wedding feasts. And then the true celebration would begin.

※

The feasting went on for hours. Day quickly became night as chalices were refilled ten times over. The quiet buzz of conversation rose into a crescendo of clinking mugs, laughter, music, and general good cheer. As the night wore on, Reyna began to relax. She gazed around the Banquet Hall packed full of tables, noting all of the happy, smiling faces.

Perhaps the Air Court wasn't as terrible as she'd once thought.

Her eyes drifted toward Thane, who sat at the head table with his mother. There were two empty seats beside him. Reyna frowned. Thane's father, Sloane, and his uncle, Lord Bowen, had not attended either the coronation or the feast.

It was very odd.

A heavy hand landed on her shoulder, and Lorcan leaned down to whisper into her ear. His hot breath tickled her skin. "Careful. You're beginning to look like you're actually enjoying yourself."

She scowled up at him. "Shouldn't you be somewhere else?"

"Our High King wanted me to keep an eye on you. He was worried you'd see the boisterous, lively feast as a fantastic opportunity to hunt down assassins again. I didn't argue. I thought he might be right."

"Honestly," she said, rolling her eyes.

The majestic doors of the Banquet Hall swung wide and two servants carried in yet another platter of food set beneath a curving silver cloche. Reyna groaned and placed a hand on her full belly. She'd had her fill. There had been warm, soft breads and peacock pie, big jugs of ale and mead, and plates piled high with red apples and pears. They'd eaten juicy spit-roasted pig with crunchy crackling and chunks of salty boar. Sweet pastries had been abundant with golden, flaky crusts. Potatoes drenched in butter and carrots drizzled in sweet honey. And, in the very center of the Banquet Hall, stood a sotiltees, a sugar sculpture carved into a golden crown.

She couldn't bear to eat another bite. However, she would happily have another chalice of rowan berry wine.

Lorcan frowned and straightened up as he watched the servants approach Thane. "That's odd."

"What is?" she asked, glancing up at him.

"I do not recognize those two."

Unease churned in Reyna's belly as she turned to take in the two servants. They wore very basic garb. Faded brown tunics and trousers. Most of the other servants had worn nicer attire for the celebration.

The two servants reached the head table and pulled the cloche off the platter. And a severed boar's head was placed before the High King, dripping in fresh blood.

The entire hall fell deadly silent. Reyna's heart thundered. A boar's head could only mean one thing. Someone wanted Thane dead. But who? She glanced around. Surely not his mother. Imogen was certainly angry that her son had challenged her claim. Reyna knew she was wicked, cruel, cunning, and rash. Was she that terrible that she would have her own son murdered on his coronation day?

Imogen tossed back her chair as she stood, her trembling finger pointing at the corpse's head. "What is the meaning of this? Who dares defile our High King?"

So, not his mother then. That kind of terror could not be false.

Reyna glanced up at Lorcan. He had moved from her side to stride purposefully toward Thane, his hand firm against the hilt of his sword. Her heart shaking in her chest, she gripped the rough edge of the wooden table. Lorcan was behind this? No, he couldn't be. He *loved* Thane.

"Guards!" he shouted in the air. "To me! Protect your High King!"

She audibly sighed. Of course it wasn't Lorcan. But then...who could it be?

Suddenly, a figure dropped down into the middle of the feast, falling from the rafters above. A dark cloak flapped around her, hiding her face from view. But Reyna recognized her in an instant. A long braid of golden hair poked out from beneath the hood. It shielded her copper eyes, but not enough. They glowed from the shadowy folds of the cloak, flickering as she landed on the floor in a deep crouch.

It was the spy. The Bloody Dagger. But why was she here to kill the High King?

Should Reyna...stop her? Certainly, she had wanted Thane dead before but not like this.

Imogen threw herself toward Thane and splayed a hand across his chest just as Lorcan reached the king's side. Mariel tossed back her cloak to reveal a bow, arrow ready to be nocked. With a slight smile on her lips, she drew back the bow and aimed.

Reyna pushed to her feet. She followed the line of the arrow. It was aimed right at Lorcan's chest.

"No!" Reyna cried out and shoved her chair aside, throwing herself toward Lorcan.

Mariel frowned as she stared down the aim at the head table. She shifted sideways, away from Lorcan. With a guttural growl, she loosed the arrow. The entire court held a collective breath as it whistled through the air. The end thunked into the center of Kelwyn's chest. The spymaster's eyes went wide in shock as blood bloomed around his golden shirt.

And then he slumped over, dead.

The Banquet Hall erupted into chaos.

The two servants that served the boar yanked daggers from the folds of their clothes. Several more servants whisked out weapons, dozens now armed and charging toward the High King. Heart hammering, Reyna ripped off her gown's arms to find her dagger hidden in the folds of the material. Then, she ripped off her skirts, revealing the hidden pair of trousers she wore underneath. She would not make the mistake of fighting in a gown ever again.

Screams filled the air.

Thane stood from his chair and backed up toward the stone dais. His face had blanched, and his lips had parted in shock. Lorcan stood by his side, swinging steel, but dozens of attackers quickly surrounded them both. Guards rushed from their own table, hurrying toward their High King, but they might not make it in time.

Reyna hesitated just the slightest of seconds. And then she shook her head and charged. She came up behind an attacker and stabbed him in the neck, ice dagger sinking deep into flesh. Yanking the dagger out, she carried on. She sliced through the back of the next. He fell with a roar, blood spilling onto the white stone floor.

She reached Thane quickly and elbowed her way to stand before him, protecting him from the rush of attackers. Another fae charged up to her. His eyes were a bright green, and his hair was silky white. There was a tall, lithe quality about him that suggested he was a wood fae. Of course he was.

That was what this was all about.

He raised his sword high, bringing it down onto her head. She darted to the side, grinning when his unmet blow caught him off guard. He stumbled forward. She shoved her blade into his heart. Eyes wide, he fell to his knees.

"Lorcan," she shouted to the warrior beside her. "Get the High King out of here!"

Lorcan caught her gaze, growling.

"I'll be fine," she whispered.

Still growling, he gave a nod and grabbed Thane's arm.

She whirled back toward the fight, her ice dagger stained red. No more attackers rushed toward the dais. Instead, the castle guards had begun to surround them in the center of the Banquet Hall around the broken pieces of the sotiltees. The crown sculpture had fallen, smashed into unrecognizable bits.

Movement caught the corner of her eye. She glanced back at the table where she and Eislyn had been feasting. Her sister's chair was empty. Terror filled her heart, rattling her very core.

"Where's Eislyn?" Reyna screamed. "Where is my sister?"

47

EISLYN

Terror consumed her as she watched the chaos unfold. Only hours earlier, the entire court had been filled with hope. Thane had taken his Seat of Power, and the Dagda had blessed him as Eislyn knew he would. She had felt the power radiating from the throne. Thane was the true High King. And he would lead the realm to a better future.

But then everything had gone wrong.

At first, she thought the assassin had been sent to kill him. But then, she'd turned her arrow on Kelwyn, Thane's spymaster.

And then everyone had started fighting.

She didn't even know who was fighting who anymore. Fear churning through her, she backed up against the stone wall, clutching her golden dress tight in her shaking hands. Reyna was busy protecting the High King. Eislyn would call out to her sister to come to her side, but she didn't want to bring any attention upon herself.

The scent of blood filled the air.

She needed to get out of here. With a shaky breath, she

turned to rush toward the heavy doors, still open from the procession of the boar's head. Rough hands grabbed her from behind. She tried to twist around to see them—a castle guard perhaps, trying to help—but their grip was firm on her arms, squeezing so tight that she ached to cry out.

They shoved her out the door, and a heavy sack fell onto her head, dousing everything in darkness. She started to cry.

"Hush," the voice said. The accent was unfamiliar. Foreign. Was this a wood fae? Had they somehow made it into the castle? Was that who had attacked Thane?

If so, where were they taking her?

Her heart banged hard against her ribcage as they dragged her down the corridor. The sound of clashing steel and screams faded in the distance.

"Where are you taking me?" she asked through the salty tears that fell onto her lips. "What are you going to do with me?"

"Keep talking and we'll knock you out," the gruff voice said. "We don't have time for stories."

Eislyn pressed her lips together.

She heard the creak of an opening door, and then felt a rush of cool wind, even through the burlap sack. They shoved her several steps forward, and the floor beneath her changed from stone to something soft. Mud. They'd taken her outside. If that was the case, surely someone would spot them.

Although...every single member of the court was inside that castle, either getting slaughtered or hiding in fear. Gritting her teeth, she tried to rip her arms away, but that only succeeded in forcing the captor to tighten his grip.

"Listen, princess. You have one more chance to be a calm, quiet little thing. You try anything else, and I will bash the blunt end of my sword against that pretty little head of yours."

"Just do it anyway," another voice growled. "No reason to keep her conscious."

"No, I'll be quiet," she blurted through her tears. "I'll be calm. I swear it."

Both males let out a grunt. Eislyn steeled herself, anticipating the blow at any moment, but it never came. Instead, two fingers tapped her knee. She lifted her leg and felt a pair of hands wrap around her suede boots. He hauled her up into the air, the other captor holding her waist. She landed on top of a horse. It neighed beneath her, its warmth soothing away some of her fear.

Eislyn was not like her sister. She hadn't spent hours galloping through the forests on the back of a speckled mare, her silver hair streaming behind her as the snow tumbled down. She had, however, enjoyed her riding lessons—the few she'd had—and the familiarity of the animal comforted her somehow.

Until a rough rope was wound tightly around her hands, tying the reins into her fingers.

She pressed her lips together, trembling, too fearful to comment.

"Hold on tight, princess," one of her captors said. "We may have to gallop at times, and we'd hate to see you tumble to your death."

Eislyn swallowed hard, gripping the soft leather reins in her hands. Suddenly, the horse began to trot. Its hooves thudded against the mud, reverberating against her skull. She shifted slightly, wondering...if she fell off now, before the horse took off into a run, she might be able to flee to the castle for help.

"By the way," a voice spoke up from her left, "if you make any move to escape, Tammon here will shoot you with an arrow. He has one trained on you now, and you should know that he's a perfect shot."

She fought back tears, despair welling up inside of her. If the fae could ride a horse and aim an arrow simultaneously, then there was no longer any doubt in her mind that he was of the Wood Court. Were they going to take her all the way to Murias, the woodland capital? Did they plan to keep her prisoner there?

It was so far from home. So far from everyone she knew and loved. And so far from safety. If they took her across the border, she'd never get back. She would spend the rest of her life inside those tree-filled lands, never again feeling the snow on her face, never seeing her father, and never finding the way to fight the Ruin.

She would never be able to save her realm. The ice fae would be doomed.

The horse slowed to a stop. She waited, listening as the creaking sounds of a rising gate grew louder. Despite her fear, she could not help but ask.

"Where are the guards at the gate?"

"Dead," the voice to her left replied. "And all the rest of Tairngire's guards are inside that castle. They're likely dead, too. The reign of the Air Court is over, princess, even if the High King makes it out of this alive."

48

REYNA

Reyna sliced her dagger through another wood fae neck and watched as his blood-soaked body crumpled onto the stone floor. She glanced behind her before charging forward. Thane was gone. Lorcan had dragged the High King to safety. Imogen had vanished as well.

And Eislyn...Reyna's heart trembled.

She took one last look at the carnage of the room—most of the assassins were dead—and spun toward the nearest corridor. Perhaps Eislyn had gotten to safety. She was a smart girl. She would have known to flee instead of fight.

"Princess Reyna," a soft voice said from behind her. She whirled, dagger raised, only to find one of the castle guards cowering in the corner, face white, hands shaking. She frowned. He should be out there fighting instead of hiding in the darkness. No matter. Some warriors did not realize they could not handle battle until death stared them in the eyes.

"The fight is over," she said sharply. "Go back into the hall and help your fellow guards with the corpses."

"Yes, your grace." He gave a slight nod, and then drew in a sharp breath. "But, you see, I just saw Eislyn being taken."

Reyna's blade clattered against the stone ground as it slipped from her hand. The world tipped sideways; everything around her turned stark white. "What?"

He nodded eagerly. "Two servants, I think they were wood fae, grabbed her and dragged her outside. They took off on horses, heading toward the front gates, I believe. I didn't hear where they plan to take her, but they left not long ago."

Fury and fear stormed through Reyna like a hurricane. She stalked toward the huddled guard, every single cell in her body shaking with pure anger. "You saw her being taken, and you didn't do a damn thing? How dare you!"

She wanted to stab him. She wanted to knock his face against the ground.

Her sister had been taken. *Eislyn* was in danger.

With a deep-throated roar, she whirled away from the guard and grabbed her dagger from the floor. She broke out into a run, rushing toward the nearest door that would lead her out into the courtyard. When she pressed into the cool air, she looked around. There was no one here. It was completely empty. A chill went through her. The wood fae had planned it like this. They knew the entire court and city would be celebrating their new king. No one would be around to see them steal a princess away.

Reyna ran to the stables and jumped onto Enbarr's back. As she galloped toward the city gates, she let out a low whistle, calling Wingallock to her aide. This time, she would not make the mistake of leaving her owl behind. Eislyn needed her, which meant she needed all the strength she could get. If the wood fae had captured her, they likely planned to take her far south, past the Mistmoor Mountains, and into the wood fae lands.

This was no simple trip through the small Witchlight Woods and into the hilly grasslands. The trip would take weeks. She had no supplies. No food. No water. But she would not stop until she had found her sister. And taken her back.

Reyna's stomach twisted as she reached the front gates of the city. The half a dozen guards that had been stationed there for the king's coronation littered the ground, scarlet blood mixing with the dirt.

Eislyn's not dead, she reminded herself. The wood fae would not have captured her if they meant to kill her. They would have just tried to slaughter her inside of the castle along with everyone else.

Wingallock soared overhead as Reyna pushed through the open gates. She dropped back her head, gripping the reins tight, and whispered the words into his mind.

Fly ahead. Find Eislyn.

Wingallock let out a long, low hoot of terror, voicing Reyna's own turmoil aloud. He rushed up ahead, wings outstretched, the white feathers glistening in the moonlight. Reyna urged Enbarr onward.

Enbarr galloped into the grasslands, the tall stalks outside the front gates untouched by the Ruin that had descended on the hilly fields behind the castle woods. They followed a close distance behind Wingallock, who could dip and soar faster than her horse.

Holding tight onto the reins, Reyna closed her eyes and focused on her familiar. Instantly, a fresh blast of power rushed through her veins, and the world brightened around her as she viewed it through the lens of her owl.

Just up ahead, she spotted three figures rushing

through the grass. They were perhaps an hour's ride ahead, but her owl's keen sight formed a clear picture in her mind. All three were on horseback, and they were moving in a gallop that was not much slower than hers. Where she had not weighed her horse down with supplies, they had. The middle of the three was Eislyn. Her head was obscured by a brown hood of some kind, but her golden gown practically glowed in the darkness.

Reyna opened her eyes, urging Enbarr ever forward. At this rate, she would be able to catch them. She did not know what she would do once she did, but she would worry about that once she'd reached them. She had her dagger on her belt, but the wood fae had arrows. Frowning, she clung tighter to her horse.

All of this was her fault. If she had not approached the wood fae alone, the Air Court wouldn't have felt forced to attack, resulting in the horror at Thane's coronation. If she hadn't had her heart set on vengeance, Eislyn might not even be in this realm. Reyna wished for nothing more than to go back in time and take it all back.

Just up ahead, Wingallock let out an agitated hoot. Reyna tensed, and then watched in horror as an arrow soared straight at her owl's heart.

49

LORCAN

Thane paced in his chambers, his fingers jammed into his long golden hair. Lorcan stood firmly with his back against the door, sword held at the ready. The bolts were all shut tight, but he would not move an inch for fear the enemy would burst through at any moment.

His mark ached, of course. It burned so terribly that tears had formed in the corners of his eyes. A little voice whispered inside of his mind, but he ignored it. No longer would he follow those orders. Never again would he send information to the shadow lands. For so long, he had been torn in two. Half of his soul had been stuck in a land where he had been unwelcome, unwanted, and cast aside. And half of it had been here. With his true brethren.

Lorcan would protect Thane's life, even if the mark killed him.

"I should not be in here hiding like a small child," Thane said, still pacing. "I should be with my people. Fighting."

"The fight has surely ended, Your Majesty. We should await word to know who has won this day."

Thane scowled. "Please. I don't want to hear you of all people use my title when my coronation was interrupted by savages."

"All right then," Lorcan said. "You need to calm down, Thane. Removing you from the situation meant protecting the crown. If the wood fae succeeded in killing you, then...well, we both know what would have happened."

"The Wood Court is trying to overthrow me," he muttered. "They're trying to seize control of this court, but not through traditional battle."

"It certainly seems that way."

"And where is my mother?" Thane demanded. "Why is she not here with me?"

"She fled before I could remove you from the hall. I wager she has taken shelter in her own chambers."

"And what of Eislyn?"

Lorcan pressed his lips together. "Reyna will have seen to her sister's safety."

But Lorcan could not help but worry about the princess, even as strong as he knew she was. When the fight had broken out, she had not done what every other courtier had attempted to do: run. Instead, she had whipped a dagger out from the folds of her gown and had ripped the skirt right off, revealing hidden trousers beneath. For a small moment, he had been distracted by the sheer beauty of it. And then he'd been forced to focus on the fight.

Lorcan knew that Reyna was very capable of taking care of herself. That did not stop him from being concerned. He had looked for her as he'd rushed Thane through the door, and she'd still been in the thick of the fight.

"Did I hallucinate or did Princess Reyna truly jump to her feet to fight for me?"

Lorcan nodded. "She did."

"She will need to be rewarded for her bravery," Thane said quietly. "Perhaps I was wrong to spurn her as harshly as I did."

"You're not thinking of changing your mind about the betrothal again, are you?" Lorcan frowned.

Thane waved his hand in dismissal. "Certainly not. This only proves that I was right about her. She is a Shieldmaiden. But nevermind all that. Why do you think we haven't had word? It has been—"

A heavy knock sounded on the door. Lorcan pressed a finger to his lip, insisting on Thane's silence. Edging sideways, he pressed an ear up against the wood, listening. Only the ragged breath of a single fae answered.

"Who is it?" he asked quietly.

"It's Vreis. Let me in, Lorcan."

"Are you alone?" Lorcan asked.

A pause. "That is a yes or no—"

"Answer it!" Lorcan growled.

"Yes," he said with a sigh. "I'm alone."

"Good." Lorcan ripped open the door to find Vreis on the other side. Frowning, Lorcan grabbed ahold of his tunic and pulled him into the chambers. Before hearing his news, Lorcan stepped out into the corridor and stared hard and long down one end before turning toward the other. All was silent, empty, and dark.

Satisfied, he stepped back inside Thane's chambers and slammed the door.

Vreis lowered himself to one knee and bowed his head. "Your Majesty. I come bearing news of the battle."

"Why are all of my friends treating me differently now? Stop that. Stand, why don't you, Vreis?" Thane scowled. "And I would hardly call that a battle. It was a slaughter.

One that will change the future of this court irreparably, I'm afraid."

Vreis stood.

"Tell me the news. If you're here, then I suppose that means that not everyone is dead."

Lorcan felt for his friend. The first hours of his rule would forevermore be tainted by this slaughter. It was a bad omen, according to some. Lorcan was not superstitious enough to believe in signs from the gods. Others were, however, particularly those who resided in Tairngire. This would haunt Thane's every step as High King. Perhaps that had been the point.

"It is over, Thane," Vreis said quietly. "All of the assassins who attacked us at the feast have been killed. Unfortunately, things are still...a bit confused. We are unsure how many casualties we have sustained. Several of the nobility, along with a few of the castle servants. Your spymaster, Kelwyn...he also did not make it."

Lorcan watched as Thane paled. He knew that the High King had never fully trusted his spymaster. But that did not mean Thane was heartless. And it certainly didn't mean that Thane was unaware of the consequences of so much death. He would be forced to strike back. If he did not, every kingdom in Tir Na Nog would think him weak.

And they would take advantage of that perceived weakness.

The Ice Court was their ally but for how long? Would High King Cos call back his daughters, desperate to remove them from the path of danger? And what of the Sea Court, who had been strangely silent for the past several years?

And, of course, there was the Shadow Court. They would be pleased by this.

"I suppose this at least means that my mother, Princess

Reyna, and Princess Eislyn have made it to safety?" Thane asked.

Vreis paled. Lorcan frowned, body taut.

"Your mother was seen fleeing, but we have not been able to locate her. We have a warrior on the way to her chambers as we speak." He cleared his throat and cast his eyes to the floor. "The Princesses...we are not entirely certain what transpired."

Lorcan shifted closer to Vreis, eyes narrowing. "What do you mean?"

"We believe that Princess Eislyn was abducted. And then Princess Reyna was seen racing out of the castle with quite the determined look on her face. We believe she has gone after her sister."

Lorcan braced his hand on the wall, steadying himself. His heart squeezed so tight with fear that he swore it might burst. Shadows pulsed along his skin, desperate to break free. Reyna was in danger. And, this time, the danger was far more than even she could take on alone.

Thane's own terror flared across his face, but Lorcan knew it was for a different reason entirely. At some point along the way, he had come to care for Eislyn. Someone must have discovered this. It was the only explanation for why they would abduct the girl. They wanted to use her, to bargain with her life. The only problem was, they would likely use her and then discard her. Eislyn was never going to return to this castle alive. Which meant...Reyna wouldn't either.

Not unless Lorcan could stop this.

Thane lifted his chin and threw back his shoulders, standing as tall as a king. "We need to gather our warriors. With haste."

"Slight problem with that," Vreis said quietly. "With the

chaos of the attack, it may take time to gather those left inside the castle."

"Those left inside the castle?" Thane asked sharply.

Confusion crossed Vreis's face. "Yes, we were told you had ordered us to protect the Witchlight Woods during the coronation. Reports came in of an army of wood fae preparing to launch an attack."

Thane let out a low growl that rumbled deep within his chest. His entire body trembled with barely-contained anger. Vreis took a step back, eyes wide. "I made no such order. Call them back. Now."

"Thane," Lorcan warned. "The order may be false but the army could be real."

"Someone lied, Lorcan," Thane said in clipped tones. "They lied about my orders, so they likely lied about the army. We have a shadow fae amongst us. It explains everything." He turned to Vreis once more. "Who gave the order?"

Vreis shook his head. "I do not know."

"Very well. Tell the army to pull back and prepare to set their sights on the Wood Court." And then the High King turned to his oldest friend. "Lorcan, you and I are going now. We cannot let the princesses die."

50

IMOGEN

Imogen ran through the corridors, her bare feet slapping against the cool stones. She cast a glance over her shoulder, certain that someone was there, following close in the darkness. Shadows pulsed against the slick walls like clouds of writhing smoke. Gasping, she threw herself forward, focusing her gaze on the safety of the Great Hall up ahead.

The looming doors had been flung wide. After the coronation, no one had bothered to push them shut. Fisting her hands, Imogen rushed inside and grabbed one side of the heavy door. She had long ago lost her enhanced fae strength, but that did not mean she was weak. With sweat-slick hands, she dragged the door shut, and then followed with the other.

Breath ragged, she slumped back against the wood and slid to the floor, her elaborate aurelian gown bunching up around her legs. Tears cascaded down her cheeks, and she brushed them away. She did not know why she was crying. Thane had survived. And so had she.

She breathed in slowly, and then exhaled, taking

control of her emotions. As she opened her eyes, she stared ahead at the empty, vine-twisting throne. For a moment during the coronation, Imogen had not been certain the throne would accept her son as the High King of the realm. He was part-human, blemished. Imogen often swore that fae was not his dominant side. Still, the throne had once accepted Sloane, who was far more human than Thane could ever be.

Imogen had often wondered if human blood worked the same way that fae blood did. If a female of the Air Court mated with a male of the Ice Court, their son or daughter would be born a full air fae. The female's side was always dominant.

So few fae had ever mated with humans that no one quite knew the result. Sloane had always seemed part-fae to Imogen, but had that merely been a front? He'd always put forth the image that he could not lie, same as anyone else. But...had that been a lie in and of itself?

Imogen was certain she would never know.

With a sigh, she pushed up from the floor and strode across the cool, slick stone toward the throne. She should find somewhere better to hide. If the assassins had pursued her, this would be one of the first places they would think to check. Even in the most holiest of places, Imogen was not safe.

She closed her eyes and called up to her god. Why had the Dagda allowed this to happen? Had she not served him well?

No, she thought, her gut twisting. She had not served him well at all. Imogen had been the one to encourage that spy to kill the former king. Even though Sloane had not been there, the damage had still been done. When Mariel had dropped from the rafters, the slaughter had begun.

Was this punishment of some sort? And, if so, when would it end?

"I am sorry," she whispered to the throne, imagining how the Dagda once looked when he sat on his Seat of Power. The strongest and tallest and most powerful of them all, black wings flaring out on either side of his broad frame. A crown of twisting thorns on his head and gold bands around his muscular arms. A pair of golden trousers spun from hoarfrost worms, the only material covering his body. Ears so long and sharp that they sliced through his long, shadow-kissed hair.

Imogen wished that she had walked these lands when the Dagda had first come here. As such, he was gone, punishing them, watching their wars and their follies from his place within the Court of Death, far beyond the lands of Tir Na Nog. Many had tried to sail there. None had ever returned to tell the tale. To sail to death meant never coming back.

He had abandoned them. Because they were corrupt, cruel, wicked, and weak.

He had let them Fall.

Breathing deeply, she stood. She needed to find her son.

Memories threatened to consume her. Memories of her other children, the ones that had been brutally taken from her so many years past. But she could not let the sorrow fill her soul. She had to pull her walls tighter around her and focus on the here and now. Thane needed her.

Imogen could feel that he was safe. She had seen Reyna jumping into the fray to protect him, and then the warrior dragging him to safety. Perhaps Imogen had misjudged the girl. Bravery in battle did not a High Queen make, but she had been far too harsh on the Darragh clan. Anyone who protected her son, she would forever be in their debt.

She could only imagine how her son felt right now. He

had only just taken his Seat of Power, and an enemy court had already attacked. His father and beloved uncle had missed the coronation. Courtiers and servants had been slaughtered. He would need his mother, for once.

Based on his training, his warrior guard would have taken Thane to his chambers, which had yet to be moved to Mistral Tower. Casting one last glance at the throne, she moved toward the door in the rear of the room.

Several cloaked figures spilled out before her, seemingly from nowhere. Imogen sucked in a gasp and took a step back. She whirled to run back toward the massive doors, but several more figures jumped in front of her, blocking the escape.

Her hands fisted; her heart thumped hard.

Face hidden in the shadows of his cloak, the figure directly before her drew an arrow from his back and slid it into his bow.

51

MARIEL

Mariel watched from the rafters of the Great Hall as half a dozen cloaked wood fae surrounded the former High Queen. Somehow, the assassins had found her here. And, if Mariel didn't do something, Imogen would die.

Heart thumping in her chest, she stared down below. Mariel had considered Imogen her enemy for quite some time. Recent events had begun to shift that perspective. Imogen had not been the one to slaughter her family. Imogen had not been the one to send so many low fae to their deaths. She had not formulated the crippling tax policy. She had not desired an alliance with a gruesome king.

Mariel had followed her here, desperate for answers on the slaughter. Clearly, it had not been Imogen's intention to draw the wood fae out to attack. The pure terror she'd shown could not have been faked. But still, she had been the one to hint at an assassination aimed at Sloane. Imogen had said there would be a signal. And yet, that signal had gone wrong.

Sloane hadn't even been there.

As a wood fae lifted his arrow to stare down the aim, Mariel knew that her questions would have to wait.

For the second time that day, she leapt from the rafters, air hurtling past her, her clothing flapping around her body like banners in the wind. She landed in a crouch as the hard stone slammed against her booted feet. Golden braid thumping against her back, she slowly stood, narrowing her eyes at the attackers.

Imogen gasped.

"I will give you one chance to leave this place. If you stay, you will die."

The wood fae pushed back his hood and sneered. "We outnumber you. Six of us. One of you. I don't count your queen back there. She's the most helpless noble of the lot."

"Does that mean you aren't going to run?" Mariel asked, cocking her head.

The wood fae glanced at his compatriot on his left, and then they both laughed. "She's hoping we'll run because she's clearly too terrified to fight us."

"Very well then," Mariel said flatly.

Speed hurtling through her, she whipped her bow from beneath her cloak and nocked an arrow, loosing it toward the enemy before he even blinked. The arrow punched into his neck, spraying blood onto Mariel's cheeks. Making a face, she wiped it away, and grabbed another arrow.

A whistle went through the air. Mariel glanced up to find the tip of an arrow flying right toward her eyes. Gritting her teeth, she jumped to the side just as she loosed her own arrow. It hit the wood fae square in the gut. He groaned and thumped to the floor.

Two more arrows flew toward her. She held up her bow to knock one to the side just as she leapt out of the way of the other. Whirling toward the attackers, she found two more nocked bows aimed right at her.

She roared and raced toward the wood fae crouching in the corner, her fingers curled tight around her wooden arrow. In an instant, she'd reached them both. She shoved the end of her arrow into one of their skulls and kicked the other in the chest.

But she missed the kick. Instead, her foot found air. The wood fae grinned and slammed his head into hers. Pain lancing through her skull, she fell hard onto the stone floor, her teeth knocking together.

She called upon her magic to dull the pain.

Spinning her legs beneath her, she pushed up into a crouch and nocked another arrow. She pulled back the string and loosed. The arrow found its mark, more blood painting the ground.

Footsteps pounded the floor as warriors clad in Air Court armor rushed into the Great Hall. The Grand Alderman strode behind them, his sleek ginger hair glistening beneath the golden sconces. He motioned for the guards to attack.

Quickly, the guards cut down the final two wood fae, and the air became thick with the scent of blood. Mariel grumbled to herself. She'd taken out four. She could have managed two more by herself.

"Oh, thank the Dagda, Aengus," Imogen said, shakily pushing up from her hiding place behind the throne. "What is happening here? What is going on?"

"Guards, take her!" Aengus shouted the words, his lips twisting into a cruel smile.

The guards rushed toward Imogen, swords raised before them. Mariel frowned and shifted to the side to block their way. She didn't understand what new horror had descended upon this court, but she did know one thing. Aengus was even more terrible than Sloane.

"Stop!" Imogen shouted, stepping out from behind Mariel's back. "What in the name of the Dagda is the meaning of this, Aengus?"

"Grand Alderman," Aengus said, still smiling. "Address me by my proper title, Imogen."

Imogen gasped. "How dare you. Guards, do not listen to this man. I may not be your High Queen now, but I have far more power than this male will ever have. I am your new High King's mother, which makes me the Queen Mother."

"None of that matters," Aengus sneered. "When you are guilty of treason."

Tense silence thundered through the throne room. Imogen gaped at her former lover, her hands trembling by her sides. Mariel shifted slightly to the side so that she faced the both of them head on. She had a feeling something terrible was about to happen, and she wanted to be ready to bolt or fight should the need arise.

"I am the queen," Imogen hissed. "Guards, take this male away from me. Throw him into the dungeons. I cannot bear to look upon his face for even a second longer."

The guards shifted uneasily in their boots, clearly unsure of where they stood. Mariel frowned. Why were they listening to the Grand Alderman over the Queen Mother?

"I have proof." Aengus reached behind his back and whipped out a wrinkled, folded parchment. Instantly, Imogen's eyes widened in fear. She hurled herself toward the Grand Alderman, a low guttural shriek ripping from her throat. The guards shifted in front of Aengus to block her way.

Mariel stayed silent, watching and waiting, biding her time.

"This letter," Aengus began, waving the parchment in the air, "is written in your very distinctive handwriting. Everyone in the entire realm could recognize your strange, jagged scrawl. Would you like to know what it says?"

"Don't you dare, Aengus. I will have you hung."

Ignoring her, Aengus unfolded the letter. "Dearest sister, I write this note to you trapped by my witless yet cunning, and cruel yet weak husband."

Mariel risked a glance at Imogen. The Queen Mother's face had gone stark white.

"I fear I may be stuck here the rest of my long—but shortened—life. He is a cruel king, and the air fae are worse off from his rule. I have come up with a plan, one intended to rid us all of his reign once and for all. I fear Thane will wish to take his place, but he is not ready. I will do whatever is in my power to stall his coronation. Oh dearest sister, I wish you were here. I could use your counsel more than ever. All of my love, Imogen."

Aengus crumpled the note and tossed it onto the floor. He drew his gaze up, his smile as wicked as darkness itself. Imogen let out a sharp cry and dove toward the floor, but Aengus quickly kicked the note out of her reach.

"Destroying the note will not help you, Imogen," Aengus said. "All of my good warriors here have already seen it. Several courtiers have as well. The ones still alive. There is nothing you can do to weasel your way out of this one. You have been caught. You conspired against the king. Both kings. By sending a letter to your sister, the Sea Court bitch who is second-in-line to take the throne there. Our *enemy*. That is treason, whether you were once High Queen or not."

Imogen rose from the floor, her entire body shaking. "*You* conspired with me. You helped me carry it out!"

Mariel frowned. This did not look good for Imogen. There was proof she'd conspired to remove her husband from the throne. Mariel couldn't care less about that. *Good riddance*, she thought. But she doubted the Air Court would let her get away with it. She was a sea fae. An outsider. They would turn on her as easily as they'd turned their backs on Mariel's family.

"Did I? Or did you merely assume that I helped just because I stood by your side?"

Imogen narrowed her eyes. "You're behind all of this, aren't you? The assassination attempts. The wood fae in the hills. The slaughter at Thane's coronation."

Aengus tsked, and thumbed the hilt of his rapier. "I'm afraid I can't take credit for that one. But I will take credit for ridding this court of your traitorous arse. I was just waiting for the right moment to play my hand. This letter has been burning a hole in my pocket for quite some time now."

The Queen Mother's mouth fell open. She shook her head, snapping it shut. "You cannot do this, Aengus."

"I can. And I have." He motioned to the guards who quickly surrounded the queen. "Unfortunately, I fear this is quite bad timing for the Selkirk family. Your son is missing, which means the Air Court has been left without a king. The rules of the court state that in a king's absence, the Grand Alderman will sit on the throne and rule in his stead. Seeing as the High King has not yet assigned the role of Grand Alderman, that leaves the throne to me. Enjoy your time in the dungeons, Imogen."

Mariel watched as the Queen Mother was quickly surrounded by guards. They handled her roughly, clasping iron chains around her wrists tightly behind her back. The scent of burning flesh filled the air. Imogen fumed, though there was a hint of terror in her eyes. She was no doubt calculating a way out of this, but couldn't find one.

Imogen's gaze swept through the Great Hall before landing on Mariel's face. Aengus and the warriors seemed to have forgotten about her presence. She inched slowly toward the back corner where she could scurry back up into the rafters, never to be seen again. As strong as Mariel was, she could not take on this many trained guards at once. She would die for many things, but not for this queen.

That did not mean she would abandon her to the dungeons and let this wicked male take the crown. There was a time and a place. This was neither of those.

Imogen's eyes widened ever slightly, as if trying to wordlessly communicate with Mariel. Mariel pressed her lips together, slightly nodding.

Don't worry, she tried to say with her eyes. *I will get you out of this.*

And then, while the guards were distracted, she stepped further into the shadows and launched up into the rafters above. She frowned down as the warriors dragged Imogen out of the room, her head hung low in defeat. Aengus stood in the center of the floor, watching his old lover be taken away. Then, he turned and strode up to the throne.

With a smile, he settled into the vines.

52

REYNA

Reyna screamed and instinctively yanked Wingallock out of the path of the arrow with her mind. Her familiar's wings suddenly faltered, and he fell hard and fast toward the ground, his body tumbling in the whistling wind. The arrow streamed overhead, its sharp point thudding into the dirt just behind her.

"Wingallock," she cried out, clinging tight to Enbarr's mane. "Here, to me!"

The owl's snowy wings stretched wide, and he caught his fall just before his body hit the ground. Hands trembling, Reyna pulled her horse to a stop. Her owl flew back to her and settled onto her shoulder, talons piercing her skin. Her heart beat in time with his, like two frightened animals pounding their feet against the ground.

Breath puffing out before her, she stared ahead at the vanishing specks. The enemy had her sister, and they knew she was in pursuit. And they were willing to shoot down her owl in order to lose her. Fury boiled in her veins. They might have slowed her down, but they would *never* stop her.

With a flick of the reins, she urged Enbarr forward once again. However, this time, she kept Wingallock by her side. That had been far too close a call. She would have to catch up to them some other way.

※

Several days had passed in pursuit, and Reyna's entire body ached. She'd barely slept, stopping only long enough to nap in the deepest parts of the night, giving both Enbarr and Wingallock much-needed rest. Both animals were far stronger than most, but they were growing weary, same as she. Every time she had been close to closing in on the abductors, they had launched arrows in her direction and then fled.

They must be as exhausted as Reyna, but they pushed forward still. She was hot on their trail, but that wasn't good enough. Once they reached the boundary between the Air and Wood Courts, she would find herself stuck. The wood fae would never allow her across the border. In fact, they would likely kill her on sight.

With a heavy sigh, she leaned forward to stroke Enbarr's coarse mane, murmuring words of encouragement into her ear. They had slowed to a walk, Wingallock circling lazily over their heads. Through his eyes, she could see another village in the distance. They had passed three others on their way, all abandoned, empty, or burned to the ground. She'd managed to pilfer enough food to keep herself from collapsing from hunger, but it had brought on a stunning revelation.

The Air Court's lands were far more ravaged by war

than she'd thought. She had not seen a single living fae since leaving Tairngire. She did not doubt they were out there, likely watching her from a distance as she passed through their lands. They would not trust an ice fae amongst them, even if they knew of the alliance between their realms.

It had been years since a full-out battle, but the effects of the war had not diminished. These villages she passed had once been right in the line of attack, along the Crown's Road from the Mistmoor Mountains up to Tairngire. The Air Court had managed to stop any attack on Tairngire itself, but so many lives had been lost. Including those of innocent villagers, slaughtered merely for being in the way.

As she approached the next village, she noted that this one seemed in better shape than the ones she'd passed before. The buildings were still dilapidated, as if they'd been struck by a terrible force and then haphazardly put together again. Roofs were made of leather scraps and straw that rattled in the fierce wind, twisting and turning like limbs in the sky.

"Wingallock," she whispered. Her owl suddenly stopped circling and came to land on her shoulder instead. After the incident with the arrow, she refused to take any more chances with her familiar.

As Enbarr's hooves thudded on the dirt ground, several fae spilled out of the nearest building. They were dirty, disheveled, and wearing rags that looked as though they had been stitched back together a hundred times. Reyna's heart hurt at the sight of them. Why had she not heard about these people back at court?

One female stepped forward from the rest. She was tall and old, with fingers of age stretching out from her deep-set golden eyes. Her garment was a ragged cloth of faded yellow, covering just enough of her body to protect her from the chill of the wind. Her feet were bare, but her hair shone beneath the glow of the sun, a life and strength emanating from her even amidst all of the ruin.

"You're Princess Reyna," the old female said. "The ice fae betrothed to our prince."

Reyna reached up and fingered her circlet. She had forgotten that she still wore it, even now. "Yes, I suppose I am…I…what village was this?"

"Was?" The woman cocked her head. "The village still is, Your Highness. It is called Varheath."

Reyna nodded. "Well, I must say, I am sorry about the state of things here in Varheath."

"We have better survived than some," the woman replied. "But such is the nature of a hundred year war, Your Highness. We still have our fields and our crops, but the crown takes half to fund the war. We have enough left over for food and drink but not much else. It has all become so impossible, having to rely on our own realm for everything we need."

Again, Reyna nodded. She understood. Her own realm had struggled without the trade from the rest of the continent. But they had been luckier than most, relying on the Fomorian trade route to survive. The air fae had not been so fortunate.

"I suppose you wish to stop for some nourishment," the female continued, waving to a small bare-footed boy who stood just behind her. He moved toward her, reaching to take Enbarr's reins.

"I couldn't possibly," Reyna said quickly, unwilling to take these poor people's food, even if her stomach was desperate to be full again. "I am in pursuit of some

COURT OF RUINS

dangerous individuals. I don't suppose you have seen them pass through here?"

"Oh yes, Your Highness." The woman wrung her hands together, the lines around her eyes deepening in worry. "Two armed strangers with a captive, who looked like a girl. It was hard to see. They had a bag over her head. We all hid inside, terrified they were an enemy looking for slaughter."

Reyna narrowed her eyes. "Yes, that's them. Please, point me in the direction they went."

The woman twisted and pointed toward the east. Reyna frowned. That was...the wrong way. The Crown's Road split there, one half leading further south to the border with the Wood Court and one half turning toward the east. The only thing in that direction would be more villages and the coast.

And Feurach Fortress, where some of the former king's family resided, where it was rumored Sloane was hiding out himself. Surely the abductors were not taking Eislyn there.

Reyna frowned. "And you're certain?"

The woman nodded. "Oh yes. We were careful to keep an eye on them. That way we knew when it was once again safe to emerge from our homes."

Reyna's stomach twisted. There was something very wrong about this. Was it some sort of trap? A way to lead Reyna onto the wrong path? An ambush of some sort? They could lead her astray, wait for her to pass, and then backtrack on this road, and then head straight down to the border.

With a sigh, she twisted toward the horizon and stared. Even if this was some sort of trap, Reyna had no other choice but to forge ahead. That was the direction her sister had been taken, so that was the direction she would go.

"Here, have this," the woman reached up and pressed a small loaf of warm bread into Reyna's hands. Instantly, her stomach grumbled in response.

"I can't take this," she said, even as her mouth watered. "You and your people, you should keep it. Feed yourselves."

The woman smiled. "We look poor because we are, but we have enough bread from our wheat. Please take it, Princess Reyna. We just ask one thing of you."

Reyna's hands tightened around the soft bread. "Of course. What do you need?"

"Can you help stop this war?" she asked, eyes wide and earnest.

The wind swept across Reyna's body, whipping at her loose hair. She lifted her eyes to see the other villagers waiting in a cluster, dirt packed on cheeks, clothing ragged. Her heart ached for them. She wanted nothing other than to tell them that everything would be all right. But how could she? Everything was a mess, and it had been for a century.

Still, she closed her eyes and nodded. "I will do everything in my power to stop this war. That I can promise."

It was all she could promise, but it seemed to be enough. A gasp rippled through the crowd, and the woman's eyes shined.

"I knew an ice fae would be more likely to understand the plight of our people." She stepped back and gave a nod. "May the Dagda be with you, Your Highness."

Stomach still twisting, Reyna urged Enbarr toward the fork in the road. She could feel the eyes of the air fae watching her, that hope shining on their faces, even after their world had been destroyed. She wished she could have made more promises than she had, but she had at least been able to give them something. She would do whatever she could to change their world for the better. The air fae might not be her people, but she felt their plight all the same.

First, she would save her sister. And then she would try her damnedest to save this bloody kingdom. One that somehow felt like her own, even if she hadn't married the damn king and killed him after all.

53

EISLYN

Eislyn had no idea how many days had passed or even if she was still in the realm of the Air Court. They had stopped to camp several times. The sack had remained over her head at all times, except when they ate and slept, which was far rarer than she would have liked. Sometimes, they would settle on the hard ground for the night, only to rush back out onto the road moments later.

Sometimes, she swore she could hear the sound of a bow being nocked, an arrow whistling through the air. But she did not know if that was merely wishful thinking on her part or her imagination running wild. She wanted to believe that Thane cared enough to come after her, to save Eislyn from his enemies.

But she did not know if he was even still alive.

Suddenly, her horse slowed to a stop. The pungent scent of brine whispered through the burlap sack. Eislyn frowned. Were they by the sea? That made little sense. The wood fae lands were far south, and the road leading there wound through the grasslands. Taking a route along the shore would add weeks to their journey time.

Rough hands ripped the sack off her head. Her face was blasted by a cool, sea-scented breeze. Eislyn did not hate the wind as much as her sister did, but she had yet to grow accustomed to the sting of it against her skin. However, for once, the fresh air brought her back to life and reinvigorated the blood in her veins.

That was until she saw the castle looming before her. She recognized it instantly, having seen drawings of it numerous times in the books she had been pouring through these past weeks. Feurach Fortress, Lord Bowen's castle where the former king was rumored to be hiding out. It was a harsh grey stone fortress sat atop the cliffs on the edge of the Mag Mell Sea. There was no city spilling out onto the grassy hillsides here. Instead, the only fae who called this castle home were some members of the Selkirk family, and a contingent of the air fae army. It looked about as welcoming as it surely was.

Dark and dreary, the short, squat fortress had four square towers that were linked by ancient stone battlements. The Air Court banner was the only splash of color, the golden sheet rippling in the wind beside the wooden gates. Several warriors stood clustered on the walls, silently watching them from above.

Eyes wide, she glanced at her captors. "Why have you brought me to Feurach Fortress? Aren't you wood fae?"

Of course, that seemed a silly question now. As they approached the castle, the gates were being opened and not a single warrior on the battlements above rained arrows on their party.

Eislyn's heart hammered in her chest. She had been wrong about all of this. The wood fae were not taking her captive.

The air fae were.

"Welcome to your new home, Princess Eislyn." And with that, the sack was shoved back over her head, once again plunging her into darkness.

Her knees dug into the stone floor where her captors had shoved her down. They were somewhere inside the castle now. From the warm crackle of a nearby fire, she assumed she'd been delivered to someone's chambers.

Who? And why would a Selkirk capture me?

That hunch was proven right when the sack was yanked over her head once again, revealing a large wooden chair and a familiar fae frowning down at her. Eislyn's heart flipped at the sight of him. Lord Bowen, Thane's uncle, the former king's brother.

An older mirror image of Thane, his golden hair seemed to glow from the light of the fire. He lounged back, crossing one leg over the other, tapping his fingers against the arm of the chair. His eyes seemed to flicker with darkness as he regarded her carefully. She had wondered why he hadn't been at Thane's coronation. Now, she knew why.

"Welcome to Feurach Fortress, Princess Eislyn," he said in that kindly, calm voice of his that had once soothed her nervous soul. Now, everything about him seemed cloaked in darkness, and the calming tremor of his voice sounded false, hiding cruelty beneath. "I apologize your visit could not have been under more...ideal circumstances."

Holding back her tears, Eislyn glared up at him. "You've been working with the Wood Court to take down your own court? How could you? Thane will never forgive you for this."

"On the contrary, I have been working with some disillusioned wood fae who wish to see an end to the war." He flashed a smile. "And *I* intend to put an end to that war. Unfortunately, you and your sister, along with that miserable queen, Imogen, has made that impossible."

Eislyn could not help but tremble. "You were the one behind the assassination attempts."

He nodded. "I do apologize for that. My original intention was not for you to get hurt. The target was your sister, of course. As Thane's betrothed, she needed to be removed."

"But why?" Eislyn asked, glancing around at the grand room, full to the brim with soft and luxurious furniture in varying shades of gold. She was stuck kneeling on the floor. "None of this makes any sense."

"My brother and I, we originally wanted to develop an alliance between the Wood and Air Courts. Thane was to marry Princess Etaine until he insisted he wanted to ally with you ice fae. At first, I thought to turn his sights back onto Princess Etaine by removing Reyna Darragh as an option. Now, I realize that Thane's affections have shifted elsewhere. To you. And he will never agree to wed the Wood Court princess if I have you killed."

Eislyn's heart sped ever faster. "Me? But Thane is betrothed to—"

"Your sister?" He raised a golden eyebrow. "Yes. But my sources inside the castle determined that he planned to switch sisters after his coronation."

Eislyn could scarcely believe it. Her feelings for Thane had been almost unbearable these past weeks. She had never been bold enough to think he could return her affections. Lord Bowen's words were everything she had hoped to hear, but not like this. Not trapped and held captive so that…what? Lord Bowen said that he wasn't going to kill her. So, what was he planning to do with her instead?

"At first, I was going to find a way to have Thane agree to marry the wood fae girl in exchange for your life," Lord Bowen said with a slight smile. "However, things have changed these past few days. Thane has left Tairngire to rescue you. Aengus now sits on the throne, awaiting Thane's return. He would be much more agreeable to a wood fae alliance, even as much as I hate the male. So, I will simply be asking for Thane to give up his reign. If he doesn't agree, well then…I will be forced to kill you both."

Eislyn felt sick. She did not know if Thane had truly planned on asking her to be his betrothed instead of Reyna, but she did know that he would never give up his rule for her. Whatever feelings he might have, they did not go that deep. His kingdom meant more to him than she ever could.

Thane was smart. He might be on his way to save her now, but he would soon realize that he was walking straight into a trap.

A trap that neither of them would escape alive.

54

TARRAH

Her chest heaved as she stared out at the fallen city. Black stone hid amongst the piles of corpses, and blood painted every wall. The city had fallen easily. Only a thousand air fae warriors had manned the once-impenetrable walls. All this time, the Shadow Court had believed the city to be protected by ten thousand strong.

They'd been wrong.

And now Findius was theirs.

King Bolg clapped her on the back. "Come. The throne is just inside. Let us go see the Seat of Power that will now be mine."

Hope and determination filled Tarrah's gut. This was what they had worked so hard for, what they had fought for, battle after battle after battle. It had taken them weeks to plow toward the border. In the end, all the blood and guts had been worth it.

For this. The Seat of Power.

She followed the king, Teutas, and Nollaig as they crept through the dark corridors of the castle. When they found the throne room, Tarrah could not help but gasp. It was larger than she had expected, the roof so high that she swore it ought to touch the bottom curve of the red sun. Everything was a gleaming black, the shadows reflecting off each other. Large pillars were dotted throughout the room, holding the lofted ceiling off the slick floor.

At the very end of the room sat the throne. It looked like the very shadows themselves.

"Made of black stone," Nollaig muttered beneath her breath as they all walked toward it with silent footsteps. "There is beauty in the darkness."

Tarrah agreed. She had never seen anything like it. It was so void of any color at all that it looked as though it could swallow one whole. Only a true king could sit on that seat and never wither and die.

King Bolg puffed out his armored chest and turned to Tarrah. "You have given this to us. This city. This power. Have you had any more visions?"

She glanced at Teutas, whose eyes flickered with so much want and desire that she almost crumbled to her knees. He had yet to even kiss her.

Soon, she thought.

"I had a vision of a silver-haired female with a circlet on her head." Tarrah's eyes swam as she recalled the vision, two nights past. She had not brought it to her king's attention as of yet. They had been so busy with the assault on Findius.

"A silver-haired female?" Nollaig cocked her head, her face still hidden beneath her dark hood. "An ice fae?"

"Aye," Bolg grumbled. "That would be one of their princesses. Which one? There's three of them now, I believe."

Tarrah's eyes blurred ever more. "I do not know a name. She had a snow owl by her side."

"Reyna," Nollaig said sharply. "She's the only young ice fae with a familiar."

It did not surprise Tarrah to know that Nollaig kept track of those with familiars. She was obsessed with her own.

"All right." Bolg frowned. "Is that it? You just saw her face?"

Her eyes suddenly cleared, the gleaming black throne sharpening before her. "She's important. I don't know why or when or how. But the outcome of this war depends on something she must do. We *have* to bring her here."

55
REYNA

Reyna hung back, crouching behind a large rock. In the distance, Feurach Fortress rose up like boxy slabs of stone, punching the dark bellies of the low clouds rolling across the nighttime sky. Only a few hours earlier, Wingallock had soared ahead to spot the two warriors taking Eislyn through the open castle gates.

By the time she had caught up, the gates had been shut tight.

She frowned as she took in the castle. A single banner flapped along the wall, bearing the sigil of the Air Court: the glittering golden crown. Unlike the sigils of the other courts, the air fae had never concerned themselves with the elemental powers that they bore. The ice fae and their frozen wings, the shadow fae and their twisting, interwoven antlers, or the fire fae with their phoenix flaming beneath an orange sun.

The air fae had always been far more concerned with absolute power than the magic of their own kind.

Which was why she did not feel surprised to find herself camped out in front of the Selkirk family's castle.

All this time, Reyna had been too concerned about the other realms to realize that the air fae had begun a civil war.

And Reyna was stuck right in the middle of it.

She had no idea how she was going to get inside of the castle to save her sister. Just as the name suggested, Feurach Fortress had been built like one, designed especially for the training and housing of troops. Sat upon a cliff, it looked down on the grasslands that stretched far and wide. A wide moat stretched just below the high, outer wall that could be filled with poisonous melted iron during an assault.

There would be hundreds of fully-trained warriors inside those gates, ready to fight at a moment's notice. As she squinted, she spotted archers dotted along the battlements. Even with no enemy in sight, they were ready to defend.

With a frown, Reyna dropped back down and huddled behind the rock. She turned to Wingallock who fed on some grains she had found along the way. She had left Enbarr in a small wooded area down the road while she scouted ahead, unwilling to tip off the castle fae before she was ready.

"What do you reckon, Wingallock?" she asked.

He lifted his head, blinked at her, and then turned back to his food.

"You're right. I have no idea either," she replied. "That castle has been built specifically for keeping intruders out. I could try scaling the wall, but they would see me before I even reached the top. I suppose I could round the castle and approach from the cliffside, but I doubt I'd be able to make that climb. It's a shame I don't have wings."

He hooted in response.

Indeed, there was only one way she could get inside that castle.

With a sigh, she glanced at her familiar. "All right, Wingallock. I need you to return to Enbarr's side. Wait for me there in the trees. If anyone discovers you, then I need you both to run."

Wingallock cocked his head and hooted in distress. With a sad smile, she reached out and ruffled his neck, his smooth feathers soft against her touch. Her soul ached at leaving him behind, but she would not do anything to put his life in danger.

"I need you to trust me, all right?" she whispered.

After another moment, he gave another hoot and then pushed off the ground. She watched him spread his white wings, returning to Enbarr's side. Her stomach twisted into knots. Would he leave the castle behind, if he must? Reyna could not be certain. As much as she felt a pull toward him, she knew he felt the same. She just had to hope he would not put himself in danger if things went wrong.

And they were very likely to go wrong.

Steeling her nerves, Reyna pushed up from the ground and stepped out of the shadow of the rock. She joined the Crown's Road and strode toward the castle gates. When she drew closer, she heard a shout echo through the battlements and felt the shudder of arrows all around her being nocked.

She slowed to a stop and called out. "I'm here to see my sister, Princess Eislyn Darragh of the Ice Court."

Several long moments stretched by. Reyna held her breath, waiting for the first arrow to punch the ground or her gut. None came. Moments stretched into hours, the distant sun peeking over the horizon. Finally, at long last, the wooden gate groaned as the fae inside pushed it open.

Warriors decked in gold-dyed armor streamed out of the castle, surrounding her in an instant.

❧

The dungeon floor was cold and hard, but there was no wind to sink into her bones. Reyna sat on a small wooden stool, staring at the iron bars that held her. They reminded her of not so long ago when she had been stuck in a cage with Lorcan, holding out hope that Thane would come to find them.

Lorcan, the shadow fae. Lorcan, the warrior who had crept his way into her heart.

Sighing, she stood and strode over to the small barred window that looked out on the crashing waves of the Mag Mell Sea. She did not know why they'd kept her alive instead of killing her on the spot. They had refused her an audience with anyone. None of the warriors had answered her many questions about Eislyn. Reyna had called out for her, hoping to hear her voice ringing through the dank musty cells. But, if she was down here, she was in some other part of the twisting tunnels.

In the distance, a door creaked open, and several guards appeared outside of her cell. They opened the door and motioned her to join them in the tunnel. For a moment, she considered giving them a fight, but her dagger had been taken from her. She wouldn't win. She would only succeed in tiring herself out. The best option at this point was to preserve as much energy as possible, just in case she ever got the chance to use it.

The guards led her up a winding set of stone stairs, through another corridor, and up through a tower. When they reached the top of the stairwell, they shoved her through an open door.

COURT OF RUINS

Before her was a study of some sort. The grey stone walls curved in close with two windows overlooking the yellow green grasslands outside of the castle. There were a few small shelves packed with books and scrolls on one side of the room while an elaborately-carved wooden desk sat on the other. A single lantern illuminated the musty space, highlighting the motes of dust swirling through the air.

Lord Bowen sat before her, his fingers steepled beneath his chin. Reyna could not help but gape. How could he be involved in all of this? He had done nothing but show care for Thane. He'd been by his side all this time, encouraging him, providing him with advice...

But he had not been at the coronation.

Reyna's stomach twisted.

"You have created quite the dilemma, Princess Reyna," he said in a soft, kindly voice that should have put her at ease. It did nothing of the sort.

She narrowed her eyes. "Good. I'm not here to make life easy on my sister's captor."

"You should not fear," he said with a smile. "Your sister is alive and well and will remain so as long as Thane does as I request."

"I see," she said. "And I suppose you want him to hand over the crown to you."

"No, indeed, I do not," he said with an eerie chuckle. "It is far too much stress for such little payoff. Trust me, I know that better than anyone. He will, however, leave the crown in Aengus's able hands."

Reyna frowned. "You want *Aengus* to be king?"

"He already is, my dear. Thane has fled the court. In his absence, the Grand Alderman sits on the throne and rules the kingdom."

Reyna's heartbeat quickened, and all the blood drained

from her face. She understood immediately what had happened. Thane, just as she had, discovered Eislyn had been taken. And he'd left his throne and his crown and his rule behind to come after her.

She wanted to believe his imminent arrival was a good thing, but surely it was not. Lord Bowen wanted him off the throne. If Thane arrived at this castle, his uncle would surely kill him.

"Aengus conspired to get the king off the throne. *Your brother*," she said. "Why in the name of the Dagda would you want him to rule?"

Lord Bowen chuckled. He shook his head. And then his laughter boomed through the small tower room. "No, my dear. Aengus conspired to get *me* off the throne."

All the blood drained from Reyna's face as she stared at the male before her. Her heart thumped hard against her ribs. Nothing he said made sense, and yet that did not stop the terror from charging through her veins.

"I don't understand," she whispered.

Lord Bowen—or Sloane—drummed his fingers on the arm of the chair. "It pleases me greatly to know that I tricked you all so well."

Tears of hatred filled her eyes as she hissed, "Tell me what is going on."

"I made a deal," he said, closing his eyes. Shadows pulsed around his golden body. "I made a promise."

The strange scent of burning flesh filled the room as a heavy mist enveloped the fae who sat before her. Reyna inched back, eyes wide, watching as the very skin on his bones seemed to quake. A moment later, Lord Bowen was gone. And Sloane Selkirk sat in his place.

He was younger than she had expected. Reyna Darragh had never met Sloane Selkirk. Or, she had, but he had not appeared as himself. Instead of the huddled old male she'd expected, Sloane was vibrant, tall, strong. His light brown hair hung to his shoulders, and his skin was clear of age.

Reyna didn't understand. She'd heard he'd been years away from death.

"What kind of deal did you make?" she whispered.

"High King Bolg of the Wood Court learned the secrets of the Unseelie god long ago," he said quietly. "Secrets that can create illusions. Secrets that can reverse age. It involves somewhat gruesome tasks. Drinking blood, eating flesh. He gave me those secrets, but they came with a price. This kingdom would become his."

Reyna sat back on her heels, eyes wide as she stared at Thane's father. "So, you...exchanged your kingdom for a longer life? And you've been killing low fae for this dark magic?"

Reyna remembered what Mariel had told her. Murder plagued the streets of Drunkard's Pit. And now she knew why. Sloane had been killing them, and...drinking their blood. She shivered.

He nodded. "Wouldn't you?"

"No," she hissed, her blood beginning to boil in her veins. "I wouldn't sacrifice my own people just for a few more years on this pile of dirt."

He steepled his fingers beneath his chin. "You cannot judge me for something you have never had to face. You are young still. Death is not knocking on your door."

"Where is Lord Bowen?" she asked in a low, dangerous voice.

Sloane sighed. "Lord Bowen, my poor brother, is dead. I had to kill him to create the glamor. He would have ruined it all regardless. He had every intention of backing Thane, who is very much misguided in his desire to continue his war with the Wood Court."

"Your own brother? And your own son? You're mad."

Reyna pushed up from the floor, rising before him. She heard the warriors shift closer as they guarded the door at her back, but she wouldn't go after Sloane yet. Not like this.

"You know, it's funny," he said softly. "I once loved Thane. Truly, he was the only person in this lackluster world who I loved. Now, I couldn't care less about my pitiful son. It seems these Unseelie powers do far more than I thought. They have freed me from the bonds of family."

Reyna's heart thumped. "How do you even use the magic? The Dagda took—"

"Took away our magic?" He chuckled again. "Your Dagda has forsaken you, but dark magic can still be drawn from these lands. It just requires sacrifice."

Sacrifice.

"What are you going to do with me?" she asked quietly. "Don't think I don't understand why you've captured Eislyn. You plan to use her against Thane. But what of me? Am I to be some sort of sacrifice for you?"

He rubbed his jaw and leaned back into his chair, the wood creaking beneath him. "That is a very good question indeed, Princess Reyna. The easiest and most obvious solution would be to kill you. However, you are awfully important. I imagine your father would like you returned to him."

Reyna's heart thumped hard. "Leave the Ice Court out of this."

"The Ice Court is in this just as much as the rest of us." He cocked his head to the side. "Your hoarfrost silk and ice glass are very valuable indeed, and the Fomorians have long favored you for trade."

"Even if you managed to get my father to make an

alliance with that tyrant of a king, the Sea Court is one that will *never* bend to you," she whispered.

He leaned forward, smiling, eyes twinkling. "Oh, I do not plan to make an *alliance* with the Ice Court, nor do I plan on doing anything other than conquer the sea fae. Neither one of you stand a chance against our armies. The High King of the Air Court will become the Emperor of you all.

"No, your father will no doubt hit us with all he is worth. And then, on the battlefield, I will hold you up before him. He and his fae will kneel. Or *you* will die."

A shiver went down Reyna's spine. She had been captured to be used as a puppet in bloody battles that had now become inevitable. She had come to the air fae lands to save her people. Instead, she had gotten them into an even worse situation than they'd been in before. They would be ruled by evil males who used dark magic for their own gain. They would be forced into endless labor. They would be beaten, starved, used.

And there was nothing Reyna could do to stop it.

56

LORCAN

"They went that way," the kindly woman said after shoving bread into Thane's hands. "Three or four days past. First, the two warriors with their captive, and then the princess alone with her owl. She did not stop for food nor rest. Poor thing looked exhausted."

High King Thane gave a slow nod, thanking the woman. He trotted back over to Lorcan, frowning in the direction of Feurach Fortress. "She seems to think they went that way, but that can't be right, can it?"

"She sounded fairly confident," Lorcan said. "Though I cannot imagine why they would head to the coast. If they plan to flee by boat, your uncle's warriors will spot them."

"Yes." Thane's frown deepened. "My uncle. Do you know, I thought it was strange he did not attend my coronation. He begged off, claiming illness, but...well, while my father suffers from his ageing bones, my uncle never has."

It was odd. Lorcan could not deny it.

"What are you saying?" he asked.

Thane shook his head. "In truth, I cannot be sure. It seems mad to think that my uncle could have anything to do with this. He has always offered me advice. He has always been so close with my father..."

Thane suddenly glanced up, eyes wide. A single thought seemed to occur to him in the same moment it came to Lorcan.

"Unless he is angry about the coup," Lorcan said quietly as they turned their horses toward the eastern horizon. "Unless he always wanted to ally with the wood fae, just like your father did."

"Until my mother got involved," Thane mumbled. "It just cannot be, Lorcan. My own family? Pitting us against each other like this? It could cause a civil war. The Air Court would never again be the same."

"I imagine he does not intend to allow anyone to cause that civil war," Lorcan said quietly.

Things were finally beginning to make sense. For too long, it felt as though they'd been walking through thick shadows while their enemies strode through the light. Nothing had made any sense until now. The wood fae had been working with Lord Bowen, who had always encouraged Thane away from Reyna and toward a deal with the wood fae. Lord Bowen had wanted Thane to marry Princess Etaine. And when Thane had turned down that alliance, his uncle had set his sights on Reyna, desperate to remove her from the court.

He had authority with the warriors. He could give them orders, and they would listen. It would explain why scouts had not been sent into the hills. And it would explain why the guards had been removed from Reyna's chambers the night she and Eislyn were attacked.

Thane's mind seemed to be following the same path as Lorcan's, for he asked, "If he is a part of this, then why has he abducted Eislyn? Why didn't he have her killed during the coronation massacre instead?"

"It seems he has decided that her life is a better bargaining chip than her death." Lorcan gave him a steady look. "Perhaps because news has spread that you have fallen in love with the girl."

Thane flushed, grinding his jaw as he looked away. "So, it is my affection for her that has gotten her into this. And my affection will get us out of it. We need to go now. Ride hard to Feurach Fortress. Save her from that place."

"And what will he do to you? Allow you to leave once you have rescued her?" Lorcan shook his head. "He has captured Eislyn to draw you into his web. Thane, my old friend, he will never let you leave that castle. Even if he doesn't kill you, you will be stuck in a dungeon for the rest of your life."

"And what would you have me do instead? Return to Tairngire and sit on my throne, all the while knowing that I have condemned an innocent, caring, beautiful fae to die? If I never show up, he will kill her just as he always planned. Tell me that isn't the truth. Tell me he will let her live if I do not go."

For once, Lorcan did not want to lie to his old friend. He saw the hurt reflected in his eyes, the fear and pain and horror of his choice. Either he walked toward his own death or he walked away from the female he loved. Lorcan knew that wasn't even a choice.

"I will go instead," Lorcan said quietly. "Reyna is there, too. I will get them both out of there alive."

Thane snorted, flicking his reins. He called over his shoulder as his horse broke out into a trot. "They will kill you on sight. Come, old friend. If we're forced to walk to our death, then at least we can do it together."

A few hours later, they stopped at a small clump of trees just off the road. The sun was beginning to set on another day, the evening orange sky bringing with it a whip of harsh wind. The cluster of trees sat beside a gurgling stream that forked off of Mill River. There, they found Reyna's speckled mare along with her owl who was circling overhead. The owl swooped down and landed on Lorcan's shoulder, hooting in what he could only translate as intense agitation.

Reyna had once told him that her soul was linked to his, that Wingallock was a part of her just as she was a part of him. Lore spoke of the ancient days of fae and familiars, where if one died, the other soon followed. They could not exist alone, nor could they spend too much time apart. Lorcan had always wondered if the intensity of that magic had faded over time. Certainly, it must have, just like the rest of the magic in the world.

But he had seen Reyna's face that night she'd been separated from her owl. He had witnessed the cold sweep across her skin. They were as linked as two beings could ever be.

"She's alive then, isn't she?" he murmured to the bird. "Otherwise, you would not be flapping around with so much energy."

He smiled fondly at the owl and ruffled his feathers. The feel of his wings reminded him of the softness of Reyna's skin beneath his hands.

He glanced over to find Thane staring at him with his refined, courtly brow arched high. "I do believe that while I have been distracted by my own worries that I have missed something incredibly important."

"Whatever do you mean?" Lorcan asked smoothly.

"Don't play coy," Thane said with a fond smile. "Reyna

clearly means something to you." He gave Lorcan an appraising look. "It makes sense. You are far more alike than any two people I've ever met. It's why you argue so much."

Lorcan held his tongue. Even if Thane's words hinted at the truth, he didn't feel ready to speak it aloud. He'd held so many secrets inside of him for so long, he didn't know how to deal with the exposure of one, even as new as the secret was.

"It is fine, Lorcan," Thane said, tossing a stone into the stream. "You know I never loved the girl. In fact, far from it."

Lorcan relaxed.

Dark forms burst out from behind the trees. Lorcan grabbed Thane and pushed the king behind him, drawing his sword from his back. He held the blade ready, eyes narrowed as he took in the enemy. There were maybe fifteen of them. Instead of the gold-dyed leather armor that signified the Air Court, these warriors donned grey scales and wielded swords forged from shadowsteel with twisting antler hilts. Their faces were partially obscured by thick metal helmets, but Lorcan could make out dark skin, dark hair, and even darker eyes.

They were shadow fae.

His heart thumped. "Back off. We have nothing for you."

He spoked the words as if they were mere thieves, aiming to rob them of their jewels. But Lorcan knew they were anything but. The shadow fae had somehow made it into the Air Court, and they had found him.

"Prince Lorcan," the nearest shadow fae said, lowering himself to kneel on the grass. "We come bearing news from your father who has reclaimed the Findius Stronghold."

57

THANE

Prince Lorcan? Thane felt punched in the gut, near to toppling from confusion. And betrayal. Prince Lorcan.

Prince.

When Thane had first met his warrior friend, he had learned that Lorcan was descended from a shadow fae father but that he had been born in the grasslands by an air fae mother. He'd said that he did not know who his father was. If these scale-clad warriors spoke the truth, then Lorcan was…the son of King Bolg Rothach, the current ruler of the exiled shadow fae.

It couldn't be true. That would mean his oldest and most trusted friend had spent years lying to him. Not only about his identity but about the brotherly bond that they shared.

Because if Lorcan truly was the son of King Bolg Rothach, then he had never been inside the Air Court as Thane's friend.

He would have been there as a spy. An enemy.

Lorcan stood stiffly, frowning down at the warriors kneeling before him. "I am afraid you must be mistaken."

Relief shuddered through Thane, even as doubt still rang in his mind. As much as Thane wanted this entire premise to be false, a portrait was beginning to form in his mind. Lorcan, the heir to the shadow kingdom, sent to undermine the strongest court on the continent. The prince, hiding in plain sight, plotting to take back his power, to end the exile from the rest of the fae. A fae who could lie, a fae who could get close to Thane, lying in wait for years until the day his kingly father made his move.

The shadow fae had been causing skirmishes near Findius these past weeks. They were on the forward assault now, desperate to reclaim their castle and their Seat of Power.

Thane's own mother and father had been the ones to banish the Shadow Court. And now they were seeking their revenge.

"We are not mistaken, my liege," the warrior said, still kneeling. "We know the truth of you. There is a mark on your arm, one that brands you as the king's own son."

Thane could not help but gasp, and his hand fell onto the comforting hilt of his sword. He had seen Lorcan's mark a few times over the years, always briefly. A tattoo, he had called it, one to remind him of where he had come.

That part must have at least been true. Because he had come from the shadow lands.

"Lorcan," Thane said quietly, taking a few slow steps back. "Tell me this isn't true. Yes or no. Answer it honestly, even if you can lie."

Lorcan turned toward him, and Thane could clearly see the pain flickering in his dark eyes. "I am a shadow fae, and I am the king's son."

Thane's eyes widened, and he continued to back away

through the trees. Now out of reach of their weapons, he drew his sword, the steel ringing in the dead silence of the night. In response, all of the warriors stood, their own swords rising into the air.

Lorcan stepped between Thane and the shadow fae, his arms outstretched. "Whoa now. No need for weapons. Your sudden arrival has startled Thane, as surely you can understand. Please put down your weapons, and tell me why you've come."

"We have come for you." The nearest warrior motioned for the others to sheathe their weapons, but he kept his sword by his side. He lowered the tip to the ground but kept a firm grip on the antler hilt. "And we have come for the air fae king."

Thane, however, did not sheathe his weapon. He kept it held before him, body tense. Lorcan's back was facing him. He could see the slick sweat on the back of his neck from where he had pulled his hair into a bun. All it would take was one slice of Thane's sword, and the Prince of the Shadow Court would be dead.

Lorcan. Thane's gut felt like writhing snakes, twisting around each other, ready to bite.

He couldn't do it. No matter the betrayal, Thane loved Lorcan like a brother. He could not find hatred in his heart for his oldest friend. Only sadness and pain. All this time, his friendship had been nothing but a lie. He'd been the only person in the entire realm Thane had ever fully trusted.

How many of his confidential mutterings had Lorcan passed along?

"Explain yourself," Lorcan said in a growl, still facing the shadow fae warrior.

"Now that your father has retaken Findius, he has insisted you return to his side to prepare for the coming war," the warrior said. "But we must take care of something else first. Him."

The warrior lifted his long sword and pointed it right at Thane.

Lorcan shifted to the side to block it. "You will leave Thane out of this."

The warrior snorted with a laugh. "We cannot leave the High King of the Air Court out of this, nor his betrothed. With no heir in sight, their absence will be felt throughout the realm like a groundquake. The air fae will tear themselves apart, every noble grappling to claim power, while we build up for the war. They will not worry about attempting to retake Findius, not while their nobles kill each other. It is the only way forward, and it is an order from our king."

"Thane," Lorcan said through gritted teeth, his body trembling. "Run."

Thane blinked at the warrior's back, confusion and fear rippling through him. "What?"

Lorcan whirled, his face screwed up in pain. He clasped his right shoulder, and his nails dug into his armor. "You need to get out of here now or they will kill you. I might not be able to stop them. Run! Go! Now!"

Thane stumbled back, his eyes wide as he glanced from the fury on Lorcan's face to the warriors now drawing their swords once again. Was this some sort of trick? Another lie?

No, he thought, as he turned his gaze back on Lorcan. There was no deceit there. Nothing but pure, unadulterated fear. Fear for Thane's life.

Understanding passed between the two friends, and memories rushed through Thane's mind. Lorcan protecting his life. Lorcan's strange veiled warnings. The shadow fae before him might have been sent to spy on

Thane, but at some point, their friendship had become real.

Thane did not want to abandon him here to fight these shadow fae alone, but Lorcan was their prince. They might be angry at his protection of Thane, but they would not kill him. He was their liege. With a nod in Lorcan's direction, Thane twisted on his heels and ran.

Even without Lorcan's help, he had to go to Eislyn. If he didn't, she would die.

58

REYNA

Reyna glanced up when the two familiar warriors appeared outside of her cell door. Sighing, she stood from her stool, and frowned when she realized their hands were empty. The sun had just begun to rise, and her stomach had twisted itself into knots of hunger. The warm bread from the village felt so long ago.

"Lord Bowen wishes to see you," the warrior grunted, unlocking the door and swinging it wide. "Make no attempts to flee or we'll be forced to shove our blades into your back."

"Sloane, you mean," she muttered.

They would do no such thing. Sloane's orders had almost certainly been clear: Reyna was much more valuable alive than dead. The former king wished to use her against her father. If she tried to escape, they would make her life a living hell, but they wouldn't kill her.

She wasn't certain if that was a good thing or not.

As the moments in the cell had stretched into hours, Reyna had been left with nothing other than her defeated thoughts. She saw no way out of this, no way to stop the battles that would destroy so much of an already war-stricken land. All her life, she had fought to become more than just a princess sitting prettily inside the safety of castle walls. But now she was even more helpless than she had ever been in her life.

Just as before, the warriors led her out of the dungeons, up the spiral stairs of the tower, and into Sloane's study. Once again, he wore the face of his brother, golden and strong. He sat quietly, bent over his desk, scribbling his quill against a curling sheet of parchment. Reyna could only imagine the contents of his letter. Another plot, no doubt.

The warriors shoved her toward the floor, and her knees cracked against the stone. They shuffled backward, blocking the door, just as they had done the previous visit.

Sloane continued to ignore her, scribbling away as if she had not just been thrown before him. Narrowing her eyes, she pushed up from the ground on shaky legs.

"It is rude to ignore guests," Reyna snapped.

He glanced over his shoulder and gave her a dismissive wave. "You are not here for a chat. I need your ring."

Reyna frowned. "My ring?"

"Oh yes." He shifted on his chair again, turning back toward his parchment. "Sources tell me that you wear that always, and it is clearly an ice fae ring, one that has been in your family for years. I require it."

Reyna curled her hand protectively around the ring and pulled it to her chest. This was her mother's ring, and she had not removed it a day in her life. She would never give it up, especially not to her enemy.

"That isn't going to happen," she said quietly.

At that, he dropped the quill and stood from his chair. As tall as she was, Sloane in his brother's form still towered over her. Lord Bowen had been younger than Sloane, and

COURT OF RUINS

he had not succumbed to the same rot and ruin that the former king had. In this glamor, he was strong, powerful, and his gaze sharpened with anger.

"I need your ring, and I will have it," he said in a low, dangerous voice. "It provides proof that I have you."

"You will have to find another way to provide proof because I am not giving up my ring," she said hotly, tossing her messy hair behind her shoulders.

Her heart beat hard. She was playing with fire, and she knew it, but she would not give up one of the only things she had left of her mother. The female who had raised her, had loved her. The female who had given up her life to save her.

Sloane chuckled. "You do realize that you do not have a choice in this matter, yes? I have hundreds of warriors here at my disposal. I am giving you the chance to hand over your ring willingly. If you do not, I will be forced to have it removed. By cutting off your finger, if necessary."

All the blood drained from her face just as a strange sensation whispered through her body. Reyna clutched her hand tighter to her chest, the ring digging hard into her palm from where she had it splayed against the ice. As she stared at Sloane, the entire world seemed to shudder to a stop.

Suddenly, something inside of her *snapped*. Electric currents rushed through her veins, almost taking her breath away. She gasped out loud. Sloane smiled, taking her shock as a reaction to his words and not to the strange energy whorling through her body.

"Perhaps you finally understand me." Smiling, he held out his hand. "The ring, Reyna."

Something in the corner of her eye caught her attention. A flash of white. Keeping her head still, she cast a gaze toward it, merely shifting her eyes to the side. Wingallock circled the air just outside of the window, outstretched wings glistening in the sun.

The owl stared at her as he flew, peering deep into her soul. She had not called him here. He had come on his own. As he continued to stare, she understood something deep within her gut, even though it made no sense at all. Even though it was absolute madness.

Holding her breath, Reyna turned her attention back upon the wicked former king. "As soon as I hand it over, you'll send me straight back to the dungeons."

He frowned. "Of course. Does that come as a surprise to you? I cannot just allow you to roam these halls, Reyna."

"Not at all," she said lightly, shifting closer to the window. "I just want a brief moment of fresh air and sunlight before you throw me back down into the dirt."

His frown deepened as she edged over to the window. Sucking in a breath, she splayed her hands across the cool stone and peered outside. Wingallock had risen just slightly as she approached. Just high enough to avoid the view of anyone inside of the room. Reyna leaned forward and looked down.

It was a very long way to the ground.

"You cannot escape that way," Sloane said dryly. "Why do you think I brought you to the uppermost room in the tallest tower? It is not because I prefer heights myself."

With a smile, she shot him a glance over her shoulder. "You really must consider me a threat to go to such great lengths to confine me. As you said yourself, there are hundreds of warriors inside of this castle."

The sky outside suddenly darkened, thick black clouds rolling off the sea. Reyna glanced up with a frown. A storm would not be ideal, but she saw no other way. She might never again get this chance. It was her one shot at an escape, and she had to do it now. And she could only save Eislyn if she were free.

Palms slick with nervous sweat, she dug her fingernails into the stone ledge. Her heart raced so fast that she swore it would burst out of her chest. Had she truly gone mad? Could she really do this?

She cast another glance over her shoulder at the former king who planned to destroy them all. And then she launched onto the ledge and jumped. Wind whistled around her as she fell, a cry of fear lodged in her throat. Her hair whipped around her face, twisting strands smacking against her cheeks.

She squeezed her eyes tight and stretched her arms wide, every single part of her screaming in fear. But a small hidden part of her had burst alive. A part that she had never known existed until now. And it truly believed that she could fly.

Wingallock's talons suddenly curled around her arms. Her body jerked in the air as the owl slowed her fall. She ground her teeth, her heart in her throat. Even though he had snatched her into his claws, they both hurtled toward the ground. Her familiar had slowed her tumble, but the ground still rushed toward them at a terrifying speed.

Arrows whistled past her ears, warriors from the battlements spotting her flight.

"Wingallock!" Reyna screamed.

Magic pulsed between them, charging through her body with white hot electricity. Her owl's mind locked with hers. She understood at once his every thought. He could not fly her away from the castle. She was too heavy. Only Reyna herself had the ability to steer their flight, by controlling his body as if it were hers. But it took time. And practice. And magic she did not think she had.

Together, they *could* fly, but having never done it before, she did not know how.

He could slow her fall just enough that she would not die when she hit the ground. But he could do no more than that.

Sharp pain ripped through her calf as an arrow struck true. She cried out in pain, writhing in the air. Wingallock hooted in alarm, struggling to hold on to her trembling arms. The ground loomed large below. Flakes of snow drifted down from the sky, and a harsh wind blasted her face.

Suddenly, her arms were ripped from Wingallock's talons. Crying, she reached out, arms outstretched. The ground slammed hard into her aching body.

59

REYNA

Tears streaming down her face, Reyna stood on her trembling leg. Heavy flakes of snow rained down from above. She tipped back her head and breathed it in, steadying her nerves, forcing away the pain. She had fallen in the courtyard as Wingallock had struggled to keep control of the flight. She had urged him away as soon as she had hit the ground. If he stayed, they would no doubt kill him to prevent another attempted escape.

Gritting her teeth, she grabbed the arrow and yanked it from her leg. Fierce pain wracked her body. So fierce that she let out a guttural scream.

Around a dozen warriors poured into the courtyard, swords raised. Reyna glanced around her, heart pounding. Blood poured from her wound, dripping onto the ground to join the falling snow. But she stood her ground, forcing herself to stay calm and in control.

Sloane stepped through a doorway, and the warriors parted to allow him through. He came to a stop before her, but kept his distance. She could only imagine how she looked. Eyes wild, body trembling from pain. Hair a mess of wind-streaked strands tumbling around her shoulders.

"Well, that was certainly unexpected," he said with an amused smile. "And I must say quite daring. Unfortunately for you, it was very much a failed effort. Did you truly believe an owl could bear your weight?"

Yes, Reyna thought. She had been certain of it. Indeed, she was *still* certain it was possible, even if it had not gone as she had hoped. Whatever had driven her out the window had been a strange knowledge deep within her gut. Wingallock *could* carry her. But just as she had needed to learn swordplay, she could not very well expect to fly without any practice at all.

Snow fell onto her face, mingling with the sweat beading on her forehead. She breathed it in, relishing in the soothing chill it brought with it.

Sloane frowned, glanced up, and wiped the flakes from his face. "I hate the snow. Such annoying things, these white flakes. They quickly turn to dirt-stained mush and get in the way of everything. I do not understand how you and your lot live with this every single day of your lives."

"Ours doesn't turn to mush," she said with a smile.

The wind picked up, gusting the snow through the courtyard.

He scowled. "You still have to trek through it. It makes fighting impossible."

Indeed, it did. For anyone other than ice fae. It was one of the few advantages they had, and it was likely why Reyna was more valuable alive than dead. It was difficult to defeat the ice fae on their own lands. Snow made everything more difficult, as did the Shard. But ice only made Reyna feel more alive.

Even the blasting wind could not dampen Reyna's spirits now. The wind swirled through the courtyard, dusting the snow and slamming it against her face. It didn't sting. It didn't even get into her eyes. Her entire body just absorbed it all, basking in the storm.

Sloane shielded his eyes and turned toward his warriors, barking orders. "Grab her. This is turning into some sort of blizzard, and we need to get everyone back inside."

Two warriors appeared behind her. They reached out to grab her arms, but she ducked out of their reach with an impossible speed. They frowned when their hands met with nothing but air. And then she hauled back her fist and punched the nearest warrior in the gut.

She smiled when she made contact, knuckles slamming into leather.

He curled over, groaning. Reyna grabbed the hilt of his sword and yanked it from his sheath, kicking him in the gut as she did. He fell back, eyes wide. She whirled toward the second warrior, sword raised high.

"Reach for me again, and I will shove this blade into your chest."

A soft clapping sounded from behind her, but she kept her eyes glued to the tall, muscular warrior before her. His long tawny hair blew into his face.

"Once again, I see I have underestimated your...brash impulsiveness," Sloane called out from behind her. "But there are hundreds of warriors here, Princess Reyna. You cannot fight all of them by yourself."

"On a normal day, no," she shouted back, smiling when the warrior before her finally drew his sword. "But in the middle of a blizzard? Oh yes. And, besides, I only see a dozen."

Reyna relished the snow as the warrior charged. She whipped her sword toward his as he brought it down on her head. The steel rang loud as their blades hit, the impact reverberating throughout her body. But instead of knocking her back, she found strength in the parry. Before he could recover, she pulled back and shoved the tip of her sword into his heart.

The warrior's eyes went wide, and blood gurgled up from his throat, spilling down his chin. She punched her foot against his body and yanked out the steel, turning to face the former king.

The blizzard had grown thick with snow and wind. Reyna spotted him a short distance away, now surrounded by half a dozen warriors. He glanced wildly from side to side, and a satisfied smile spread across her face. She might be able to see him, but he could not see her.

With a roar, she charged, no longer feeling the pain in her leg. These warriors were loyal to Sloane, so long as he still lived. If she could take him out, they would answer to her.

A warrior jumped into her path. She grabbed his tunic, throwing him onto the ground with a strength she didn't know she had. He tumbled to the ground with an *oomph*. She gripped her sword and swung the steel toward his head, but a hand grabbed her arm and yanked her back.

She whirled to face the new arrival. A tall male, almost twice as tall as she. He wore full-plated armor and a helmet that hid his face from view. His bulky form stalked toward her, a massive two-handed sword held high.

Reyna swallowed hard, tightening her grip on the hilt. All of her lessons rushed through her mind, and the words of the Shieldmaidens rose into her mouth. She had never spoken the vows aloud, but she felt them all the same.

And they had never before felt as important as they did now.

I swear I will be the sword that rings true.

I swear I will protect the realm with the ice in my veins.
I will not cower when faced with the darkest enemy.
I will never run from the shadows in the night.
My life for theirs. My soul for theirs. My everything for the realm.

The wind whipped faster around her, blasts of snow stinging her face. The warrior charged. He swung his sword wide, the steel slicing straight at her gut. Reyna ducked low, only just in time to feel the *whoosh* of the air pass over her head.

She stumbled back several feet and slid to the right as he launched his next attack. The warrior was fast. Far faster than any she'd fought so far. He might even be faster than she.

As he rushed toward her, Reyna jumped to her feet. She held up her blade as he threw his sword toward hers once again. This time, she blocked his blow, but the force of it threw her onto her back.

The air hurtled from her lungs.

He's not only fast. He's strong, too.

Reyna would have to fight far better than this if she was going to survive.

From behind her, she heard the unmistakable cackle of Thane's father. That was everything she needed to get the blood pumping through her veins.

Go on then. Mock me.

With a roar, she rushed toward the warrior, catching him off guard. So far she had only defended and not attacked. She threw her strength behind her sword and swung. He stepped back, and the end of the blade whispered across his chest. It left only a slight tear behind.

Even though she couldn't see his face, she swore he smiled.

He rushed her. His feet slammed into the ground. With a gasp, she darted to the side, but his hand grabbed the back of her tunic. He roared and threw her to the ground. Pain lanced through her back as she wheezed against the force, her sword tumbling out of her hands.

The warrior twisted his sword to the side and slammed the blunt end against her aching wound. Pain screamed through her, blinding her, filling her eyes with blood. Nothing existed but the fire rushing through her leg.

She felt his sword whistling toward her. Eyes shut tight, she tumbled to the side, missing his blow by seconds. He slammed his sword down again, missing her face but only just.

Gritting her teeth, she opened her eyes to see him looming above her.

The sky rumbled. Lightning cracked through the thick snow. A strange sensation curled inside her gut, and she gasped as black flakes tumbled down from above.

The Ruin. It's here. It's found me again.

White wings speared through the storm. Wingallock swooped down and landed on the warrior's head. Sucking in a sharp breath, Reyna scuttled back, grabbing her weapon and jumping to her feet.

Wingallock flapped hard against the volatile wind, his talons gripping tightly to the warrior's helmet. And then the owl pulled it away, revealing the wide, angry face of the air fae within.

He ground his teeth and whirled toward the owl. Reyna screamed as his blade sliced toward Wingallock. Her owl screeched, dropping the helmet to the ground. He spun away into a sky full of ash, escaping the warrior's blade.

Reyna smiled and charged. While her opponent had been distracted by Wingallock, he hadn't noticed her forward advance. She leapt up from the ground with an impossible speed and aimed her sword right at his forehead, her feet high off the icy ground. The blade *slurped* as it sunk deep into his flesh, killing him instantly.

She grabbed his sword as he fell and then whirled on her feet. Sloane's face had paled as he'd watched the fight in horror, but his eyes were now locked on the sky above. Black flakes of the Ruin hit her face, slamming against her, prodding at her skin. But the swirl of snow flicked them away just as easily. And her body did not yield. With a smile, she stalked toward the former king.

The handful of warriors surrounding him had scurried into the safety of the castle. Another black flake hit her face as she advanced. And the snow brushed it aside once again.

"Where are your hundreds of warriors?" she shouted into the wind. "It appears they have abandoned you."

He nervously wet his lips. "They're not here. I sent them to join the wood fae army a week past. There's no need to point your blade my way. I can't command them to kill you if they're not even here. Only a dozen remain, and they've gone inside."

Reyna smiled, power still tumbling around her trembling body. Ash and snow whipped through the courtyard, masking everything in a hundred shades of grey. "Your mistake. My gain."

With wide eyes, Sloane spun on his feet to race into the castle halls.

She grabbed the back of his shirt and threw him onto the ground. Towering over him, she placed the sharp tip of her sword against his bobbing neck. Narrowing her eyes, she leaned down and hissed, "Where is my sister?"

He let out a chuckle, though his eyes were wide in fear. Black flakes landed on his face, and his skin began to sizzle. "You are making a terrible mistake. I am the High King's father. By killing me, you're starting a war."

"The war started a hundred years ago," she said in a low growl. "*Where* is my sister?"

His laughter died on his lips just as his glamor faltered, revealing the true fae beneath the mask. A pitiful former king with no power and no one to save him anymore. "She's in the dungeons, same as you've been all this time. Now," he said, licking his lips and wincing as another black flake landed on his nose. "Go to her and let me live. It's better for the realm if you do."

"No," Reyna said, shaking her head. "I don't believe it is."

With the wind, snow, and Ruin swirling around her, she shoved her blade deep into his neck. A sickening *crunch* echoed through the storm, the sound of a life ending in the dirt. Blood spread across the newly-fallen snow, fingers of bright red that flared bright against the white.

Reyna left the sword where it was, the hilt pointing straight up toward the stormy sky. And then, with the snow urging her on, she went to find her sister.

60

THANE

Horror churned through Thane's gut as he stood just out of reach of the storm. Feurach Fortress had been consumed by...something. He didn't quite understand it. Whatever it was, it wasn't natural. Thick, bulging clouds hung low over the square stone towers. Snow and ash swirled through the air.

Not ash, he thought. *The Ruin.*

Eislyn and Reyna were stuck inside that castle. They would be trapped inside their cells while destruction rained down from above. Sorrow churned through him. How could he stop it? How could he save them? This wasn't a battle he could win or a lord he could manipulate. Winds whipped around the castle in a frenzy, creating a blizzard of epic proportions. Thane could barely even see the familiar towers jutting up toward the sky.

He glanced behind him. The shadow fae had not followed. Lorcan had stopped them somehow, and Thane couldn't squander that by standing on a hillside, gaping at a castle in fear.

Thane would have to go into the storm. There was

nothing else he could do. The Ruin might kill him, but he would never be able to forgive himself if he didn't try.

The princesses were inside. *Eislyn* needed him.

Just as he squared his shoulders, two silver-haired figures stumbled out from the whirlwind of snow and ash. They both glanced behind them at the castle, and then raced through the waist-length grasslands, avoiding the road where he stood.

They hadn't seen him.

He opened his mouth to call out, relief churning through his veins. But something stopped him. Frowning, he stayed rooted to the spot and watched them flee. Reyna's hands were covered in blood, but that ever-present wildness clung to her like a pulsing cloud of pure power. Wingallock hooted as he soared overhead and joined the two ice fae running from their terrible fate. Enbarr, the mare, soon followed.

Thane continued to watch as Eislyn leapt toward the horse and wound her arms around her neck, burying her face in Enbarr's mane. He smiled. Eislyn was alive. She was okay. And she was free.

She was safe now.

And she didn't need Thane at all.

In fact...Thane's heart twisted. Eislyn had been in danger from the moment they had met. One attempt after another. Assassins, abductors, and power-hungry uncles. His own family had gone after her, and he knew it would not stop, even now. *Especially* now.

It all came back to Thane's rule over the realm. He had wanted to bring peace to his kingdom, to provide a kind of stability that the air fae had long since had. Instead, he had created nothing but turmoil. His reign had begun in bloodshed.

It was a bad omen.

He wanted nothing more than to run toward Eislyn and wrap her up in his arms, and then return to the castle so they could wed. He wanted it fiercely. So much that he almost tossed aside his fears and doubts. His selfish desires wanted to drown out everything else.

But Eislyn would never be safe as the High Queen of the Air Court. His enemies now knew what she meant to him, and they would use his love for her against him time and time again.

Until the day they took her life.

She will be safer with me gone, he thought.

Indeed, the entire realm would be better off.

He gazed toward her, watching her hug her sister and then jump onto the back of the mare, committing every part of her to memory. Her bright smile. Those gleaming silver eyes. The way she stuck her tongue between her teeth as she read.

And then, before the sisters joined the Crown's Road, Thane rushed toward the sea. His uncle had boats. Thane would take one. Where he would go, he did not know.

But he knew he had to leave.

As he reached the docks where the boats bobbed waiting, he heard another set of footsteps pounding the ground behind him. Light filled his chest as he whirled toward the sound, hoping to find his oldest friend standing behind him, hoping that Lorcan had escaped the shadow fae.

But his heart quickly sank when he saw who had found him.

"Oh. It's you."

61

REYNA

Reyna clutched Enbarr's reins as they began their trek back to Tairngire. She walked beside her while Eislyn sat on the mare's back, half-asleep as they plodded along. She had found her sister in the dungeons only two tunnels away from where Reyna had been kept. They'd embraced and then fled, escaping the Ruin before it could sink into their skin.

Reyna tried not to think about her seeming immunity to the disease. Or her strength and speed gained from the storm. She wasn't even certain that was what had happened. She had heard tales of warriors on the battlefield, gaining fleeting strength in the height of the battle, frenzy pouring through their veins.

Still...was that what had happened? Or had it been more than that?

Whatever it had been, it had left her now. She had never ached more than she did in that moment. Her body begged for sleep. Her eyes burned with the need to shut tight against the glare of the midday sun.

As soon as they'd left the castle, the storm had stopped. It was the strangest thing…

"Look!" Eislyn suddenly cried out.

Reyna stopped, heart hammering. What new horror would they face now? She shielded her eyes against the sun, and spotted a familiar figure cresting the distant hill. Dark hair pulled back into a bun, impossibly muscled arms. She dropped the reins and ran toward him, leaving all her anger behind.

When she reached him, she launched into his arms. Her feet left the ground as her arms wound tight around his neck. Lorcan was here. He was solid. And real. And he had come for her. Who cared if he was a shadow fae? Who cared if he'd lied to keep it secret? She wasn't perfect either.

After several moments, he gently lowered her back to the ground and pushed the wind-swept hair out of her eyes. "You're alive."

"Did I cheat you out of a brave and daring rescue?" she said with a smile.

"Yes, you should apologize immediately," he said. "And then return to the castle to get captured again. That way I can rescue you properly."

"Hmm, yes. That might be difficult." How did she explain this to him? "The castle is likely destroyed. The Ruin hit it while we were escaping."

He shielded his eyes and stared at the distant horizon. "The Ruin? Again? And this far south?"

Reyna shrugged. "I know. I don't quite understand it."

She fell silent as Enbarr clopped up next to her. Whatever was happening with the Ruin, she did not want to scare Eislyn.

"Where's Thane?" her sister asked. "Did he stay in Tairngire?"

Reyna could hear the disappointment in her voice. She had clearly hoped he had come for her. In truth, Reyna was shocked he hadn't. He might be High King now, but he was still Thane inside. Unless the attack on the coronation had claimed his life.

For the sake of them all, she fiercely hoped not.

My, how things change...

Lorcan's jaw rippled, and he glanced away. "He was with me until we were attacked by a band of assassins. It seems there is a contract out on his life. I told him to run and hide somewhere safe, where no one would think to check."

"What?" Reyna asked, lips parting. "He went into hiding? But he is the High King. He can't just...go away."

Eislyn's face had gone white, and she clutched Enbarr's mane in her trembling hands. "So, he's alone out there?"

"He's alone, but he is safe," Lorcan said, still avoiding Reyna's gaze. "I'm sorry. There was nothing else I could do to save him. We were heavily outnumbered."

Reyna frowned. She wanted to trust Lorcan. She did not wish to doubt him. But his story did not make sense.

"How were you able to get away from the assassins then? If Thane ran and you fought?" she asked.

"They were not interested in me. I fought a few, but they quickly gave up when they realized that I would not be an easy mark."

Reyna narrowed her eyes but didn't probe further. In truth, she was far too weary to do anything but steel herself for the long trip back north. Her aching bones needed a bed. She'd charged hard and long to reach Eislyn in time, and then had spent far too many nights in a cramped, dirty cell. And then she'd fought harder than she'd ever fought in her life.

She needed...rest.

"Ah," Lorcan said, wrapping strong arms around her as her vision went dark, her tired body finally giving out. He held her tight to his chest, and then lifted her from the ground. "I've got you."

Almost a week later, the trio arrived back in Tairngire to find a very different court than the one they had left. They were stopped at the gates by guards who proclaimed to be loyal to Grand Alderman Aengus, who had seized the throne in Thane's absence. They were taken straight to the Great Hall and questioned extensively by the de factor ruler. He'd wanted to know everything about their disappearance.

"And where is the High King now?" he asked, leaning forward on the throne, arm braced on his knee. He'd even put a golden crown on his head.

Reyna exchanged a weighted glance with Lorcan. For some reason, she felt confident that the less said, the better. She cleared her throat. "His guard, Lorcan, was the last to see him."

It was a hint to Lorcan. *Lie.* She could only hope he understood her implication. If Aengus knew that Thane was somewhere hiding, he would tell the entire realm that their High King was a coward.

The Grand Alderman turned his attention to the warrior who stood just behind her. "And what say you? Where is the High King?"

"We got split up during the chaos," Lorcan said easily. "He should be on his way back now. He'll arrive any day."

Aengus arched a brow. "Based on what the princess here has said about the…what do you call it?"

"The Ruin," Reyna said through gritted teeth.

"That's it. The Ruin," Aengus said. "Based on its attack, could the High King be dead?"

Reyna's heart thumped. The last thing the realm needed was for the Air Court to believe that Thane was dead. Thane had no heir. He had no wife. And he had never named a Grand Alderman. Which meant...Aengus would become the next High King unless someone decided to challenge his rule.

Sloane was dead. Imogen had been imprisoned. Lord Bowen, Sloane's closest relative, was also dead. Sloane had no other siblings, and Imogen's family were sea fae. Any other claims to the throne would be weak.

That left Aengus.

The kingdom needed hope that Thane would return.

Reyna cleared her throat and glanced at Lorcan.

He pressed his lips tightly together. "Neither Thane nor I were assaulted by the Ruin. As Princess Reyna explained, she alone freed her sister and escaped as the castle crumbled into the dirt. The last I saw of our king, he was nowhere near the Ruin."

Aengus sat for a moment, lips pursed, clearly trying to decide if he would make more of Thane's disappearance than he should. Finally, after a long while, he nodded and leaned back into his throne.

"Until he returns, I rule in his stead. As his betrothed, you are of course welcome to continue your stay here in the castle." He turned to Lorcan. "You may continue your role as guard. Unless any of you wishes to make argument against my place here. If you do, then you will have to join Imogen in her chains."

Reyna had never been good at holding her tongue. Aengus should not be squatting on the throne. He had been Imogen's Grand Alderman, not Thane's. And he had thrown her into the dungeons. He could not be trusted to rule with a steady hand.

But she had to trust that Lorcan was right. Thane would return and soon, and then everything would be put back to right. She almost laughed out loud at her thoughts. Only a few months ago, she wanted nothing more than to murder Thane for everything he had done to her people.

And now, she wanted to protect his rule.

So she would.

Lorcan accompanied Reyna back to her chambers. When she pressed into the familiar, sea-facing rooms, a strange ache formed around her heart. As much as she had hated her place here when she had first arrived, she could not help but feel immense relief at once again standing inside these stone walls.

If only it were under better circumstances.

"You wanted me to lie," Lorcan said quietly, shutting the door behind him. "I thought you did not approve of that."

Sighing, she turned to face him. "I don't, but I'm quickly understanding how important some falsehoods can be. Aengus cannot know that Thane has gone into hiding. He would use that in the worst way possible."

"I believe Aengus has been playing a very dangerous game," Lorcan said with a frown. "He is the reason Sloane stepped down, and he is the reason Imogen has been arrested. Something tells me this has been his goal all this time. Seize the throne for himself."

"And now he has it," Reyna said, shaking her head. While they'd all been too busy worrying about assassins and wood fae attacks, Aengus had quietly been making his moves. The only way to remove him now was with Thane's reappearance.

"Why hasn't he come back?" she asked, twisting her hands together. "You said assassins found you. Do you think they've been able to track him down again?"

Lorcan shifted away from her and moved toward the window. The light breeze rolling off the sea ruffled his dark hair. He had been oddly distant since they'd returned to Tairngire. She still felt as though he was hiding something, though she hated to doubt him after everything they'd shared.

He sighed. "I cannot be sure. I wish I could head out into the grasslands to look for him. The longer he is gone, the more sure-footed Aengus will become."

Reyna smiled and strode up beside him, resting a hand on his arm. He glanced down at her, and his eyes churned with sadness and dread. "You're a good friend to him. If you want to go in search of him, I'll come with you. If you'd like."

Reyna's heart beat hard in her chest. She knew what she was suggesting, and he would, too. That path was a dangerous one. She knew that if they travelled together, alone, they would only end up in each other's arms again. Her father would hate it. She would risk her place in the court. But she no longer wanted that place. Thane, while not perfect, was a far different male than she had first thought. Vengeance would not save her people.

Lorcan twisted toward her and placed a warm palm against her cheek. Warmth flooded her body, and she instinctively stepped toward him. Their chests brushed, and his thumb caressed her cheek. She leaned into his touch and sighed.

"We should wait. If he doesn't return within the next few days, we will go look for him."

"We." She smiled.

"Of course," he said, but then he turned away again. "Reyna, I worry about the Ice Court. How will your father react when he learns you have run off with a warrior?"

"He has dealt with far worse when it comes to me," she replied. "I never wanted to be a princess. A life has a Shieldmaiden has always been my calling. I've been...distracted these past few months. I forgot who I truly was inside and what I stand for. Being here, being with you, it has reminded me of what I am. My father may not like it, but he will understand. I am my mother's daughter. I always have been."

His eyes softened. "And you are certain you shouldn't return home? It hasn't been safe here for you and Eislyn. What of your sister?"

Reyna let out a heavy sigh. "My dear sister has fallen in love with the king. I doubt I could drag her away from this city, regardless of what I say. Besides, Sloane, the traitor amongst us, has been defeated, and we've stopped the Wood Court for now. Things could get better here in court, as soon as Thane returns."

Lorcan winced. "And you truly believe that?"

"No," she said with a laugh. "As much as I want to believe otherwise, I have quickly learned one thing about the Air Court. Life will never be easy here. But, perhaps together, we can make it better than it was."

62

IMOGEN

Once she got out of this cell, Imogen was going to murder Aengus. She glared at the guard who strode through the dungeon tunnel, his flickering torch highlighting the dirt and grime that clung to the ancient stone walls. He carried a small loaf of bread in his other hand, a sight that caused Imogen's growling stomach to echo around her.

He came to a stop before her. Imogen recognized this one. The one with the short hair and the mismatched eyes. He had been a member of Thane's personal guard. Vreis was his name. Narrowing her eyes, she pushed up from the ground on her bare, dirt-flaked feet.

"I've brought you some food," he said when he reached her cell door. But instead of opening it, he flipped the small hatch to the right and shoved the bread through. Greedily, she grabbed it and sunk her teeth into the soft, warm dough. It had been far too long since she'd had a proper meal.

Vreis nodded and turned to go, but she quickly pressed

up to the rusted bars and spoke around her mouthful of food. "What news of my son?"

Most of the guards had refused to speak with her about Thane. She knew that Aengus would have no right to his rule once her son returned from going after that insufferable princess, but she did not know how many days had passed. The hours blurred together in these dungeons. She did not even have a window to tell whether it was day or night.

The guard paused but kept his focus forward instead of turning to face her once again. "Our High King has still not returned from his mission to rescue the princesses."

Imogen sighed and slumped back against the bars, wincing as the iron burned her. She wanted nothing more than to see Thane's twinkling golden eyes, to hear the rumble of his voice. The two had never fully seen eye-to-eye, and they had disagreed more often than not. But her heart ached for him. She would do anything if it meant his safe return, even if that meant sacrificing herself.

Vreis cleared his throat, causing Imogen's head to jerk up. With an uncomfortable set in his jaw, he edged closer to her cell and dropped his voice low. "There is other news, however. The princesses have returned. They were with Lorcan. They believe the High King is alive, but they do not know where he is."

Imogen's heart sank. "They believe it, but they do not know?"

"I'm afraid not," he said quietly. "There was a fight, and they all got separated. Lorcan and Princess Reyna have suggested that they will go in search of him, but the...ah...Grand Alderman has ordered that they stay."

Imogen's hands fisted. Aengus could toss her into the dungeons. He could get her husband to give up his throne.

And he could sit on the damn throne himself for as long as he could.

But he would *not* put her son's life at risk. He was all she had left. The world, *the shadow fae*, had taken everyone else.

"I would like to see Princess Reyna," Imogen said, scarcely believing the words coming out of her mouth. Of all people, she never would have expected to pin her hope on her. "Please. And do not tell anyone else of this request."

63

EISLYN

Eislyn found herself standing outside the door that led into Thane's chambers. His rooms were still in the North Tower, far enough away from the Grand Alderman that she wouldn't be spotted lurking around. Thane had never been given the chance to move his belongings into the chambers of the High King, located deep within Mistral Tower.

Sighing, she pushed open the door and stepped inside. The antechamber spread out before her. Lush furniture sat around a fireplace that hadn't been lit in days. Thick golden rugs stretched across the stone floor, and the window overlooking the sea shuddered from the force of the wind.

Eislyn closed the door behind her and sat hard on the nearest chair. They had returned to the castle three days past, and there was still no sign of Thane. Reyna had insisted that she and Lorcan would go and find him, but they had been stopped in their tracks. The Grand Alderman had forbidden it. If they went regardless of his orders, he had threatened to have them hanged for treason.

Eislyn wasn't entirely certain that Aengus *could* even do such a thing. However, she did know that he would try it.

With tears in her eyes, she pulled her knees up to her chest and stared at the empty fireplace. She had come to this court to find a cure for the Ruin. Instead, she had failed. She had gotten herself captured. And she had been the reason that Thane had become lost to the grasslands. The High King. The one person over all others that the air fae needed more than anything.

It was becoming clearer every day that Aengus did not care about the low fae. He had heard no complaints from the city. He had not listened to any pleas for help. Instead, he had holed up in his tower discussing military strategy with a very select group of nobles.

No one knew what he plotted up there. Reyna had theories, of course. Even though Aengus had not been involved in the wood fae plot, she worried that they had somehow gotten to him as well.

Regardless of what he was doing, one thing was certain: the war was nowhere close to an end.

Eislyn wiped the tears from her cheeks and stood. There was no sense in moping around Thane's chambers. It did nothing. It helped no one. It only made the ache in her heart grow worse. There was nothing for her to do but return to her studies.

As she strode away from the chair, she spotted something through the open doorway leading into Thane's study. His desk, normally neat and orderly, was a mess of books and papers that threatened to topple to the floor. Curious, Eislyn strode to the door and poked her head inside. There were a couple of books stacked on the nearest edge that she recognized. Books they had poured through together, hunched over their lanterns late at night.

She went closer and gingerly picked up the top book. A part of her hated to even lay a finger on the tome. She didn't want to disturb his research or snoop through his things, but something about the sight of all these papers called to her.

Gently placing the book back where she found it, she moved around the side of the desk to peer at the others. She picked up one and read the title. It was a detailed history of the Fire Court. Frowning, she moved to the next. This one traced history back even further with theories on how the fae had come to these lands.

What had he been researching?

Eislyn's fingers drifted toward an unmarked book at the very edge of the desk. Breath tight in her throat, she flipped it open.

A Detailed Investigation Into the Origin and History of The Ruin

By Thane Selkirk

Eislyn gasped. She flipped the next page and drank in the words.

> *I write these pages in hope to assist the Princesses Eislyn and Reyna of the Ice Court. I may have made some interesting connections, but I wish to further investigate before bringing my findings to the princesses, in case this research amounts to nothing more than a dead end.*

With her heart in her throat, Eislyn greedily continued to read page after page of notes. Instead of focusing on the recent hundred years, Thane had turned his attention to centuries past. All this time, he had been locking himself up in his study and pouring through ancient tomes...all to help her kingdom.

Overcome, Eislyn dropped into the desk chair and stared at the monumental pages and books laid out before her. Thane must have really thought he was on to something, if he spent this much time and effort on these studies.

There was a lot to pour through, a lot to understand. With a deep breath, she stood and padded back over to the door that led out into the tower corridors. She could not risk anyone venturing inside Thane's chambers to discover this themselves. Particularly no one loyal to Aengus. She did not trust him not to destroy this information.

Before she could lose her nerve, she rushed back over to the desk and gathered all the papers and books in her arms—what she could carry, at least. She would return for the rest in only a few moments. This research would be far safer in her own chambers than here.

As she headed for the corridor, she paused and took one fleeting glance behind her. Despite the excitement of finding Thane's notebook—or perhaps because of it—the pain of his disappearance felt like a shard of ice through her heart.

"Thank you," she whispered to the empty room, tears burning her eyes. "But please come back soon. I don't want to do this without you."

64
MARIEL

Mariel plopped two overflowing tankards onto the wooden table and sashayed through the tavern, nodding as her regular patrons shouted out their orders. Things had returned to normal in the days since the coronation, as much as could be considered normal in the poor streets of Tairngire.

She had not yet been able to extract Imogen from her cell—the dungeons were too heavily guarded at the moment. Aengus no doubt worried that some seeds of disloyalty had sprouted amongst the courtiers. They would regard him as an outsider, someone who had toppled their carefully-constructed world.

The High King was still missing. Rumors about his disappearance had swept through the city. Some believed he was on a coronation trip throughout the realm, bestowing good wishes on villages and towns he passed by. Others believed that the Grand Alderman had thrown him into the dungeons with his mother. And many others believed he was dead.

"Mariel," her brother called out as she poured two more

tankards of ale. He jerked his head, motioning for her to join him at a table where he sat with two grubby boys wearing patchwork garb.

Frowning, she wheeled through the pub, depositing mugs of mead, before finally stopping at her brother's table. "You calling me over for drinks? You can poor the damn ale yourself, you know. We've a busy crowd here this night."

"Sit." He motioned to the chair, his voice grave.

Unease rippled through her. She took the seat.

"I know I said I don't like you doing your...erm, business, but I thought you should hear these two boys out," he grumbled.

She sat a little straighter in the chair, her heartbeat picking up speed. Since Reyna had killed Sloane, the murders in Drunkard's Pit had completely stopped. Apparently, he'd been using the poor low fae as sacrifices in order to extend his pitiful life with dark magic. Now that he was dead, the streets were safer than they'd once been.

Or so she'd thought.

She turned to the boys, eyeing them. They were both young, though most fae looked young to her ancient eyes. Perhaps fifteen or sixteen years. Fresh-faced fae with hard eyes. The eyes of the street. Their tawny hair was ratty and dirty, the sweet color dimmed by grime. Her heart ached for them. Once, this city had thrived. The low fae had never had the riches of the nobles, but they had done far more than merely survive.

"Tell me what you've come to say," she said quietly. "You can trust me."

The older of the two nodded and wet his lips nervously. "There's talk on the streets. Something the Grand Alderman knows but doesn't want found out."

Mariel frowned. "I'm listening."

The boy swallowed hard. "They say the High King was half-human."

"Wait. Sloane?" she asked, eyes bulging wide. "He was *human*?"

"Part, ma'am. Half."

"Huh." Mariel sat back in her chair. Well, that certainly explained a lot. He had aged far too quickly. Some believed it had been due to the stress of his position. Others believed him to be far older than his peers. But if he had always been half-human, then...it was shocking that he even lived as long as he did.

"That is very interesting information, boy," Mariel said, "but why are you bringing this to me now? Sloane is dead."

"Well," the boy said, glancing to his brother. "There's more."

Mariel's heart thumped hard.

"Some say that he traded secrets with the Wood Court on how to extend his life, using Unseelie magic. He promised them our kingdom in return."

Mariel nodded. "You're right. He did. But his promise died with him."

"But he didn't know the full truth of it. The shadow fae have been using the wood fae's king as a pawn all this time. They set up that plot as a way to disrupt these lands. To get us to fight amongst ourselves instead of focusing on what they're doing down south. And it worked. Now, they've taken back Findius. And soon, they're going to march to war."

65

TARRAH

Shadow fae from all across the kingdom had fled to Findius to watch their High King take his throne once and for all. A ripple of excitement had spread through the land, a spark that lit the fire. For so long, the shadow fae had lived in exile. Backs bent, faces turned down, shrouded in mist.

Things were changing now. Tarrah could feel it in the air. It was the ripple of electric energy before a storm. The arrow that started a war.

She beamed as she stood in the front row of the audience, donning a new set of grey scale armor that glistened beneath the torchlight. The shadow sigil had been stamped onto her breastplate, twisting antlers spreading wide. The throne room had been packed as tight as it could and fae had to elbow themselves into a spot inside the lofted room. Some were even forced to stand outside. Others waited in the courtyard for the chiming of the bells. But the High King had insisted that Tarrah be placed right up front. He wanted her with him every step of the way.

The door behind the throne cracked open, and the king

strode into the room. A hush fell across the crowd at the sight of him. Even as slight as he was, he looked tall. He wore his shadow court garb, glinting scale armor and a cloak so dark that it looked as if it led to a whole other world. He held a black staff made from antlers that clicked on the ground as he walked. With a wide smile, he stopped at the edge of the dais.

An Unseelie priest in black robes hurried to his side, a crown of twisting antlers in his hands. It was almost identical to the crown the king had once worn, but this one was far larger than the first.

It was the true crown of the Shadow Court. It had been waiting here in Findius all this time.

"Shall we begin, my liege?" the priest asked, lowering his bald head.

"Wait," Bolg said, voice booming through the expansive space. "I wish for my champion to stand by my side as I take my vows."

Confusion rippled across the priest's face. "My lord, that is...out of the ordinary."

"I do not care about the ordinary," the king replied firmly. "My champion is the reason we have taken back this city. She is the reason I can now truly reign over this kingdom. She will stand by my side."

"Very well," the priest murmured.

And then the entire court turned to stare at Tarrah.

She swallowed hard, nerves shooting through her belly. This she had not expected, nor had she intended. She did not feel the need to be revered. All she wanted was to return the shadow fae to their rightful place as part of Tir Na Nog.

"Tarrah." The High King motioned for her to join him on the dais. "You are my champion. Please join me as I pledge to rule this realm and all that it entails."

With a nod, she strode forward, her armor clinking as she moved. She took careful steps up to the dais, her face flushed as she took her place beside the throne. And then she lifted her eyes toward the crowd. A strange wave of exhilaration went through her at the sight of so many eyes staring her way. Most held hints of admiration in them. They were awe-struck by their champion. Some reached out, as if in hope of touching her arm. With a smile, she lifted her chin, basking in the admiring gazes.

She should not feel shy. She *had* saved them, after all.

"Now, we may begin," the king finally said.

The priest took the court through the coronation quickly. These were all vows the king had made before, just never in this holy building before the true Seat of Power. He was making his pledge before his realm, in front of the Unseelie god himself. It was binding in way that his previous vows had never been.

Finally, Bolg knelt before the priest, and the twisting crown was placed on his head. Smiling, he stood and thumped his staff hard on the ground. A gasp rippled through the crowd as he slowly lowered himself to the gleaming black stone throne.

And then he sat.

Power rumbled beneath Tarrah's feet as the seat churned from the king's touch. It rattled her skull. She had to grit her teeth against the force of it. Several fae in the crowd stumbled at the quaking ground, clasping each other's arms to hold themselves steady.

The rumble soon stopped. Silence punctuated the air. And then the entire court burst out into cheers.

With tears in her eyes, she glanced down at the king. His back was tall and straight. Determination set his jaw. He looked proud and hopeful and as powerful as he should have always been. Nothing could stop them now.

As the crowd died down, the king waved his hand for silence. His booming voice echoed through the room. "Now that we have taken back our city, we cannot stop. The Unseelie god would not have brought us here unless he had a reason."

Another round of cheers lit up the room.

"We may have a long, hard road before us, but there is one thing we have that they do not." At that, he glanced up at Tarrah and smiled. "My champion, who the Unseelie god himself speaks to. She has brought us this far. She will take us to the wood fae lands and beyond."

More cheering. Tarrah smiled. They liked her. No, they *loved* her. Her soul filled with light from how good that felt.

"So tell me, champion," the High King said, pressing the staff into her hands. "What would the Unseelie god have us do now?"

Her fingers curled around the antlers as she stared out at the crowd. Expectant faces blinked back at her. Her visions had been clear. They had been all along. She knew exactly what their god wanted them to do.

She cleared her throat and then spoke loud so that her voice carried to the very back of the room. "It is time for us to press forward. It is time for war."

66

LORCAN

Lorcan stood with Reyna outside of Imogen's cell. She had called them for a meeting, desperate to know the status of her son. It seemed that Vreis had been willing to give her the information she craved. Lorcan's old friend felt guilty for his past actions, even if they had not been solely his fault. Listening to what he thought to be official commands, he'd redirected scouts away from the hills behind the Witchlight Woods and then had instructed Lorcan not to stand guard for Reyna the night of the attack. Sloane had been pulling the strings for weeks, controlling the guards, the warriors, and the scouts before making his final play.

There had been no reason for the guards to suspect that "Lord Bowen" was not who he had appeared to be. And Sloane, as Lord Bowen, had never outright lied. He'd only ever made suggestions.

The truth may be twisted but never false.

"Please, Reyna," Imogen said, her dirty fingers curled around the rusted cell bars. They burned her skin, but she scarcely seemed to notice it. "I know you're able to get out of this castle without being seen. Aengus may have forbidden it, but do not tell me that you are afraid of him. We may never have gotten along, but I *know* you."

Reyna's lips were a thin white line. "I fear what he will do to my sister if I disobey his orders and leave."

"Send her back to your kingdom. She will be far safer there than here."

Reyna shook her head. "I have tried to convince her to go. She will not have it. It seems she has fallen in love with your son."

Imogen blinked back, clearly shocked by this revelation.

Lorcan cleared his throat. "We will see what we can do. There might be a way."

Hope flickered across Imogen's face. She clutched the bars tighter and pulled her face as close as she could. "You have always been there for Thane. Please do not abandon him now."

Lorcan clenched his jaw and nodded. The trouble was, things were far more complicated than he had let on to anyone. Any day now, his father would send word. And if he ignored it...

"Lorcan is right," Reyna whispered. "I can't pretend that it is going to be easy, but we will not leave Thane out there to fend for himself. We will find him. It just might take us some time."

Imogen reached through the bars and grasped Reyna's hand. Her eyes swam with tears, and the pain that flickered across her face was too much for Lorcan to bear. Not when he knew he would only let her down.

"Thank you," Imogen whispered.

Back in her chambers, Reyna started tossing a few of her tunics into a small leather satchel. She opened her wardrobe and grabbed her hoarfrost cloak before adding it to the pile. Wingallock clutched a pair of trousers and tossed it onto the satchel, assisting his human soul. As they worked, Reyna stopped to shoot Lorcan a frown.

"Come on, Lorcan. We cannot wait any longer. It's been days now."

He knew it had been days. They had stretched out long as he had stalled for time. And it seemed that Reyna would refuse to be stalled any longer.

He steeled himself as a knock sounded on the door. Lorcan knew who was there before he even opened it.

"What about Eislyn?" he asked as he opened the door. A messenger stood on the other side, holding out a folded piece of parchment.

"For you," the messenger said before nodding once and disappearing down the corridor. Heart thumping, Lorcan shut the door behind him and turned to face Reyna. She was still whirling around the room, throwing open drawers and rifling through her things.

"We will just have to convince Eislyn to return to the Ice Court or come with us," Reyna said.

Lorcan arched a brow. "Come with us? Your sister has many strengths, but she is not a warrior, Reyna."

Not like us, he thought with sadness. Lorcan had never met a female like Reyna and he doubt he ever would again. And soon, she would hate him.

"She'll be safer with us than here by herself." She stopped and propped her fisted hands on her hips. "What's that letter?"

"Oh. Well, let's see." Heart pounding, Lorcan unfolded the note.

My son,

The boat is ready. My spies have informed me that you have agreed to my proposal. Be warned: if you do not fulfill your end of the bargain, I will be forced to follow through on my threat. We have Thane. Try as you might, you did not prevent my spies from capturing him. I do not wish to cause you pain, my son, but this must be done for the sake of our kingdom. Use the vial I have sent to you, if you must.

With regards,
High King Bolg Rothach of the Shadow Court

Pain squeezed around Lorcan's heart as tight as a twisting snake. His father had out-smarted him, time and time again. While Lorcan had been distracted with one band of warriors, another had chased after Thane. He'd never had a chance to escape.

Lorcan had known this day was coming. He had tried to work out a way to avoid it, but he had come up empty. The time had finally come. The day he had to betray the only female he had ever loved.

"It is nothing. Just news that there has still been no sign of Thane."

Reyna's face fell. "Well, only more reason for us to leave here as soon as possible."

Before we go," Lorcan murmured, turning away from Reyna's trusting face. "Let us have a toast. It is often done between air fae warriors before battle, and I fear that is exactly what we're heading into."

"A toast?" Reyna continued to rustle through her things. "Sounds a bit too lighthearted for what we're about to do."

"It is for good luck," he said, wincing at his own lies. He strode over to a table by the wall where two golden chalices sat waiting with a bottle of wine. Blood roaring in his ears, he pulled a black vial from the folds of his leather and poured the contents into one of the chalices before filling it the rest of the way with wine.

Then, he poured a drink for himself, sans poison.

Lorcan hated himself in that moment.

Grinding his teeth together, he turned and handed Reyna the poisoned chalice. She took it with a nod, though her eyes kept cutting back to her half-packed satchel. She was so eager to get out there and search for Thane. Lorcan loved her for it.

And yet, his love for her had turned into *this*.

Wingallock hooted.

"Right," she said, lifting the chalice. "How does this toast tend to go?"

Lorcan lifted his own chalice, anger burning his veins. Everything inside him felt hot with dread, like his own insides would melt. "We toast to our journey. Deep into the grasslands we go, in search of our High King. May we return."

Reyna nodded. "Short and sweet. I like it."

She clinked her chalice against his and then took a large gulp of the wine. Lorcan downed his in one go, hoping the wine would dull some of the pain. Reyna lifted a brow, watching him, and then she followed suit. When she finished it, she slammed her empty chalice on the table, and then moved back to her bag.

Blood thudded in Lorcan's ears as he watched her. It would not take long for the poison to take effect. He braced his hand on the wall and held himself steady. There was nothing he could do now. The damage had already been done.

And, if he did not do this, Thane would surely die.

"Oh," Reyna said, suddenly pressing her hand to her head. She stumbled to the side, grasping at her wooden bedpost. "I do not feel so well."

Lorcan rushed to her side and wrapped his hands around her waist, holding her steady. "Perhaps you should lie down."

"No," she said, stubbornness shining through even as her words slurred in her mouth. "We must leave. Now. While we can."

She slumped back toward him, her body trembling in his arms.

"Just lie down for a moment, Reyna. A dizziness has overcome you."

He held her steady, hoping she did not fall from his arms and hurt herself. Even as he poisoned her, the last thing in the world he wanted was for Reyna to feel pain.

She twisted toward him and wrapped her arms around his neck, burying her face into his chest. His heart pounded hard against her cheek, and it was all he could do not to tip back his head and shout his anger at the world.

"Lorcan," she moaned. "Something is wrong..."

"Shh," he whispered into the top of her head. "It is all right. I've got you. I won't let you go."

Then, her arms loosened around his neck as her body went slack. He tightened his grip around her and lifted her into his arms before she could fall. Unshed tears burned his eyes. Wingallock hooted at him, flapping angrily in the wind.

"Come along," he said to the owl. "But don't let yourself be seen."

Lorcan grabbed Reyna's satchel from the bed and strode over to the door where he kicked it open. He stepped out into the corridor, hoping no one would spot him. It was late at night—that was why they had chosen now to visit Thane's mother. He should be able to sneak out through the tunnels easily enough.

The boat would only wait for an hour, and then it

would be gone.

He took one last glance behind him, knowing it might be the last time he ever saw these halls. It was time for him to return to the Shadow Court.

67
REYNA

Time seemed to have no meaning. Hours or days passed in a blur, Reyna's mind too numbed by a strange, intoxicating illness that left her weak and confused. She would only wake for moments at a time, long enough to see a crack of light or a shadowy face before she drifted back into darkness.

Sometimes, she hallucinated. She would hear the caw of seagulls and smell the scent of brine. The world seemed to tip beneath her like waves upon the sea. And sometimes, she awoke just to vomit on an unfamiliar floor and find herself in a strange bed of straw.

She swore Lorcan was nearby. His voice echoed inside her head, though nothing in his words made sense.

Southeasterly winds, he'd say. *The captain is concerned.*

But she could scarcely breathe, let alone hold onto her thoughts. And so, she drifted away like an unmoored boat across the sea.

She pried open her eyes and was momentarily blinded by a strange red light that speared across her face. Squinting, she pushed herself up from the bed and tried to shake the clouds out of her head.

What the hell is happening? How long has it been? What in the name of the Dagda has plagued me for so long?

Because it had been a very long time. Reyna wasn't certain how she knew, but she did. Weeks, at least. Maybe more. Her body felt the days, along with her mind.

Finally, she managed to open her eyes long enough to see an unfamiliar room and an iron-barred window looking out at a very red sky. Frowning, she gingerly stepped out of the bed and moved closer to the window. And then grasped tight to the ledge to hold herself steady.

What lay before her was...well, it was not Tairngire. In fact, it was anything but. The strange city stretched out before her like a hulking mass of black. There were hundreds of buildings, windows lit up with light. They were all made of black stone, roofs covered in black bricks. The sky was thick with a strange, eerie mist that obscured the sun, transforming it into a blob of bloody red.

Reyna's heart thundered in her ears as she stumbled away from the window. It was barred, clearly meant to prevent an escape. She'd been taken captive. By who, though? And when? She and Lorcan had been ready to leave for their adventure when...

Wingallock hooted and settled onto her shoulder. Her heart soothed at once at the soft feel of his feathers on her face. Wherever she was, at least she had him.

"Tell the king she's awake," a voice mumbled on the other side of the door.

She whirled to face it, heart banging hard in her chest. A horrible realization washed over her as she took a quick glance around the room, searching for anything that could be turned into a weapon. Someone was coming.

But the furniture was sparse, if not luxurious. The room held a large bed covered in black silken sheets, along with a small chair that set in front of an unlit fireplace. A soft rug covered the floor beneath her feet. Other than that, the room had been emptied.

Soon, the door cracked open and a dozen warriors in scaly armor swept inside. They formed a circle around her, ushering her into the center of the floor. She could see none of their faces, all hidden by thick, grey helmets. Eyes wild, she clutched at her shirt. Wingallock's talons tightened on her shoulder.

"Your Majesty," one of the warriors barked.

A small fae stepped through the door, his form engulfed by black armor. A twisting crown of antlers squatted on top of his head, and a large silver medallion hung from his thick neck. Reyna knew at once who he was. This was the High King of the Shadow Court. And she had been taken prisoner by them.

He stepped into the door, flanked by two warriors, one of whom was a young, hollow-eyed female who wore an air of superiority far better than even the king. She stood beside him in her own set of grey scale armor, giving Reyna an appraising gaze.

"Princess Reyna of the Ice Court," the High King said in a loud, commanding voice. "Welcome to the Shadow Court. I apologize your visit here is not under better circumstances."

"What do you want with me?" Reyna asked. "Where's Lorcan?"

"I realize that you are not a part of this court, but you will address my son by his title," he replied.

Reyna blinked. "Your son?"

"Oh." The High King's eyes widened. "He did not tell you then."

Blood roared through Reyna's veins. Lorcan was...the High King's son? Her head swam, her bones shook. She wanted to reach out to grab something to steady herself, but the only thing near her were the warriors. And she would not let them see just how much they had shaken her.

"No, he did not," she said softly. "I suppose *he* is the reason I am here."

It was all beginning to make horrible sense now. She remembered him acting strangely the night they'd planned to leave Tairngire, suddenly aloof and cold about their rescue of Thane. He'd wanted to toast to their adventure when he never had before. Reyna's stomach twisted.

That was what had happened to her. She hadn't fallen ill. He'd poisoned her, all to make her pliant enough to steal her away. And the scent of the sea. The rolling of the waves. He had sneaked her out of Tairngire on a boat.

Reyna needed to sit.

Tears threatened to fall from her eyes. Even when she'd discovered the truth about his shadow fae origin—or, perhaps, the half-truth was really what it had been all along—she had trusted him. More than she had trusted almost everyone else in the world. She had felt for him. It had been real. And she'd thought he'd felt the same for her.

But it had been a lie. In a war-torn land, love was always a lie.

"Do not be angry at my son," the High King said, clearly reading the turmoil on her face. "I ordered him to do this. He did not have much of a choice."

But he *did* have a choice. There was always a choice, even if it was a difficult one.

"What do you want with me?" Reyna asked through gritted teeth. "Why am I here?"

"My champion here," he said, motioning to the strange, hollow-eyed warrior beside him, "has had a vision that you will be important in the coming war. She does not know why or how as of yet, but she is insistent that you remain our captive."

Reyna shook her head. "You did all this because of a vision?"

It sounded absurd. And yet, the High King looked remarkably serious.

"Yes." He nodded toward the warriors that surrounded her. "You will be provided for, of course, though heavily guarded. You may have all the food you'd like, and you may request entertainment. And, of course, your familiar may remain with you. You can thank Lorcan for that one. As long as you do not attempt to escape, there will be no need for you to live in the dungeons."

"And then what?" Reyna demanded. "You cannot just keep me locked in here forever. What do you plan to do with me?"

The High King of the Shadow Court smiled. "We will do whatever my champion commands."

※

***The Fallen Fae* continues in...**
Kingdom in Exile
(The Fallen Fae, Book Two)
Available for Preorder Now

Join Jenna's reader newsletter to be notified on release day and to receive exclusive free stories not found anywhere else.

The World of Tir Na Nog: Find extra information about

the books, including a larger version of the map, a Spotify playlist, upcoming release dates, and more at www.thefallenfae.com

Jenna's Court of Books and Readers is a Facebook group with early access to cover reveals and sneak peek chapters.

GLOSSARY OF TERMS

Adhradh - a building of worship for followers of the Dagda

Airgead - the coin of the six kingdoms in Tir Na Nog

Alchemist - a healer in Tir Na Nog who specializes in herbal treatments

Alder - a tree found within the Wood Court lands that turns to an orange red when cut

Animal familiar - an animal whose soul is linked to the soul of a fae

Beltane - the yearly celebration that takes place at the beginning of summer

Brigantu - one of the two moons

Court of Death - the mysterious home of the Dagda

GLOSSARY OF TERMS

Dagda - the god worshipped by all of those in Tir Na Nog, other than the shadow fae

Danu - one of the two moons

Druid - a religious leader in the faith of the Dagda

Elemental Arts - the powers that were once available to fae based on their lineage

The Fall - the event where every fae upon Tir Na Nog fell to the ground, losing the magic given to them by the Dagda

Fomorians - the mysterious people of the Empire of Fomor, found across the impassable sea

Grand Alderman - the right hand of the High King and the second most powerful position in a kingdom

High King - the highest ranking noble in the kingdom who controls the Seat of Power

High Queen - the highest ranking noble if there is no High King

Hoarfrost silk - expensive, valuable silk obtained from the hoarfrost worms only found in icy terrain

Ice glass - a strong, sturdy glass found in the mines of the Ice Court that can be used to create jewellery and weapons

Priest - a religious leader for the followers of the Unseelie god

GLOSSARY OF TERMS

Rowan - a tree found in the north yielding berries that can intoxicate

The Ruin - a terrible magic that falls from the sky, destroying everything it touches

Seat of Power - the coronation seat in each of the six kingdoms that bestows power and strength

Shadowsteel - a powerful steel forged from metals only found within the Shadow Court lands

Shieldmaiden - a female warrior who vows to spend her entire life protecting her people no matter the cost

Tamaris steel - a strong, sturdy steel forged within the Fire Court lands

Tir Na Nog - the continent of the six fae kingdoms

Unseelie - the dark magic god that bestows powerful gifts, but requires sacrifice in return

The Wild Hunt - the rumored hunt by Fomorians every Beltane where they kill every fae they see

Winter Solstice - the yearly celebration during midwinter

Yew - a poisonous tree found throughout the continent

ALSO BY JENNA WOLFHART

The Fallen Fae

Court of Ruins

Kingdom in Exile

The Paranormal PI Files

Live Fae or Die Trying

Dead Fae Walking

Bad Fae Rising

One Fae in the Grave

Innocent Until Proven Fae

All's Fae in Love and War

The Supernatural Spy Files

Confessions of a Dangerous Fae

Confessions of a Wicked Fae

The Bone Coven Chronicles

Witch's Curse

Witch's Storm

Witch's Blade

Witch's Fury

Protectors of Magic

Wings of Stone

Carved in Stone

Bound by Stone

Shadows of Stone

Otherworld Academy

A Dance with Darkness

A Song of Shadows

A Touch of Starlight

A Cage of Moonlight

A Heart of Midnight

Order of the Fallen

Ruinous

Nebulous

ABOUT THE AUTHOR

Jenna Wolfhart spends her days tucked away in her writing shed. When she's not writing, she loves to deadlift, rewatch Game of Thrones, and drink copious amounts of coffee.

Born and raised in America, Jenna now lives in England with her husband, her two dogs, and her mischief of rats.

www.jennawolfhart.com
jenna@jennawolfhart.com

Printed in Great Britain
by Amazon